The Lady in the Tower

From the moment Anne Boleyn appeared in Henry VIII's life it was clear that she was destined for distinction. She was singled out for her elegance and a quality which was more exciting than beauty. There was no one like Anne Boleyn. Even her physical defects – which her enemies said were the marks the Devil set on his own – she turned to advantage. Proud and independent, sharp-witted and talented, she was completely alluring.

Anne is at the heart of controversy, surrounded by those who played notable parts in the country's history – men like Cromwell, Wolsey and Cranmer. Dominating them all is the glittering figure of Henry, sometimes sentimental, always ruthless. Then Anne herself, impetuous, reckless, heading for danger and realizing this only when it is too late.

This is the love story which rocked the foundations of the Church and changed the course of English history, the story of an obsessive love which turned into a murderous hate.

JEAN PLAIDY

The Lady in the Tower

FONTANA/Collins

First published by Robert Hale Ltd 1986
This edition first issued in Fontana Paperbacks 1988

Copyright © Jean Plaidy 1986

Made and printed in Great Britain by
William Collins Sons and Co. Ltd, Glasgow

CONTENTS

The Prisoner

Here I lie in my dark prison. I hear voices in the night – those who were here before me, those who had suffered as I am suffering now, numbed by fear, without hope, the prisoners of the King.

They came for me yesterday, and we glided along the river to the great grey Tower. Many times had I seen it before but never with such fearful clarity. Once I came here in great pomp and glory – and that only three years ago – and never for one moment then would it have seemed possible that one day I should be brought here – a prisoner.

It was May then as now and the people crowded the river banks to see me pass. I was proud, so confident, so sure of my power. At the prow of my state barge was the stem of gold with branches of red and white roses – symbolic of York and Lancaster, which the King displayed on every occasion to remind people that the Tudors had united the warring factions; and among those roses was my very own symbol, the White Falcon, with the motto 'Me and Mine'.

How had I come to pass from such adulation to bitter rejection in three short years? Was it my fault? I must be in some measure to blame. When did I cease to be the adored one and become the outcast?

The people had not cheered me even in my day of triumph. They did not like me. All their affection was for Queen Katharine. They did not accept me. 'We will have none of her,' they cried. 'Queen Katharine is our true Queen.' They would have abused me if they had dared. The people were my enemies, but I had greater and more powerful enemies than they were. Now they would be openly gathering against me; even during the days of my triumph they had sought to destroy me; how much more assiduously would they work against me now! And they had succeeded for I was the King's prisoner.

As I passed through the gate the clock was striking five, and each stroke was like a funeral knell.

Sir William Kingston, the Lieutenant of the Tower, was waiting for me. I murmured to myself: 'Oh, Lord help me, as I am guiltless of that wherefore I am accused.'

I turned to William Kingston and said: 'Mr Kingston, do I go into a dungeon?'

And he replied: 'No, Madam, to your lodging where you lay at your coronation.'

They took me there and I laughed. I could not stop laughing, for I, who had come in such pomp and glory just three years ago, now was here in the same apartment . . . a prisoner.

Had they brought me here purposely to remind me? Was it a touch of that exquisite torture which so many of my enemies knew so well how to administer?

My women tried to soothe me. They knew the nature of that wild laughter; and in time I was quiet.

I thought: I will write to him, I will move him with my words. I will remind him of how it once was between us.

I wrote and I destroyed what I wrote. Again and again I took up my pen and tried to appeal to him.

'Your Grace's displeasure and my imprisonment are things so strange unto me that what to write or what to excuse, I am altogether ignorant . . . '

That was not true. I did know and I would not make it easy for him. I knew him well – his reasoning, his sanctimonious excuses, his mean, hypocritical nature, his passionate desires all cloaked in piety. No, I would not make it easy for him.

My angry pen flew on. My lack of discretion had often turned people against me, but I was reckless. I was fighting for my life. I would let him know that I was aware of the real reason why he wanted to be rid of me.

' . . . that Your Grace may be at liberty, both before God and man, not only to execute worthy punishment on me as an unfaithful wife, but to follow your affections already settled on that party for whose sake I am now as I am . . . '

Angrily I wrote – more vehement perhaps because *I* was now in the position of the discarded wife.

He would be angry. He would try to pretend that it was not because he desired another woman that he wished to be rid of me. He was a past master – not of deceiving others, for those about him saw through his utterings and posturings as clearly as I did – but of deceiving himself.

He was superstitious, fearful of ill luck; he committed his sins with one eye on Heaven hoping to pull the wool over the eyes of God and His angels as he thought he did over those of his ministers and courtiers.

'But if you have already determined of me that not only my death but an infamous slander must bring you the joying of your desired happiness, then I desire of God that He will pardon your great sin herein and likewise my enemies, the instruments thereof and that He will not call you to a strait account of your unprincely and cruel usage of me . . . '

I was again on the verge of hysterical laughter. I must calm myself. Others had suffered like this before me. This place was full of the ghosts of martyrs. What was so important about one more?

I sealed the letter. I would send it to the King. I wrote on it 'From the Lady in the Tower.'

It must give him twinges of conscience. His conscience was important to him. He referred to it constantly; and knowing him well, I believed that it did exist.

I could see him in my mind's eye so clearly – those days at Hever and at Court – his little eyes alight with desire for me, his cruel mouth suddenly soft and tender – for me. How he had wanted me! He had fought for me with that tenacity which was a part of his nature; he had been determined to have me. For me he had shaken the foundations of the

Church; and however much he declared he did it to satisfy his conscience, he knew . . . the whole world knew . . . that he had done it for me.

So where did it change? There must have been some point where I started to go downhill. When? I could have stopped myself perhaps.

I remembered early days at Blickling and Hever and later at Court where I was surrounded by those who loved me. My dearest brother George, my friends, Thomas and Mary Wyatt, Norris, Weston, Brereton – the wits and poets of the Court. We had talked of life and death, of ambition and achievement; we had come to the conclusion that we were all masters of our fate. The wise knew how to recognize danger before it reached them, to step aside and let it pass by. We were what we made ourselves.

That was George's theory. Some of the others disputed it; and in a Court where living was precarious and once-great men could be brought low in the space of an hour it was a debatable conclusion.

But in my heart I believed there was some truth in it, for if a man or woman did not wish to face danger he or she could stay away from where danger would most likely be – and nowhere in the country was that more than at Court.

So where did I go wrong? Where was that moment when I could have averted the danger?

I could have produced a son; but that was not in my power. I had my sweet daughter Elizabeth and I loved her dearly, though I did not want to think of her, for I greatly feared what would become of her. She had her governess, a good friend of mine. I trusted Lady Bryan for she loved the child well and her husband was a kinsman of my family. When the power had been mine I had always looked after my own family.

But I must not think of Elizabeth now. It was too distressing and could do no good.

But if I had had a son this would not have happened. Henry would have been unfaithful, but the ambitious Seymour brothers would not have been able to guide their silly sister; she would have become his mistress no doubt and I should have been expected to accept that. I should have raged against them; I should have been insulted and humiliated, but I should not be in this doleful prison in the Tower.

No. I had taken a false step somewhere. All through the waiting years I had managed – with consummate skill, all would agree – to hold him at bay, to refuse him until I could take an honourable position beside him. Suppose I had not done this? Then I should now be a cast-off mistress instead of a Queen in a Tower.

I put my fingers to my throat. It was long and slender. It added an elegance to my figure. I accentuated it as I did all my assets and I disguised my defects, with success, I believe. I could almost feel the sword there.

All through the waiting years I had known I must hold him off. I knew him as the hunter and his delight in pursuit. As long as it remained the chase he was determined to succeed. But the joys of capture were brief.

I should have known. I should have realized even as the crown was placed upon my head that it was there precariously.

I knew well the man on whom my fate depended. None knew him better. I should have realized that my life depended on one who was not to be relied on. His fancies faded as quickly as they came. I had been bemused because he had pursued me so ardently and with such persistence. The years of the chase had been long; those of possession short. When had he begun to weary? When had he begun to realize all he had done for me and to ask himself whether it had been worthwhile? What did he think now of his public quarrel with the Pope and the power of Rome – all for a woman who had ceased to interest him?

I should never have become involved with him. I should have escaped while there was time. I should have married Henry Percy. I should have died of the Sweat. Then this would never have come to pass.

Somewhere along the years the fault lay with me. Where? I would seek it. It would occupy me in my prison. It would keep my thoughts in the past, away from contemplation of the fearful future.

I would go back to those happy days at Blickling and Hever, to the glitter of the Court of France, my return to England – a young girl knowledgeable beyond her years, brought up in the most sophisticated and elegant Court in the world. That was what had made me what I was, and what I was had brought me to my present state. I wanted to recall it in detail . . . and while I waited here in my prison I would do so.

The Death of a King

The first time I saw the King was in the cavalcade on the way to Dover where his sister, the Princess Mary, was to embark for France and her marriage to the King of that country. To my surprise I was a member – though a very humble one – of that glorious assembly. This was the most exciting experience of my young life so far and I was in a state of constant apprehension lest I should act without due propriety and be sent home before we embarked because of some deficiency discovered in me – my youth, my inexperience or because I did not know how to behave with due decorum in the presence of the great. True, I had been assiduously schooled by my governess, Simonette, and I spoke French with a fair fluency; but I was realizing that the cocoon of safety which had enclosed me at Blickling and Hever was no longer there. I had left my childhood behind me for ever.

And there I was in close proximity to the King himself. He was big – surely the biggest man I had ever seen, which was as a king should be. He was twenty-three years old then. His hair shone golden in the September sunshine and he wore it short and straight in a fashion which had come from France where, Simonette told me, all the best fashions came from. There would have been no need for any to be told that he was the King; all would have known just to look at him. He glittered. The jewels in his garments were dazzling; he laughed and joked as he rode along and the laughter of those about him seemed to punctuate every remark he made.

On one side of him rode the Queen and on the other the Princess Mary. Beside him the Queen looked almost sombre – a peahen beside a glorious peacock. She had a serious, kindly face and the cross she wore about her neck called attention to that piety which we all knew was hers.

The Princess Mary bore a strong resemblance to her brother; she was strikingly beautiful, but at this time she wore a sullen expression which indicated that, however much others might be delighted by her marriage, she was not.

I thought how alarming it must be to be despatched off to a husband whom one had never seen and who had already had two wives – the last one recently dead and the first put away because she was hump-backed, ill-favoured and could not bear children. I knew this because Simonette had thought it necessary for me to know what was going on in the world about me, and as I was called precocious and Simonette said I was wise beyond my years, I listened to what I was told and remembered it.

The marriage had been arranged to indicate friendship between France and England who had until recently been at war with each other. England's allies had been the Emperor Maximilian and Ferdinand of Spain; but Maximilian and Ferdinand had been uncertain allies and Louis of France was a wise man who saw the futility of war and sought to end it. This he did, breaking up the alliance by offering his daughter Renée as a bride for Maximilian's grandson Charles and to Ferdinand he offered Navarre on which Ferdinand had long cast covetous eyes. That left England to fight France alone; but Louis was prepared for that. Why not a friendship sealed by his marriage to Henry's sister? It must have been hard for our King to turn away such a glittering prize. His sister to be Queen of France! So, smarting from the humiliation inflicted on him by the perfidy of Maximilian and Ferdinand and knowing a good bargain when he saw one, he agreed. It was too good to be resisted so Princess Mary was being led most reluctantly to the altar. It was small wonder that she looked sullen.

As we came into Dover the fierce wind was rising and a feeling of apprehension swept through the company. None of us looked forward to crossing that strip of water which

14

separated us from the Continent of Europe. Storms blew up suddenly and I had heard people talk with horror of what had to be endured on a storm-tossed ship.

So we came to the castle where we should stay until the sea was calm enough for us to set out.

The great fortress loomed before us, its basements dug into the solid rock. It was known as the Gateway to England – a formidable building which could house two thousand soldiers and which had stood for centuries overlooking the sea. It was said that King Arthur of legend had inhabited the castle and that William the Conqueror had had difficulty in taking it. Of course it had changed since those days; it had been restored and added to, to make it the great fortress it was today; and here we must stay to await the King's pleasure and that of the sea.

*

As I lay in bed listening to the wind buffeting the walls of the castle I thought of how my life had changed so quickly. It had begun with the death of my mother two years before.

I believed I would never forget that day at Blickling. The Wyatts – Thomas and Mary – were with my own sister Mary, my brother George and myself in the garden. We saw a great deal of the Wyatts because our father and theirs had been appointed joint Constables of Norwich Castle; and when we were in Kent – they at Allington and we at Hever – we were close neighbours. We were great friends. I found Thomas exciting to be with and Mary a comfort.

Thomas was a vital person. He wrote poetry and he used to read it to us. Sometimes it made us laugh; sometimes it made us think. I was always happy to see Thomas; and his sister Mary was a girl who never said an unkind word about anyone; she was serious and quite clever. I think I liked Thomas more than anyone except my brother George, who was also a poet and a great talker. I loved to be with them both although I was

15

expected to listen; and I was not allowed to speak for long, they being so much older than I was.

As for my sister Mary, she admitted that she never listened to what they said. Her mind would be flitting off on lighter matters such as what ribbon she would wear in her hair or whether her dress should be blue or pink. That was Mary – not so much stupid as having a lack of concentration. But she was good-hearted and we all loved her.

I was not quite six years old but I seemed much older, perhaps because my father had insisted that Mary and I should be given a better education than most girls of our station, and I profited from it, even if Mary did not. Daughters of minor aristocracy were usually sent away from home at an early age to some noble household where they would learn to read and write, to sing, to dance and play the lute, to ride side-saddle, to curtsy, to wash their hands before and after a meal, to handle a knife with grace and to dip it into the salt bowl, take a delicate portion and never pick it up with the fingers. That was not good enough for my father. So we were kept at home until the right place could be found for us, which was not easy, for his aims were high and opportunities had to be waited for.

I knew why, of course. I had heard George talking to Thomas Wyatt. We did not have to look far back into the family history to see what great progress we had made. Our great-grandfather, the founder of our fortunes, had been a mere merchant trading in silk and wool cloth. It was true he was a very special merchant, for he had acquired a title and become Lord Mayor of London. His greatest cleverness, though, was in his marriage, for his wife was the daughter of Lord Hoo – and her father's heiress at that. They had a son, William, my grandfather, who had married the daughter of the Earl of Ormond; hence more blue blood was injected into the Boleyn circulation. My father had done best of all, for he had married Elizabeth Howard, daughter of the Earl of Surrey, who in due course became the Duke of Norfolk; and the Dukes of Norfolk considered themselves – most danger-ously – more royal than the Tudors.

That was the pattern, said George, and our father planned for us all to continue with it. Therefore his children must receive a special education. They must be prepared to stand equal with the highest in the land. They should therefore not only learn the social graces but have the education which was generally reserved for royal children.

Our governess, Simonette, was aware of this. She was a worldly woman with the fatalism and realism of her race. I was her favourite which was strange because Mary was more lovable as well as being outstandingly pretty. She was hopeless with her lessons, because she would not – or could not – give her mind to them. So I supposed that was why Simonette favoured me.

I must dance as the French danced, walk as they walked in France; and I must speak French as it was spoken in that country. I was fond of her because she admired me and I had always yearned to be admired. I was very conscious of being less pretty than Mary and I confessed this to Simonette.

'No, no, no,' she cried. 'You have the grace. You have the charm. You will be the one, little Anne. Mary . . . oh yes . . . very pretty . . . loved for a while because she is giving . . . too giving . . . and that can pall. Oh, *mon amour*, I should want to see you older . . . a little older, yes. Those eyes . . . they are *magnifique* . . . yes, *magnifique*. And I tell you this: you know how to use them. It is something you are born with . . . for I have not teach you . . . They will allure, those eyes.'

I studied them critically. They were large, making the rest of my face small in comparison. They and my thick dark hair were compensation for the mole on the front of my neck and the beginning of a nail on the side of my little finger which made me think that God had intended to give me a sixth finger and changed his mind, leaving me with only the nail.

I hated it. I could not understand it. I found myself staring, fascinated, at other people's hands.

My brother George said: 'Never mind. It makes you different. Who wants to be the same as everybody else?'

'I do,' I said vehemently.

Simonette also tried to comfort me. 'Sometimes it is more *chic* to have a little imperfection ... more human ... more exciting ... more fascinating. You will see.'

Then came that summer's day when we were all in the gardens. I remember so well that feeling of impending doom. I knew that something fearful was going to happen. The household was subdued. Even George and Thomas Wyatt were quiet. Mary was trying to fight off the evil as she always would by pretending that it did not exist.

But we knew that all was not well, for they had sent to my father, bringing him home from the Court and that would be something no one would dare do unless it was very important.

My mother was dying. This was not just another of those yearly illnesses which beset her. This was not what they called 'another disappointment'. This went beyond that. The doctors were there with the midwife.

I thought of her. She was tender and loving to us children, but we had seen little of her. When she was well she accompanied our father to Court and it was only when he was on embassies abroad that she returned to her family. When she grew heavy with child she would be with us. Then would come the confinement and the brief rest before she joined our father. It was a pattern which seemed to go on for ever.

Neither George nor Thomas Wyatt could talk as usual on that day. We had been silent, glancing every now and then at the house, waiting.

It was Simonette who came to tell us. I knew as soon as I saw her walking across the grass as though reluctant to reach us.

To lose one's mother when one is not quite six years old is not only a tragic but an illuminating experience. It teaches one that life is not as pleasantly predictable as one had thought it to be. There comes a terrible sense of aloneness and the alarming knowledge that nothing will ever be the same as it was before.

Our father went away on a mission to the Netherlands and was absent for a whole year, and when he came back there was more change in our household. He was clearly rather pleased with himself. George told us that he had had to conclude a treaty with Margaret of Savoy, Archduchess of Austria, by which the Emperor Maximilian, Pope Julius and Ferdinand of Spain, should, with England, make war on France. This was the treaty which was soon to founder; but at that time my father believed that its conclusion was a great success for him. There was something else which was equally pleasing to him. My sister Mary was to go to the Court in Brussels over which Margaret reigned as Regent of the Netherlands.

George said: 'This is what our father always wanted – to get his children into royal circles.'

So I lost Mary and as George was soon to go to Cambridge – and Thomas Wyatt with him – our little group was much diminished and Mary Wyatt and I did our best to console each other.

I remember well the long summer days at Hever or riding over to Allington, feeding the pigeons with Mary Wyatt. I was fascinated by the pigeons; they had light brown feathers, different from the ordinary grey ones. I thought the reason why they were there was so romantic. I had first heard it from Thomas who told it so beautifully – as he did everything.

His father, Sir Henry, had been the prisoner of Richard III because he had not supported his accession to the throne, and on account of this had been thrown into the Tower. There he was severely tortured and when he had fainted with the agony, mustard and vinegar had been forced down his throat to revive him. When he refused to give way, he was put into a cell and left to starve.

Sir Henry had thought his end was near but one day he saw a cat on the windowsill. He staggered to the window, delighted to have contact with some living thing; he put his hand through the bars to stroke the cat's fur. Instead of repulsing him the cat had purred. He felt the better for it. The cat went away but shortly afterwards came back with a pigeon it had caught and killed. The pigeon was for Sir Henry. It was food and he was almost dead of starvation. He ate the pigeon.

The next day, the cat appeared again with another pigeon, and thus did that cat keep Sir Henry alive all through the time of his captivity. So he lived to see the defeat of Richard at Bosworth Field and the arrival of Henry Tudor, who, wishing to reward him for his fidelity to the House of Lancaster, immediately freed him and restored his estate to him.

Sir Henry never forgot. Whenever I saw him at Allington it was with a cat . . . not the same one which had kept him alive, but a descendant of that cat; his cat was like a faithful hound; it followed him wherever he went, slept on his bed and was constantly in his company; and to remind himself of how he had been saved, he had pigeons brought to Allington and he said they would be there as long as there were Wyatts in the castle. And the strange thing was that the cat and the pigeons of Allington were friends. They lived together amicably in the castle – symbols of Sir Henry's survival to serve with loyalty the Tudor Kings.

So Mary Wyatt and I were often together at Allington or Hever until I heard that I was to go to France in the service of the King's sister.

So here I was about to embark on this great adventure.

*

When we arrived at Dover Castle a gale was sweeping in from the sea and white horses were flinging themselves against the white cliffs in an abandon of fury that sent a shiver of alarm through me.

Lady Guildford, who was in charge of us, came to the

apartment to which we had been taken and told us that we should not be embarking yet but that we must be prepared to leave as soon as the sea grew calm which, she stressed, could be at any time.

Seeing us settled in our apartment, she went back to the Princess and I was left with the other ladies who were inclined to look down their aristocratic noses at me. I was considered to be the outsider by my companions, Anne and Elizabeth Grey, the two sisters of the Marquis of Dorset, the sister of Lord Grey and the daughter of Lord Dacre. Who are these Boleyns? they were saying. True, I was the grand-daughter of the Duke of Norfolk – he who considered himself more royal than the Tudors – and he had actually been in the cavalcade with his son, the Earl of Surrey, but they had pointedly ignored my father as though to disclaim the family connection; and I supposed these ladies took their cue from the Duke. I had always known that he deplored my mother's marriage into a family which had its roots in trade. So I was of little account – and not only because of my youth.

They talked over my head as though they were quite unaware of my existence. This infuriated me. Who were they? I asked myself. The Greys were descended from Elizabeth Woodville, and who was she before the King married her? I had always liked the story of how he came across her in the forest and had fallen in love with her and secretly married her, and when it was a *fait accompli* he had confronted his ministers with what he had done. This was the glorious Edward IV, grandfather to our present King, and, as some said, the two were very much alike.

Edward had triumphed in the Wars of the Roses but he was known to be the most profligate man in England, and his mistresses were legion. Our King had not had the same success in battle and he was, I had heard Tom Wyatt say, moderately faithful to his Queen. So perhaps it was only in appearance that they were similar.

I listened avidly to the talk around me.

'I am sorry for the Princess. She is so angry,' said Anne Grey.

'Who would not be, buffeted about like a shuttlecock . . . first betrothed to one, then to another. And the Princess of all people. We know her temper.'

'I thought the King might relent right at the last moment. He is very indulgent with her.'

'But this is politics. It has to be. I think she is a little glad to escape from Charles. By all accounts he would not have been the bridegroom for her.'

There was laughter. 'And you think poor old Louis is?'

'Hush. *Lèse majesté*. You are speaking of the King of France.'

'Well, even so, everyone knows he is all of fifty-two. Just think of our beautiful Mary with that old man.'

'She will make him dance to her tune.'

'Of course she will. But how angry she is . . . and how she longs for Suffolk!'

'I was sure at one time the King would give way to her.'

'Oh no . . . not even to his beloved sister. It is all part of the treaty. That is what royal marriages are about.'

'I long to know what she will do when she *sees* him.'

'You will. She will let us know. She will let everyone know.'

'When her temper flares out . . . '

'As it will.'

'But the King loves her well. That is why he is waiting here to say goodbye to her.'

'Perhaps,' said Elizabeth Grey, 'he fears that if he does not see her off she will come back to Court . . . or run off with Suffolk.'

'How she would like to do that!'

'And knowing her, do you think she might attempt it?'

And so they continued to talk while we were in our beds but I was so tired that I was soon fast asleep.

The next day I came face to face with the Princess herself. She took my chin in her hands and studied me. She was in one of her good moods apparently. 'Little Boleyn, is it?' she asked. She added, 'Fine eyes you have, child.' And she gave me a little tap on the cheek.

That, said the ladies, was indeed a mark of approval.

I said I was amazed that she should have noticed me.

'Oh, it is only because you are so young,' I was told by Anne Grey. 'Lady Guildford is really very put out because you are here. She said did they expect her to look after children.'

I heard one of them whisper something about Thomas Boleyn always being on the lookout for favours.

But it did not worry me unduly that I was resented. Everything was so novel to me and to be here in the castle waiting for the wind to change, being ready to embark at short notice, was very exciting.

The time came at four o'clock on the morning of 2 October. Everyone had been growing more and more uneasy the longer we stayed, for the year was advancing and October was notorious for its gales. We should have waited for the spring, but matters of state have to be concluded, whatever the time.

I shall never forget that voyage. I thought it was the end of my life and that I should never see France. We had not gone more than a few miles when the storm arose and the fleet was scattered. Never in my wildest imaginings had I thought of anything like this. The ladies were terrified; and Lady Guildford hovered round the Princess, who seemed less concerned than the rest of us.

I realized then how she must be dreading her marriage for she cried out, laughing rather wildly: 'I rejoice for perhaps I shall not be Queen of France after all, Mother Guildford.' She always called Lady Guildford 'Mother' because they had been together since the Princess's childhood.

How unhappy one must be to welcome death! But later I realized that she, who was so full of life, would cling to it with her entire being; it was just her reckless and extravagant way of talking. The Princess Mary could not be quietly sad, she had to be tragically so and let everyone know it.

So we were flung about – too frightened to feel even the horrible sickness which had begun to affect most of us. We could think only of one thing: death in that angry sea.

We were making for Boulogne – I heard later that some of the ships put in at Calais and some even went to Flanders – and the ordeal seemed to go on for hours. Then suddenly someone called: 'Land!'

But that was not the end of our troubles. The Captain could not get the ship into the harbour and we ran aground outside it. But at least we felt comparatively safe then, for although we were still surrounded by sea we could see people watching on the shore.

We were all on deck, drenched to the skin, our hair wildly flying, and soon they were sending out little boats to bring us in. One gallant gentleman waded out and shouted that he would carry the Queen ashore. Mary was lowered into his arms and we watched him take her to dry land.

Then it was our turn; but no gentleman came for us. We must, with great difficulty, get into the little rowing boats and ride the waves again.

But at last the ordeal was over. We had arrived.

It had been a terrifying experience.

*

The Princess Mary was in fact already the Queen of France for the proxy ceremony had taken place at Greenwich (with the Duc de Longueville standing in for the King of France; and in France with the Earl of Worcester incongruously taking the place of Mary) but we had been apt to think of her still as our Princess and should do so until the ceremony had been performed between her and King Louis. This was due to take place in two days' time.

The day after our arrival we were to make the journey to Abbeville where the King would be waiting to greet his bride.

24

It was amazing how quickly we recovered from our ordeal. Few would have recognized the bedraggled creatures who had come ashore in those rowing boats as the dazzling company who prepared to journey with the new Queen to meet her bridegroom.

I had thought a great deal about her and how tragic it was for one so beautiful to be sent to a loveless marriage, particularly when – as I had gathered – her love was for someone else. Had I been older, with more knowledge of human nature as I was to come to know it later, I should have felt less sympathy perhaps. It was true that Mary was in love with Suffolk, and Mary, being a Tudor, was subject to intense emotions, loving and hating more violently than most people; it was true that she was being forced into a marriage with an old man who might be repulsive to her, but Mary's nature was such as would enable her to exploit any situation to her advantage and emerge from it unscathed and with the determination to have her own way in the end. As indeed it proved for her.

How beautiful she looked in white cloth of silver with a jewelled coif on her lovely hair; her skin was smooth and pink like her brother's. I envied her fairness.

Our clothes, which had been carefully chosen for this occasion, had been safely brought ashore – for which we were thankful – and our dresses were of crimson velvet. I was glad of this for it was a colour which was most becoming to my dark hair and eyes. I noticed one or two ladies glance at me; they said nothing, but I could see by their looks that they were reluctantly admiring me, which pleased me very much.

The King had sent over horsemen and archers to accompany us – a gentle reminder, no doubt, of our fighting strength, even though, through this marriage, we were the friendliest of neighbours.

We were just leaving Boulogne when a party of horsemen rode up. At the head of them was one of the most striking men I had ever seen. He was tall – as tall as the King of England –

and one rarely saw men as tall; but where Henry was dazzlingly fair this man was dark. He was dressed with extreme elegance and here and there a jewel gleamed about his person to suggest good taste rather than ostentation. Oddly enough, the first moment I saw him, I found myself making comparisons with the King of England.

He was clearly a person of high rank. This was obvious by the attitude of those about him. I quickly learned his identity. He was François de Valois, Comte d'Angoulême and the Dauphin of France. I had heard of him, for Simonette had often talked to me of her country. If old Louis did not get sons, François would be King of France.

I wondered how François felt to see this lovely young girl coming into his country to marry the King. If the marriage should be fruitful, it would be the end of François's hopes.

There was something secretly sly about him, I thought, though his manners were as exquisite as his garments. He leaped from his horse and bowed low as he took Mary's hand. His eyes surveyed her and he managed to convey a great deal by his expression for if he had said he found her beautiful, charming, very exciting and completely desirable, it could not have been more explicit than his looks.

He addressed her in musical French telling her of his great joy in her arrival. He was welcoming her to France and was proud to have the honour of escorting her to Abbeville.

His glance travelled over the ladies. It even included me whom he must have found uninterestingly youthful. Then he rode beside Mary and we made our way to Abbeville.

When we were within a short distance of the town a party of horsemen came riding towards us. They pulled up sharply and one of their number moved forward and came to the Princess. I guessed who he was, for the Dauphin had leaped from his horse, removed his cap, bowed his head and stood at attention. I noticed a slightly sardonic smile on his handsome face as he did so. Was he guessing that the bride was comparing the King of France with the Dauphin?

The King looked small and insignificant beside François. His eyes were big and rather prominent; his neck was swollen – with some disease, I imagined; but there was something kindly about him and I liked him for that.

He was looking at Mary and was, I believe, unaware of the rest of us.

She sat there on her horse, glowingly healthy and beautiful – pink, white and gold and a little Tudor arrogance. She was very sure of herself and I fancy made a little happier by such obvious admiration.

'The Dauphin has taken good care of you, I trust,' said the King.

Mary replied in rather charmingly accented French that indeed he had and so had all since she had set foot in France.

The King took her hand and kissed it. 'They deceived me,' he said. 'They just told me you were beautiful – but not how beautiful.'

Mary replied that His Grace was too kind.

The King said he had told his courtiers that he was going to hunt but he had been unable to curb his impatience. He would now have to leave her; and he was going to let the Dauphin conduct her to Abbeville. Then she would know that the cheers of the crowd were for her alone.

He rode off. François leaped into the saddle and brought his horse close to hers. It was obvious that he was attracted by her.

And so we came into Abbeville.

*

The next day they were married. My grandfather, the Duke of Norfolk, and the Marquis of Dorset rode with her to the Hôtel de la Gruthuse.

I wondered what she was thinking of her sickly bridegroom with the bulging eyes and the swollen neck. Of course he had a crown to offer her. Did she think it was worth it? I knew she did not, for she yearned for the Duke of Suffolk. Everyone knew this, for she made no secret of it. I was glad it was not yet time for me to be married and I wondered who would be chosen for me. I would rebel if I did not like the choice. But then I was not royal. I was thankful that I should not be a clause in a treaty.

The ceremony took place in the great hall of the Hôtel de la Gruthuse which had been made very grand for the occasion. Cloth of gold and silver with beautiful tapestries lined the walls; the glass windows had been designed to show pictures of the life of the town's saint, Wulfran; they threw a tinted light on the cloth of gold and silver, making it shimmer, which added a magical touch to all the elegant furniture which had been put into the room for this very special time.

A canopy was held over the bride and one of the bearers of this was the Dauphin, the other the Duc d'Alençon who was the husband of the Dauphin's sister Marguerite.

Thus Mary Tudor became truly Queen of France.

It was at this ceremony that I was first aware of the Princesse Claude, daughter of the King, for, to my amazement, I had heard that she was the wife of the fascinating Dauphin. What an incongruous pair! She was slightly deformed, had a limp and looked sickly. Her marriage had obviously been made by a treaty. François, the future King of France – providing Louis did not get a male heir – would naturally have to marry the daughter of the reigning King. It was all very neat, but I did wonder what the thoughts of Claude might be as she watched her fascinating husband, and even more did I wonder what was going on in François's mind. That he was ambitious, I had no doubt. So what would he be feeling now to see the King married to, and so enamoured of, this beautiful young girl? If this marriage was fruitful, what of François's hopes for the crown?

It was an interesting situation and now I had recovered from that fearful sea crossing, I was beginning to feel normal again and most exhilarated to be here, away from those backwaters, Blickling and Hever, out in the world where extraordinary and exciting events took place.

There was a great deal of giggling and whispered conversation in the apartment that night. They were all talking about the new Queen of France and the old King.

Lady Guildford was very sad. She had been with the Princess Mary from her childhood and regarded her as her own child. She spoke sharply to the ladies for she guessed the gist of their conversation and it upset her.

'They will sprinkle the bed with holy water,' said Anne Grey. 'They will bless it and pray that it will be fruitful.'

'Just imagine her . . . listening to all that. It is a beautiful bed, they say, with a canopy of velvet and everywhere the golden lilies of France. They know how to make things look beautiful.'

'It won't make up for the man she has to share it with.'

'Well, what about François . . . '

They whispered together.

'Hush. Don't forget the little Boleyn. Why did they send babies with us?'

'Her father snatches every opportunity. He evidently found one here.'

'He is very sharp. He gets that from the silk merchants.'

I wanted to hit them. I wished I could. I was often impulsive and acted without thought; but I remembered that if I did anything like that I should be sent home immediately. Lady Guildford would be only too glad of the excuse to be rid of me. Simonette had often told me that I acted first and thought afterwards, which was a very unwise thing to do.

So, as the last thing I wanted was to be sent home, I meekly hung my head and shut my ears; and I lay in bed thinking about the King of France and his new English Queen.

*

The next day a great shock awaited us. The ladies who had

come from England to serve the Queen were all to be sent home.

There was great dismay in our apartment. Lady Guildford was too shocked to speak. There was chatter and speculation. 'Is this how he intends to treat her? She will never allow it. She will storm and rage.'

I think they were right about that. But the King had great dignity and determination. I had heard before that when royal personages married into foreign lands their attendants were invariably replaced. Naturally, the Queen of France must not be surrounded by English attendants.

Lady Guildford was incensed when she recovered from the first shock. Had she not been with her Princess since her childhood? How could Mary manage without her?

But Mary did manage without her. She had to.

The strangest thing of all was that the King had said she might keep one of her retinue – the little girl. I could not believe it. I had been selected as the only one to stay! It was naturally because of my extreme youth for I would obviously be considered too young to indulge in political scheming and such like. So . . . I was safe.

Perhaps Mary was not sorry to see the last of her attendants – except, of course, Lady Guildford of whom, I was sure, she was genuinely fond. Mary, whom I was to know more intimately after the others had left, was tempestuous by nature; she would flare into anger but very soon afterwards would have forgotten her rage; she was generous at times, mean at others; but there was a certain shrewdness in her which never really allowed her to forget what would be advantageous to herself; and whatever impetuosity she was involved in, she would always stop short of disaster.

I think she had made up her mind that the King of France could not live long; whatever she had to endure could not last and for this reason she was more amenable than she would otherwise have been, for when she was free of her husband she should have complete charge of her own affairs. Moreover, in place of her ladies, she had the Duchesse d'Alençon, that very talented and fascinating sister of François, and, as I was to learn later, her company was a great deal more enjoyable than that of the discarded ladies. The Princesse Claude was also sent to comfort her, and I think Claude did not displease her either. She was, after all, her stepdaughter, and the fact that she was married to the exciting François did intrigue Mary a little.

I was glad to discover she took a fancy to me.

'You are all they have left to me!' she cried, looking at me quizzically.

'I am sorry, Your Highness,' I said.

'Sorry! That you are to serve me?'

'Oh, no, no . . . sorry that I should be all that is left to you. Sorry for Your Highness, pleased for myself.'

That answer seemed to amuse her.

'Well, little Boleyn, we have to make the best of what comes to us, do we not?'

There were occasions when she was almost affectionate towards me. She would show me jewels the King had given her.

'Poor man,' she said. 'He tries so hard to please me.'

She liked me to brush her hair. Then she would smile at me and let her thoughts run on. I think at times she forgot my youth. Very soon she was telling me about her lover – the incomparable Charles Brandon, the Duke of Suffolk.

'There was never a more perfect man on Earth,' she declared. She invariably used exaggerated terms. 'He is *always* the champion at the joust.'

'Does he joust better than the King your brother, Madame?' I asked innocently.

'Well, it is advisable for a subject to be just a little less good than a king. You should know that.'

'But what is the *truth*?'

'Ah, the truth! The truth is that my Charles is the most

31

wonderful man on Earth and does everything better than anyone else.'

'So . . . he allows the King to win?'

'Little Boleyn, you are asking me to utter treason against my brother.'

I looked alarmed, so she took the brush from my hand and put an arm about me.

'I'll not betray you,' she said, her laughing face close to mine. 'I'll not have you sent to the Tower. I'll not have you put on the rack, even. There, little Boleyn. I really think I have frightened you. Now . . . just within these four walls. Charles is the finest man in the world and nobody . . . nobody compares with him.'

Then she would sit thinking of him with a dreamy look in her eyes, and suddenly seem to remember that she was married to the King and her eyes would grow stormy with anger.

I used to sit watching her, waiting for her commands; but sometimes she seemed to forget that I was there.

But in a way she was fond of me then; she often sent for me. She liked me to be there alone, I believe, so that she felt free to talk to herself – which was what she was really doing. I was too young to matter. I expect she felt a little lonely at times in a foreign land. I was after all the only English attendant they had allowed to remain with her. I liked to hear about her love for Charles Brandon. I had even on one or two occasions very carefully prodded her to talk about him when I saw her staring dreamily into space and would ask something about the Duke of Suffolk and she was only too ready to talk.

'I knew as soon as I saw him that he was the one for me.'

'Did he know?' I asked.

'He knows now.'

Then she turned to me and caught my arm. 'One day, little Boleyn, Charles will be my husband. You see, a Princess must marry for state reasons . . . but when she has done it once . . .

32

the next time she should be free to choose for herself. Do you agree?'

'Oh yes, Madame.'

'So shall I . . . when . . . when . . . ' She put her fingers to her lips. 'The King is very old.'

'Yes, Madame.'

'And I am young. Do you know, before I came to Court he used to go to bed at six . . . and now he does not go until midnight. I arrange that. Would I want to go to bed at six . . . with him, do you think?'

'I do not think you would, Madame.'

'No. There are entertainments now. We feast . . . and there are balls, ballets and suchlike . . . as you know, do you not? Poor Louis . . . he has lived such a quiet life with his saintly Anne of Brittany, but he is not married to *her* now, is he? He is married to Mary Tudor and that is a very different matter.'

'Marrying Your Highness has changed his life.'

'And mine, little one.' She put her lips close to my ear. 'We live merrily . . . but how long will it last, think you?' I was too astonished to reply and she went on quickly: 'How long do *you* think it will last? Not forever. And then . . . I shall be free. And the second time I shall make my own choice.'

I learned a great deal from her.

She told me of the King who was so enamoured of her.

'He is so much in love with me,' she said, smiling at her face in the mirror with complacent pride. 'I seem such a child to him. He has had two wives before me . . . and never a really beautiful one before, poor man. Sometimes I am rather sorry for him. He is touching in his devotion. But when I compare him with my Charles . . . but then all would suffer in comparison with him. Louis is a good king. The people appreciate him. He is a moderately moral man . . . as moral as the French go. They have had some wild monarchs. Of course he is not like St Louis. Saints turn up very rarely. But he is not licentious like Charles VII, or coarse like Louis XI or very, very immoral like Charles VIII. You see, it is easy to

33

follow such. So my Louis has the respect of his people. They don't love him, he is not handsome or romantic enough. It is strange, little Boleyn, that kings are not always loved for their virtues. But they are respected for them. My father was respected but not liked. But how they love my brother! Why? Because he is big and handsome and merry. My father did much that was good for England but they love my brother . . . who has not made any great reforms yet.'

'He has not been long on the throne . . . only five years.'

'Is it then? How knowledgeable you are, little one.'

'I had a very good governess.'

'And those big eyes saw all . . . and often what was not intended for them, I'll warrant. And those little ears were always on the alert. That's so. And I talk too much to you, Mademoiselle Boleyn. Now I am going to shut my mouth like a trap and tell you nothing.'

I was downcast. I had been foolish to display my knowledge and remind her that I could remember what I had heard.

But of course she did not stop her confidences, and what she said one moment she had forgotten the next.

She told me about Louis's previous wives. 'He had to marry Jeanne. She was the daughter of Louis XI. She was very ugly and had a hump on her back. But she was very good, saintly in fact. I suppose it is easy to be good if one is ugly.' She sighed. 'I shall never be a saint. Why do you smile? I'll tell you this: you will not be one either.' Then she laughed and hugged me for a moment. She was very familiar when we were alone. She went on: 'You amuse me with those big, wondering eyes. You are not in the least pretty, you know. But you have something more. You are going to find life very amusing, I am sure. You will not be like saintly Jeanne, I promise you. Poor girl, she could have no children. What store these kings set by children! Sons, sons, sons – that is what they want. It is an insult to our sex, is it not? Louis hopes I will have a son. François, his mother and sister live in daily terror that I shall have one – for if I did, what would become of bold François's

34

hopes of the crown, eh, tell me that? Sons . . . sons . . . Well, poor little hump-backed Jeanne could not have any and Louis – my husband now – begged the Pope to annul their marriage.' She paused and laughed.

I waited eagerly and then I said: 'And did he, Madame?'

'But of course he did. You see, this Pope was the notorious Alexander VI – Roderigo Borgia. He had a son. Ah, you say, but Popes do not marry. No, little one, you are right. But it is not necessary to marry to have sons . . . and this Pope had a son called Cesare Borgia. He loved him dearly and sought great favours for him. Now Louis was in a position to be of great use to this young man, and in return for favours to Cesare, the annulment was granted.'

'What happened to Jeanne, Madame?'

'What do you think? She accepted her dismissal with quiet resignation. Would you have done so? I would not. But we do not belong to that band of worthy females. Louis was free and he married another saintly one – Anne of Brittany – the widow of the previous King. But she was not quite perfect. She was lame, but pretty, they say, very witty and clever. Both she and Louis had great respect for each other; and although she could not give him sons – fortunately for François – she did produce two daughters – Mesdames Claude and Renée whom you have seen at Court.'

She paused and I almost held my breath. I was always afraid that she would remember that she was talking too much, and stop. For the first time in my life I was glad that I was of little account.

'They were married for fifteen years,' she went on dreamily. 'Fifteen years . . . think of that! She was a very good ruler, though some say she had more care for Brittany than for France. But she was greatly respected and Louis was very sorry when she died.'

'He is sorry no longer since he could not have married Your Grace if she had not died.'

'Oh, he is not sorry now. He is living as he never did before.'

Then she laughed and studied her face carefully in the mirror.

'So much gaiety,' she whispered. 'I say to him: "Why does not my lord retire early? I will be at the revels in your stead. I will represent you." But he says, "No. No, my Queen, I shall be there." Poor tired old man! And he comes to his bed so wearily at night that there is nothing else for him to do but sleep the sleep of the exhausted.' She smiled. 'He is afraid, you see, because . . . '

She looked at me steadily and I cast down my eyes and tried to look innocent and to hide my eager desire to hear more. 'You see . . . he is afraid of François. I believe that François is in love with me . . . a little.'

'You are so beautiful that it is not surprising,' I told her.

She shook her head. 'François is passionately in love with all things beautiful. Fine buildings, fine music, poetry, pictures, statues and beautiful women. But most of all he is in love with himself. So, my clever little Boleyn, he would not have a great deal of love to spare for one person. He would like to make love to me – and the prospect is all the more enticing because he would be afraid to. What if I were to be with child . . . by him! What a situation! It is enough to make the gods laugh. He wants me . . . very much he wants me. He says so with his eyes. I know. But what if he gave me a child? That child would be the King of France because all would think it was the King's. His son would be a king, but it is himself he wants the crown for.'

She stopped suddenly. 'What am I saying? You are a witch. You are probing my secret thoughts. Go away. You are dismissed.' Then she caught my arm and held it so tightly that I could have cried out with the pain. 'If you ever mention a word of what I say to anyone . . . I'll have you in the Tower. Yes, I shall send to my brother and say, "The child Boleyn is to go to the Tower. She is a traitor." '

36

'I will never say a word ... '

'Go away. I don't want to see you. I want to go home. I want to see Charles again.'

I crept away. I was heartbroken for I did not know what I had done to displease her.

Time dragged heavily when I was not with her.

*

Those months were full of revelations for me. I think I grew up then. The Court was rather sombre for the King had a reputation for parsimony. He was a good king and did not want to tax his people to pay for his extravagances which was a habit most kings indulged in; and because of this they called him mean. He hated war, therefore they called him unadventurous. France prospered under him more than it had under his predecessors, but the people did not love him because he was not the glittering figure they liked their kings to be. I often thought how difficult it is to please the people; whatever one was, whatever one did, there would always be the other side of the picture to bring complaints.

Of course I saw him only from a distance, but I did realize how he doted on his beautiful young Queen. He often looked pale and fatigued; his eyes seemed to have grown more prominent, his neck more swollen. In the evenings at revelries – which I was sometimes allowed to attend – he looked as though he needed nothing so much as sleep. But the Queen would be there dancing – often with François, laughing and coquetting. I thought it was not very kind; but I knew from these monologues at the dressing-table how she yearned for her Charles, and that her one idea was to get to him. I could understand that need in her but it did occur to me that she planned these feasts and revels with the great idea of tiring her husband so that he would be too weary for anything but sleep in the big canopied bed decorated with the fleurs-de-lys ... and perhaps to hasten his end.

There were three women at Court who interested me. Perhaps it was because of their connection with François, who himself was the most interesting as well as the most attractive man at Court. These three were François's wife Claude, his sister Marguerite d'Alençon and his mother, Louise of Savoy.

Claude was good and kind. She was like her father in that she tired easily; she was delicate in health and walking exhausted her because of her limp.

She took notice of me because I was so young and she thought that it was wrong for a child of my age to be sent away from her country to live with foreigners. I told her that I was very happy to be here and serve the Queen.

'Ah, the Queen,' she sighed. 'What a beautiful and healthy lady she is!'

There was no malice in her, but she must have hated to see the way in which her husband danced attendance on the Queen. I wondered what she felt like being married to such a man. She accepted her husband's infidelities as a matter of course. She had no doubt been brought up by the excellent Anne of Brittany to do her duty whatever it was, and as the daughter of the reigning King it was her duty to marry the heir presumptive to the throne – and this she had done.

They were hardly ever together; he was usually beside some dazzling beauty. He treated her with courtesy. François's exquisite manners would not have allowed him to do anything else, but at the same time it must have been very hard for her.

I liked to talk with her and really it was great condescension on her part to notice me. She made me read with her and insisted on correcting a slightly imperfect accent. She insisted that I learn to do very fine embroidery and *petit point*, which I quite enjoyed. She was very gentle and I could not help being fond of her.

But she was not as interesting as François's sister. There was a woman who amazed me. She was very beautiful and extremely well educated. She was noted for her cleverness;

she wrote verses and was interested in every new idea which was presented to her. I saw her often with her brother, their arms entwined. In fact, one would have thought *she* was his wife. They loved each other with a fierce passion. The Queen told me that if anyone said a word against François Marguerite would be ready to slay that person. 'Of course,' she added, 'no one ever does say a word against François . . . except the King, and even Marguerite could not slay him. The King is really worried about François. Not so much now but he thinks of what will happen after he has gone. You know how the King cares for the people. He does not want them to be subjected to taxation and hardship, nor to be involved in wars. I heard him say to one of his ministers the other day, "We are labouring in vain, The Big Boy will spoil everything when I am gone." The Big Boy, of course, is François. Marguerite did not hear that or she would have stormed into the royal chamber to castigate the King.'

Marguerite had noticed me even as Claude had.

She said: 'You are young to be in a foreign Court,' just as Claude had. She questioned me and she must have been pleased with my answers for she gave me a book to read.

I read it avidly and when I returned it she questioned me about it. I felt gratified because I could see that I had impressed her with my intelligence.

She was twenty-two years old at the time – two years older than François. At the age of seventeen she had been married to the Duc d'Alençon; but it was clear to everyone that her feelings for him fell far short of those she cherished for her brother. Everyone paid homage to her – not only because of her wit, learning and beauty but because she was the sister of the man they expected shortly to be King and when he was in that supreme position, she would be his chief adviser; in fact, she would rule beside him.

The other who aroused my interest was Louise of Savoy. She had always ignored me; in fact, I do not think she was even aware of my existence. She was a very grand lady, very much aware of her royal connections. She had married Charles, the son of Jean d'Angoulême whose grandfather had been Charles V – hence François's claim to the throne.

Louise doted on François with the same idolatry which was bestowed on him by Marguerite. Mother, daughter and son were irreverently referred to as 'the Holy Trinity'. And thus it was. From the date of François's birth Louise had been hoping for him to ascend the throne. It was said that she had refused all offers of marriage after she became a widow, because she wanted to give her entire attention to her son.

When he was a little boy, the possibility of his ascending the throne must have been remote and it would have seemed to Louise like a miracle when King Charles VIII, on his way to watch a game of tennis with his Queen Anne, had struck his head against a stone archway and died as a result. Consequently Louis d'Orléans became Louis XII and Louis was at that time married to crippled Jeanne who had no hope of bearing a child. That was why he had decided to rid himself of her and had done so with the help of the Borgia Pope; and then he married the late King's widow, Anne of Brittany.

Having seen what I had of Louise of Savoy, I could imagine her rejoicing. She was the sort of woman who would let nothing stand in the way of ambition and that ambition was for her son, her Caesar, as she called him. To her he was perfect; all his rash acts, his daring exploits, his love affairs, his infidelity to his wife, they were all regarded with indulgence by the devoted mother and sister. It was indeed a trinity – if not a holy one.

I was amused – and I knew the Queen was, too – to see the anxiety of this haughty lady now that the King had married a young wife; and so deeply were her hopes and ambitions involved that she could not hide her feelings.

The Queen said to me: 'She fears I may be pregnant. Oh, what if I were! What if I bore the King's son? What of François's hopes then? I think it would kill his mother.'

'Is it . . . ?' I was rash enough to begin.

She looked at me and taking my cheek between her finger and thumb pinched it hard.

'You must not take liberties, little Boleyn. Just because I show you favour.'

I cast down my eyes; and it occurred to me that it was not easy to tread safely when dealing with royalty.

But I was completely enthralled by life at Court and what I dreaded most was to be sent away.

*

The Queen was growing restive. December had come and, although the King often looked fatigued, he still attended the masques and entertainments which Marguerite and François devised. I believed that they, like the Queen, were anxious to tire him out.

Poor man, I thought. In a way it is a gentle sort of murder. How dreadful that people should want to be rid of you so much that they are prepared to kill you . . . even gently. But what goals these people had! For the Trinity there was the crown; for the Queen there was Charles Brandon, Duke of Suffolk.

I wondered if Louis knew. He was a very astute man, so it might have occurred to him.

I think he was longing for the Queen to be pregnant so that he could foil François's hopes. If what I heard was true, he was apprehensive about leaving the crown to François. He was a good king who cared about his country. I wished that I knew more about French history. I did know that there had been a hundred years' war which the English had lost and that one of the Charleses – Charles VII, I believe – had been crowned because of the success of Joan of Arc who had been burned as a witch. But it was the present in which everyone was interested now and it seemed as eventful as anything that had gone before.

As the weeks passed the tension seemed to be rising. The

Queen was aware of it and did all she could to intensify it. She liked to tease. I had quickly realized that. I had seen her when in the presence of the Duchess Louise, being aware of how closely the older woman watched her, giving some little sign which might mean that she was *enceinte*.

She used to laugh about it. 'Well, why not?' she said. 'Let us give the lady some excitement. Did you see her eyes on me? She would like to bore through me. Is she? Is she not? I can see the question in her eyes. And if she is . . . *mon dieu, mon François* . . . my god, my Caesar . . . deprived of the crown. The good God cannot be so cruel. What a King he will make! And that poor, feeble old man struggles on when there is my incomparable François . . . '

She gave a good imitation of the Duchess which made me laugh.

I think she was beginning to feel that we were reaching some climax, for she talked more frankly now. Charles! It was always Charles. I would not have thought such a mercurial creature could have been so faithful, so single-minded. But however much she flitted from one enthusiasm to another, she was always true to Charles.

'I would be happier in a little house . . . right away from everyone . . . if Charles were in it with me,' she told me wistfully. 'These fine clothes, these jewels . . . this flattery . . . this homage . . . I would give it all for a quiet life with Charles.'

I was not sure that I believed her. She seemed to have been born for her position, just as her brother seemed to be for his.

She was talking more and more of Charles. I would brush her hair and she would close her eyes. I heard her murmur once: 'How much longer?'

I almost said: It is only eight weeks since we came, Madame. But I had learned my lesson. It was unwise for me to comment; and at times she was really talking to herself.

Sometimes she seemed depressed and then she would talk of Charles to me, how he had first come to Court with little hope of promotion save for one thing.

'His father was the standard-bearer to my father at the battle of Bosworth Field. His father died defending mine. We Tudors remember our friends . . . and our enemies. When my father was declared the rightful King and the usurper Richard was dead, he remembered the faithful standard-bearer and sent a message to his widow to tell her that if his son came to Court there would be a place for him. And that was how Charles came to Court. He was put into the house of the Duke of York. Perhaps he would have preferred to be in that of the Prince of Wales. But fate works strangely, does it not? For the Prince of Wales married Katharine of Aragon and very soon he was dead and his brother, Henry, Duke of York, became Henry Prince of Wales . . . and now he is the King instead of going into the Church as they intended him to. Every time I think of Henry as a Cardinal, I want to laugh. Well, it was the crown for him, and much more suitable, too. And Katharine did not lose by it. She was Arthur's widow but now she is Henry's wife. So you see, Charles was in the right place after all.'

She was silent for a while, musing.

'They are alike. So tall . . . both of them . . . my brother and the man I love. I love them both, of course. Henry is very dear to me but there is no one like Charles. Charles is six years older than my brother . . . so my love is not a silly, beardless boy.'

'He is indeed a man,' I said, feeling the need to say something.

'Such a man! There was never one like him. At Court he learned to joust and ride and fence . . . and being Charles he could do it all better than anyone else. He and my brother became the closest friends. They are so like each other. They might be brothers . . . so tall, so fair . . . both of them, and excelling in all sport. You cannot be surprised that I love him.'

'No, Madame,' I said.

'Go on with the brushing. It soothes me. You are thinking if he is six years older than the King why is he not married?'

I was afraid to say yes, though it was what I was thinking.

'Well . . . he has been married. Twice. But that is of no consequence to me. I would not want a foolish, inexperienced boy.'

'Of course not, Madame.'

'And what do you know of such things?'

'Only what Your Highness tells me.'

'I believe there is more going on in your head than you would let us know.'

'Oh no, Madame,' I said in some alarm.

'Well, there should be,' she said. 'I do not want stupid little girls about me.'

I did not know what to reply to that. But she was smiling at me.

'He has told me all about his marriages,' she said. 'There are no secrets between us. Did you know that Margaret of Savoy wanted to marry him?'

'I did not,' I said.

'Well, she did. When he was on an embassy there, she fell in love with him. We can understand that, can we not? She might have married him. What a catastrophe! But fate was kind. Though perhaps it was the Emperor. He would never have allowed it to happen . . . however much she wanted him. And you may depend upon it, she did want him. Any woman would be mad not to want Charles.'

I waited because I was afraid to speak, lest what I said did not please her. I found these sessions with her fraught with apprehension and delight. Her conversation was so racy, so indiscreet. I was sure a great deal of what she told me was exaggerated, but that made it all the more exciting.

She went on: 'When he was very young, he fell in love . . . or thought he did . . . with the daughter of the Lieutenant of Calais. Of course he was not really in love. He has never loved anyone but me, but when people are young they hear the minstrels singing of love and they become enamoured of love

44

... for love's sake. So it was with Charles. This girl, Anne Browne, was, of course, madly in love with him; but she was very young and the marriage was delayed; and after a while Charles realized that it had been a temporary infatuation and that he would be a fool to marry someone in such a humble position, for by that time my brother had become King and Charles was his constant companion. It is a very different matter to be King of England from Prince of Wales with a stern father to keep one in check. You understand me?'

'Oh yes, I understand.'

'Charles is human and all young men have desires. They must satisfy them for it may be that they do not meet the only one in the world for them until they are passing out of their first youth. So it was with Charles ... '

She was silent for a while. Then suddenly she dismissed me – and that was the end of her confidences for that time.

But later she took up the story where she had left off.

'He was visiting his grandfather when he met Margaret Mortymer. She was young, lusty and a widow; therefore it was a great hardship for her to be deprived of a husband; and of course as soon as she saw Charles she wanted him. He was young. He cannot be blamed. It was natural for him to take advantage of the situation. It would be a poor sort of man who did not. He was only a boy then ... very inexperienced – and she was far from that. She initiated him, as you might say. Well, it had to happen. Do you understand what I am talking about, little Boleyn? Sometimes I forget what a child you are. There seems to be so much wisdom in those dark eyes. Perhaps I talk too much.'

'Oh no ... no, Madame ... '

She laughed and gave me a slap on the hand. 'You have to grow up. And if you stay long in this Court you will need all your wits about you. It will not be long before the men begin to notice you ... ' Her eyes were dreamy again. 'This woman was of a better family than poor little Anne Browne; her father was a Marquis. The fact is that Charles married her. He was very upset about little Anne, because she was expecting to marry him – but he got carried away by the voluptuous widow. He did not know then that people get tired of a relationship which depends on erotic excitement for its continued existence. There should be love, little one. Nothing else matters ... jewels ... power ... nothing. Let it all go for love. My brother was very interested in Charles's affairs. He was his confidant, you see. So he said why not get the marriage annulled which might not be so difficult as there was a pre-contract with Anne Browne. Luckily for Charles, Margaret had come to the same conclusion as he had about their marriage, so there was no conflict between them. Charles was soon free. He married Anne. So you see, he was very impulsive.'

I was afraid that she was going to stop but she merely sighed and went on: 'They say there is one person in the world for each of us and the lucky people are those who find that one ... at the right time and the right place. I have found Charles and he has found me ... but there are many obstacles for us to overcome.'

'Your Grace will overcome them.'

'You are right. For he is free now. Anne died. She was a delicate creature. He has two little daughters – Anne and Mary. He loves them dearly and so shall I. I will be a good mother to them when the time comes. Soon ... '

She looked at me and smiled; but even she realized it was not wise to say what was in her mind.

She was pensive suddenly, for her moods changed quickly.

'We had some happy days at Court ... my brother, Charles and I. We were always together. When there was to be a masque it was for us to devise it. We would plan it together. Henry knew how it was between Charles and me. Oh, he is my dear brother but there are times when he remembers he is the King; and of course, as his sister, I am a useful pawn in the game he has to play. Much as he loves Charles, when he puts on his crown he says, "My sister must marry into royalty." '

I thought of what Simonette had said: 'The Tudors have to stress their royalty at every turn simply because they only came into it a short while ago. When one has descended from a long line of kings, one's royalty is apparent; it is only when the glory is short lived that it must be stressed and none be allowed to forget it.'

'My brother wanted to make Charles richer and more powerful so he appointed him Keeper of the Royal Manor and Park of Wanstead, Ranger of the New Forest and then Knight of the Royal Body. Before he had been only a Squire. Henry wanted him to have a grander title so he thought of Elizabeth Grey, a little girl who was the sole heiress of her father, Viscount Lisle. He planned to make her Charles's ward and when she was old enough Charles could marry her and take the title. There was a wealthy estate to go with it.' She sighed. 'You see how fate has always worked against us.'

'And did he . . . ?' I ventured and stopped. She did not like me to ask questions. Perhaps because she did not greatly care for the answers. I was thinking that he only had to tell the King that he was in love with someone else and was not tempted by the title and wealth he would get by marrying the girl.

'He dared not offend the King, of course. And you know that when a gift is offered it is churlish not to show gratitude. Charles visited the young girl. He is delighted because she is only a child and it would be years before he could marry her. So he is safe . . . for a long time . . . and by the time . . .'

She smiled, looking into the future.

'He is so brave . . . so good. He rescued a child from the river . . . a little thing of only two years, and when he found that she was an orphan, unwanted by some aunt who had a brood of children of her own, he sent her to be brought up with his own children. That is the sort of man Charles is.'

'How noble,' I said.

'You speak truth. It was then that he was sent to the Netherlands.'

'My sister is there, in the Court of the Duchess of Savoy.'

She was not interested in my sister.

'Margaret fell in love with him and wanted to marry him. You see there are so many who want to marry him. Wherever he goes, it is inevitable. Charles had been with my brother during the invasion of France and had been made a Duke . . . the Duke of Suffolk. There will be no marriage with Margaret of Savoy . . . no marriage with Elizabeth Grey . . . for when Charles marries it will be with me.'

She put her finger to her lips; then she stood up and taking me by the shoulders, shook me gently.

'Talking to you is like talking to myself. You are too young to understand what I am talking about, are you not, eh? Answer me.'

'Yes, Madame,' I said.

Then she laughed and there was a warning look in her eyes. 'Remember,' she said. 'You are only a child.'

'Yes, Madame,' I said again.

*

The festivities of Christmas and the New Year were celebrated at the Palais des Tournelles. The Queen was growing more and more reckless. She confided in me less, but I could feel the rising tension of the Court.

Mary was constantly in the company of the Dauphin. There were whispers that he was neglecting his mistress and that all his thoughts were now for the Queen. I was alarmed at this, knowing her impulsive nature; and if she had not talked to me so fervently of her love for Charles Brandon, I should have suspected her of having a love affair with the Dauphin.

He was so very much the leader of the Court. The masques he and his sister devised were elegant and witty; and he was always at the centre of them; but he had drawn the Queen into the play to share the honours with him.

I was aware of his mother and sister watching him anxiously. Louise of Savoy was such a formidable lady. Before, there had been such accord between her and Marguerite and François; they had seemed to think as one person. How well the epithet Trinity fitted. And now François was acting apart from them and giving the greatest cause for anxiety. I understood their feelings well. They knew their darling's nature. I had heard that ever since he was in his early teens he had enjoyed amorous adventures. They were part of his life. And now he was unable to hide the desire he felt for the young Queen. Mary knew this and revelled in it. I had seen her lay her hand lightly on his arm and gaze up at him, sparkling and dewy-eyed. I wondered what the King thought of the outrageous Big Boy's fondness for his lovely young Queen. I knew what Louise and Marguerite felt. Nothing could convince them that Mary was not madly in love with François, because they thought every woman must be. They had not heard those monologues that I had listened to in which she had showed so clearly that there was only one man for her. But being Mary she was enjoying the situation; and I believed it made those months tolerable to her.

Meanwhile the terrified mother and sister were watching, sure that Mary would not be able to resist their Caesar. And if François was the successful lover, what if there should be a child? They would think this very likely in the case of their virile paragon. The son of François King of France! No! No! That was not what they wanted ... for the son would never be recognized as belonging to François and what use was that to the Trinity?

I wondered whether, in secret, they begged him to take care.

And what of the King? Louis was no fool. Did he see what was going on? I was amazed that he did not put his foot down, put an end to this flirtation – for it could be nothing else – which was going on between his wife and the Dauphin.

I think he was bemused by Mary. She was indeed a very lovely creature – so young and fresh with that magnificent reddish gold hair and the beautiful blue eyes; but it was her vitality which was her greatest charm. Louis had been married to poor deformed Jeanne and later to Anne of Brittany, and in complete contrast was this young girl – wayward but beautiful and spirited.

He made an effort to live up to her, although it seemed to be killing him. He would look on smiling while François beguiled her with his witty conversation; he watched benignly while they danced together or rode side by side. It sometimes seemed as though he was pleased to have François to charm her in his essentially French manner. It was as though he were saying: 'This is France. Notice the courtesy of our gentlemen, the wit, the charm.' If anyone could show her these things, François could.

King Louis had changed his way of life completely, I understood. With Anne of Brittany he had retired early. It would have been a staid routine, devoid of excitement. I supposed that much of the time they were together was spent discussing matters of state. There had been two daughters, it was true – neither of them healthy. Mary must seem very charming to him. But he was obviously an old man trying to keep pace with a young and lively wife.

There was a little verse which he had been fond of quoting before the arrival of Mary:

> *'Lever à six, diner à dix,*
> *Souper à six, coucher à dix,*
> *Fait vivre l'homme dix fois dix.'*

That was the rule he had followed. Now it was hardly likely that he would live to a hundred.

It seemed to me that everyone was watching him. How long? they seemed to ask and particularly during those Christmas revels. I wondered whether he was in pain. He would sit there smiling but he seemed to be very weary, and his eyes to grow more prominent and his neck more swollen.

Like everyone else at Court, I was aware of what was going on and wondered what the outcome would be. I knew my mistress perhaps better than most; and it was my belief that she was faithful, not so much to the King as to Charles Brandon. I did not believe in this love affair with François; what I did believe was that the sense of mischief in her wanted them all to draw that conclusion. I believe she enjoyed leading François on and watching the acute anxiety of his mother and sister.

François was almost at the post. He could not be cheated now; and Mary was amused by the watchful eyes which studied her so closely, wondering all the time. Was she pregnant? Or wasn't she? Was this the end of hope for the Trinity?

Mary was not naturally unkind; but the only way she could endure the intolerable situation which had been thrust upon her was by extracting some amusement from it. She did not dislike the King; that would have been difficult for he was a very kindly man; he could not help it if his appearance was repulsive to her and she was yearning all the time for handsome Charles Brandon. The King had been ailing before she came – and she longed for freedom.

At this moment Charles was free. But how long would he remain so? The right time ... the right place ... it was necessary for the lovers to be there when the moment came.

It happened on New Year's Day. They had retired to their room. It was midnight.

He lay in his bed completely exhausted. The last words he said were that he wished to be laid beside his Queen, Anne of Brittany.

Mary wept a little and her tears were genuine.

'He was a good man,' she said, 'but it had to be.'

Then a certain radiance came into her face. I knew that she was thinking: I am free. I married once for state reasons. Now

51

my reason will be my own.

*

There was deep mourning throughout the capital. The *clocheteurs des trépassés*, according to the custom, went through the streets ringing their 'death bells'. Dolefully they spoke of the passing of the Father of his People. They remembered that not since St Louis had there been a king to care for his people as had this king. His frugality and thrift, which had been called meanness and avarice during his lifetime, became virtues. Reforms which had been introduced, abuses which had been abolished were remembered. But putting aside the vacillating affections of the people, when the facts were looked squarely in the face, there must have been evidence throughout the country that Louis had been one of the best kings they had ever had. He had worked hard to keep the country out of war and if he had not always succeeded that was not due to a lack of trying; people had prospered under his rule; they should have been grateful to Louis XII – and although it had taken his death to make them realize his virtues, they did at this time. So there was genuine mourning throughout the land.

Mary went to the Hôtel de Clugny for the traditional six weeks and she took me with her.

The Hôtel de Clugny had been the home of the Clugniac monks – hence the name. It was situated in the rue des Mathurins. During the mourning period she was expected to remain most of the time in *la chambre de la reine*, an apartment made gloomy for the occasion with the daylight shut out and wax candles giving the only light.

Mary herself was dressed completely in white.

She was troubled a little by her conscience. That was inevitable. The King was dead and she had wished him dead. Now she recalled his virtues. He had been so indulgent. He had wanted so much to please her.

'He was always gentle with me,' she said. 'It is sad that it had to be thus.'

But she was soon remembering her freedom.

'Six weeks,' she said. 'It seems a lifetime. And I am expected not to go from this gloomy chamber until that time is passed. Tell me, little one, who, do you think, will be most anxious to see me?'

I was glad to see the mischief returning to her eyes.

She began to laugh. 'They won't be able to wait. They are all agog. How long will it be before they can be sure? You are too young to know these things, my little wiseacre. But you may depend upon it that Madame Louise and Madame Marguerite are beset with anxiety as to the future of their darling. And what of the darling himself? The crown hovers over his head. Is it going to sail right past him? I could die of laughing.'

I was so pleased to see the change in her. I smiled with her.

*

As the days passed, she grew happier. Her conscience had ceased to worry her.

'He was old,' she said. 'He was half way to the tomb before I came.'

Although she was shut away it was permissible for some to visit her; and of course one who would have special privilege was the Dauphin. He lost no time in coming.

She looked very beautiful in her white mourning clothes as she went to receive him, and when she returned from that interview she was her old sparkling self.

'His great concern was that I might be carrying the King's child,' she said. 'Poor man, his thoughts could not go beyond that. Oh, he is so clever, so courteous, his choice of words exquisite. He could not ask the question outright as my brother or most Englishmen would have done. That would have been crude and vulgar. Is it not amazing that these

French – the most licentious people in the world, I believe, flitting from one lady's boudoir to another with impudent bravado and discussing us at length afterwards – should be so delicate in their outward treatment of us? Oh, I am having fun with François, little Boleyn. I let him think . . . yes, perhaps. "How is your health?" he asks with concern. I say to him . . . listen to this for it is clever . . . I say, "I am as well as can be expected in the circumstances." You should have seen his face. Even François with all his beautiful manners could not hide his alarm. What did it mean? Was I referring to my widowhood . . . or my coming motherhood? I shall amuse myself while I am in this doleful place. Six weeks . . . and then I am free.'

And amuse herself she did.

Louise and Marguerite came to see her. They could not hide their anxiety. After all, this was the most important time of their lives. Ever since Caesar had been born his mother had had her eyes on the crown, and even though in the early days it had seemed a remote possibility, I believe she thought that even God must realize that. He must work a few miracles for the sake of this incomparable boy. They went away in a fever of apprehension.

And when Mary summoned me, she was so amused that she found the mourning chamber tolerable.

*

She shared the secret with me. She was afraid to impart it to anyone else. I was flattered to be the one she trusted; but I think it was because of my youth. Moreover she would take me by the shoulders and tell me that if I betrayed her she would have me sent to spend the rest of my days in a dungeon in the Tower.

I would never have betrayed her.

She had taken to wearing extra petticoats. 'How does that look?' she would ask. 'It must not be too much. I could be three months with child. But perhaps we had better make it two. That would be more likely. How does one look at two months? Not much to show, I fear. Let us make it three. After all, it is a possibility, and my husband was in better health when I arrived than he was later. Oh we are going to deceive them.'

When the Duchesse d'Alençon called to see her, she sent a message saying she was a little ill. She added: 'It is to be expected.' Leaving her in that uncertainty as to whether she referred to her husband's death or her pregnancy.

She used to tell me what they said to her.

'We are anxious about your health,' said the Duchess of Savoy. 'Marguerite would like to come here to be with you. Oh, I know you must be alone, but Marguerite could come and stay at Clugny . . . just in case you felt the need to see her.'

'Dear Duchess,' she replied. 'You are too kind. I am as well . . . as I can expect to be. A little sickness now and then and I confess to feeling the need to rest more than I did.'

Mary went on: 'She was in a panic. I thought at any moment she was going to shake me. Oh dear, the Trinity is suffering, I can tell you. And what is so amusing is that, if I am with child, whose it is – the King's or François's? It is clear that he wanted to be my lover and his devoted mother and sister do not believe that anyone could resist him. Oh, it is an amusing situation. I wish you were older . . . then you could understand how amusing.'

I wanted to say that I did understand. I knew how children were born; I had learned a great deal at the French Court. There was always gossip; I had picked up the language and could understand most that was said; and I really was knowledgeable beyond my years.

The game amused her; and the visits of Louise and Marguerite were frequent. She was always very merry when they had gone and would sometimes talk to me and at others remain silent. But being Mary she played the game to excess.

Her bulk increased too rapidly. She made me pad her with quilting. I was the only one in the secret.

The result was that one day the Duchess called and while Mary was talking to her, the quilting slipped. Completely sure of herself now as the mother of the King, Louise actually laid hands on the Queen and shook her until the padding dropped out.

The game was over.

It was one of those occasions when she could not keep to herself what had happened. Almost hysterical with laughter she described the scene to me.

'The Duchess was infuriated. Oh, little Boleyn, you are *wicked*. You did not fix me well enough. The padding fell below my knees. She pounced on it. She even shook me. She said in a thunderous voice: "You have deceived us." It would have been horrifying – if it had not been so amusing. Then Marguerite laughed. But Madame Louise does not forgive so easily. I had to think quickly. How to extricate myself from such a delicate situation? It was not going to be easy. She was right. I had deceived them – and in that moment they realized what very important people they had become. I said: "Madame, I know now and so do you that I am not to bear the King's child. *Vive François Premier!*" There! You see how important it is to choose the right words. Remember it when you are in a difficult situation. There I was – exposed. I had tricked them for weeks and now we were facing the truth. But those were the magic words she had been waiting to hear for twenty years; and she could not be anything but pleased to hear them spoken with such conviction. And I, with all my wickedness exposed, was forgiven because I said *Vive François Premier*.'

The French Court

So he was King at last.

He came to see Mary at Clugny. There was a subtle difference in him; his anxious days were over, he was safe on the throne.

I wondered what he would have to say to Mary, whether he would reproach her for the trick she had played on him, withholding the good news from him for several weeks and moreover putting him into a fever of despair.

He was with her for some time and when he left she sent for me. She was very pensive and, I think, alarmed, so I thought he must have expressed his displeasure.

But later I learned this was not so. François's sense of gallantry would never allow him to upbraid a beautiful woman.

Mary could not keep her anxieties to herself and I was the only one to whom she could safely unburden herself.

She said to me: 'It shall not be. I have endured all this, have I not? And was it not on the understanding that, having married once for state reasons, the next time it would be for my own. That silly little Prince of Castile. That his name should be Charles is an outrage. I'll not have it. I will not.'

I stood by silently. She put the brush in my hands and signed for me to brush her hair. It soothed her in some way. She turned and looked at me. 'My brother is negotiating a marriage for me with the Prince of Castile.'

'Your Grace will not submit . . . '

'Not I!'

'And the King of France?'

She laughed. 'He was amused by the trick I played . . . so was his sister. Madame of Savoy less so. I think she would like to punish me very severely . . . and she would, if she could.'

'Oh no, Your Grace.'

'Yes, she would, but she cannot, can she? She would be afraid of offending my brother if they harmed me in any way. She will content herself by seeing me off . . . right away . . . out of France forever. But the King of France has other plans for me. Do you think I am very beautiful, little one?'

'Oh yes, Madame.'

'So does he. Oh, what elegant phrases! I wish I could understand them better. I shall be glad to speak English again. That is what is so pleasant with you. We can talk together . . . sensibly. It seems that between them the King of England and the King of France have decided my future. Just as though I were a piece of baggage. Shall we send her to the Prince of Castile or shall we keep her here for the King of France? I'll not have it. I told François so. He is greatly enamoured of me. The trick I played has not changed the feelings he had for me from the moment he saw me. Rather has it enhanced them. He likes women of spirit. We laughed together over the padding. I told him that you were the only one in the secret. He said, "Oh, the little one with the big dark eyes." What do you think of that?'

'I . . . I am surprised that he should have noticed me.'

'Oh, he sees all women. Just as he notices a painting or a building . . . but especially he notices women . . . and although you are but a child you are a woman, too. He says he is madly in love with me and will be desolate if I leave France. He plans that I shall marry here. He has even selected my bridegroom. He thinks the Duc de Savoy . . . another Charles if you please. He will be a complaisant husband, and François and I can embark on an idyllic love affair, which we were meant to do from the moment our paths crossed. It is a pity, he says, that he cannot make me his Queen. It would have been following the pattern set by my late husband with Anne of Brittany. But alas he is already married to Claude. But Claude is the most obliging of wives. Who would not be

58

obliging to the handsome, charming, witty King of France? That is how matters are arranged in France. But there is one who will not fall in with these charmingly expressed arrangements. I think he was a little taken aback. He is not accustomed to refusals . . . and I made myself very clear to him.'

She was silent for a few seconds. Then she went on: 'I told him there was a reason why I was not in love with him. I had already given my heart to another. I said there could only be that reason, for I, like the rest of the world, could not be unaware of the charm of the most attractive man in France. Oh, I was on dangerous ground, was I not? But I had a certain pleasure in treading it. He was so charming, he expressed himself envious of my Charles. He said something about bartering his crown to be in his place which made me want to laugh. Did he really think I would believe that? But he was kind. He had to live up to his reputation for chivalry. He said that, since I had so honoured this man by loving him, then he must be his friend. Nothing else would do . . . and if he could do aught to persuade my brother to give way to my will, he would do so. What think you of that?'

'That it is indeed good of him.'

'The point is, little one, does he mean it? Often there is something hidden behind these flowery phrases. But I really think he wishes me well . . . that is, if my good can bring no harm to him. One thing I am determined on: I shall never take that snivelling little boy from Castile.'

She dismissed me soon after that, and when I saw her again she was radiant. She could not stop herself giving me the news. Her brother, hearing of Louis's death, was sending an embassy to France to offer condolences and talk with the new King; and at the head of that embassy was to be Charles Brandon, Duke of Suffolk.

She would see him soon. 'And this time,' she vowed, 'I shall not let him go until we are married.'

*

During all this time I was anxious about my own future. I had seen how cursorily her maids of honour had been dismissed in the days after her marriage. I only had remained and that was on account of my youth and unimportance. I was wondering what would happen to me if she married Charles Brandon. Should I be sent home? The thought of returning to the life at Hever or Blickling was a little depressing. I had grown accustomed to the French Court. I liked listening to the chatter, picking up pieces of gossip and scandal; I liked very much the dresses. I was interested in fashion and enjoyed helping the Queen to dress. She said I had a feeling for colour and often she would say to me: 'Should I wear this, little Boleyn? What think you?' She would pretend that the question was merely rhetorical, but she sometimes took notice of what I said.

I was growing up fast. If I had been precocious when I arrived, I was more so now. I missed little. I knew when men and women were lovers, though many of them thought they carried on their intrigues secretly. Now and then I plucked up courage to bring a scrap of scandal to the Queen's ear which greatly amused her.

I was changing. I was no longer the innocent child. Such an environment was a forcing ground. The ladies of the Court took little notice of me. I was a child to them and they often behaved as though I were not there; that was when I gleaned my scraps of gossip. They did not realize that I understood their language better than I spoke it – although I was doing that more fluently every day.

I was enormously interested in everything that went on around me, and my great fear was that any day I might hear the dreaded news that I was to leave this colourful scene and return to England.

The Queen did not talk to me as much now. Her thoughts were on one subject: her meeting with her lover. She was silent often and would sit staring into space with a beautiful smile on her lovely face; I knew then that she was dreaming of the meeting.

François was naturally very eager to be crowned King of France. No monarch feels that his position is secure until he has been crowned. But he was in a dilemma. To hurry on the coronation would seem like disrespect to the late King; and yet he could not bear to remain uncrowned.

François compromised. Much as he would have loved a glittering spectacle of a coronation, he decided it would be better to have a simple one if he could have that without delay. It was usual for Kings of France to be crowned at Rheims. But the people would have expected a very grand occasion if he had followed that tradition. So to Rheims he went but that was just for the ceremony of the 'sacring' which meant the anointing with the *sainte ampoule* which was performed in the Cathedral St Rémi. This took place at night and afterwards he went to St Denis – where before this, only the Queens of France had been crowned – to complete the coronation with as little fuss as possible.

So François was the crowned King of France.

At this time we heard that the English embassy had arrived in France. François had had a meeting with the Duke of Suffolk and I heard afterwards that Suffolk had thanked François on behalf of King Henry for the comfort he had given his poor widowed sister; and François replied that he hoped the Queen would let her brother know how lovingly he had behaved towards her. He was not, of course, referring to the dishonourable overtures he had made to her, but if I knew the Queen, her brother would hear of that in due course. He told Suffolk that he had hoped the King's happy marriage would have been of long endurance. I could imagine his sardonic smile as he uttered such a blatant falsehood.

The meeting had taken place at Noyon; and when it was over the English party made its way to Paris, where it was to witness the ceremonial entry of the King into his capital.

If the coronation ceremony could be called a little subdued, this did not apply to the celebrations which followed.

The coronation had taken place on 25 January – just over three weeks after the death of Louis; but François did delay his entrance into the capital until 13 February. By this time the Queen had just completed her six weeks' retirement and, although still in mourning, she could emerge – though not take part in the celebrations, but she could watch them from a window as they passed.

I was, of course, beside her.

There was no doubt that the French welcomed their new King. Louis might have been good for the country but he had sadly lacked that glittering presence, those handsome looks, the young and sparkling vitality which could not fail to fill the people with admiration and hope for the future under such a magnificent creature.

The streets had been hung with damask and tapestry and the people were out in their thousands. Recklessly they climbed to the highest points of buildings to get a better view, and they refused to be dislodged.

And what a splendid sight he was! François was dressed in white satin and silver damask; over this he wore a cloak of silver edged with silver fringe. His white velvet hat glittered with gems and sported a plume of white feathers.

There was a hush as he appeared. I was sure none of these people had ever seen anyone like him. Very tall, athletic, yet perfectly graceful, he must have seemed like a god. He was indeed the supreme specimen of manhood – and most royal personages of the past had been small, sickly and even deformed in some way. The French habit of tightly swaddling their babies probably accounted for a certain stunted growth which I had noticed was rather prevalent. Following Louis with his swollen neck and protruding eyes, François was a glorious contrast. Louise must have made sure that her Caesar was not tightly swaddled in his babyhood; his limbs must have been free to expand as nature intended them to. In any case he was a magnificent figure. He had a natural elegance, as had quite a number of the noblemen who attended him. This was something I missed later in England where there was a decided lack of that quality and where people adorned themselves with dazzling jewels instead of using them with discretion as François and the members of his Court did. I learned to follow the French modes and that I think was one of the things which set me apart later on.

The cheers for the King, the music from the trumpets, sambucas and hautbois was quite deafening and not always harmonious but one could not fail to be caught up in the excitement.

The officers of the Crown in their cloth of gold and damask, the nobility in crimson and gold, the ladies in their litters, all passed below us. I saw Louise seated with little Renée, the late King's daughter; and in another litter was Marguerite d'Alençon with old Madame de Bourbon, who was the daughter of Louis XI.

All this was to be the beginning of six weeks of festivities. François wanted the people to know that under him there would be no cheeseparing. His reign must be heralded by this indication of the good times he was going to give them.

There was no doubt of their appreciation.

During the procession Mary sat beside me, tense, waiting.

And at last the moment came, for part of this brilliant cavalcade was the English embassy which had come to visit the King to offer condolences and congratulations and no doubt lay the foundation for further friendship between the two countries.

The Duke of Suffolk rode at the head. He was undoubtedly handsome – tall as the King of France and as fair as François was dark. He did bear a resemblance to Henry VIII, and I could quite understand why Mary had become obsessed by him.

He glanced up at the window as he passed and I saw the looks they gave each other. Mary was radiant. She was breathing deeply and her clasped hands lay in her lap.

I hoped she would be happy. Perhaps she would take me back to England with her into her household. That would not be so unusual. Young girls did go into households of noblewomen; and I believed that she did have a fondness for me.

Events moved quickly after that. That very day there was a meeting between Mary and Suffolk. Afterwards she was in a state of great excitement – of wild optimism and despair.

They had had such a short time together, she told me; but that was going to change. 'That arrangement with Elizabeth Grey is nothing . . . nothing. And I am free now. I tell you this: nothing is going to stop us.' Then she was sunk in melancholy. 'There are so many against us. They know of our feelings for each other.'

I thought: 'Seeing you, Madame, who could fail to be aware of it?' But I said nothing.

'They hate him. They are jealous of him. Who would not be? That is understandable. They will try to turn my brother against him. I do believe that Henry might agree to this match . . . if it were not for those people around him. They think he would become too important . . . married to the King's sister. It is intrigue . . . intrigue. He loves me . . . as I love him. He said it might cost him his head if he married me. Wolsey is not against the match . . . and Wolsey and my brother together . . . who would dare say nay if they said yes?'

She paced about the room. I wished she would be calmer for I was sure that would be wiser.

'François has spoken to him. Do you know what he said to him? These are his exact words: "My Lord Suffolk," he said, "there is a bruit in this realm that you have come hither to marry the Queen, your master's sister." Poor Charles. He was so taken aback, for he did not understand how François could have known about us. But, of course, it was I who told him. François said he would help us if he could for he had a great affection for me and he knew the strength of my feelings.

64

That was good of him. But I don't trust him. I wish I could speak to my brother. I will write to him. That is it. I will remind him that I married once to please him, and for this I was promised that next time I should please myself. I shall warn him of my enemies who surround him and will try to do me ill.'

I brought the writing materials and she wrote.

I shared her tension, for my anxiety regarding my own future was growing. She said nothing about what would become of me; I could understand that there was no room in her mind for anything but her own affairs.

All during those days when the jousting, balls and banquets and rejoicing in the new reign continued, Mary alternated between joy and despair. She did not attend the festivities of course, for although the six weeks were up, she was still supposed to be mourning the late King.

She had one or two meetings with Suffolk which carried her to the pinnacle of delight; then she would be plunged into melancholy.

'Charles is afraid,' she told me. 'He says our love will destroy us. My brother knows of the love between us. He made Charles swear before he left England that he would not persuade me to plight my troth to him, nor take the opportunity which being here he might find.'

'And did he promise, Madame?'

'My brother would insist. Oh, he is bluff and hearty but he can be ruthless if any go against him. I know his temper. I should, because it is very like my own. But as I know him, so should he know me and when I set my heart on something, I shall have it ... as he would. There is a strong feeling between us because we are so much alike. We know each other well.'

'But if my Lord Suffolk has promised ... '

'*I* have been promised. My brother has promised me that, if I married for state reasons, the next time I should have freedom of choice.'

I could understand her feelings. She was ready to brave her brother's wrath; she was his beloved sister, but Suffolk, whatever the friendship between himself and the King, was only a subject.

Then something happened which upset her a great deal, not because of what actually took place but because it was an indication of the power of those who were working against her marriage.

Her confessor came to her and told her that a certain Friar Langley had arrived from England and it was imperative that he have speech with her immediately.

I was with her when he was brought in.

I curtsied and was about to leave when she said to me: 'No. You may stay.'

The friar looked at me with displeasure but he seemed to come to the conclusion that my presence was of no importance. I had always been allowed to witness a great deal because of my youth.

Mary said haughtily: 'What is it you have to say to me?'

'I have come to warn Your Grace.'

'To warn me? Of what?'

'Of one who has come hither in an embassy.'

'I do not understand you, Friar.'

'I have come to tell you the truth about the Duke of Suffolk.'

The colour flamed into Mary's face. 'What of the Duke of Suffolk?' she asked haughtily.

'I believe Your Grace has been deceived by this man and have shown him much favour. It has been impressed on me that I should come here to warn you that he traffics with the Devil.'

She was seething with rage and controlling it with more success than she usually displayed.

'And who, may I ask, has done this impressing?'

He was evasive, evidently wary of betraying those who had sent him.

'All know that Sir William Compton – a rival with the Duke for the King's favour – suffers from a virulent ulcer of the leg,' he said.

'I fail to see what connection this has with the Duke of Suffolk?'

'The King has made an ointment which is a cure for ulcers. It fails to work on Sir William.'

'Is that so?' Her voice was dangerously calm. I thought: In a moment she will fly at him. Clearly he did not know her temper.

The friar lowered his voice. 'The Duke of Suffolk is a friend of Wolsey and it is well known that *he* is one of the Devil's disciples. How could a butcher's son rise to such greatness?'

'By shrewdness, wit and very special qualities which others have not.'

'No, Madame. Through the Devil.'

'Sir Friar, you should be careful how you speak of my friends.'

'It is because I fear for your safety that I have come here to warn you.'

She went close to him. 'Go back to *your* friends,' she said in a low voice, 'and tell them I know their motives well. Tell them this: I shall make sure that when I return to England the King is informed of your perfidy towards those he loves . . . and if you have any sense in your addled pate, you will get out of my sight at once. I never wish to look on your sly and silly face again. And if you pass on any of these lies which you have uttered to me, I'll have you in the Tower and there they will discover who it was who led you to this act of folly.'

'Madame . . . '

'Go,' she cried.

He went.

She looked at me and said: 'You see, I have my enemies. They will do everything they can to prevent my marriage. They would destroy my happiness . . . if they could. But they are not going to.'

*

Nor did they. Fortunately for Mary, François had decided to help. Looking back, I think he was rather pleased to do this – not because of his affection for her. François's feelings towards her were entirely lustful. He might have been piqued because she preferred someone else, but I think he rather admired her tenacity. He was romantic at heart; at least, at times, it pleased him to see himself as such. One could never be sure of François; but I certainly think he took a pleasure in flouting the King of England.

There was a rivalry between them which was intensified because they were of a kind – both young, handsome, both following serious predecessors who had lived without pomp. It must have amused François, who would surmise that Henry would be obliged outwardly to disapprove of the marriage of his sister to a man who had come from a comparatively humble background because it would annoy the great families of England whose favours he could not afford to lose.

So, with François's help, Mary was married with great secrecy in the chapel at the Hôtel de Clugny.

I saw her briefly after the ceremony. Worried as I was about what would now become of me, I could not help but rejoice in her happiness. She was radiant with joy – there in her simple gown, so different from the gloriously apparelled young woman who had been married such a short time before in the Hôtel de la Gruthuse.

Only ten people were present in the little chapel, but one of them was the King of France himself.

*

It was a daring act, but characteristic of Mary. I believed that without her determination it would not have taken place, for

68

Suffolk knew the hostility it would arouse.

The King of England was most displeased and for a time they were afraid to return to England.

But I learned something of the King's nature much later, when I went to England. He was very sentimental and he truly loved his sister. He liked Suffolk, too, and it was not long before a compromise was arranged. For such a flagrant act of disobedience they could not go unpunished, so the King would take possession of Mary's plate and jewels; for he had incurred great expense in sending her to France in the appropriate manner and he wished to be reimbursed for that. They were to pay him yearly instalments of £24,000 and naturally they would not be able to come to Court for a while.

It seemed harsh punishment, but Mary did not seem to mind. She was so deliriously happy that I supposed Suffolk was all she had believed him to be.

'We shall be poor,' she said, 'living in the country. How I shall love that! I am heartily sick of courts. I shall have my Charles and we shall be a country gentleman and his lady. It is what I have wanted more than anything in the world and now it is mine.'

Queen Claude sent for me.

She was very gentle and kind – not like a queen at all. She was surrounded by ladies just like herself. They spent most of their days doing good works, like sewing for the poor and visiting convents; they prayed a good deal. She was such a contrast to her flamboyant husband that it was amazing that theirs should be – after a fashion – a successful marriage – perhaps due to that realistic view of life which is characteristic of the French.

'Come here, Anne,' she said. 'I have some news for you.'

I waited in trepidation, certain that she was going to tell me to prepare to leave for home.

She smiled her very gentle smile and said: 'I have had word from your father. He trusts that you have given satisfaction during your stay at our Court. I think Queen Mary would agree that you have, for she has kept you close to her.'

I was silent but my heart was beginning to beat very fast.

'Your father thinks that a stay at our Court is good for you
... for your education and all you have to learn besides. He
therefore asks me if I can find a place for you here so that you
may remain when the Queen-Duchess returns to England,
which she will shortly be doing. And I have decided that I will
take you into my household.'

I was so delighted that I must have shown it, for she seemed
pleased and patted my head.

'One of the ladies will tell you where you will sleep and
explain your duties to you. They may be a little different from
those you did with the Queen-Duchess.'

'Thank you, Madame.'

She smiled and nodded, and I left her in a daze.

I was reprieved.

So, with the coming of April, I joined Queen Claude's
household; and Mary and her husband went back to England.

*

Life changed a great deal for me. Attendance on Queen
Claude was indeed very different from waiting on my previous, volatile mistress. Claude always seemed surrounded by
quietness; she was so kind and fundamentally good that while
one admired her one felt a certain resentment of such virtues,
perhaps because it seemed a reproach to one's own less than
perfect nature. I learned how to do the finest embroidery; my
French improved; and although I was one of the Queen's
attendants, I did know what went on beyond our circle.

The Court was, as ever, dominated by François. In every
field he distinguished himself. He was always champion of the
jousts; he was the most skilful swordsman in the country; in
wrestling none could overthrow him. Perhaps royalty came to
his aid on one or two occasions but it was never obvious; I do
not think he would have resented a rival in those arts but

welcomed him. King Henry seemed a boy set side by side with the King of France. François had been born with wisdom, it seemed; but perhaps he had learned that at the side of his sister, who must surely be the cleverest person at Court, male or female. Not only was François the leading sportsman, he was the arbiter of elegance. He set the fashion which always tended to show off his own perfections. He was quite dazzling. It seemed that he had all the outward gifts of sovereignty. The French could not fail to be pleased with their monarch.

His love affairs were numerous. Love was the great theme of the Court at that time. Poets wrote of it; musicians sang of it; courtiers talked of it. François was always gallant and charming; and he gathered about him men of similar tastes. It was said that if a man did not have a mistress he regarded him with suspicion. He liked to talk of women with other men and to hear how their love affairs were progressing; he would press for intimate details, and yet he could get angry if he considered any did not pay due respect to women.

To my mind it was all rather puzzling; but I did realize later how important my upbringing was in making me the sort of person I became.

In spite of his notorious infidelity to my mistress Claude, François was always gallant to her and showed her the respect due to a Queen. She was constantly pregnant. I believe he delighted to see her in that condition for then he need not spend his nights with her until after the child was born and the time came for him to father another. It was really very decadent and the greatest offence was not wickedness but vulgarity. It was quite different from the Court of England of which I was to learn so much later.

Queen Claude herself took an interest in my education and very soon I was immersed in my quiet life. Those months which I had spent with Queen Mary seemed very far away. I often thought of her; and I heard that she was indeed living quietly in the country, for the Court was too expensive for her and her husband in view of their debts. I thought the King must soon free her of that obligation, for she would surely add to the brightness of his Court. I did hear also that she was deeply contented and I rejoiced with her. It seemed to be one of the few marriages which were truly happy.

As for myself, perhaps because of my youth, I was able to settle into the new life with the utmost ease. Not long after I joined Queen Claude's household, the King left to go to war. He wanted to prove to his subjects that besides being a handsome gallant he could be a conqueror. I heard these matters discussed and I was alert for what I could discover. Thus I learned that François was determined to bring conquests to France. He was gathering an army together on the pretext that he wished to make Burgundy secure against attacks from the Swiss, but it was believed – and this appeared to be the truth – that he was contemplating an invasion of the Italian States. Ferdinand of Spain was urging the Pope, the Swiss, the Emperor Maximilian and the Duke of Milan, Maximilian Sforza, to join a league for the defence of Italy. The Pope, however, refused to join, declaring himself, as Pope, to be father of them all.

The conquest of Italy had been the policy of the last two Kings of France and François was determined to continue in this. He appointed his mother Regent of France and went to war.

Soon we had news of his great victory at Melegnano over the Swiss. François had done all his country expected of him. In a short engagement he had beaten the Swiss, disconcerted his enemies and entered Milan in triumph. Maximilian Sforza, after taking refuge in the castle there, surrendered and agreed to retire to France with a pension. The Pope, seeing the way in which events had gone, invited François to meet him at Bologna, where they could discuss the future as the good friends the Pope and the Most Christian King must be.

I did not understand all this at the time, but it fell into place later and when I look back I see clearly how these events shaped my future.

François became enchanted by the art of Italy and grew much attached to Pope Leo. Leo was a most cultivated man, which might be expected of the son of Lorenzo the Magnificent. Intellectual, witty in conversation, astute in matters of state and a patron of the arts, he had all the gifts which would appeal to François. He was fond of music and enchanted by theatrical performances; he encouraged writers and artists as his father had done. It was small wonder that François was only too ready to dally at the Papal Court; he was in his element surrounded by works of art; and he found the women of Italy beautiful and gave his rapt attention to all.

Ferdinand of Spain had control of Naples on which François had set his heart. Ferdinand was getting old and was ailing, Leo pointed out. He could not live long, so would it not be wise to postpone the attempt to take it and wait a while for Ferdinand's death, when it might be quite easy for François to attain his desire without going to war?

Having proved his military skill, François was ready to take that advice; and when he returned to France, he brought the great artist Leonardo da Vinci with him; he was so enamoured of his work that he wanted him to work for him. He gave Leonardo the Château Cloux in Touraine, near Amboise, as his home. Unfortunately the great man did not enjoy it for long and died four years later in 1519, which was perhaps not unexpected as he was in his sixty-seventh year. François had the utmost respect for artists of all kinds. Once he said: 'Men can make kings, but only God can make an artist.'

During the years that followed, I became so much a part of the French Court that I forgot I was English. I was growing up and very different from the seven-year-old who had arrived. I enjoyed looking on at the Court without being an actual part of it. It was like watching through a window. I was rather relieved about this in a way. I could see how easy it would be to be caught up in actions which might prove detrimental to

73

one's dignity. I was very much aware of dignity. But perhaps I came to that state later, after what happened to my sister Mary. Looking back, it is not always easy to remember when one began to change.

I really enjoyed my role of observer. I felt I was being prepared for the day when I must emerge and take part in the scene. The King's favourite mistress at that time was Françoise de Foix, one of the most beautiful women I ever saw. Many envied her her place at Court; they said François was her slave and he certainly acted as though he adored her; but he was not faithful to her and it all seemed to me like a masque without reality. I thought I would not care to be Françoise de Foix for all the adulation which came her way. Tomorrow it would all be gone. It all depended on the fickle King and he was playing a game most of the time. But it was interesting to watch.

François had come to the throne in a haze of glory; he had appeared to have all the kingly qualities, but his extravagances had to be paid for, and the time must come when the people realized that a monarch who was as handsome as a god and amused them with his outrageous adventures might not bring them so much comfort as a sick old man who had the welfare of his people at heart. Under Louis life might have been dull for the citizens of Paris, but the streets were quiet; following the example of the King, the people had retired early, and if any had reason to be out late, they went without fear. That had changed. Bands of roistering young men roamed the streets. It had long been the law that anyone out after dark should carry a little hand-lantern, and these were maliciously knocked out of their owners' hands; dissolute young men humiliated the women, taking liberties with them during these drunken brawls. There had been occasions when the mischief-makers were revealed and seen among them were noblemen; and there had been seen the most familiar face of all – the long-nosed, handsome, sardonic features of the Most Christian King.

The sober citizens were shocked; they were disillusioned; they began to talk nostalgically of the good old days.

A party of players had roamed the country amusing the people with their comedies; and in the past they had often performed their little playlets at Court. A feature of these was the satirizing of well-known figures. The late Louis had often watched them and been amused to see himself portrayed not always flatteringly, counting his money, the parsimonious monarch who liked to keep the Treasury at a high level – for all they knew that this was not for himself but for the country's needs.

Now they were bringing into the sketches a new monarch – a figure of elegance to whom the cut of a coat was of the utmost importance, who flitted from one *amour* to another; it could only be a parody of François. But it was not the portrayal of François which was so disconcerting as that of his mother, the Duchess Louise. The people had to have a scapegoat and François, being young and charming, could be forgiven for his foibles. 'High spirits. Youth,' said the people indulgently. The extravagances necessary to placate these high spirits were laid at the door of the Duchess Louise, who had taken charge of affairs to such a great extent since her regency that the people complained that she ruled the country. In the play she was *Mère Sotte* and was seen plundering the Treasury and leading her youthful son astray.

François might have shrugged this off – not so Louise. She was incensed. The criticism was directed against her and she wanted revenge. This was a blatant example of *lèse majesté* and, she declared, punishable by law.

Consequently the players were arrested and taken to Blois, where they were kept in dungeons.

I think they would probably have been left there to perish had it not been for Queen Claude. She was really distressed about the incident. I thought that, in her quiet way, she was very wise although there had been times when I had been inclined to despise her for her meek acceptance of her lot.

After all, she was a king's daughter. Had I been in her place, I should have insisted on being treated with more respect. I should have refused to feign indifference to François's love affairs, for it must be feigned. She must care. She must feel humiliated. And when the time came, she just meekly accepted his return to the marriage bed, remaining calm and continuing with her good works.

She asked a great many questions about the players and thought it was quite wrong to imprison them for what they had done with impunity in the previous reign. 'The people will not like it,' she said. 'I must speak to the King.'

And she did. She was like many people who appear weak; she was indifferent enough over matters which seemed of no great moment to her but when she really felt strongly she could stand very firm.

François admired her – if not physically – for her character. The people loved her. Although they were amused by the King, they respected those who led saintly lives; and they respected Claude.

I could imagine the scene, although, of course, I did not witness it. Claude would clearly state that she thought the players ought to be set free. She would explain her reason, and clever François would see the logic of it. He knew his mother would be furious if he gave them their liberty and he hated to offend her, but he could see that Claude was right. Graciously and gallantly, he said that he could not refuse his wife's request; and for once Louise was impotent to act. I was sure she raged in private and must have wondered if Françoise de Foix was loosening the bonds between her and Caesar.

However, the players were released unconditionally, to the satisfaction of all except Louise.

François was too intelligent not to realize that his grip on the people's affections was slackening and he knew that it was always wise to give the people some lavish entertainment. The Romans had realized this and they instituted their circuses.

François, so well read, so well versed in history, decided to do the same.

Queen Claude, more popular than ever over the matter of the players, had never been crowned. That honour must be given her and at the same time it would give the people something to think about other than their growing dissatisfaction with the new reign.

The preparations threw our circle into a state of great activity. I was to be in the procession and we were fitted with new gowns of rich velvet and we were to wear hats made of cloth of gold in the shape of crowns.

So we rode to St Denis on elaborately caparisoned mules. Even Claude looked beautiful, accepting all the acclaim as calmly as she had the neglect. The people cheered her wildly, calling her St Claude. They remembered she was the daughter of the king whom they had failed to appreciate when he was alive, but they now knew his worth; and her mother had been the great Anne of Brittany whom they had all respected and loved.

I was pleased to see her appreciated.

Then there were the entertainments which always followed these occasions, during which the King had a chance of winning back some of his lost esteem by performing with grace and skill at the jousts.

It was after the activities were over that the Queen sent for me.

She bade me be seated and then she said: 'I have some news for you. I have received letters from your father.'

My heart sank. I was going to be sent home. But she went on: 'He is very happy that you are here and I have sent him a good account of your behaviour.'

'Oh, thank you, Madame.'

She nodded. 'You are a good child, and you have talents. Your speech has improved greatly since you came to me and your needlework is good.'

I thanked her again.

77

'He has been a little anxious of late about your sister – Mary, I believe.'

'Yes, Madame. Mary.'

'He has asked me if I can find a place for her here . . . with you.'

I looked at her in astonishment. She was smiling her gentle, sweet smile.

'I have written to tell him that I am willing to have her here. So, Anne, you will soon be seeing your sister. She is, in fact, on her way to us now.'

I was amazed. So Mary was coming to France! It was so long since I had seen her and those days with my brother George and the Wyatts in the gardens of Blickling and Hever seemed far in the past.

It would be wonderful to see Mary. I smiled and the Queen gave me one of her benign looks of approval.

I murmured: 'Thank you, Madame.'

*

Mary and I were emotional when we met. It was quite four years since we had been parted; and at first we did not recognize each other. She had changed considerably from the little girl who had been sent to Brussels; she was plumper, more voluptuous. She must be twelve years old but she looked older.

She told me how glad she was to come to the French Court. That of Brussels had been quite dull and she had heard that, since the reign of the new King of France, life here was very amusing.

Her eyes sparkled at the prospect, but I quickly disillusioned her. We were in attendance on Queen Claude and that was a little circle apart.

She pouted and said that perhaps there were ways of breaking out of the circle.

She laughed a good deal. I asked her about affairs in

Brussels but all she could tell me was what the people were wearing; and when I explained about King François going to war and his meeting with the Pope, she looked at me blankly and I could see that her attention was wandering. She had not changed; she was the same girl who had sat with us in the gardens and not listened to a word of those interesting conversations between George and Thomas Wyatt.

She was easy-going, happy-go-lucky, and I noticed, in a few days, that she was more interested in the men than the women. When she caught a glimpse of François she was overwhelmed with admiration.

'Surely,' she said, 'there has never been anyone like him.'

'I imagine he is unique,' I said.

'I think he smiled at me.'

'He smiles at all females.'

'Oh . . . I thought he smiled specially at me.'

I began to think she was inclined to be foolish, but it was pleasant to have someone of my own family near me; I was amazed what a joy it was to be able to converse in English.

After a while she settled in, as Mary always would, I supposed.

An important event occurred soon after her arrival. There was a great deal of talk about it, and the King's sister, Marguerite d'Alençon, showed a lively interest.

Some said it was an attack on the Church and struck at the very roots of religion; but Marguerite said that every new theory must be given attention.

The fact was that a priest called Martin Luther was so incensed by the sale of indulgences – which meant that by paying a sum of money, men and women could be forgiven their sins – that he drew up ninety-five theses on the subject and nailed them on the church door at Wittenberg. This had caused consternation throughout the Catholic world. The chief offender in Martin Luther's eyes was a Dominican friar named John Tetzel who had established himself at Jüterbog, where he carried out what Luther called 'this shameful traffic'. 'God willing, I will beat a hole in his drum,' declared Martin Luther. At one time Luther would have been seized and no more heard of him, but times were changing. Luther had his supporters and Tetzel was forced to retire to Frankfurt. This caused quite a stir in Court circles, and people thought that Martin Luther was striking a direct blow against the established Church.

Who was this upstart monk? people were asking. He should be taught a lesson.

But Marguerite insisted that the question was worth studying. The man had certainly raised some interesting points and it was nonsense to say that the Church could not profit from improvements.

Sometimes she would be walking in the gardens and a little group would gather round her and there would be an interesting discussion. I had been attracted to Marguerite from the moment I saw her. She was very beautiful but it was for her cleverness that she was noted. She and the King were on terms of intimacy such as he shared with no one else, not even his mother. I had heard it whispered that there was an incestuous love between them, but I did not believe that. François might be capable of indulging in it but I did not think Marguerite would be. Her adoration of her brother was not physical, although when one saw them walking in the gardens with their arms about each other one might think so. But although he was the King, it was Marguerite who would decide the nature of their relationship; and I have always believed that that relationship was far stronger and of greater durability because there was no sexual side to it. They were perfect in each other's eyes; and although it was clear that Marguerite had a greater regard for her brother than she had for her husband, I would be ready to swear that physical contact did not play a part in it.

Marguerite had one quality which the other two in the Trinity lacked: modesty. And I think this was due to her greater wisdom. She and François had grown up together; she was his senior by two years; she it was who had taught him to read, who had told him stories of great heroes, who had, in a measure, made him the man he was. To him she was always the elder sister, the greatest love of his life; although his devotion to his mother never wavered, being François, realistic and highly intelligent, he must see the faults in Louise; but he found none in Marguerite.

Marguerite wrote constantly; I had seen her on occasions sitting with the King – just the two of them because François made it clear that at that time he wanted no other company than that of his sister – his arm about her shoulder, while she read her poetry to him; I had seen them in animated conversation or laughing together; I had rarely seen such amity between two people.

I remember a verse she had written in her youth. The translation ran something like this:

> Such boon is mine to feel the amity
> That God hath putten in our Trinity
> Wherein to make a third, I, all unfitted
> To be the number's shadow, am admitted.

But to my mind – and perhaps this will be borne out by future generations – it was Marguerite who was the wisest member of the Trinity.

François would have forbidden any approval of Martin Luther in his Court. Was he not, after all, the Most Christian King? But Marguerite was above such laws; she was one who must give her attention to what she considered important, and the King would not dream of forbidding her to do what she thought right. And she certainly considered Martin Luther worthy of her attention.

One day I saw her talking to a group of people and wandering up, I stopped to listen.

She was saying: 'The Pope at the moment is inclined to shrug this aside. He thinks Luther a clever priest ...

interesting . . . expressing new ideas. But the Cardinals see danger here. They believe Luther is striking at the foundations of the Church. This may well be, but should we go on accepting these old laws and traditions? Should we not take them out of storage and give them a closer look? This is interesting. I do not believe it is the simple matter some people think. There is a good deal to the friar. I'll swear he will be sent for . . . to Rome, and if he goes, it may be that we will hear no more of Martin Luther, for he is certainly causing disquiet in some circles.'

Everyone listened intently – among them myself – and a few gave their opinions. She must have noticed me for when she stood up to leave she called to me.

'You are Anne Boleyn, I believe,' she said. 'The little one who stayed behind with Queen Mary and now serves Queen Claude.'

I told her this was so and she went on: 'You were listening to the discourse.'

'Madame, I am sorry . . . I saw no harm . . . '

She laughed. 'You have long ears, I believe,' she said and pulled one of them playfully. 'Tell me, what do you think of this man Luther?'

'I . . . I have not seen the theses.'

That amused her. 'Many people are giving judgement without seeing them.'

'I . . . I think one should see them first.'

She bent towards me and said: 'We think alike.'

Then she dismissed me, but after that she would speak to me when she saw me; and sometimes she would have a little chat – just the two of us – which I found most exciting.

The attention she bestowed on me had its effect and people were a little more respectful to me than before.

It was about this time that Raphael's masterpiece, *St Michael*, arrived in France. Having persuaded Leonardo da Vinci to take up residence under his shelter, François had tried hard to induce Raphael to do the same. Raphael, however, declined the invitation, but at least François succeeded in having two of his pictures brought to France. *St Michael* came and *The Holy Family* was to follow.

When *St Michael* arrived, it was treated with a respect which bordered on idolatry. François had the picture hung in his grandest gallery. It was hidden by a rich velvet curtain and only those who, in François's opinion, could appreciate great art were invited to the unveiling.

'It is sacrilege,' said François, 'to display great art to those who do not understand it.'

So it was a great privilege to be at the ceremony.

Marguerite sent for me. Eagerly I went to her. I had lost my awe of her and enjoyed these occasions when I would be seated on a stool close to her and listen to her reading poetry, often her own. She had discovered in me a love of the artistic. I had always been interested in clothes and I was allowed to design my own, which I did in a humble way; I invented a special sleeve which hung over my hand to hide the sixth nail.

Marguerite had admired them and when she knew the reason why, she admired them still more. She had decided that I was worthy to attend the unveiling; and so I was present on that great occasion.

It was thrilling when the curtains were drawn aside and the masterpiece revealed.

Afterwards François came to his sister and I heard him say: 'Who is your little guest?'

'Anne Boleyn,' she told him.

'A protégée of yours?'

'An interesting child.'

He surveyed me and I cast down my eyes. He took my chin in his hand and turned my face up to his. He stroked my cheek gently.

'Charming,' he said. His smile frightened me a little. Marguerite saw this and laid a hand on my shoulder, drawing me away from him. His smiles were then all for her.

'Her sister has now joined her,' said Marguerite. 'Anne has

been with us for some time.'

He nodded and seemed to forget me. I was glad of that.

It was soon after that that I became a little anxious.

Mary began to be absent for long stretches of time. There was a change in her. I often saw her smiling to herself as though she found something very amusing.

When I asked her what was happening, she giggled a little. I realized suddenly that others were whispering about her.

One day I said to her: 'Mary, what has happened? I know it is something.'

'Happened?' She opened her blue eyes very wide and I could see the laughter behind them. It was a certain gratified laughter.

'Please tell me,' I said. 'You seem very pleased about it. Let me share your pleasure.'

That sent her into fits of laughter.

'You are too young,' she said.

Then, knowing the morals of the Court, I feared the worst. Mary was twelve years old . . . soon to be thirteen. Girls were often married at that age.

I said: 'You have taken a lover.'

'Rather,' she corrected me, 'he has taken me.'

'Oh Mary,' I replied, 'it will do you no good.'

'But it will. Wait until you know who.'

'Please tell me who.'

'Guess.'

'No, I can't. Tell me.'

'You'll never believe it.'

'I will if you tell me.'

'The King.'

'François?'

'I know of no other King in France.'

'Oh Mary . . . you *fool!*'

Mary tried to be angry; it was not easy for her. She was astonished at my stupidity, in not understanding the honour – as she thought – this was. She seemed to think she had gained

84

the greatest possible prize because she had been seduced by the most profligate man in France.

'He is delighted with me.'

'For how long?'

'What do you mean?'

'Do you know that he seduces girls as frequently as he sits down to meals?'

'He likes me a great deal. He calls me his little English mare.'

I felt sick with shame. I thought of elegant, witty Françoise de Foix and the other Court ladies who had enchanted him briefly. How long did Mary think she would last?

I said: 'You have disgraced the name of Boleyn.'

Then I almost laughed at myself. Who were the Boleyns? Descendants of merchants who had done good trade and married into the aristocracy. But however humble the family, it should keep its honour.

*

Even now I would rather not dwell on that time. My sister Mary was one of those women – and this quality always remained with her – whose main purpose in life seemed to be to satisfy her sexual desires and those of her partners. I did not know whether she was a virgin when François discovered this . . . I call it a failing . . . in her, but he was the kind of man who would be aware of it at once and seek to exploit it.

Mary must have been born with a sexual competence; she would know how to attract and how to satisfy. This was the purpose of her life, I suppose, her *raison d'être*. It had been present in those early days, only I had not recognized it. Perhaps Mary herself had not.

She amused François for several weeks, which was longer than I expected. Everyone was talking about his new mistress, a girl . . . very young . . . but not too young. How long? was the question on everyone's lips.

It was not very long. His ardour waned very quickly, and Mary's visits to the royal bed grew less frequent. This was not to be tolerated by Mary's overwhelming sexuality, and very soon there was a new lover, who no doubt felt himself honoured to take that which had delighted the King.

Mary was reckless. She accepted the loss of royal favour with equanimity. There were others – plenty of them.

There was nothing subtle about Mary. She enjoyed her sexual encounters as did those who shared them with her; and in her opinion that should not be the concern of anyone else.

Perhaps it would not have been, if the first to take her up had not been the King.

She was now referred to not as the King's mare but the mare anyone could ride at any time it suited him. This was a very willing little English mare.

Marguerite understood my shame.

'Your sister is a foolish girl,' she said. 'She does not understand our ways as you do.'

'I have remonstrated with her,' I replied.

This made Marguerite smile. 'Oh, poor little sister. You are so much wiser than she. You will learn from her mistakes. You would never act as she has, I know.'

'Never,' I said fervently.

'Your sister, as I said, does not understand us. She is not exactly wanton. She is innocent, which sounds strange in one who leads such a life. She is like a child who takes too much of what seems to her so good, and does not think of the effects it is having. There are others likes her. Do not think she is unique. But where is her discretion? they are asking. How many have ridden the King's mare? Poor child. That is detrimental to her. The King cannot have the morals of his Court so corrupted.'

I looked at her in astonishment and she laughed.

'It is not that she has taken many lovers that is so disastrous; it is her manner of doing so. She blatantly enjoys it. It is almost as though her actions have become a public spectacle. People talk of her ribaldly. That, my brother will not endure. He declares he honours all women and will not have our sex humiliated . . . and that is what your sister is doing.'

I was bewildered and as always in our encounters Marguerite wanted me to explain my thoughts.

I said: 'But it was the King himself who seduced her. He it was who called her his mare.'

'He did all this discreetly. It was only natural that she would find him irresistible and that in time he should have tired of her. Then she could have taken another lover . . . discreetly. In time the King might have found a husband for her. That often happens in such cases. But Mary could not wait. She must dash into the next available bed. She should have bargained.'

'That seems worse.'

'It is . . . in a way . . . but it is etiquette and let me tell you this, Anne, my dear child: it is not what is done in my brother's Court which is important, but the manner in which it is done.'

'But Mary would never barter. She would *give*.'

'That is true. But to give too freely is not good manners. It is humiliating our sex. You are puzzled, as well you might be. But this is how things are at my brother's Court.'

'Mary is young . . . she is simple really.'

'Ah, there you have it. She is too simple to be acceptable at the Court of France.'

'What will happen to her?'

'She is to be sent back to England.'

'Sent back in disgrace!'

'Her presence is no longer required at the Court of France.'

I covered my face with my hands. 'And I?' I asked.

'My dear child, you are not responsible for your sister. Why, you are even younger than she is. I have grown fond of you. You interest me. My brother has noticed you, too.' She looked at me steadily. 'You will always remember your sister and never, *never* make the mistakes that she has.'

I nodded.

'We wish you to stay at our Court. I am sure your father will agree to that – though your sister must go.'

So Mary went.

My father was horrified that she should be sent home – and for such a reason. I heard later from her that she was made very unhappy for a while. But she had had such an exciting time at the Court of France that she would remember it for ever.

My father had married again and Mary was not welcome in the household. She was in disgrace.

But Mary's nature was not to be sad for long, and a year after her banishment I heard that she was married; her husband was a William Carey – a nobleman but poor; he came of a good family from the West Country – not the sort of match my father had anticipated for his daughter. It must have seemed to him that all his efforts on Mary's behalf had been wasted. But Mary was happy; she would always be happy; and perhaps if she were married to a man who pleased her – and she would not look for great riches – she would be contented.

Mary's experiences had a great effect on me – one which I should never forget. I did not know what plans my father had for me, but I guessed there would be plans. I was the only daughter left to keep up the Boleyn tradition for advantageous marriages.

And I was growing up.

I felt I wanted to hold back time. I wanted to go on living in this most elegant Court. I wanted to serve Queen Claude in the cloistered atmosphere of her apartments from which I could escape now and then to the stimulating society of Marguerite d'Alençon. I wanted my girlhood to go on and on.

Never, *never* must I follow in Mary's humiliating path. Remember it, always, I told myself.

One does not always realize at the time what effect historical events have upon our lives.

In the year 1520 I was thirteen years old, getting dangerously near the time when I should be considered marriageable. It was something I refused to think about.

Momentous events were afoot. The Emperor Maximilian, who had been one of the leading figures in European politics for so long, died. François immediately announced to his rival, Charles of Austria, who was now King of Spain, his claim to the vacant suzerainty. There was a great deal of discussion in Marguerite's circle about this. I heard it mentioned that the King of England believed he also had a claim.

The choice rested with a council of German Princes and Archbishops besides the Duke of Saxony, the Margrave of Brandenburg, the King of Bohemia and the Count Palatine of the Rhine. They were the only ones who could make the choice. Their verdict was a blow to François. He had thought he had a chance, though not an overwhelming one. Charles of Austria and Spain was elected and so became known as the Emperor Charles.

The result of this was to draw the disappointed candidates – France and England – together and it was arranged that a meeting should take place between them.

Much discussion went on between the two countries. Each was determined to show its power and glory to the other. So there was to be this meeting between the two Kings; if I were present with the Court, it would be the second time I had seen the King of England and I was excited at the prospect.

The matter was often discussed in Marguerite's circle, of which I was happy now to be a member. Queen Claude put no obstacles in my way; she thought it an excellent opportunity for me to be received in such intellectual company, which I could not enjoy with her.

I was naturally interested in comments on England. They spoke quite frankly in front of me. I think they had forgotten I was English – so French had I become.

Marguerite used to laugh about King Henry's vanity. We heard many stories about him because ambassadors were constantly coming back to the Court of France after having been to that of England and they liked to gossip. Marguerite encouraged this. We knew that the King of England had a tendency to play boyish games, that he liked appearing at masques in disguise, although it was never difficult to see through those disguises, for he could always be recognized by his height and reddish hair. He took a boyish delight in being treated familiarly and then suddenly revealing himself with: 'I am your King.'

There was a great deal of laughter among Marguerite's friends – not always kind. Henry was a little naïve in the manner in which he betrayed his interest in François. They were more or less of the same age and in similar positions. Henry would have heard of François's good looks and elegance. He himself was considered handsome – a fine figure of a king – and he wanted to make sure that he was equal to – or, better, excelled – François.

When the Venetian ambassador called at the Court, he had just come from England and he repeated a conversation between himself and Henry which was typical.

Henry wanted to know whether the King of France was as tall as he was. The Venetian ambassador replied that he could not give a definite answer; they were both unusually tall and must be about the same height.

'Is he as stout as I?' asked Henry.

'No,' replied the ambassador. 'He is slender.'

'What sort of legs has he?' asked the King of England.

'Very slender.'

'Slender!' cried the King. 'Then they cannot be shapely. Look you, man.' He held up his leg. 'Look at this calf. Just look at it.'

The ambassador did as he was told and had to admit that the leg of the King of England was very fine indeed.

There was a great deal of laughter. 'And what are your legs like?' became a catchphrase throughout the Court for a while.

But the growing power of the Emperor Charles meant that the Kings of France and England, whatever the rivalry between them, would have to watch the Emperor, and it was politic for them to show him that they were good friends, at least outwardly.

These three men stood astride Europe – the Emperor Charles, the King of France and the King of England. They were all young. Henry of England was the eldest, being three years older than François, and François was four years older than the Emperor. They were all eager to prove themselves – all energetically dedicated to the struggle for power.

As a result of this situation the King of England sent an embassy to Paris, there to make arrangements for the meeting between the two Kings. It was with some apprehension that I learned that my father was a member of this embassy.

Our meeting was rather a painful one. My father studied me closely. I saw at once that he was not displeased with me but the shadow of Mary's disgrace hung over us.

I curtsied and kept my eyes downcast.

He said: 'It is a long time, daughter, since we met.'

'Yes, father.' I was uneasy, wondering whether I should have to return to England with him.

'I have had good reports of you,' he said, and I had the impression that he was pleased with me. I would have given a good deal for a sign of fatherly affection, but that, of course, would have been asking too much. I found myself wishing that George had been sent instead of my father. What a different meeting that would have been!

I think he did not mean to be unkind, but he did not know how to show affection to us – though when I returned home and saw him with my stepmother, I realized that he could be fond of someone. It was a strange marriage because she was of no great family and by marrying her he had gone against the Boleyn tradition. I was to come to love her in time, for she was a wonderful woman – even though her blood might not be noble; and when I compared her with my cold grandfather, the Duke of Norfolk, and my indifferent uncle, the Earl of Surrey, I was glad my father had for once allowed his affections to get the better of his family pride.

He could not, it seemed, show affection to his children; but I think he must have suffered acutely over Mary.

'You are now a young woman . . . almost,' he said. 'How old are you?'

Odd that he, who had begotten me, could not remember. 'I am thirteen years old, father.'

'Growing up. Growing up. They have been good to you at the Court of France?'

'Very good.'

'And I hear that the Duchesse d'Alençon has shown some interest in you.'

'She has been very kind to me.'

'You will be returning home . . . in due course.'

I lowered my eyes. I did not want him to see the apprehension in my face. I dreaded that summons home. It would mean either a life of boredom at Hever or Blickling . . . or marriage. But perhaps a place at Court? I wondered. Could Mary have disgraced us all so much that that would be impossible?

'I doubt whether I shall be coming with the King's party,' said my father.

I was relieved at that.

'I shall make the arrangements. I have certain discussions with the French foreign minister . . . and then I shall return home.'

'Yes, father.'

'Is there much talk here . . . of your sister?'

'She is hardly ever mentioned. It is forgotten, I think.'

'Idiot,' he said. 'Well, she is off my hands now. Carey . . . '

he grimaced with contempt. 'She was lucky to get even him after her disgraceful conduct.'

'I don't think she realized . . . '

'I don't know how I could have offended God to be cursed with such a child.'

I knew it was no use trying to explain Mary to him. As far as he was concerned, she was a bitter disappointment, an utter disaster.

I saw him once or twice at Court; he was often hurrying to some meeting. I was relieved when he left.

*

That meeting between the two Kings which is often referred to as 'the Field of the Cloth of Gold' because of the lavish extravagance which was given to it, is well known in history.

I was old enough to be struck by the falseness of life at Court – and not just the French Court. I supposed that all courts were more or less the same. This meeting had not been devised so that two rulers with similar aims might be together in friendly fashion and talk of the peace of nations. It was an encounter between rivals, each eager to display his wealth and power to the other. While they talked friendship, they planned treachery, and the main object of the meeting was to show their successful rival, the Emperor Charles, that they would stand together against him.

My father had arranged that the two Kings should meet in France. There had been a certain amount of manoeuvring about this, for Henry of England thought he might demean himself by crossing the Channel; François no doubt felt the same.

After much argument it had been decided that the meeting should take place in Picardy but that the headquarters of the King of England should be at Guines, which was not far from Calais and in English territory, while those of the King of France should be at Ardres, which belonged to France.

Preparations were extensive. I expected it was the same in England, for each King was determined to outdo the other. There was great consternation when it was learned that the Emperor Charles had landed in England in order to have a conference with Henry before he set sail for France, which made it clear that he must be disturbed to contemplate this show of friendship between the Kings of France and England.

There were always a great many secret missions going on between all countries; visitors arrived constantly at Court who were, I was sure, spies and they brought news of what was happening in England. It appeared that Henry had gone to Dover to meet Charles when he heard he was about to land and the two monarchs had journeyed to Canterbury where they visited the Cathedral and the shrine of St Thomas à Becket.

The Cathedral was resplendent with all the precious gifts which had been brought to the shrine over the years, and it seemed that Charles was very impressed by such honour done to the saint – an indication, he said, of the piety of the nation.

There was a very disturbing piece of news which I heard Marguerite discussing, and that was that the Emperor Charles had made a friend of Cardinal Wolsey.

Wolsey was a name I had heard frequently whenever my country was mentioned. Wolsey, it was said, had the ear of the King; and Wolsey it was who kept a tight grip on affairs in England. The King honoured him; he was a brilliant statesman; when one considered how England would act, one thought of Wolsey.

The Emperor, it seemed, had promised Wolsey that he would help him in his life-long ambition, which was to become Pope. François had no such bait to offer him.

Everyone was talking about the preparations for the meeting of the Kings. Right from the beginning the rivalry was apparent. Henry had chosen eleven hundred workmen from Flanders and Holland – the most skilful in the world at their particular trade – to build a wooden palace in the shape of a quadrangle. On one side of the entrance was a fountain and in this a statue of Bacchus had been set up. Not water but wine flowed in this fountain. And on it was written in letters of gold: Make Good Cheer Who Will. On the other side of the entrance was a column held up by four lions and on the top a statue of Cupid, arrow poised. As if this were not enough, Henry had had a large statue placed opposite his palace depicting a Herculean figure with the inscription: He Whom I Back Wins.

There could be nothing more likely to arouse feelings of rivalry in the French and they set about scoring over the English, but with good taste to match ostentation.

François had had erected close to the town of Ardres a great tent, the dome of which was covered in cloth of gold. The inside was decorated with blue velvet spattered with stars so that it looked like the night sky. Though I did not see it, I heard that it was magnificent and made Henry's wooden palace seem vulgar.

However, a few days before the meeting was due to take place, a storm arose and the wind, being almost of hurricane force, tore up the tentpegs and ruined the cloth of gold, destroying François's magnificent tent. The superstitious wondered whether it was an omen.

François immediately took possession of a castle near Ardres and made light of the ominous event.

I wish I had seen that meeting of the Kings. It must have been impressive and at the same time a little amusing to see those mighty monarchs, so wary of each other and making such efforts to show what good friends they were – and thereby showing that they were not. There had been a great deal of discussion as to how the meeting should take place. Neither must give way to the other. There must be no sign that one side was the weaker.

They must have looked splendid; they were both head and shoulders above most men, both vain of their appearance and but newly come to kingship – and for neither of them had the possession of the crown been a certainty. Henry had had to take second place to his brother Arthur for years; François had lived in a state of anxiety even after the death of Louis. That must have made the crown doubly precious to them both.

They were to meet in a valley between Ardres and Guines. On the way there Henry's horse stumbled. I can imagine the consternation that ran through the English community. Was it a sign? Henry, however, ignored the incident as François had the destruction of his tent – and went on to meet his friendly foe.

They regarded each other for a moment or two. Knowing Henry so well now, I can imagine his little eyes taking in every detail of that truly elegant figure before him; and knowing François too, I could picture his cool assessment of his rival.

The two Kings greeted each other and embraced before they dismounted; and then arm in arm they walked to the tent where Wolsey and de Bonnivet – François's chief minister – awaited them.

Their words, were of course, recorded by observers and repeated.

'My dear brother and cousin,' François said, 'I have come a long way and not without trouble to see you in person. I hope that you hold me for such that I am, ready to give you aid with the kingdoms and lordships that are in my power.'

Henry replied: 'It is not your kingdoms or your divers possession that I regard, but the soundness and loyal observance of the promises set down in treaties between us two. My eyes never beheld a Prince who could be dearer to my heart, and I have crossed the seas at the extreme boundary of my kingdom to come and see you.'

In the tent agreements were drawn up regarding the marriage of the Dauphin and Henry's daughter, Mary, who was just four years old.

It was a good beginning. I learned afterwards, when I knew Henry very well indeed, that he had been greatly impressed by

François's appearance, and it had depressed him a little because he always wished to shine more brightly than anyone near him, and he was afraid that François might be considered the more attractive. Then he remembered that François's legs were short. He looked at them and rejoiced. Of course François looked well on a horse. His own legs, he believed, were beautifully proportioned and François, being so slender, did not have that rounded calf which the King of England was so proud to possess. He often said much later when referring to François: 'He had short legs and big feet. He was not quite perfect.'

Now I can imagine his feelings on that celebrated occasion. The celebrations were to last for sixteen days and the time would not be devoted merely to meetings between the monarchs. There would be jousts and tourneys, such entertainments as had never been seen before. Neither King had spared his attempts to impress the other with his wealth and power. It was said that those nobles who had accompanied the Kings to Guines and Ardres carried their lands and houses with them, so had they impoverished themselves in order to make the journey.

But during those magnificent celebrations there was a hint of that tension which we all felt. There was such falseness behind the expressions of good will.

It was arranged that the King of England was to go to Ardres to dine with Queen Claude, and that at the same time François was to go to Guines to be the guest of Queen Katharine.

During the time the Kings were in foreign camps they should be hostages for each other. The suggestion had come from the English, and François laughingly agreed to it.

The next morning François rose very early – which was unusual for him – and, taking only two gentlemen and a page, he rode over to the castle at Guines. The English guards were astonished to see him almost alone in their midst. I suppose the English were far more conscious of security than the

French; they were after all in France, and certainly they did not trust the French. It was because he understood their feelings so well that François acted as he did that morning.

He demanded of the guards the way to the chamber of the King of England.

'His Grace is not yet awake,' the guards told him.

François laughed and walked straight into the chamber where Henry was in bed.

Henry was dumbfounded. He at once realized that he himself was in no danger, but François had taken a great risk by walking right into the midst of what could have been the enemy.

Henry was immediately aware of the trust which was being shown him.

He said: 'Brother, you have done a better turn than any man ever did another. I see what trust I should have in you. I yield myself your prisoner from this moment.'

Henry was wearing a jewelled collar worth fifteen thousand angels; he took it off and begged François to wear it for his sake.

François, guessing something like this would happen and that there would be an exchange of gifts, had brought with him a bracelet which he insisted Henry accept and wear for *his* sake.

François had judged accurately. The bracelet he bestowed was worth thirty thousand angels. The French must outdo the English in all things. That was a little touch typical of François.

He then said that he would be the King of England's valet and it was he who warmed Henry's shirt and handed it to him.

When François returned to Ardres, his ministers were shocked that he had gone almost unaccompanied into the English stronghold, but François only laughed at them; and when he touched the collar which Henry had given him, and thought of the bracelet which he had given Henry, he was much amused.

There was another incident which did not end up in quite such an amicable way.

This was on the occasion of a wrestling match, when, as in all the tournaments, the excitement was increased by the rivalry of the French and English.

Henry had brought the champions of the sport with him from England, and as soon as the match began, it became clear that the skill of the English was superior to that of the French. I heard many a grumble that the best French wrestlers, who came from Brittany, had not been invited to take part. It was an oversight which was very regrettable to the French but delighted the English, for they won all the prizes.

I could see that François was disconsolate when the winners came to the ladies' loge to receive the prizes from Queen Claude.

Afterwards the Kings went into one of the pavilions to refresh themselves with a drink together. Henry was delighted with the success of the English, and he thought to crown the glory by wrestling with François and overthrowing him.

He turned to him and said: 'Brother, I must wrestle with you.' He thereupon seized François and sought to trip him. He must have forgotten – or perhaps he did not know – that François was one of the finest wrestlers in France. In a few seconds Henry was thrown to the ground.

Embarrassed and angry, Henry rose.

'Once again,' he cried. 'Once again.'

But the French King's friends reminded him that supper was just about to be served and, as none could start without them, it would be a breach of etiquette to arrive late. The wrestling match would have to be postponed.

I can imagine François looking down his long nose at Henry and laughing inwardly, and Henry's humiliation to have been thrown. Fortunately it was only those close to the Kings who had seen it, but he knew the story would be all round the Court by tomorrow – as it was, and that was how I heard of it.

But although François might have gleaned a momentary satisfaction, the incident did him little good, for after all, he was trying to win Henry to his side in the conflict with the Emperor; and Henry was a man who remembered slights.

I vividly recall the dinner at which Queen Claude entertained the King of England. It was the occasion when François was dining with Queen Katharine. As one of Claude's attendants, I was present, so I had a greater opportunity of observing King Henry than I had ever had before.

He was extremely affable and none could be more charming when he wished. I think the absence of François made him feel more at ease. He was gracious and very attentive to Claude; he had heard much of her saintliness, he said; and that was a quality he most admired in ladies. He was honoured to be in the company of a lady of such goodness.

I remember the gown I wore on that occasion. It was red velvet – one of my favourite colours – with a long skirt open in front to show a brocade petticoat. It was drawn in tightly at the waist and my long wide sleeves fell gracefully, well below my hands, hiding that sixth nail which always bothered me.

The King complimented the Queen on the excellent food and wine and afterwards he spoke to all of us.

He lingered a little with me – I supposed because I was English. He seemed particularly amused to hear that I was Sir Thomas Boleyn's daughter.

'A good servant, Sir Thomas,' he commented. 'And you are an English girl.' He slapped his thigh. 'I could have sworn you were French.'

'I have been long at the Court of France, Your Grace.'

He put his big face close to mine and said jovially: 'Well then, you must have been nothing but a baby when you came.'

'I was seven years old, Your Grace.'

'Beautiful girls should be where they belong,' he said. 'In their own country.'

I smiled and he passed on.

I thought he was very friendly, which was obviously because I was my father's daughter. I knew that he had progressed amazingly at Court during the last years.

The great occasion of the Field of the Cloth of Gold was over by 24 June and I left with the royal party for Abbeville, while King Henry and Queen Katharine led their cavalcade towards Calais where they were to make the crossing to England.

The next day François was furiously angry and that anger seemed to reverberate throughout the Court, for the King of England, instead of going direct to Calais, had gone to Gravelines, where the Emperor Charles, with his brother Ferdinand and his wily minister Chièvres, were waiting to meet him.

So this was what the protestations of brotherly affection and friendship were worth! No sooner had the King of England said goodbye to his friend François than he was meeting the Emperor Charles; and Heaven knew what treaties they would be drawing up together.

One thing was certain though – they would bring no good to the King of France.

*

That year seemed to flash by. I was fourteen years old. I knew in my heart that I could not go on as I was much longer. There would be plans to get me married. Already I was aware of the glances of young men which seemed to follow me everywhere I went. I smouldered with resentment for I was sure some of them were remembering Mary and judging me by her.

I had a ready wit which was gaining me quite a little reputation. Then I began to enjoy the admiration of the young men – which did not arouse in me any desire whatsoever – because of the opportunity to repulse them. I was so anxious to show them that I was not like Mary that I think I developed into being sexually cold. When I saw some of the women giggling together and recounting their amorous adventures, I felt disgusted. I was so determined not to be like Mary that I made myself so.

Oddly enough, instead of being a deterrent, my studied indifference to the advances of young men seemed to make them more eager to pursue me. I could play the lute very well indeed. I have never believed in false modesty and I would say that few of the ladies could compare with me in that respect. I could sing well and could dance even better. In fact, I had been taught all the social graces and I had learned my lessons well.

I had always been interested in clothes and because I had two defects to hide – my sixth nail and the mole on my neck – I designed my own clothes and I had become good at it. I could mingle colours artistically and I knew exactly what suited me, and that was what I was going to wear, even though I must sometimes snap my fingers at fashion. So well did I succeed in this that *my* styles had started to become the fashion. Everyone wanted to wear them, but I heard it said that they did not look quite the same on others as they did on the little Boleyn.

Suddenly I had emerged. I was no longer a child. I was a nubile woman. I was fashionable. I had acquired an elegance; and I looked different from other women at Court. There was, after all, a similarity about beautiful women like Françoise de Foix. Big blue eyes, fair curls, straight little noses, red lips and pearly teeth. I was not a beauty, but I was myself. Large, deep-set eyes which held some mystery, for nobody understood what I was thinking; long black hair which I liked to wear hanging loose about my shoulders, scorning the elaborate hairstyles; pale skin and slightly prominent upper teeth, oval face and a long, slender neck. People noticed me before they did these beauties. My clothes designed by myself were different and when others copied them I changed my style. Oh yes, I was beginning to be noticed in the Court of France.

My attitude towards my would-be suitors baffled them. They did not know that the shadow of my sister walked constantly beside me – a dreadful warning.

As soon as the festivities of the Field of the Cloth of Gold were over, the Court started its summer season of travelling throughout the realm. This was almost like a repetition of those weeks at Ardres; there was feasting and tournaments at every *château* where we rested.

François was perhaps a little subdued. He was too clever to deceive himself, and he knew that in the Emperor Charles he had a formidable enemy who seemed to flout him at every turn. It might be that all the expense incurred through the meeting with Henry was wasted, since Charles, lurking at Gravelines and with very little pomp and ceremony, had proceeded to undo all the good François had done. It had been a master stroke to offer to help Wolsey to the Papal crown; nothing could win over that wily statesman more than such an offer. François knew that in spite of his youth the Emperor was more than his match.

But at this time my mind was full of my own affairs.

Little incidents occurred which disturbed me. It was becoming clear to me that François's attention had alighted on me.

When I played the lute, he would compliment me in most fulsome terms; I would find him at my side; he often partnered me in the dance. A great compliment, some thought, but it filled me with apprehension.

I knew that François was not always scrupulous in courtship. On the surface he was the chivalrous knight; but he would employ all kinds of devious means to reach his desires. There was a rumour that his one-time mistress, Françoise de Foix, had been a lady of great virtue, having been brought up in the pious Court of Anne of Brittany; and a marriage had been arranged for her with the Comte de Châteaubriand, which had been a happy one. François had seen her, desired her and urged her to come to Court, but she listened to the entreaties of her husband and remained in the country. François had heard that her husband had a very unusual ring and they had made a pact that, if they were ever parted and he sent his ring to her, she was to come to him at once. François had a copy made of the ring and sent the Comte away on an embassy. Then he sent the ring to Françoise with the instruction that she was to come to Court without delay.

Of course, if Françoise had been a truly virtuous woman, she would have gone straight home when she realized she had been duped and I am sure François would have been too chivalrous to prevent her. But one had to remember that François was a very attractive man – apart from his kingship, and the power which came from that made him irresistible. However, Françoise succumbed. She had three brothers who were hungry for promotion and François could give so much. So that was the end of the virtuous existence of Françoise de Foix.

There were many such stories of François and some may not have been true, but knowing him I guessed they had their roots in fact.

Thus, when I saw his eyes on me, I began to suffer small anxieties.

If I had been different, I might have been willing. After all, he was the King. I should never be like my sister, of course, but without her example might I have fallen into temptation? Should I have enjoyed flaunting my power at Court as the King's mistress? I was not sure.

I was helped a good deal by Marguerite.

She adored her brother and thought him perfect in every way, but that did not mean she could not see other people's points of view.

She used to read to me quite frequently. She was interested in me. In fact, there was a similarity between us. I lacked her erudition and her clever mind, but I found great pleasure in listening to her discourse.

It was she who kept me informed of events and one of her great fears at this time was that our countries would go to war. The meeting at Ardres and Guines? She shrugged that aside. It was merely two kings displaying their wealth and power. That was not how treaties were made. Did I think it furthered friendship? It was rivalry all the time. What are tournaments but competitions? When it is between two knights, that is very worthy, even though it engenders jealousy, but when it is between rival countries, then the danger is acute.

'Then why . . . ' I began.

She shook her head. 'Who can say? It was a gesture . . . while it lasted. If it had been a meeting to discuss ideas . . . Oh, it was said to be so, but what was important? Who won at the jousts? Who won at the wrestling? Who had the greater strength? The greater power . . . the greater wealth . . . And all the time there is that young man . . . the most powerful man in Europe. He is young in years but in wisdom he is already an old man. I hate the thought of war.' Then she looked at me and said: 'But you, Anne, have a distant look of late. Tell me, what is on your mind?'

I hesitated and she urged me to go on. I said: 'It is the King.'

'François?'

'He . . . he looks my way.'

She nodded, smiling. 'Ah, he is a lusty boy. He always was. He is strong . . . such a man. He adores beauty. He is going to build beautiful *châteaux* all over the country. You know he brought Leonardo da Vinci here. Poor man, his stay was short. Genius should be above mortality. It should be granted eternal life. He tried for Raphael. You see, he would bring all the great painters, writers and architects to France so that his country becomes the centre of art. He lives for beauty and he sees that in women. Women are essential to him . . . as art is. And he has seen something in you which attracts him.'

'I do not want . . . '

She understood as she always did.

'I know. You are young. You are not of an amorous nature . . . like your sister.'

I shuddered.

She said: 'Yes, I understand, Anne. You felt it deeply. It was a great disgrace and humiliation to you. Of course, she was young and innocent. There are others here who do all that she has done . . . and more . . . and yet here they live as respected members of the Court. Your sister was not clever enough; she was not devious; she was too open. She enjoyed sexual encounters so much that she could never resist them. There are some women like that. She became a byword at the Court, and that is what could not be endured. There are women at the Court who could not tell you how many beds they have slept in . . . they are so numerous. But here they stay while poor innocent little Mary is sent away. And the gentlemen . . . led by the King . . . if they have not a mistress, they are regarded with suspicion. Yet your poor little sister is sent away as a prostitute.'

'She was never that. She had numerous lovers . . . yes . . . but she gave all the time. She never asked for payment.'

'I know. And you think that since you are her sister it might be assumed that you resemble her.'

'Yes, I believe that is so.'

'My dear Anne, nobody could think you resemble your sister. You are a person in your own right. I cannot have you disturbed. I am not surprised that the King is attracted by you. How old are you?'

'Fourteen.'

'It is a charming age. And you have never had a lover?'

I drew back in horror.

She laughed and said: 'You have answered.' She took my hand. 'Yes, you are indeed different from so many girls of your age. You have a dignity and respect for yourself. That is it. I shall speak to the King.'

I became alarmed.

'Oh, don't be afraid. You know of this special bond there is between us. We can talk intimately on any subject. It has always been so. I it was who taught him to read. We used to sit under the trees at Cognac and I would tell him stories I invented for him. He was such a beautiful child . . . clever too. We adored him, my mother and I. I would have done anything for him. I must tell you this little story about our childhood, and then you will learn something special about him. I was six years old; François was four. I had put away my dolls long before. François liked to look at them and he asked me why I no longer wanted to play with them. I said it was because I was too old. He replied that I wanted a real baby not a doll. Then he said he wanted one too . . . I to be the mother, he the father. You look shocked. It is hard to imagine François innocent, but he was then. He thought that babies just arrived when people wanted them. He already knew that he was the precious one – my mother called him Precious and my King, my Caesar, even at that age. So he believed if he wanted a baby, he would have one.'

I murmured: 'How you love him!'

'He is my life,' she said. 'Nothing else means the same to me. I want all the best for him now as I did then. Outside the *château* there was a cottage, and before it a baby was playing on the grass. François said: "There is our baby." So we picked up the child and took it into the *château*. We washed it because it was not very clean and I found some of François's garments. They were rather big but we dressed the baby in them. The child was soon missed and traced to the *château*, and when they wanted to take it home, François was so unhappy. He pleaded to keep it. It was his, he said. He was its father, I was its mother. It was our baby. The result was that the parents – who were poor – realized what a good life the child could have at the *château*; and in the end we were allowed to keep her. We had nurses for her and we called her Françoise, which was the nearest we could get to François' name.'

'What a charming story,' I said. 'What happened to the girl?'

'She was brought up in the *château*, and when she was a little older a home was found for her with some wealthy people. That is not the end of the story. There was a very strange sequel. It is one of those coincidences in life which often bewilder us but which happen now and then. François liked to go about incognito, and he favoured the dress of a student. One day he went to church in this guise and saw there a beautiful young girl and was immediately enamoured of her. She was gentle, obviously not wealthy but of good breeding. He followed her to her home – a very pleasant house but quite humble, of course, compared with what he was accustomed to. He did not speak to her immediately but watched her. It was an exciting game to him. Finally she became aware of him and he spoke to her. He said he wished to be her friend but she replied that there could not be friendship between a humble girl and the Dauphin. You see, she knew him. Then she told him who she was. She was our baby Françoise. She insisted that there could be no love between them because she was a virtuous girl and could not be any man's mistress. François was desolate. He came to see me as he always did when disturbed. I felt rather indignant with the girl for refusing him. It was always my desire to give François what he wanted – and I thought then that she should be proud to be loved by the Dauphin.'

She paused, smiling.

'I suggested that he should have her abducted and brought to him. When he had seduced her, she would forget her scruples. He was well versed in the arts of love. He would know how to please her. He was delighted. He embraced me and told me that I had always had an answer to his problems.'

I said in a shocked voice: 'You could tell him that!'

'I did. You see, I believed that she must be happy and proud to be loved by François. I thought she just had bourgeois scruples which would be swept away by her delight in him. It would be such a beautiful ending to our story. It would make the whole thing full of meaning.'

'So you would abduct the young woman as you did the child.'

'I know you are thinking that I assume royalty has special privileges. Well, has it not?'

'People's lives are their own. They should decide what to do with them.' I spoke boldly, for Marguerite had always encouraged me to say what I thought.

'Sometimes they need a little guidance, a little push in the right direction. Shall I tell you the rest of the story?'

'Please do, Madame.'

'She was brought to him, and he told her he had fallen in love with her and how delighted he was that she was his Françoise whom he had named and who had given him such delight when he was a little boy. Then he sought to make love to her, to take her by storm. She wept; she entreated; she implored. François, as you know, sets great store by chivalry. He has always been the perfect knight. She declared vehemently that, if he dishonoured her, she could not live; she would kill herself. François believed her. He saw that she was not feigning reluctance. He was immediately contrite and assured her that she had nothing to fear from him. He loved her and she should go on her way unmolested by him. She fell on her knees and thanked him. François was very touched. She went away. He has not seen her since, but always he enquires after her; and he will see that she is well looked after all her life.'

'What a happy ending to what might have been a sad story. I am so glad it happened like that.'

'I tell you this story so that you understand him. You know how I love him. Do you think I would give so much of myself to someone whom I considered unworthy?'

'No, I do not,' I said.

'I will tell him of your fear.' I lifted my head in protest but she waved that aside. 'Oh yes, I will tell him. I will explain that

109

you are not like so many ladies of the Court. He will understand. I will remind him of the day we found little Françoise. I will say the little Boleyn is young yet. She is not yet a woman. Because she is wise beyond her years, you think she is. Physically she is immature, though mentally advanced. She knows what she wants. She will always know what she wants; and she is not to be trifled with.'

'You could say this to the King?'

'He is my brother first, my little François – the King second.'

I said: 'Thank you. I shall always remember your goodness to me.'

She shook her head. 'You interest me. I shall follow your future . . . wherever you are.'

François's attitude towards me changed after that. He regarded me with an amused glint in his eyes; he talked to me now and then – but I had the idea that he had ceased to pursue me; and I felt a great sense of relief.

*

The months passed. It was more than a year since the meeting of Ardres and Guines. There was a great deal of uneasiness, for the rivalry between François and the Emperor was growing dangerous. There was talk about King Henry, for much depended on whose side he came down. At this time he was hovering between the two – a very uncertain ally. True, the little Dauphin was betrothed to Henry's daughter, the Princess Mary, but everyone knew how easily such contracts could be broken.

One day the English ambassador came to see me.

He said: 'I have word from your father. You probably know that war is imminent.'

'I have heard talk of it, and it does seem that France will soon be in conflict with the Emperor Charles.'

'It is more than likely, and for that reason your father thinks it is wise for you to leave the Court of France.'

I was overcome with depression. I had been here seven years. This was my home. It could mean only one thing: England would soon be at war with France.

I stammered: 'Leave here . . . '

'It would seem to be wise. I am sending all the students home. Your father thinks that, now your education has been completed, you should return.'

'When?' I asked.

'It would be advisable to begin preparations at once. You should leave not later than January.'

Of course, I had known it had to come. I thought back over all those years, to my arrival here and how exciting it had been serving Queen Mary; and after she had gone I had settled into the household of Claude. I had learned to love the company of Marguerite. And now I was to be uprooted.

Those days were gone for ever.

I was desolate but there was nothing I could do. I must say goodbye to my friends at the French Court – to kind Queen Claude, to dangerous François and to the one I loved best – my teacher and mentor, Marguerite d'Alençon.

I realized fully then – though perhaps I had always known it – that I, who tried to regard myself as an individual, was nothing more than a pawn to be set on a chequerboard at the spot where I could be most useful to those who commanded me.

I guessed my return might have something to do with a marriage. I was at last being called upon to play my part in the family game.

I was apprehensive and very sad to leave; but there was no escape; and in January of that year 1522 I set sail for England.

A Visit to Hever

It was strange to return to a home with which I had been so familiar long ago and had not seen for seven years. I had forgotten the feeling of security I had always experienced when I crossed the moat and passed under the portcullis and stepped into the enclosed courtyard. How often had I sat there listening to my brother and Thomas Wyatt! I felt a thrill of pleasure because I must see them soon. How well I knew the buttresses and the embrasures where Mary and I had played hide and seek. A castle was a good setting for such a game.

France seemed far away, and whatever my feelings would be later, I was home.

One of the most pleasant experiences of my homecoming was meeting my stepmother. I took a great liking to her from the first moment I saw her. She was no grand lady but she had a pleasant face and a lovable manner; there was nothing fashionable about her; she was a country woman; I believed she had lived near Blickling and that my father had met her when he was staying there.

That he had recognized her worth and married her endeared him to me; it lifted my spirits to realize that he had made such a disinterested choice. But I was sure she had brought him more than lands and blue blood. Perhaps he was not the cold, ambitious man I had always thought him to be – or at least not in all things.

She was nervous of me, which made me feel protective towards her. I guessed it was not easy to be presented with a family of grown-up children. I put her at ease by calling her Stepmother and showing that I bore her no resentment for taking my mother's place. I could, at all events, remember very little of my mother.

An obvious relief settled on her, and she was too open and frank to hide it.

She said: 'Your room is ready. They told me which one it was, and I thought you would wish to have it while you are at Hever.'

I thanked her and said it was what I had hoped.

I sat looking around my room at the panelled walls and the furniture I remembered so well – the bed, the chairs, the table and the muniment-chest. It seemed smaller than it used to, perhaps because I had become accustomed to the vastness of the palaces of France.

After a while my stepmother came up and asked me if there was anything I wanted. She advanced into the room and stood with her hands on her hips, looking at me tentatively. Her gown was of a brownish colour, which was not very becoming, and I immediately thought her dress would not be fit for life at Court. I supposed it was fit enough for the country, but surely she must sometimes accompany my father to Court? But she was at home in the country now and she looked like a country woman – not like the wife of a man who was an associate of the King and advancing fast at Court.

But I liked her looks, her fresh, open face and her obvious desire to do what was right and be liked.

I smiled at her.

'Are you sure you have everything that you wish?' she asked anxiously.

I told her that I had.

She sat on the bed and looked at me. 'I have been a little nervous of meeting you,' she said. 'I know Mary and George now . . . '

'I am the youngest,' I said. 'You should not stand in awe of me.'

She smiled. 'I don't know. But you are . . . rather grand.'

'Grand?' I laughed. I realized she was referring to my clothes. 'It is how we dressed at the Court of France.'

'You are glad to be home?'

I hesitated. I was not sure. I should see George and Thomas Wyatt. That would certainly make me glad. But I should be apprehensive until I knew for what purpose I had been brought home so suddenly.

I said: 'It is a little strange at first. I have been away so long.'

'It will seem quiet here in the country, but I daresay it will not be for long.'

'Do you know what is intended for me?'

'Your father will explain everything. He will be here soon . . . and your brother and sister, too.'

'They are well?'

'Indeed, yes. Your brother said he would be here almost as soon as you arrived. He is most eager to see you.'

'And I him. And my sister?'

'She is at Court.'

'Mary at Court!'

'Yes.' She lowered her eyes. 'Her husband has a post there in the King's household.'

'Oh, I see. And she is well and happy?'

'She is well and seems happy.'

'I am glad. I look forward to seeing them.'

'We must have some talks while you are here. You must tell me about the Court of France. It must have been very interesting.'

I nodded.

She went on: 'If there is anything . . . '

'Thank you. You have been so kind to me.'

She flushed a little and, smiling a little uncertainly, left me.

I thought: Mary at Court! Then she must have recovered from her disgrace. My stepmother knew something and, if I had read her aright, she believed it was not her place to tell me. Well, I must be patient and wait until it was revealed. But I had made up my mind that I would not be forced into a marriage which I did not like.

To my great joy, George arrived next day. I saw him from

114

my window as he rode into the courtyard and my heart leaped with pleasure. My dearest brother, how handsome he was! Tall and distinguished-looking . . . yet still the same George, whose special favourite I had been in the days of our childhood. I ran down to meet him.

He leaped from his horse and I was in his arms.

I touched his face. I laughed. I was so happy. Whatever happened afterwards, this was a moment to savour.

'Let me look at you,' he said, holding me at arms' length. 'Is this elegant lady my little sister?'

'Is this handsome gentleman my brother George?'

Then we laughed and were hugging each other.

'It has been a long time,' I said.

'I have thought of you constantly.'

'And I of you. There is so much to talk of. Let us go in, shall we?'

Our stepmother came running to meet George. He kissed her affectionately and I could see that he had the same opinion of her as I had.

'I am so glad you are here,' she said. 'Anne has been most impatiently awaiting your arrival. Will you have some food now . . . some refreshment?'

'Later please,' said George. 'I want to talk with my sister first.'

Arm in arm we went up the staircase and into the gallery with its ornamental stucco ceiling, past the embrasures – favourite spots in which to conceal ourselves in our games – to that room where we used to gather with our friends – usually the Wyatts – and sit and talk and listen to Thomas's poems and play the lute.

'There are many things I want to know,' I said. 'What are you doing now, George? And Mary . . . what of Mary? I hear she is at Court.'

'Oh yes. Will Carey has a post there. Esquire to the Body.'

'But after what happened in France . . . '

'You are thinking of Mary. Oh, Mary is reinstated. She is

quite a personage at Court . . . if Mary could ever be that. No, in spite of everything, she is still the same. She never asks for anything.'

'What do you mean, George?'

'I thought you might have heard. There must have been gossip. Mary has found favour in a high place.'

'You can't mean . . . '

He nodded. 'The highest place of all. The King finds our sister enchanting. He has selected her as his little playmate.'

'Oh . . . no!'

He nodded. 'Sweet little Mary, the friend of Kings! I wonder whether she finds the King of England different from the King of France. One could never get Mary to tell. Not that she would know. Mary is intent on one thing and as long as she gets that she is content.'

'And what of Will?'

'Oh, the King likes him well enough. He is such a complaisant husband.'

'George, I find it . . . shameful.'

'No, sweet sister. Such goings-on are only shameful among the undistinguished. To be the mistress of a peasant is disgrace indeed, but to be the mistress of a King . . . well, that is a great honour.'

'Don't be cynical, George. This is our sister, and after what happened to her at the Court of France one would have thought she would have been wise enough to see that it did not happen again.'

'The Court of England is not the Court of France. Here there is a high moral tone. *Amours* are not flaunted here. François's affairs were too numerous for the people not be be aware of them. Our King is different. He would be a saint . . . if his nature would let him. François is more realistic. He knows he can never be a saint, even if he wanted to be . . . which he doesn't. He loves the world too well. So does Henry, but between you and me, Anne, he knows how to deceive himself. He feels very saintly since he wrote his book against

Martin Luther, *Assertio Septem Sacramentorum*. It has earned him the title of Defender of the Faith. Mind you – again *entre nous* – Wolsey had a hand in it and Thomas More is responsible for a goodly part of it; but it is put forth as the King's work, and it shows him to be an upholder of the Church. You see, he wants to show the world that he is a *good* man. Half of him is . . . but we are all complex characters . . . you and I . . . and even His Grace the King. So . . . he tells himself that he is faithful to his Queen . . . in thought, he is . . . it is only these little forays on the side. And our Mary is at the centre of one.'

'How long has it been going on?'

'Almost since she went to Court. He noticed her at once. Mary is like that, you know. Her appeal is immediate. It is not beauty . . . it is promise. I think that is the answer. That in some cases is the essence of the attraction between the sexes. I am ready. That is what Mary says: I am as eager as you. I want nothing but our union. It is only the satisfaction I can give you and you can give me, that I crave. There you have it, Anne – the secret of Mary's appeal to all men. Who could resist it? Certainly not the King.'

'She has learned nothing from what happened in France!'

'This is different from France. There, when the King threw her aside, she took lovers . . . anyone . . . openly. Men boasted that they shared the King's mistress. But there were so many of them that it became the talk of the Court. That was considered crude by the French. Not good manners . . . not polite behaviour. That is the real sin over there. Mary is in her natural environment here. I don't see why she should not last quite a long time with the King.' He laughed at me. 'Don't fret,' he went on. 'You need never worry about Mary. She will always come up smiling. It is her nature.'

'So our sister is the King's mistress. What does our father say?'

'He says, "Well done, Mary." He is getting along well at Court. The King favours him. He has made a success of his

117

embassies and more than that he has begotten a daughter who pleases the King.'

'I would he had earned his success in some other way.'

'The path to success is a thorny one, and the way is steep. There are many pitfalls. It is a fool who does not take advantage of a helping hand when it is offered.'

'Oh, George, it is good to be with you and listen to your talk. I have often thought of it all. Do you remember the gardens with the Wyatts?'

'I remember.'

'Why have they brought me home? Do you know?'

'They have a bridegroom for you.'

'Who?'

'Well . . . you probably didn't hear that a few years ago our great-grandfather, the Earl of Ormond, died. He left, in addition to his title, vast estates in Ireland. The inheritance was expected to come to the families of his two daughters – one of them our grandmother. Our father has long been expecting this. However, the Earl's second cousin, Sir Piers Butler, is claiming the estate.'

'How can he do that? He is not in the direct line.'

'It is rather complicated. It is an Irish peerage. The Earl took up his residence in England because he was tired of the continual conflict reigning in Ireland. Sir Piers is something of a brigand. He is suspected of having murdered another member of the family who might have a claim, so his intentions are obvious. He had been taking care of the Irish property and is one of the few lords there who can be trusted to work for the English against these tiresome people who have always – and always will – created trouble and mischief. So Sir Piers is in high favour at Court. In his will the Earl rewarded Sir Piers for his services but left his estates to his daughters' heirs. The case was brought forward and Sir Piers was commanded to come to England and state his claims before a court of law. His reply was that he was too busy fighting the King's wars. This was true and as Ireland was –

as usual – on the verge of rebellion and Sir Piers was one of the few men on whom Henry could rely, the King was loath to offend him. As a result, the case has hung fire while Sir Piers continues to use the land and revenues as though they belonged to him.'

'What has this to do with my marriage?'

'A great deal. Sir Piers has a son – James Butler. The King wants Sir Piers to stay working for him in Ireland. Therefore he must keep him happy. He was in a dilemma until our uncle Surrey came up with the suggestion that marriage was the answer to this dispute. Sir Piers has a son; our father has a daughter. If those two were brought together in matrimony, their offspring would naturally inherit the estates. Simple, it seemed to Surrey . . . and the King. It has been decided and, as Master Wolsey gives his approval to the plan, it is as good as accomplished.'

I was furiously angry. I said: 'They have settled it without asking the opinion of those two to whom it means most.'

'It is the way of the world, sister.'

'George, I will not have it. I will not be bartered like this.'

'You will find it hard to stand against it, Anne.'

'I will tell our father when I see him.'

'It is not only our father. It has become a political matter. The King wishes it. Wolsey wishes it.'

'What could they do to me if I refused?'

'I do not think it would be wise to attempt to find out.'

'But I won't have it, George! I won't have it!'

He tried to soothe me. 'Some arranged marriages work out very well. One man is very like another. You will make this James dance to your tune, I do not doubt.'

'Among the Irish bogs?'

He laughed. 'A far cry from the Court of France, I'll swear.'

'I'll not do it.'

'Don't despair. It may be something will happen. You never know. Often life does not turn out the way it was planned.'

'This is certainly not going to.'

What I had learned had considerably dampened my pleasure in being home, although I had expected to hear something like this. Ireland! I had not thought of that. I could not imagine myself, after having grown accustomed to the elegance of the French Court, exiled into a savage land. I had read somewhere that it was populated by barbaric chiefs who roamed about the country bare-footed, wrapped in saffron-coloured robes, making war for no reason at all except that it was a state they revelled in.

I was shocked because my father was profiting from Mary's degradation. I remembered how violently he had spoken against her in France, how he had reviled her for her immoral conduct; now, it seemed, when it suited him, he applauded it.

I thought of all the good that had come to him through his daughter's shame. True, he had been advancing in favour before Mary came along to help him on his way. I remembered hearing how he had been one of the four people to carry the canopy over the Princess Mary when she was christened. That was quite an honour. Soon after that he had been appointed Sheriff of Kent. All this before Mary. He had pleased the King and proved an able ambassador.

I felt I wanted to escape from the cynical attitude to life where an action was deplored only when it did not bring material advantage.

*

A few days later Thomas Wyatt came riding over from Allington.

I was in the courtyard. He dismounted and, coming towards me, lifted me in his arms and held me, looking up at me.

'Anne! So my lady deigns to return to us at last.'

'You haven't changed, Thomas,' I told him.

'Did you expect me to? I'd always be the same to you.'

He set me down and we stood for a moment regarding each other.

He was tall and, if not exactly handsome, very attractive. Memories came flooding back. I remembered how much I had cared for him.

'As soon as word reached me that you were here, I had to come,' he said.

'How is everyone at Allington? Your sister Mary?'

'Mary is well. You will see her soon. But I was impatient. I had to come at once.' His eyes ranged over me. 'So elegant,' he said. 'Indeed the Court lady. So this is what the French have done to you.'

'I was a long time there, Thomas.'

'To our loss.' He took my hand – the one with the sixth nail – and kissed it. 'Do not leave us again,' he said.

'Come into the house.'

'One moment ... Let us be alone ... for a while.'

We sat on one of the benches close to the wall where the creeper grew. It was like going back in time to be there with Thomas.

'George is here?' he asked.

'Yes.'

'And rejoicing to have his sister home, I doubt not.'

'He says so.'

'We were a pleasant company, were we not? I often think of the old days in Kent and Norfolk.'

'It seemed like fate that our two families should be together in the two counties ... almost as though it had been arranged.'

'Whoever arranged it grew careless ... sending you to France. You must never go away again.'

'They are planning to send me away now. I won't have it. Do you know about this Butler affair?'

He nodded. 'It is not just a family affair. It's political. The King wants the Butlers to fight for him in Ireland.'

'Therefore I and this poor young man have been chosen to

unite the warring factions.'

'It's an old story, Anne.'

'It may be but I do not intend to be taken up and used to bring it to the required ending.'

'If your sister had not married, she would have been the one.'

'Perhaps Mary would not have minded,' I said bitterly. 'This James Butler is a man . . . that is all she would ask.'

'Well, Mary has gone her way and that leaves you. But Ireland! It is a wild and savage place.'

'I have made up my mind not to go.'

'Your father will insist, I fear.'

'And so shall I.'

'They will force you, Anne.'

'Can people be forced to take marriage vows?'

'It has been known. What of all the princesses who have been brought to their stranger bridegrooms and all the young men who have been presented with their brides. It is the penalty of position. It is one of the burdens which families like ours are called upon to bear.'

'*I* will not bear it.'

'Have you seen your prospective bridegroom?'

'Oh, they did not think it necessary that I should! They plighted my troth in my absence.'

He turned to me and taking my chin in his hands looked searchingly into my eyes. 'There is no one like you,' he said. 'So perhaps you will succeed where others have failed.' Then he kissed me on the forehead. 'Anne, why did you not come back sooner?'

'To be thrust into marriage at an earlier age?'

'No. That I might have shown the same spirit as you will. Now that you have come back, I remember so much. When I came, whom did I look for first? It was always Anne with the serious probing eyes and the wild black hair. George and I were the blustering braves, were we not? We looked down on our little girls . . . but my heart was always lifted at the sight of you . . . and so will it always be.'

'I think I looked for you, too. I admired you . . . and George, of course. You were the heroes – we girls your minions. I loved your sister Mary. She was comforting to be with . . . but the excitement came from you and George.'

'If they had not sent you away . . . it would not have happened. I should have stood out against it. It was advantageous, you see. My father thought it an ideal match. I was careless, forgetful . . . I thought it had to happen some day. What I am trying to tell you, Anne, is that I have a wife.'

'Thomas! You!'

He nodded sombrely.

'When?' I asked. 'And who?'

'Just over a year ago. She is Elizabeth, daughter of Thomas Brooke, Lord Cobham.'

'Congratulations. A worthy match.'

'My family consider it to be.'

'And you . . . are happy?'

He looked at me sadly and said: 'There is only one who could make me happy . . . completely.'

I did not answer. I was rather moved by Thomas; I was certain that I could easily have fallen in love with him and I felt a bitter disappointment that he was married. If it had not been for the political elements in this Butler affair, Thomas Wyatt might have been considered a worthy husband for me. I pictured weeks of exhilarating courtship – Thomas would ride over from Allington to woo me. But my father had risen beyond Sir Henry Wyatt in the King's favour and would, no doubt, in accordance with Boleyn tradition, have wished for a greater marriage for his daughter even though the Wyatts were old friends, good neighbours and of excellent family. But what was the use of thinking thus? Thomas was married and I was destined for Sir James Butler.

He repeated then: 'Oh, why did you not come back earlier?'

'Where are you living now?' I asked. 'At Allington?'

'I am mostly at Court. I have a post there.'

'What post is that?'

'I am one of the Esquires of the King's Body.'

'Then you know Will Carey well?'

'I do.'

'And you must see my sister frequently.'

He nodded.

'You know, of course.'

'That she is the King's mistress? Everyone knows, but no one refers to it. The King likes to keep his little peccadillos secret and as you know we must all bow to his wishes.'

'Life is lived more simply in the country,' I said.

'But you would not want the simple life. You would soon grow tired of it. The intrigues at Court . . . the excitement . . . the fighting for one's position and the even harder battle to keep it . . . that is what we enjoy. There are the masques which I help to devise . . . The King loves nothing better than a masque in which we wear disguises. No disguise could hide his identity, of course, but he likes to think it is possible, and he has great delight in revealing himself: "It is your King!" he cries and everyone gasps with feigned astonishment, pretending to try to remember if they had been guilty of *lèse majesté* . . . knowing full well they have uttered nothing but what the King wanted most to hear, being aware all the time to whom they were speaking. It is a farce . . . a game of pretence; but it gives me a chance to hear my verses spoken and sung. You should come to Court, Anne. Your father must find a place for you.'

'He has found a place for me . . . in Ireland.'

'It must be delayed as long as possible.'

'I fear it will not be. They have brought me home for this, but I shall not let it happen. I will not be told whom I am to marry. When I marry *I* shall choose my husband.'

'Anne . . . would you have chosen me?'

I drew back from him. 'You chose to marry . . . so how could I?'

'If you had been here . . . '

'It is too late to take that view. What does it matter what I should have done if it is not possible for me to do it?'

He shook his head sadly. Then he said: 'I have a son, Anne. He is not yet a year old.'

'Again congratulations. That must be very gratifying.'

'I admit to a fondness for the child.'

'I must come to Allington to see him and to meet your wife.'

My brother was coming out into the courtyard.

'Oh, so you are there, Tom,' he said. 'What do you think of my sister?'

'A very grand lady with Frenchified airs.'

'Exactly my view. Have you caught up on old times?'

Thomas nodded. 'I have been upbraiding her for staying away so long.'

'Come in,' said George. 'My stepmother heard your arrival; she has some of her own wine to offer you. Now, Tom, you must let her know you like it. She is proud of her brews.'

And as we went into the house I was thinking of the old days and Thomas and what might have been.

*

When my father arrived at Hever, I expected the storm to break.

George had gone back to Court and so had Thomas Wyatt. I had been over to Allington and renewed my friendship with Mary Wyatt. I had found a certain peace in our gardens which I had always loved in the past. I rode out quite often. I should have had a groom with me. My stepmother worried about this but I assured her I was quite able to take care of myself, and she was always anxious not to impose her authority upon me.

She used to busy herself in the kitchens. I think she was not yet accustomed to living in a house like ours. She came of good yeoman stock; her father was a landowner, but we had become very grand since my father was doing so well at Court – and, I thought bitterly, since Mary had found such favour in the very highest place.

My stepmother never referred to that aspect of Mary's life, though she had grown fond of her as she had of us all.

From my window I saw my father arrive. He travelled in some state, as became a gentleman of his importance. He was on terms of friendship with both Cardinal Wolsey and the King. He had kept the French wondering which way England was going to turn and he had completed a successful mission at Oudenarde with the Emperor Charles. He was rich; honours had been showered upon him. That made me angry. Could he not forget the Butler revenues for the sake of his daughter's happiness? Apparently not.

When I heard of his successes and his growing wealth, I was more determined than ever to stand firm against his attempt to use me to add to them.

I was expecting to be given instructions as to what I must do and was amazed when there was no mention of this – until I understood the reason.

There was one thought in his mind at that time and he could give no attention to anything else. The King was doing us the great honour of paying a visit to Hever Castle. It was for this reason my father had come home. He wanted to supervise preparations. We must all realize what an important occasion this was. There was so much to be done. It was one of the greatest honours which could be bestowed upon a subject. It was an indication of the rising fortunes of Thomas Boleyn.

He greeted me in an absent-minded fashion. I had seen him once or twice during my stay in France when he had been on embassies there and he had no doubt thought that he must spare a little time to see his daughter; but those visits had been of a perfunctory nature. I had been too young to interest him then; it was only when his daughters were of marriage-able age that he took notice of them.

I was surprised to see the affection between him and my stepmother. It set me wondering about the strangeness of human nature. Somewhere in that granite-like exterior was a softness, and my humble countrified stepmother had somehow managed to find it.

I felt a little kinder towards him, though not much – considering his plans for me.

My stepmother was in a flurry of dismay.

She came to my bedroom to talk to me, for we had become good friends by this time.

'The King . . . here . . . What will he think of me?'

'He will think what we all do . . . that you are good, sweet, kind and gentle . . . and he will like you for that.'

'Oh, Anne, you seek to comfort me. Never did I think . . . What shall we give him to eat? How shall we entertain him? How can we compare with the Court?'

'We don't have to. He is escaping from the Court. For that is what kings do on these peregrinations. I am sure he will never have tasted food better than that which you prepare. You are so clever with food. We never ate so well before you were in charge of the kitchens.'

'I . . . I shall have to be there . . . the hostess . . . beside your father.'

'Just be yourself and remember that he may be the King but he is only a man after all.'

'How can you say such a thing!'

'With conviction. I was at the Court of France, remember. I knew the King of France well. He was even more elegant than this King . . . and he was only a man.'

'You comfort me.'

'All you have to do, my lady, is be yourself.'

'I shall be so nervous.'

'He will see that and love you for it.'

'How can that be?'

'Because, from what I know of him, he will enjoy seeing you in awe of him. He will be very gracious. He will like your manners. I can swear to this . . . because I know the ways of royalty.'

'Bless you, my dear. I am so happy that you are here.'

What a bustle there was in the kitchens. The smell of roasting filled the castle. Beef, mutton, sucking pigs, boars' heads, fish of all kinds, fruits, enormous pies which were to be made into fantastic shapes and all adorned with Tudor roses.

We did not know when the King would arrive. He would be hunting on the way and it seemed one could never be sure. My stepmother was in despair. When should the pastry be made to ensure perfection? My father, too, was nervous. Everything must be in order. No expense must be spared. I had heard that noblemen throughout the country, while they craved the honour, dreaded it because it almost ruined them.

I refused to allow myself to be caught up in all the excitement. I had caught a glimpse of the King at Guines and I had had a close view of him when he had dined with Queen Claude and I was in attendance. He had actually spoken to me then. Accustomed to being with Marguerite, who had talked so much about her brother, had brought me into very close contact with royalty, and I had ceased to be overawed. Therefore I was not as excited about this visit as the rest of the household seemed to be. As two days passed without the royal arrival, it occurred to me that the King might have decided not to come after all – which I knew was what my father feared and my stepmother hoped.

I had made up my mind that this must be so. In any case my thoughts were filled with the Butler affair.

My father had taken little notice of me since his arrival, which, in the circumstances, was understandable, but I was sure that when the King's visit was over I should be informed of what was expected of me. I wanted to prepare myself for that. It was a greater matter of concern to me than the King's visit.

There was a small enclosed rose garden at Hever – a favourite spot of mine. There I felt at peace. I would sit there for hours and think of the past and wonder about the future and how my father would act when he realized I was set in my determination not to be forced into marriage.

On this afternoon I went there. It was a warm spring day, I remember, and quite windless in the garden. I sat on the wooden seat contemplating the pond with the little figure of Hermès poised above the water, trying to rehearse what I would say when my father brought up the subject of James Butler.

And as I sat there I heard a footfall, and through the gap in the hedge there came a figure. I gasped and felt my heart begin to beat very fast. There could be no mistaking him. He seemed bigger than I remembered. Perhaps he was a little more corpulent than when I had last seen him. His padded coat, reaching only to his knees, so that the well-formed calves of which he was so proud were displayed in all their glory, was puffed and barred with elaborate appliqué so that it made him look very wide. It was of deep purple velvet, his waistcoat of purple satin, and there was a design of roses – Tudor, of course – embroidered on it; on his head was a hat with a curled feather of pale yellow. I could see the jewels glinting on his garments. He was a scintillating and splendid figure.

I myself was most simply clad. My father would have been most put out if he could have seen me thus. I was wearing a red gown, open from the waist to the hem to show a satin petticoat of a lighter shade of red which toned perfectly. My hair was loose about my shoulders. Apart from the long hanging sleeves which I always wore and which gave a certain style to my gown, I might have been a simple country girl.

Half embarrassed to have been caught thus and half amused, I felt more than a little mischievous and I determined to play a trick on him. He liked to disguise himself so that people should not know he was the King until he surprised them with the news. Well, I would pretend I did not know who he was.

He stared at me and came towards me. I remained seated until he was close. I think he was expecting me to fall on my knees. Instead I said coolly: 'Tell me, are you of the Court?'

He was obviously taken aback for I saw him start. Then his lips twitched slightly. I learned afterwards that it was not difficult to judge his moods by his expression. I supposed he usually felt he had no need to cloak his feelings since his will was law. In fact, I was to see a look reduce people to terror.

He said: 'I am.'

'Ah then,' I went on, 'the King must have come.'

'I believe that to be so.'

'And you are of his Court? I should say: "Welcome to Hever," but your late arrival has caused much inconvenience. We had expected you earlier.'

He was looking at me intently and I felt a rising resentment at the manner in which his little eyes grew brighter as he surveyed me. It was a kind of softness and lustfulness which I had seen in others. I immediately thought of my sister Mary. Did he know who I was? He must. Here I was in my father's house. He would have heard of me through the Butler matter. That was another thing which aggrieved me. I was not so much a person as a means of acquiring a fortune for my father and a warrior for the King. He would not remember our first meeting. Why should he? I had been just a young English girl at the Court of France ... almost a child, too young to interest him. But I was older now ... as old as Mary probably was when he first noticed her. Anger mingled with resentment. Did he think I was like my sister?

'Had I known I should find you here, Mistress,' he said, 'I should have spurred on my horse.'

'You are gallant.'

'Tell me,' he said. 'Are you the daugher of the house?'

'I am.'

'Then you are Mistress Anne Boleyn.'

'Clearly so.'

'I doubt not that you have been most excited by this visit of the King.'

I shrugged my shoulders and looked at him from under my

130

lashes. Little angry lights had shot into his eyes. I should be careful. But no. I had seen that other light in the blue eyes. This would do no harm.

'Not so?' he asked.

'I have been abroad. I have spent many years in the Court of France which I believe is even more splendid than that of England.'

'Who tells you this?'

'None, my lord. It is my own conclusion.'

He seated himself beside me. He was very close, his splendid brocade breeches against my dress.

'You are a forward wench,' he said. 'What do you know of the King's Court?'

'I know only the French Court and of that I know a great deal. I was in attendance on the Queen of France. I went with the King's sister on her marriage to King Louis and was with her until she returned home. Then I was with Queen Claude and the Duchesse d'Alençon. Perhaps you did not know that she is reckoned to be the most erudite lady in France – and that may well be in the whole world.'

'I take it amiss that you, who have not been at the King's Court, should speak of it with such scorn.'

'I did not speak with scorn, my lord. And if I know nothing of the English Court, what do you know of the French?'

He shifted in his seat. I thought he was getting angry. He had had enough of the game. Now he wanted to say, 'I am your King!' And then in the game I should fall at his feet and beg pardon for my forwardness. He would allow me to plead while his brow would be heavy with displeasure. Then the little blue eyes would twinkle slightly, for I could see that in spite of my simple garb and loose hair – or perhaps because of it – he liked the look of me; he would be remembering that I had a sister with loose morals and probably had the same. Then he would graciously forgive me, perhaps kiss me and expect to be received into my bedroom that night – with my father's consent, of course.

I only had to think of that for my anger to rise against my father and against all men who humiliated women.

So the game was not going to end yet.

'I like not the French,' he said.

'I found so many of them charming.'

'Perfidious ... cheats ... breakers of promises ... ' he muttered.

'Oh, my lord, they could say the same of the English.'

'You are a bold chit,' he said. 'Are you not afraid that I might carry your words to the King?'

'I would not care if you did.'

'Do you think he would be pleased to hear your praise of our enemies?'

'I hope he would be wise enough to see these enemies as they really are.'

'I think, Mistress, that you should have a care.'

'We should all have care. But sometimes is it more fun to be a little rash. Do you not agree, my lord.'

He tapped his knee and said: 'It may be so.' Then he turned to me and laid a hand on my arm. He gripped it firmly. 'I will give you a word of advice. Watch your tongue, sweetheart.'

'Please do not address me so. I am not your sweetheart.'

'If you were,' he retorted, 'I would teach you a lesson.'

'If that impossibility should be, I might teach you one.'

He laughed then and moved closer to me, but I shifted my position away from him.

'What do you do here all day?' he asked.

'I read. I sing. I play the lute. I ride. I walk. I write a little. When I was with Madame d'Alençon, I used to read with her. Have you heard of the *Decameron*, my lord?'

'I have.'

'And not read it, I dareswear.'

'Why should you so dareswear?'

'Because gallants like you spend all their time adorning themselves in their pretty clothes and making love to ladies.'

'You are, forsooth, a saucy wench.'

'I speak as I find.'

'So that was how it was at the French Court?'

'With some.'

'With the King?'

'All know of his *amours*. There will always be some who think it an honour to be a king's mistress.'

'And you would not be of such an opinion?'

'Indeed, sir, I should not sell my honour so cheaply.'

'Cheaply! I'll swear the ladies in question did not feel their honour had been lost in such case.'

'Why so?'

'You should know it is an honour to be honoured by the King.'

'Think you so? I have been led to believe that a woman should save herself for her husband.'

'A lady gains dignity by being favoured by the King.'

'Dignity? Worldly goods, do you mean, sir?' I felt angry, thinking of Mary. 'A lady's honour is beyond price. I would never demean myself by being anyone's mistress . . . not even a king's.'

He stood up, glaring at me. He was now angry. I had gone too far. I had been carried away by Mary's humiliation at the Court of France. He was going to forget his designs on my virtue. I had been too sure of myself. After all, most women would be ready to succumb to him at a moment's notice. Who was I to play childish games with this mighty monarch? But it had been hard to suppress my desire to tease him and I was drawn to him a little because in spite of his royal presence there was a certain innocence about him. That love of childish games . . . it was the pursuit of someone who had not quite grown up. I was beginning to forgive him for his love affair with Mary. After all, Mary was anyone's for the taking. Why should I be so resentful?

'I asked you, my lord, if you had read the *Decameron*. Have you? Please tell me,' I said quickly.

'I have, and if you were an innocent maid you would not have done so.'

'I have always thought it a mistake to shut one's ears and eyes to what goes on. How does one ever learn anything if one does? The Duchess and I read it together. She herself is writing a similar book. She showed it to me. I was fascinated.' I quoted some of the poetry I had learned from Marguerite.

He listened intently.

I looked sideways at him and said: 'This one is set to music. It is a haunting tune.'

I started to sing it. There was a glazed look in his eyes. Music affected him deeply.

He said: 'You have a pleasant voice.'

'It needs the lute to help it along.'

'It is good to hear even without it. You must sing for me again.'

'I might . . . if our paths cross.'

'It might be arranged that they should. Tell me more about this Court for which you have such a high regard. I'll warrant you I can cap your stories with what happens in ours.'

So I described some of the masques, the exquisite dancing and singing, the wit. 'The French you know set a great store by wit,' I said. 'It has to be light as thistledown and sharp as a rapier. The King of France loves art. Did you know he brought Leonardo da Vinci to France?'

'Filched from the Italians. Aye, and tried for Raphael! That one loved his country well enough to refuse the bribe.'

'Once he said that men can make kings but only God can make an artist.'

'Do you believe that?'

'I do, for it is true, is it not? Have you seen Raphael's *St Michael*? There was a ceremony when it arrived in France. The King himself unveiled it. Surely only God can give a talent like that. As for kings . . . it is certainly men who make them . . . and unmake them. Think back over history . . . a battle here . . . a victory there . . . and that decides a king and a line of kings.'

Oh, this was dangerous ground! Was he thinking back to Bosworth Field and how easily it might have gone the other way? What of Henry Tudor then?

I was surprising myself. I had been brought up close to the King of France but Henry of England was of a very different calibre. I was foolishly putting myself in danger. My father would be beside himself with fear and fury if he could overhear this conversation. If it had not been for the glint of desire which kept showing itself in the little Tudor eyes I might have been terrified myself. But instinct told me that would save me. I could go a long way before his wrath would be irreconcilable.

He was silent, glowering.

I went on quickly, thinking it advisable to call a halt: 'But for a battle we might not have the glorious House of Tudor reigning over us now. What a calamity that would have been!'

He did not hear the touch of irony in my voice. He was happy again. There was indeed a childish element in his nature.

'So,' I said, 'I make my point.'

He grunted that that was so, but he had had enough.

'You have been talking to me . . . singing to me . . . telling me of yourself, and you have not yet asked my name.'

'Well, I will ask it now.'

'It is Henry.'

'Henry! A good English name. And one you share with a great and illustrious personage.'

He had stood up. I remained seated looking up at him. His eyes were narrowed, his legs astride. Some majesty in him made me rise and in doing so I betrayed myself.

'You know who I am!' he cried.

He was angry now. I had gone too far. He would denounce me. *Lèse majesté* – the crime for which the French players had been thrown into dungeons. This man, I believed, would be more deadly in defence of his royalty than the King of France.

Feverishly I searched for the answer. It came easily.

I fell to my knees, threw back my hair and lifted my eyes to his face. He was looking at me with a kind of wonder and I thought: It can be all right if I find the right words.

They came: 'Your Grace, in your presence who could fail to be aware of who you are?'

He was a little mollified.

'So it was a game, eh? You thought you would play a game with me! Well, let me tell you this: you did not deceive me. I let you go on just to see how far you would go.'

'I trust our little game did not displease Your Grace. I know I need not fear that it did. Your Grace has too fine a sense of the ridiculous . . . I have heard of it, and how well you like these little masquerades.'

He was rocking on his heels, keeping me kneeling before him. I wondered what punishment he was going to inflict. But the little light of lust was still in his eyes.

I heard voices. People were coming this way. They were very likely looking for him. I said: 'I must go. They must not find me here.'

He put out a hand and caught a strand of my hair.

But I was up and away.

I sped out of the garden. I hid myself among the shrubs. A party, led by my father, came into sight. They were obviously looking for the King.

*

I ran to my room. I looked at myself in the mirror. My eyes were sparkling; my cheeks had an unusual faint colour; my hair was untidy.

What had I done? What had led me to behave in such a way? I had been in a strange mood. I was so angry about the Butler affair and determined to show the world that I was not, like other girls of noble houses, to be pushed this way and that. But to become involved in such an exchange with the King was sheer madness.

I wondered what action he would take. He would not let the matter rest, I was sure. He had been really angry at some points; but there had been something in my looks which had touched him in some way. Although I was a virgin, I was not ignorant of the ways of men; I knew of those animal desires which were somehow unpredictable but when they came could obliterate all else. François and the gentlemen of his court were mostly young and lusty and they pursued women as they did the deer. They only had to see one and they were off. One knew exactly the meaning in their glances. With Henry it was a little different. I remembered what George had said of him. He did not flaunt his love affairs and they were not numerous like those of the King of France. There was definitely in Henry a certain moral and sentimental streak. I had sensed a touch of cruelty too – such as had not played a part in the character of François. François would have been amused by my effrontery; I was not sure of Henry.

There would be a great feast tonight, with my father straining every effort to entertain the King in accordance with the custom of those noblemen whose houses he visited during his journeys through the country. As the daughter of the house I should be called upon to show my talents . . . to sing, to play the lute; and he would watch me and think: She is comely enough for the night here. She is doubtless a little like her sister. And Mary had been pleasing him for some time. She had lasted longer with the King of England than she had with the King of France.

I could not go down there tonight. I could not bear it. I would not submit to these people. I would not be like my sister Mary.

Then what could I do?

I took off my dress and slipped into a nightgown. I lay in my bed listening to the bustle in the castle. There were voices below my window. I knew by the sycophantic laughter that he was there. My father's voice sounded unctuous. Was he begging the King to forgive his wayward daughter or hoping that his humble home would not displease His Grace.

Someone was scratching on the door. It was my step-mother. She looked horrified to see me in bed.

'But Anne,' she cried, 'the King is here! You must come and be presented to him. Oh dear, I'm in such a flurry. I know not which way to turn. I am terrified. He is even more grand than I thought. Anne, what are you doing in bed?'

'I am ill,' I said. 'I cannot leave my bed.'

She was all concern and I felt very tender towards her.

'What is wrong? What can be wrong?'

'I have a cold. I think I have a fever. I could not come down. The King would never forgive us if he caught something from someone in our household.'

'I must get you a posset.'

'No . . . no . . . Do not worry . . . I . . . I had these turns in France.' It was a lie but it served. 'All I have to do is rest and in a day or so I am well. I need no posset. You go and do not worry about me. I shall not be missed.'

'Your father . . . '

'Tell him of my illness, he would not want me down there in this state.'

I closed my eyes and tried to look ill.

My poor stepmother! I was sorry for her. I knew I was unnaturally flushed and that alarmed her. I should have been down there to help her. But I dared not be. He would still be smarting from some of the things I had said. But it was not that which alarmed me so much as the look in his eyes. I had seen the same look in those of François. But Marguerite had understood about that and had helped me. This was different; every instinct I possessed told me that I must not see the King again while he was at Hever.

My stepmother leaned over the bed. She touched my forehead.

'You are rather hot,' she said.

138

I nodded feebly.

'Oh dear God, that it should happen now!'

'Don't worry. Just forget it. The King will like you. I am sure there is a kindness in him for all his splendour.'

Then I closed my eyes once more and she went out.

Shortly afterwards my father came in. He stood by the bed glaring down at me. I was afraid that he would order me to get up, dress and join the party.

I said in a small faltering voice: 'I'm sorry, Father. My head is so heavy . . . and I am rather hot.'

'At such a time!' he cried.

He stood for a few seconds and then went out.

I breathed a sigh of relief and told myself that in future I must curb my impetuous nature. The urge to tease him had come and I had given way to it. But it was as well that I had, for if he had seen me at the banquet and heard me sing and play the lute, he might have expected further entertainment from me.

So while the sounds of feasting and music went on in the castle, I lay in bed. I thought of the future and what would happen when I was presented to James Butler. I knew that I had some special attraction for the opposite sex – even as my sister Mary had. Someone had once explained Mary's allure as Promise. That was possibly true because it was obvious, merely by looking at her, to see that she enjoyed sexual encounters and that the preliminaries of courtship could be curtailed and the conclusion quickly reached. How different I was! I was cold towards them; I did not feel a vestige of desire for them. I should hate to be submitted to the humiliation Mary suffered in France. Why then did I see desire in men's eyes for me? Was it because I was different from other women? There was something distinctive about me . . . apart from my sixth finger. Thomas Wyatt loved me – or was ready to; François had had designs on me; and now I had seen something which I feared in the eyes of the King of England. Who would have dared speak to him as I had this afternoon?

Only one who was desired. I liked the power this gave me over men. I felt that I wanted that power. But I could see that it would not be easy to hold it once one had surrendered.

I was in a state of apprehension, cowering behind my pretence of illness; and I was afraid of the outcome of this day.

It was midnight and still the revelries went on. I hoped the King was pleased with the hospitality of Hever and did not report to his host the ill behaviour of the daughter of the house.

I slept little that night, and when my stepmother came into the room next morning she was alarmed at the sight of me.

I was sorry to give her this concern and tried to reassure her. I knew these attacks well, I told her. They soon passed. 'Tell me,' I said. 'How was it last night?'

'All went well,' she told me. 'The servants excelled themselves and there were no mishaps in the kitchen. I had given them their orders – but of course *I* must be sitting on the right hand of His Grace, and I was in such a state that I was shaking like one of my jellies. He noticed it and patted my arm. He said: "You must not be afraid of us. We do no harm to gentle ladies." Then he was laughing and I was laughing and everything seemed well. He was so splendid and he liked well the sucking pig. I told him it was a recipe I had brought with me from my home – and he did not seem to mind my nervousness at all.'

'He liked you for it,' I said. 'It indicated how much you were in awe of him and that you were overwhelmed by his greatness.'

She was not listening. She was smiling, thinking of the evening.

'The tumblers were very good and so were the minstrels. Your father had thoughtfully arranged for them to sing one of the King's songs, which pleased him mightily.'

'It would,' I said.

'And do you know . . . he asked about you.'

I felt a tremor of alarm. 'What did he say . . . of me?'

' "Your daughter Mary is at my Court," he said. "Your son, too. But I believe there is another . . . a younger . . . " I said to him, "Your Grace, that is Anne. She is laid low in her bed. She is not well." "Oh," he answered, "What ails the wench?" "It is nothing much, she assures me," I replied. "A headache . . . and a little fever." "I should have liked to see her," he said. "Is it true that she plays on the lute?" I told him how beautifully you played and sang and how you have put us all to shame with your grace and your fine clothes and that you have been in France. I don't think he liked that very much for he said, "It would be well if she forgot she has lived in France and took up with our English ways." I said quickly that I knew you soon would. Then he said "Headache, eh? Tell her she must have lingered too long in the rays of the sun." '

'Did he really say that!'

'Yes – exactly that. I was about to say that the sun was not very strong just yet but felt that might sound like contradicting him.'

'Is that all he said . . . of me?'

'Yes, that was all, for the dancing had begun. You should see him dance. He leaps higher than any. You would know that he was the King if nobody told you. What a pity that you had this attack . . . now.'

'When is the party leaving?' I asked.

'Today. Your father will be going with them. How quiet it will seem when they have gone!'

'And peaceful,' I said.

'Now rest, my dear. I will send up some broth . . . something soothing. You must try to take it.'

'I will try,' I said feebly . . . 'to please you, dearest Stepmother.'

*

They had gone. When I heard the clatter of departure, I sat

up in my bed and laughed.

It had been quite an adventure and I had rescued myself very cleverly, I thought. Now that it was over, I did not regret anything. He had obviously been displeased. He had spoken figuratively when he had remarked that I had stayed too long in the rays of the sun. Did he believe in my sudden illness? I wondered. But he would no doubt have forgotten the incident by now. I was just a saucy wench who had played a little trick on royalty; but wenches did not play such tricks, particularly those with ambitious fathers.

Oh well, it was over now.

It was strange that my father had not mentioned James Butler. I supposed it was because he had been so taken up with the King's visit, which was certainly enough to make him forget anything else; still, there might have been a reference to such an important matter.

At first I revelled in those peaceful days. I sat often in the rose garden and went over that scene again . . . word by word, and laughed at it. How daring I had been! But all was well. He had forgotten all about me by now. He probably dismissed me as a foolish girl. I thought perhaps he might speak to my father about me, but if he had, I should surely have heard.

George and Mary were at Court and so was Thomas Wyatt. I saw Mary Wyatt often, and our friendship carried on where it had left off in our childhood. I became more and more attached to my stepmother, but her interests were in the herb garden and the kitchens; she was a perfect housewife, and I was quite different from that. I did feel the lack of stimulating conversation; I often thought of those days in France with Marguerite and I became very nostalgic.

Every day I expected to hear that James Butler was on his way to Hever and I was to meet him. But nothing happened.

I used to sit with my stepmother while she worked on her embroidery, for in accordance with her housewifely excellence she was very clever with her needle; and she would tell me of her humble life in the country and how she was at last fitting into our castle ways.

'It amazed me,' she said, 'that your father should have chosen me.'

'He is a clever man, my father,' I reminded her.

'And that he should bring me here . . . where I have actually met the King! I would not have believed it possible.'

'I can understand it – and I think it is my father who is the fortunate one.'

'And such a charming family I inherited! You . . . who are such an attractive young lady . . . so worldly in your way . . . and your beautiful clothes and your manners and playing and singing as you do . . . to bother to talk to me!'

I was touched and said: 'Dear Stepmother, it is you who honour us.'

And indeed I felt it was so, for there she was with her goodness – which I felt none of us shared.

'Your brother George . . . he is so clever . . . but always kind to me. And Mary . . . ' Her eyes clouded a little for, affectionate as she was, her strict upbringing would not allow her to approve of Mary.

I said: 'Mary is the King's mistress.'

'Poor Mary. She will suffer remorse.'

'Not Mary. She revels . . . not so much in her position but in the relationship. You know she was also the mistress of the King of France.'

'That scandal, yes . . . I do know.'

'Don't waste your sympathy on Mary. She will always be as she is.'

'It's a pity . . . and that nice husband.'

'He is weak. He just stands by.'

'He has to, your father says, because of the King.'

'He should not. If he were a real man, would he?'

'The King is very powerful.'

'I do not admire Will Carey,' I said firmly. 'And what do you know of James Butler?'

'I hear he is a very charming young man.'

'That is what they would tell me. I will not be bartered. They will have to look elsewhere. I am no Will Carey.'

'Oh dear, I hope there is not going to be trouble.'

'You have married into an ambitious family, dear Stepmother.'

'I wish there was less of that in the world.'

'No one would strive to get on but for ambition. Life would be peaceful ... but static, dear Stepmother. I do not think that would be entirely for our good. The point is, passions have to be moderated; they have to be used by us; it is only when they begin to use *us* that they become dangerous.'

'You are too clever for me, my dear. But it is nice to hear you talk. I hope beyond all things that you will find a nice husband whom you love and who loves you ... and be happy for ever more.'

I kissed her. I thought she was more like a mother to me than my own had been.

She made Hever very pleasant during my stay there.

It did not last very long.

One day a messenger came from my father. He had found a place for me in the Queen's household. I was to be a maid of honour and should prepare to leave without delay.

The peaceful time was over. I was not entirely sorry, for peace to one of my nature was not always desirable for long. I found the atmosphere of Hever without my brother and Thomas Wyatt rather boring. And much as I loved my stepmother, she was hardly a stimulating companion.

So I could not help feeling a sense of expectation and excitement as I prepared to leave Hever.

Love Affair

And so I came to Court to be a maid of honour to Queen Katharine.

I was struck immediately by the difference between the French and English Courts, though oddly enough they were both presided over by a young, forceful, monumental figure of a King and a Queen who was retiring and pious. Manners were gallant at Henry's Court but less affectedly so; there was a lack of that intellectual quality which had been inspired by Marguerite and followed by François; culture was less in evidence here, although the King was a lover of music, poetry and all the fine arts. This was of a more robust nature. The masques were less subtle, the dances more strenuous, given to leaping, bounding and athletic prowess rather than grace. There was a vitality in the English Court which replaced the languid elegance of that of France.

It was very interesting to me and I felt alive as soon as I arrived. I realized, more than I had before, that the country was no place for me.

I was quickly initiated into my rôle of maid of honour. I was allowed a servant – a woman, of course – and one dog, which should be a spaniel. I was given a certain allowance of food for myself and my dog, and it was far more than our needs. Food was plentiful at Court, served plain, without the fancy sauces so beloved of the French; my maid, my dog and I breakfasted on bread and beef; and more ale than we could possibly drink was supplied to us. There were hens, pigeons, rabbits and all kinds of pies served for dinner and supper; and on Fridays we had salted eels, plaice, gurnet and whiting . . . and almost any fish one could think of.

I had never been interested in food – but it did show a

concern for our welfare.

My sister Mary was one of the first to greet me.

She was well and happy and showed no sign of any shame, though it was well known what terms she was on with the King. He had been right when he had said it was considered an honour to be chosen by the monarch.

Mary was looking very pretty and pleased with life. When I came to think of it, she always had. She had not been entirely crestfallen even when she had been expelled from the Court of France. Mary took everything in her philosophical way.

She embraced me warmly and said how pleased she was to see me at Court.

'You will find the Queen a little ... serious.' She grimaced.

'I imagine she is rather like Queen Claude.'

Mary nodded.

'She is very much the daughter of the King and Queen of Spain ... and never forgets it. And she is very religious. There will be a great deal of praying. Your knees may get sore.'

'And you, Mary?'

She laughed. 'I do very well.'

'And what of Will?'

'He does very well, too.'

'Of course I know about you and the King.'

She laughed in that carefree way of hers and dimpled prettily. I thought how strange it was that I should have such a sister. There could scarcely be two people less alike than Mary and myself.

'The King is very kind to me.'

'Mary ... do you *love* him?'

'Of course.'

'And Will?'

'Will is my husband. Of course I love him.'

I could see that it was impossible to come to any understanding about these matters with Mary. She loved everyone

. . . particularly men. She could see no harm in coupling, I gathered. How could there be anything wrong in giving pleasure? She pleased the King; she pleased her husband. Of course, Will had to accept the fact that the King liked her. This he did with good grace, for being Will, he had not the strength to do anything else. He was a Squire of the Body. It was as good a post as Will could expect; and neither he nor Mary thought of asking for special privileges.

It was true that our father had profited from the relationship and was rising high in the King's favour. He was a good ambassador, a loyal and faithful subject, but he was rewarded also because he had a beautiful daughter who pleased the King very much indeed.

I said to Mary: 'Has the King ever said anything to you about the visit he paid to Hever?'

'Yes, he did mention it. He said our stepmother had talked to him of recipes, and he attributed the excellence of the table to her good work.'

'Was that all?'

'He thought it a pleasant spot. I can think of nothing more.'

So he had not thought of me after that strange interview. But perhaps he cared for Mary too much to bother her with an account of her sister's deplorable behaviour.

I was greatly impressed by the Queen when she received me, which she did with the utmost grace. Regality sat naturally upon her. One was immediately struck by her calmness. She had an oval face with rather heavy features. I noticed at once her high forehead. Her figure was rather squat and solid; she had endured much childbearing, although the only royal child so far was the Princess Mary, who must have been some six or seven years old at this time. If Queen Katharine had been beautiful once, she was no longer so. She was dressed in very dark blue velvet which was almost black; her straight sleeves were ruffled and slashed at the wrists and a great crucifix hung about her neck. She had no need to proclaim her piety; it was obvious. Moreover we all

147

knew that she fasted on Fridays, Saturdays and all saints' days. She was with her confessor twice a week at least, although what sins she had to confess it was hard to imagine; and she received the eucharist every Sunday. Each day one of her attendants read to her for two hours after dinner from a book of devotions – a task which often fell to me, for she said I had a musical voice.

I had a great respect for her but she was not the sort of person to whom one could get close. I think she always felt she was in an alien land.

Maria de Salinas, who had accompanied her as a maid of honour, when she came to England from Spain, and who was married to Lord Willoughby d'Eresby, was one of the few women friends she had. For the rest of us she showed a rather gentle tolerance. But she was always considerate of us and kindly towards us. We liked her but it was hard to feel that affection which I had had for Queen Claude or the deeper feeling I had cherished for Marguerite.

I knew her story, and in a way it seemed rather a tragic one. She had only been sixteen when she had come to England to marry Prince Arthur who was fourteen at the time. I could imagine her childhood and the rigorous upbringing in the Spanish household. There would have been a lack of warmth, a formality which must have been rather frightening to a young child. Yet she had had a passionate adoration for her mother, Queen Isabella. Her father, Ferdinand, had shown a rather cynical disregard for his daughter after her mother had died. So, as an innocent girl of sixteen, she had been married to Prince Arthur, who had died a few months after the ceremony. The marriage had never been consummated because they had all been afraid for Arthur's health and they thought that exertion and excitement, to which he was unaccustomed, might kill him. Poor boy, he had died without that excitement, and there had followed for Katharine, the virgin widow, a time of great anxiety. Her mother, whom she adored, and who would have brought her back to Spain, had died and the poor little widow was left bereft in an alien land where her only worth seemed to be through her dowry, over which King Henry VII and Ferdinand of Spain were haggling for a long time. Consequently for eight years she lived wretchedly in England with very little money, until the old King died and the new King, eighteen-year-old Henry VIII, came to the throne and, flushed with romantic chivalry and having a certain fancy for the daughter of Spanish kings, married her.

From then on Katharine should have reached a haven of happiness, but ill luck was hers. Desperately the King wanted a son, but for some reason, although the Queen was fruitful, disappointment after disappointment followed.

Within a year of her marriage, she had raised her husband's and the country's hopes by giving birth to a child. A daughter, it was true, but still-born. The next year there was a son, who brought great joy just for one month before he died. Two years later there was another son, born dead, and a year later a premature delivery. After that a healthy child, but a girl. The Princess Mary, the only one who had lived. More miscarriages followed and the King, in his despair, had been heard to say that some evil fate was working against him.

I was sure that this caused the Queen great unhappiness. But at least she had the Princess Mary on whom she doted.

Perhaps the failure to produce the children for whom the King so longed had made her more pious than ever. I was aware that she derived little pleasure from the masques and banquets which so delighted her husband; but she certainly found great comfort in prayer and books of devotions.

She was interested in serious discourse, and people like Sir Thomas More, a man of great wit, charm and erudition, was a great favourite of hers. I had occasionally heard her laughing with him over some witticism; but it was obvious she could not share wholeheartedly in the festivities of the Court, and although she tried hard to fall in with the spirit of these things, she could not express the required surprise when the King emerged from his disguises to show himself as the monarch.

She did not show any rancour towards my sister Mary. It might have been that she realized that if the King must have a mistress it was better she should be a girl like Mary than some grasping female who would make all sorts of demands. Mary at least did not flaunt her position; she was just there, smiling placidly, available when required and, when she was not, quite contentedly giving herself the pleasure of warming her husband's bed.

I believed that Elizabeth Blount had been less retiring, though her day was over before I came on the scene. She had a son by the King of whom he was very proud, because he was a boy and had survived. In his heart, I believed he had feared that the inability to produce a healthy boy might lie with him – but this boy of Elizabeth Blount's proved that the fault lay with Katharine.

Having been in such close contact with Marguerite and listened to her discourse, I had come to realize how important affairs of the country were to individuals; and I was very interested in what was happening politically.

Our ally was now the Emperor Charles – a fact which greatly delighted the Queen because she was his aunt. It must have been very distressing for her when Henry and François were courting each other. Yet she had successfully hidden her feelings at Guines and Ardres. I realized now what she must have been suffering to know of the plotting which was going on against her nephew.

Now, however, Charles was our friend and François our foe. The Princess Mary was no longer affianced to the Dauphin – that betrothal which had been made at the Field of the Cloth of Gold; and to the Queen's delight there was talk of an alliance with the Emperor, even though the poor child was only seven and he was twenty-three.

But the man who was most talked of, whom people most feared and who was said to have the King's ear in all matters, was the great Cardinal Wolsey.

I was interested to learn how a man of humble origins could have risen so high as to dominate not only the Court but the King himself. Of course he was a man of great and rare intellect, of immense purpose and a certain charm, which he exerted with the utmost success over the King. I wished I could have discussed him with Marguerite. I was sure she would have found the secret of his success. That he was exceptionally clever was obvious – but it was more than that.

I learned all I could about him – and there were plenty to tell of his origins. 'A butcher's son. His father had a shop in Ipswich,' they jeered. Such a man would inevitably engender envy which I was beginning to recognize as the most deadly of the seven deadly sins as well as the most prevalent. Let them sneer at him for his humble origins; it seemed to me that all the more credit was due to him for his spectacular rise. He must be almost twenty years older than the King, and it was said that Henry looked upon him as a father. Every problem which arose was taken to Wolsey and it was rarely that the King did not take his advice.

I think the butcher must have been a man of some means; he probably owned land on which he grazed his cattle. However, Thomas Wolsey was destined for the Church and, as was to be expected, once he had taken Holy Orders, made rapid strides in his chosen profession. Before he was forty he had been promoted to an archbishopric; he had graduated and was a BA at the age of fifteen and was known as 'the Bachelor'; there followed his MA and eventually he became chaplain to Sir Richard Nanfan, Deputy of Calais, who, amazed at his brilliance, spoke of him to King Henry VII.

That was the big step Wolsey had been looking for. Henry VII was too astute to be affected by a man's origins, and Wolsey was soon in his confidence. Men of influence began to notice him, and one of these was Richard Fox, Bishop of Winchester. Wolsey was climbing high to the pinnacle of his ambition which was clearly the Papal Crown.

There is a story that Henry VII decided to try him out as a

diplomat and sent him on a mission to the Emperor Maximilian in Flanders. The matter was urgent, said the King, and he wished Wolsey to act with all speed. Three days later the King, looking from a window, saw Wolsey making his way towards the palace of Richmond. He sent for him to come to him at once; he was preparing to reprove him for delaying so long before setting out, but Wolsey replied that he had been to Flanders, completed the mission and was about to present himself to the King to report on this when he had been summoned to his presence. That he could have acted so quickly and successfully surprised the King and he realized from that moment that he had a very rare servant in Thomas Wolsey.

There were many stories about him – his brilliance, his determination, his ambition, his love of ostentation. His houses were as grand as palaces; he had as much power as the King. He became Dean of Lincoln and, when Henry VII died, his son made Wolsey his Almoner and began to shower honours on him. In the year 1515 Pope Leo sent Wolsey his cardinal's hat with a very valuable ring, and there was a great gathering of bishops when the hat was placed on Wolsey's head in the Abbey. He had become the most interesting and important man at Court.

I was enjoying my life there. In France I had been aware of my youth until the last year, when my coming to maturity had raised problems with which I had feared I might not be able to deal. It was different here. Now, at sixteen, I was no longer a child and I felt I could take care of myself. Having been brought up in the French Court, I stood out among the others. I found that I attracted attention and I had many admirers, which pleased me. I was not pretty, as many of the girls were, but I knew that I made them appear commonplace. My dark hair and eyes, my choice of clothes, designed by myself, set me apart; and although others tried to imitate my gowns, they could not do it – or the garments did not look the same on them. I could dance better than any of them and play the lute to bring tears to many an eye; and I could sing so as to affect them in like manner. I was a success.

I saw the King on one or two occasions. He did not appear to notice me. I wondered whether he remembered our encounter in the garden at Hever and this was his way of showing disapproval. I did not care if it was.

Being a member of the Queen's household meant that one was engaged in many duties other than pleasure. I should have liked to take part in the masques more frequently, but there were always certain tasks we had to perform. We had to sit with the Queen at our embroidery while one of us read from a religious book. There were prayers to be attended.

But there were occasions when the Queen and her ladies were expected to attend the revels; and this gave me a chance to shine. I always paid a great deal of attention to the clothes I should wear and I hoped I should not have too many imitators. I loved to dance, and when the King and his friends danced with the ladies, I often wondered whether he would come to me and if so what conversation would pass between us. I half hoped and was afraid that he would do so. I should have to curb my tongue. I had no wish to be banished from Court.

At one of these occasions I saw a new face among the gentlemen – a young man who was quite good looking, perhaps lacking in elegance and with an air of not belonging to the Court.

I could see that he was watching me intently.

In the dance he made his way to my side.

'Mistress Anne Boleyn?' he said. I nodded and he went on: 'Your servant James Butler.'

I felt myself flush and turn cold. This rather gauche but not ill-favoured young man, the husband they had chosen for me!

'I think,' he said, 'that we should talk.'

He took my hand and looked round.

'Let us leave the dancers,' he said. 'We could sit awhile . . . there.'

153

I sat down looking at him.

'I think it is time we became acquainted,' he went on, 'in view of the plans for our future.'

'I must tell you at once,' I said, 'that I have no intention of being hurried into marriage.'

'It has been arranged by our families.'

'I know that well, but I am not of a temper to be forced to go against my will.'

'This is the will of our fathers.'

'I know that.'

'It is also the King's will.'

I said: 'When I marry, it will have to be *my* will.'

He smiled. 'Oh, I know I have not the grace of these Court gallants, but I would be a good husband, I promise you.'

'That may be so, but I fear I should not be a good wife.'

'I would do everything I could to make you happy. I would be ready to wait . . . to let you get to know me . . . I myself felt reluctant at first. I said, as you did, I shall not be forced into marriage. But now that I have seen you . . . '

I said: 'We are unfortunate . . . as so many have been before and no doubt many will be after. I have always believed that men and women should have freedom of choice in what concerns them most.'

The music had stopped. There were no dancers in the great hall. There was a buzz of conversation. The King was seated beside the Queen at the great table, and I saw that he was looking straight at me. For a few seconds I could not take my eyes from his face. It looked thunderous. A little while before he had been smiling, applauding the music; now, having seen me, he must be remembering that scene in the garden and was angry.

I thought: He has recognized me; he has suddenly realized that I am here and he is annoyed that I am a member of his wife's household.

I lowered my eyes.

James Butler was saying: 'Do not be afraid, Anne. We shall

grow to know each other. We shall grow to love each other. We will go to Ireland.'

I shuddered.

'Oh, it is not all bogs and savagery, you know.'

I said: 'I would not wish to hide the truth from you, but I would never be forced into marriage.'

He touched my hand gently.

'There is time . . . ' he said.

I rose and joined the ladies.

I was very disturbed, not so much by James Butler but by the anger I had seen in the King's eyes.

*

I waited for dismissal. It did not come. Then I breathed more freely. I supposed it was just a momentary memory. It was too insignificant to occupy his mind for long.

When I saw Mary, I asked if the King had mentioned to her that he knew her sister was at Court.

She looked surprised. 'Why should he?'

'I wondered if he had noticed me.'

She laughed aloud. 'I know you have admirers, Anne, but I do not think the King is one of them.'

'I did not think he was admiring me. I just wondered if he had said anything to you. After all, I am *your* sister.'

She shook her head.

I decided I had worried unduly.

'I have met James Butler,' I told her, 'he whom they have decided I shall marry.'

'Oh? Is he pleasant?'

'I suppose so.'

'Oh, Anne, I'm glad for you.'

'Then don't be. I have no intention of marrying him.'

'Why not? It's what everyone wants.'

'Except me; and I happen to be more involved than anyone.'

155

'Does James Butler object?'

'Apparently not.'

'It'll be all right, Anne. You'll get used to it.'

'Mary, I am not like you.'

'That I know well.'

'I cannot take pleasure in just any man.'

'You must fall in love with him then.'

'Is it as easy as that?'

'Oh, it's very easy.'

I saw that I could not make Mary understand.

James Butler used to seek me out and talk to me. I quite liked him. He was gentle and eager to please me. I could not help finding a kind of pleasure in his admiration, although I supposed it would have been easier if he had found me repulsive. I was vain enough, however, to be pleased that he did not, even though it made the situation harder. He talked about Ireland and the life he could offer me out there. We could come to England frequently. I would soon get used to his Irish ways.

And I would sit there listening and saying to myself: Never. Never.

One day he came to me in a puzzled frame of mind.

'Has anything been said to you?' he asked.

'About what?'

'About our marriage.'

'Why should anyone say anything about that?'

'It has been arranged not only by our families but by the King and the Cardinal. You know, of course, that the Earl of Surrey, your uncle, is most anxious for the marriage. It was he who suggested it.'

'I never liked him.'

'I spoke to him yesterday. I said, "I have now made the acquaintance of Anne Boleyn. I love her already and I am sure that, in time, I can bring her to love me. I think there should be no delay and Anne should be persuaded that our betrothal should be announced." And what do you think he said?'

156

I shook my head.

'He said: "There is to be no more talk of this marriage."'

I felt my spirits rising. But like James I was bewildered.

He went on: 'I asked why. I said, "I have come here to court Anne Boleyn as I was told to do by my father. Why is there to be no talk of it?" He said to me, "You are a boy and understand not these matters. You are advised to say nothing of this. But there must be no more talk of a marriage with Anne Boleyn." "But I cannot understand it," I cried. "What of those estates?" He frowned at me and said angrily, "Cannot you understand my words? I have told you there is to be no more of this . . . " There! What do you make of it?'

'That they have found some other solution to the problem.'

'I shall not leave it at this. I shall approach the Cardinal.'

'Approach the Cardinal! Do you think the great man would concern himself with our trivial affair?'

'This was no trivial affair, Anne. I know our marriage was to unite the families and secure the title and fortune for our children and so satisfy two sides; but the marriage was an affair of state, suggested by your uncle Surrey to the King and the Cardinal because they wished to keep the service of my father in Ireland. The position is still the same. They need my father and they want to satisfy your father's claim. Why this sudden change?'

'I know not.'

'I shall not let it rest.'

Nor did the ardent young man. He very foolishly attempted to see Wolsey; he must have been very persistent, for he succeeded.

He told me afterwards that the Cardinal was very short with him and told him not to meddle. There was no longer to be a marriage between him and Anne Boleyn.

It was good news to me, but I was rather sorry for James. He was very sad; and shortly after that he went back to Ireland.

*

A great burden had been lifted from me. I no longer had to fight for my freedom. I was in my element. I enjoyed the days; Court life suited me. I was not averse to the serious side as some of the ladies of the Queen's entourage were. In spite of my love of dancing, singing and masquing, I loved to read, and to write too. I tried my hand at verses, which, although they were not great poetry, had a certain charm. I missed Marguerite and I wondered what was happening about the changes in the Church which Martin Luther had suggested. Marguerite would have been up-to-date with developments. There was no chance of such discussions here. The Queen was completely devoted to the Church of Rome and believed – in spite of her gentle nature – that heretics should be burned at the stake, which was what the Inquisition, which had been so ably assisted by her mother and Torquemada, was doing in her own country. The King had written his book and was the Defender of the Faith. I could imagine the sort of opinions I should find here if I attempted to discuss the matter.

There was a great deal of excitement at Court because the Emperor Charles was visiting England, and there would, of course, have to be lavish entertainment to welcome such an important man.

François was now our enemy and the Emperor our friend. To the delight of the Queen, the latter was coming for his betrothal to the Princess Mary. There would be masques in plenty and we ladies should escape the religious duties imposed on us by the Queen, to join in.

I was in attendance on the Queen at Greenwich, where the Princess was to be presented to the Emperor. Poor little girl! She was the same age as I had been when I had gone to France. How would she feel about being presented to the man, so much older than herself, who was to be her husband; the Dauphin would have been more her age. This is the fate of women, I thought, to be bandied about to whatever suits their rulers best at the time. I would never be so treated. Once more I was thankful for the extraordinary turn of fate which meant I did not have to go into battle over the Butler affair, uncertain what the outcome would be.

We stood at the door of the great hall of Greenwich Palace, the Queen holding the little Princess by the hand while the barge came up. There was the King, great and glittering, his considerable size accentuated by the padded garments he wore – richly coloured velvets scintillating with jewels. The Emperor looked almost insignificant beside him.

The King surveyed the scene with pleasure; his docile Queen, his pretty little daughter whom he was giving to the mighty Emperor as a sign of the amity between the two countries.

His eyes swept over us. Did they pause for a fraction of a second as they alighted on me? Did I glimpse the expression of anger? Was he going to remember every time he saw me, and one day, perhaps when he was in an ill temper, would he give vent to his resentment? The result of that would be – exit Anne Boleyn from Court.

But this was a happy occasion.

Little Mary behaved just as her mother had taught her to, and after that we went into the Palace.

Inside, we ladies talked together and someone said that when the Princess was twelve years old she and the Emperor would be married.

'Providing,' I said, 'nothing happens to prevent it.'

'Hush,' I was told. 'You should watch your tongue, Anne Boleyn.'

Was that not what the King had told me? It was true. I should, if I wanted to remain at Court, and there was no doubt in my mind that I did.

There were to be some exciting entertainments for the Emperor even though he was the sort of man who would rather be discussing politics. But the King must show him honour and what a brilliant Court was his. So there would be lavish festivities.

Charles had brought with him a large company of diplomats who were perhaps a little more eager to enjoy the merriment than their master was.

It was an exciting time for us all. We sat with the Queen and watched the jousting in the courtyard. The King was much to the fore. He was always the victor. I smiled to myself. Who would dare score over him; I had tried – in a different way of course – and now here I was expecting every moment to be banished from Court.

He really was a magnificent sight. I often thought of François when I watched him. François glittered less; he never padded himself so outrageously; he wore subtle colours which always blended to perfection. The purple and gold of Henry would have been condemned as vulgar by him. He would say that the Tudors were *nouveau riche*, newcomers to power and glory and determined that no one should doubt for a moment that they now possessed it.

The joust always amused me, for there was an element of romantic love involved in it. The knights were supposed to be jousting for the honour of the ladies whom they would seduce and discard with impunity if given a chance. Henry himself rode a horse resplendent in silver, with the motto in black and gold: *Elle mon côeur a navera*. Who was she who had broken his heart? Certainly not the Queen. Certainly not my sister Mary or any of the ladies whom he honoured. It was a game and he was always a player of games. In that respect he never grew up.

Of course he was triumphant. He came to the Queen afterwards and bowed before her, playing the faithful husband who had been true to her over the years in spite of the fact that she had bitterly disappointed him in not giving him the son he longed for.

After the joust there was to be a banquet at York House, the Cardinal's splendid palace which rivalled the royal residences. There was to be a masque afterwards in which I was to take part.

It was a most brilliant occasion. The hall was decorated with rich brocade and tapestries, and lighted with what must have been a thousand candles. But what was so exciting was that the floor had been covered with green material to resemble grass, and at one end of the room had been erected a building which was the exact replica of a castle in miniature. Banners hung from the towers, from which came the sound of music.

At the sight of it everyone gasped with admiration. Only my lord Cardinal could go to the expense of providing such a setting for the night's entertainment, they said.

At the battlements of this mock tower sat eight ladies all clad in white satin; they had been chosen for their fair hair, blue eyes and very white skins. They were the Virtues and they all bore placards – Beauty, Honour, Kindness, Constancy, Pity, Mercy and so on. Seated on the mock greensward at the foot of the castle were the opposite of the Virtues, the Vices. I was amused – and a little piqued – that they had chosen brunettes to play the wicked Disdain, Danger, Unkindness, Jealousy and other failings.

Then the knights came into the hall, dressed in blue satin and cloth of gold. They carried labels on their feathered and jewelled caps such as Loyalty, Pleasure, Youth; and they were led by one more magnificently attired than any of them, who was recognizable at once by his size if by nothing else. The King was Ardent Desire. I failed to see that that was necessarily a virtue.

He led the attack on the castle. The fair ladies welcomed the knights – presumably they were intended to be prisoners of the wicked brunettes who tried to hold off the knights. Cannons outside the palace were fired to add to the effect. A brilliant idea, said everyone. Trust Wolsey to do something different. The dark ladies pelted the knights with rose petals

161

and sugar plums; the knights' weapons were dates and oranges.

Evidently the oranges and dates were the more effective weapons, and soon the castle was in the hands of the valiant knights, the Vices defeated and the Virtues rescued.

Then the galliard began.

The King, of course, was the centre of the dancing. I wondered what Charles and his ambassadors thought of this. They looked rather pleased, so perhaps they thought that one who took such delight in this kind of entertainment would be easy to outwit in the diplomatic field. Perhaps so. But they could be forgetting the Cardinal.

As one of the ladies of the Queen's household, I joined in the dance. I was close to the King and again was aware of his attention. Of one thing I was certain now – he had not forgotten that scene in the garden and still held it against me.

I shall always remember that night because during it I first became aware of Henry Percy.

He was in the household of Cardinal Wolsey. We danced together and afterwards sat engaged in conversation. It was obvious to me that he admired me, and there was a quality in him which appealed to me. He was modest and rather gentle. He told me that I was quite different from the other ladies at the Court, and he left me in no doubt that he found the difference pleasing.

'You have not been long at Court,' he said. 'I have seen you now and then . . . but only recently.'

'Are you often at Court?'

'I am in the Cardinal's household and have to attend on him every day. That often brings me to the Palace.'

'I am with the Queen's household.'

'Yes, I know. You are Mistress Anne Boleyn.'

'How did you know?'

He flushed a little. 'I . . . I asked your name. I know that you have come recently from France. Do you think the Court here different from that of France?'

162

'In many respects, yes.'

'Do you regret leaving France?'

'Only now and then.'

'Are you regretting it now?'

'No,' I said honestly, 'I am not,' and we laughed together.

'I have been here so long,' he said. 'My father was insistent that I should be brought up in the Cardinal's household.'

'It is a good training for Court life, doubtless.'

'That will be my lot. When possible, I go back to the North.'

'So you come from there? You know my name. What is yours?'

'Henry Algernon Percy.'

'You come from the North. Your name is Percy. Then you must be related to the Northumberlands.'

'The Earl is my father.'

'And do you long to go back home?'

'It is so long since I lived at Alnwick that it no longer seems to be my home. I have been back of course . . . then when I leave it I feel homesick. The air is different there . . . free and fresh.'

'How is the Cardinal?'

'Well, I think.'

'I mean as a master?'

'He does not concern himself with his pages.'

I laughed. 'You are of a noble house and he is the son of a butcher yet you must consider it an honour to be received into his house. Does that not strike you as strange?'

'Put like that, perhaps. But he is a brilliant statesman and I the not very clever son of the house. My father does not think much of me. I believe he wishes one of my brothers were the elder.'

'Parents are rarely satisfied with their children. But then, are children always satisfied with their parents? What a pity we cannot choose each other! That would be more satisfactory.'

'But difficult to arrange.'

'Tell me about yourself.'

'Do you really want to know?'

'Of course I do. What of these brothers who are so much more worthy than you?'

'Thomas and Ingelram? We get along well together when we meet, which is not often, my being down here in the service of the Cardinal, and they . . . lucky creatures . . . being up there in the North.'

'How you love that place! I should like to see it.'

'One day I must show you Alnwick.'

'The family home . . . '

'Home of the Percy clan for generations. It is very ancient. Of course it has been added to and altered since it was first cut out of the deep ravine on the south bank of the River Alne. It was there before the Norman Conquest and was the home of Saxon lords. It was the year 1309 before it came into the possession of the Percys. Now it is very much ours. We have put our stamp on it.'

'Very different from Hever, my home. That, I believe, was acquired by my great-grandfather, who was a merchant and Lord Mayor of London. A little better than a butcher perhaps – but trade none the less.'

He looked at me admiringly. 'I can only applaud him for being the great-grandfather of the most charming lady at Court.'

'You know how to pay compliments.'

'I don't usually. But now I have only to speak the truth.'

'They are beginning to dance,' I said. 'Shall we join them?'

'I am a poor dancer.'

'I am a good one, and all you have to do is follow me.'

It was true that he was no dancer, but I liked him the better for that. There was a delightful honesty about him.

He said: 'I liked better talking to you, which one cannot do seriously in the dance. I like to look at you because I have never seen anyone like you. I cannot believe you really exist

. . . unless I keep my eyes on you.'

'I assure you I am no phantom.'

I bantered a little with him, but he was very serious. I enjoyed his admiration, and I felt drawn to him as I never had to any other person.

'I shall look for you,' he said. 'I come to the palace every day with the Cardinal to wait on the King, so I shall be near you. The Cardinal is often closeted with him for a very long time.'

'And his attendants must wait for him?'

'They can wander round the gardens . . . providing they do not stray too far.'

'I see.'

'And the Queen's maids of honour?'

'They, too, often wander in the gardens.'

'I shall look for you,' he said.

I smiled and thought, though I did not say it: And I shall look for you.

*

That was the beginning. Our friendship grew. Friendship? It was more than that. I awoke each morning in a state of such happiness as I had never known before, asking myself whether I should see him that day. I realized that this was falling in love.

He was different from the other young men. He was earnest and sincere. It was not surprising that, in a Court of shams, I should prize these qualities.

It had never occurred to me that I could fall in love so easily. I had seen too much of the relationships between the sexes to trust them. There were the flowery phrases, the *billets doux*, the compliments, the flattery . . . and then it was all over. I had never thought that something doomed to be so ephemeral was worth the trouble until now.

But Henry Percy was not like the others. When he said I

was different from all others, he meant it. When he said he had thought of nothing else but me since we had met, he meant that too. Trust was a wonderful thing to have for another person; and that was what I had in him.

The weeks began to pass. I used to watch for Wolsey's arrival at the palace. He came in his barge often – a splendid figure in his Cardinal's robes with his attendants all about him. He travelled with almost as much state as the King. I would look among those young men about him, and my gaze would come to rest on one of them.

As soon as he saw me, a beautiful smile would illuminate his features. He was not handsome, and I liked him the better for that. He would never be the champion at the jousts, and I was glad. He was without that pride of which I saw so much. I loved him and part of my love was protective. I wanted to look after him. I wanted to leave all this meaningless pomp and go with him to that windswept castle where, he told me, the Percys were kings of the North as surely as Henry was King of England. 'Kings . . . under kings,' he said. 'But the people of the North would have no one to rule them but the Percys.'

He would take me over the castle and show me the sally port which was one of the sixteen towers flanking the castle; he would show me that spot they called the Bloody Gap, the name given to a breach in the walls made by the Scots during the Border Wars which had raged intermittently throughout the centuries. He would show me Hotspur's Seat, which had been a favourite spot of his gallant ancestor, the fierce Hotspur who had died at the Battle of St Albans. He made me see the castle keep, the gatehouse and the statues of warriors placed at intervals along the parapet as though to remind all comers of the might of the Percys.

And it seemed that there was an understanding between us that day that we should be together always.

Being in love changed everything. I even looked different. I was absent-minded. 'What is the matter with Anne Boleyn?' asked my companions. 'I believe she is in love.'

Was it so obvious?

I would wait for the coming of the Cardinal and, if for some reason he did not come, that was a sad day for me, one to be got through as quickly as possible.

We sat in the gardens and talked. People noticed, of course.

I told him how I had come to Court full of misgivings because I had feared they would try to force me into a marriage with James Butler. I had determined to hold out against that, but I was delighted that the matter had been set aside and James Butler had now left the Court, presumably to return to Ireland.

Then he told me that when he had been a child his father had talked of a marriage for him with Lady Mary Talbot, who was the daughter of the Earl of Shrewsbury.

'I suppose he thought that an alliance between North-umberland and Shrewsbury would be a good one,' I said.

'There is only one I would take for my wife,' he replied; then we clung together and I thought: This is perfect happiness. This is how it will be for evermore.

What a lot I had to learn!

*

I could not imagine that my father would put any obstacle in our way. It was clear that the need for me to bring the Butler estates into the family was no longer acute, and my father had lost official interest in the match – I presumed because of some change in the Irish situation. He could surely raise no objection to a match with the Northumberlands. They were one of the most noble and ancient families in the country. No doubt the Howards would consider themselves superior, but the Northumberlands would certainly not agree. As for the Percys accepting *me* . . . well, it was true that my origins were not of the most noble, but my father was rising high in the favour of the King, and my sister was certainly a woman of some consequence at Court. How strange that I should have counted Mary's affairs a boon. But I was in love. I was ready to accept anything which brought me to the goal on which my happiness depended.

In the apartments of the maids of honour there was a great deal of gossip, and they were naturally interested in my relationship with Henry Percy.

I was unprepared for the storm.

One day Henry did not arrive in the Cardinal's company when the great man called on the King. My disappointment was intense. What had happened? Was he ill? That was my first thought.

I asked one of the young men who was in the Cardinal's household.

'He is not ill,' I was told. 'He has greatly displeased the Cardinal, so I heard.'

'Then where is he?'

'He is not in attendance on the Cardinal.'

I was very anxious. What would happen? Would he be sent home? To displease the Cardinal was often to displease the King. If he were sent back to Northumberland, perhaps I could join him there. We could be married. But marriages were not arranged as simply as that. What could this mean? What could he have done?

For the rest of the day I was in a state of terrible uneasiness. It will pass, I kept telling myself. After all, even Wolsey must take care how he treats the son of Northumberland.

The next day the Cardinal came and I was watchful in the gardens. One of Henry's friends came to me and told me that Henry would try to come and see me, but it must be secret, and if he did not arrive I must understand that he had failed in his attempt to reach me.

Now I knew that something was seriously wrong.

It was difficult to contrive the meeting, but the maids of honour were ever ready to assist lovers, as were Henry's friends, and by a certain manoeuvring they helped us to the meeting. It was brief and completely shattering.

He came up the river to Greenwich and we went to a secluded part of the gardens. I could see that he was in great distress.

He said: 'They are determined to stop us. The Cardinal called me to him and addressed me in a most hectoring and insulting manner. He said he marvelled at my folly in attempting to contract myself to you. He said, had I forgotten the estate to which God had called me, for when my father died I should inherit one of the noblest earldoms in the kingdom, and therefore how could I think of marrying without the consent of my father and also that of our King. I had offended not only my father but the King in this folly. He suggested that the King had a special interest in your future. I know not what he meant by that.'

'I do,' I said bitterly. 'He can't forget that I once played a little game with him. He liked it not and ever since has been determined to repay me for my insolence.'

'Then everyone is against us. I never thought of this opposition. Your father stands high at Court; he is in the King's favour; and your mother was a Howard. I could not believe this. I would pass over my inheritance to my brother. I wish I were not the eldest son. I told the Cardinal that I was old enough to choose my wife and I would beg the King's favour for the match. I was sure that, if he did give it, my father would also.'

'And then?' I asked.

'The Cardinal looked very shocked. I was not alone. That made it worse. Several of our company were there witnessing my humiliation. He turned to them and said: "You see how this foolish boy lacks wisdom. I thought, Henry Percy, that when you were made aware of the King's displeasure you would have repented your folly and sought at once to end it." I told him that you and I had already plighted our troth and I could not give you up. Then he said he would send for my father. And that is what he has done.'

We looked at each other in despair.

'What can we do?' I asked.

He shook his head. 'There is nothing we can do.'

'Do you give up so easily, Henry Percy?'

'My dearest, we could run away together. How far do you think we should get? We should be put in the Tower for that.'

'Why should they behave like this? Am I so far below you in birth?'

'I would not care if you were a serving maid. But I do not think that this is a case so simple.'

'But your father wanted you to marry Mary Talbot.'

'It was long ago that that was talked of. I will see my father. I will talk to him. It may be that I can explain to him. It may be that when he sees you ... '

'But the *King* ... '

'It may be that the Cardinal only mentioned him to make me give way. I cannot see what interest the King could have.'

'I think he seeks revenge on me.'

'But, my dearest Anne, there are many ways he could have done that had he wished. He could have refused to have you at Court.'

'I do not understand him. I see him watching me sometimes and there is anger in his eyes.'

'It is your fancy. Wait until I see my father. Do not give up hope, my love.'

'No. I will cling to it. I cannot bear to do anything else.'

'I must go. The Cardinal must not know that we have met.'

We parted.

A fearful premonition was creeping over me that there was some evil force working against me.

*

I did not see him as I had hoped. But I heard what had happened.

It seemed that my enemies were going to extraordinary lengths to ruin my life.

As the meeting between the Earl of Northumberland and his son did not take place in private, there were gentlemen of the Cardinal's entourage to bring news of it to the ladies of the Queen's household, and from them I learned what had taken place.

The Earl must have been amazed to receive a summons to come to Court just to listen to an account of the misdemeanours of his son in engaging himself with a girl who was not considered worthy of the House of Northumberland.

The interview took place in the great hall of Wolsey's palace. The Earl had previously been in consultation with the Cardinal for some time; then he went into the gallery where his son was called to him.

The Earl berated Henry, calling him proud, licentious and an unthinking waster. Such abuse, as all must know, was so untrue that it astonished and maddened me to hear of it. His son had no regard, went on the irate Earl, for his father or his King. He might have brought disgrace on his father and his noble house. He had done his best to ruin them both. But by good fortune, his sovereign and the noble Cardinal had seen fit to warn him of what his profligate son was doing; and therefore he had learned of what sorrow was being brought to his house. He had come to tell his son that he must desist from his folly without delay. He was considering disinheriting Henry and naming one of his brothers as his successor, for the Lords of Northumberland had great duties in the North and these could not be performed by a profligate waster.

Poor Henry! I could imagine his distress to have his character so misrepresented simply because he had fallen in love and wished to marry. I knew that he was not quick with words as I was; his temper did not rise as mine did. It was those very differences which had attracted me. I wished I had been there. I would have told the Earl – and the Cardinal, too – what I thought of them. I knew in my heart that my poor Henry was not fitted to deal with them.

I could imagine his standing there accepting the abuse,

stammering that he loved me, telling them of my perfections. That was not the way to handle them.

And then the Earl turned to the Cardinal's servants, who were listening to this harangue, and told them not to make excuses for his son's faults, and to treat him harshly when the need arose. Then he went out to his barge in a state of great anger.

I sought to cheer myself. It was not the end. The Cardinal's men had been told not to spare him, which meant that he would stay in the Cardinal's household. At least he would not be far away.

But even that hope was soon past.

A few days later I heard that Henry was banished from Court and that he had already left for Northumberland.

I wanted to see the Cardinal, to demand to know what it all meant. Why was everyone so determined to destroy my future happiness? I would have them know that I had Howard blood in my veins. Perhaps they would care to throw insults at the Duke of Norfolk. In private I stormed; I raged; I made up conversations between myself and the Cardinal in which I flayed him with my tongue until the man cringed; but of course it was only my own angry face which looked back at me in the mirror, not the bland one of the great Cardinal. In my thoughts I argued with the King. Why did you have to do this to me? I know you have not forgotten that time at Hever. I see you watching me. Is it possible that a great King could want revenge just because for a few minutes a young girl made him feel foolish?

But these imaginary conversations did nothing but increase my fury.

I was very sad, very hurt and very angry. I supposed it was called broken-hearted for I was listless and had no interest in anything.

My father summoned me to his presence.

He looked at me coldly. 'So you have disgraced yourself with young Percy,' he said.

'Disgraced! We were to have been married.'

'Foolish girl. You should know that the marriage of the future Earl of Northumberland must be arranged by his family.'

'We are as good as they are ... almost.'

'You have displeased the Cardinal.'

'Why should my affairs displease him? If he is so worried about my low birth, let him look to his own.'

'You are too forward. You are lacking in modesty. Your presence at Court is no longer needed.'

'Do you mean ... ?'

'What I mean is that you are to leave at once for Hever.'

So I was banished too.

*

It did not matter to me very much where I was. What was the use of being at Court if he was not there?

Over the moat, under the portcullis, into the familiar courtyard ... I was home, banished from Court, banished from joy for ever more.

My stepmother greeted me with pity and affection. She knew of the broken love affair.

'You will feel better at home,' she told me. 'I will look after you.'

I fell into her arms and, for the first time since it happened, I was weeping. I think I alarmed her, for it was so unlike me, and as always with me, my tears were more tempestuous than those of other people – just as my anger and my pleasure seemed to be.

She was a great comfort to me. I was able to talk to her. She understood how much I had cared for him and why. I told her of our meetings and our plans; and she listened and wept with me.

She assured me that I would recover in time. 'Time is our friend in trouble,' she said, 'because it tells us that the sorrow

173

cannot last for ever.'

I was sure mine would.

'I shall never forget him,' I told her. 'He was not in the least like the man I should have expected to marry. He was no great warrior. I am surprised that I could care for such a man as he was . . . but as soon as we were together I knew that I was for him and he was for me. He was not like any of the others and nor am I . . . but the difference between us was great. Oh, it is good to talk of him . . . to someone who I think will understand.'

'There, my darling child,' she said. 'Talk to me. Tell me . . . and if you would be quiet, then we shall just sit together . . . close like this . . . and you will know my thoughts are with you.'

I do not know how many weeks passed thus. I lost count of the days. Sometimes I lay in bed from sunrise to sunset; and my stepmother would come up and sit by my bed.

'There is nothing to get up for,' I told her.

And she would sit there, so that if I wished to talk to her I did and if I was silent it did not matter.

I have never forgotten what she did for me at that time.

Then one day a messenger came from Court from my father.

Among other things he brought a letter for my stepmother. He wished to know how I was faring. Was I sulking in my disappointment?

'She should be told that Henry Percy is now married to Lady Mary Talbot for whom his father has always intended him.'

So it was really over. Before that, I had had wild hopes that some miracle might happen, and that one day I should see him come riding into the castle.

This was the end . . . and I did not care what became of me.

*

174

I do not know how I lived through the weeks that followed. I was ill for a while. I had some sort of fever and I lay in my bed unsure where I was for long stretches of the day – for which I was grateful.

Mary Wyatt came over to Hever to see me. She read to me and we talked a great deal about the old days when we had all been so happy.

'Thomas is at Court,' she said. 'He writes more now. He produces many of the entertainments there. The King likes his work.'

I did not want to hear about the Court.

Mary went back to Allington, but it was comforting to know she was not far away.

My stepmother tried to interest me in some embroidery stitches she had learned. She was working on an altar cloth for the church and wondered if I would care to help her.

I worked with her listlessly, taking no interest in it.

And so the weeks passed.

Then one day a messenger came from Court. We were to prepare for a visit from the King. He would be with a hunting party in Kent and as he would be near Hever he would spend a night at the castle. My father had written out a list of instructions for my stepmother. It was possible that the Cardinal would be a member of the party.

I felt sick with rage.

'I shall not see them,' I said. 'I shall take to my room and they must be told that I am ill ... which I shall be at the thought of seeing them.'

My stepmother reasoned with me. 'You cannot do this. It will not be allowed. You will be commanded to come down to greet the King.'

'I refuse.'

'Have you forgotten that when the King came before you stayed in your room pleading illness?'

'I remember the occasion well,' I said grimly.

'You must steel yourself, my love. It will not be so bad.

Remember, it is only for one night. It will soon be over.'

'No,' I cried. 'I will not.'

The next morning I had a return of the fever, and this was not feigned. I think I must have conjured it up. I lay in my bed, hot and uneasy, assuring myself that in no circumstances would I see the royal party.

What if they forced me? They could, I supposed. They had shown me how powerful they were. If they were capable of ruining my life, they could surely insist that I leave my bed and join them.

I lay there fuming with hatred. I was not calm and gentle like my stepmother. I could not mildly accept the fate which had been thrust upon me. Whenever I closed my eyes, I saw the sinister figure of the Cardinal. How I hated that man! How dared he humiliate my lover! How dared he speak of me as he had!

How I should love to have my revenge on him! If ever the opportunity arose, I would gladly take it. I would never forget, never forgive.

It was absurd to think that the King was interested in my affairs. It was the Cardinal who was making the trouble. After all Henry Percy had been of his household. He wanted to have charge of all those there; he looked upon them as his minions. He was an arrogant man.

And as I lay there I thought: There is only one way to be sure. I must not be here when they come.

I rose from my bed. I felt better now that I had a plan of action. The fever had miraculously subsided, so it must have come to my aid as it had now so conveniently left me.

I put on my riding habit and rode over to Allington Castle. Mary received me warmly.

'I must talk to you,' I said. 'I need your help.'

'You know I shall be happy to give it.'

'The King's party is coming to Hever. The Cardinal may be among them.'

'What an honour!'

'I do not see it as such, Mary. I cannot be there. I cannot face them. I think if I did I should do something . . . say something which would damn me and my family for ever '

'Anne, you must restrain yourself.'

'Restrain myself when they have taken away the only man I shall ever love, when they have ruined my life!'

'Anne, be calm. Tell me your plan.'

'I intend to be away from home. I want to come and stay here during their visit.'

'Might they not come here to seek you?'

'Why ever should they?'

'I don't know. Your father might be angry and send for you.'

'That is true. My stepmother will help. She has been wonderful to me. I shall ask her to say that I am with you and we are going to visit a friend of yours and she does not know who it is.'

'He could send to see if you were here.'

'Then we could make your people pretend that I was not. Would they do that?'

'There would be talk.'

'I know. But I must try. May I come and stay . . . just for a few days. Leave it to me. I will do the planning.'

I rode back to Hever.

My stepmother was in a panic. 'I heard that you had gone out riding alone, Anne. You know . . . '

'Dearest Stepmother, I am old enough to ride alone and the sky is full of daylight. No one would harm me. You are going to help me in this.'

So we went to my room and we talked. I told her that I was going to Mary Wyatt. She was to make them believe that the arrangement had been made before the King's visit to Hever had been proposed. While the royal party was in Hever, I should be elsewhere. As a safety precaution she must tell them that Mary had arranged for us to visit friends so that we should not be all the time at Allington. When the King's party had left she should send a servant over to Allington to tell me. Then I would return to Hever.

She needed a certain amount of persuasion. She hated to lie to my father, but she was very worried about the state of my health, and she feared I would fall into a fever if I were crossed. So at length she agreed.

In due course I rode over to Allington.

Mary welcomed me and I talked to her freely of my hatred for the Cardinal, who I reckoned was at the root of my trouble.

Mary could not understand why he, who was so involved with the politics of Europe, should concern himself so deeply about the marriage of two young people at Court.

I could not understand it either, but it was clear to me that he was behind all my troubles.

'Cardinals are not allowed to marry, so perhaps they resent other people's finding happiness in that way.'

It seemed as good a reason as we could think of, and somehow it made me hate the Cardinal more than ever.

Those days were fraught with fear. Every time I heard the sound of horses' hoofs in the courtyard, I was alert. But it proved to be no fateful messenger.

I fed the pigeons with Mary; we rode together; she showed me some of Thomas's poems which I had not seen before; and so the days passed.

One day a messenger arrived at Allington. He came from my stepmother.

The royal party had been to Hever and departed.

So I could go home.

The Outcast

Weeks passed into months and a year sped by. During that year my father had been awarded several stewardships and he was now a very rich man; it was clear that he was a favourite with the King. He had been considerably successful as an ambassador, but I was of the opinion that the King was saying: Thank you for giving me Mary.

One cannot grieve forever. There were days when I forgot my love for Henry Percy. I did not wonder all the time what was happening in the castle which he loved so much; I did not continue to ask myself what Mary Talbot was like, whether he still compared her with me and thought of those days when I had waited for him to arrive with the Cardinal. One must grow away from sorrow. But the scar was there; and always would be. Now and then something would remind me ... inconsequential little things like the dew on the grass, the shape of a cloud in the sky, the smell of a flower ... sights and feelings one has marvelled at when one was in love ... and I was back in the past.

My stepmother understood me well and she tried so hard to wean me from my unhappiness that I felt I had to respond and pretend that I was forgetting – and that helped me to forget.

She would consult me about the management of the house, and although I was not really interested, I would feign to be just to please her. I rode a good deal; I walked; I hunted; I hawked; I was often at Allington Castle, and Mary often came to Hever.

My father paid rare visits. He did not reproach me as I had expected him to; he behaved as though the matter was closed. But he did not speak of my future and I began to feel that I was to be left at Hever for the rest of my life. It was at least peaceful, and I had grown to love the surrounding country. It was home in a way. But I missed the Court. I designed my dresses but what was the use if no one was there to see them except the local people and a few country friends. They understood nothing of fashion.

Mary came visiting us once. She was sparkling with pleasure. Life was very good to her. My stepmother was in a flurry of excitement, making sure that all was befitting for such a personage as my sister had become. I laughed at these preparations. 'She may be the King's mistress,' I said, 'but she is still only Mary.'

Mary was as little likely to give herself airs because of her position as she was to feel shame because of it. She lived by simple rules and it was not long before she was betraying a few secrets to me.

When we were alone together, she slipped easily into the rôle of a sister who, although she might be older, had always been dominated by me to a certain extent. She had never seemed to understand discretion and it was easy to learn what one wanted to from her.

She told me something of what had happened about Henry Percy and myself. Being close to the King she had seen what effect it had had in royal circles. Not that she was in the least discerning, but even she could not fail to be aware of such a *contretemps*, particularly when it concerned her sister.

She said: 'The King was in a mighty rage. He sent for Wolsey. I don't know what he said to him, but Wolsey was with him for a long time. I did hear the King say something about "those upstart Boleyns". I thought that was the end of me. He shouted: "Send for Northumberland." The Cardinal left him, and the King did not send for me. I only knew that he was very angry because one of our family had dared to think she could marry with the mighty Northumberlands. It was a surprise to me. After all the King had done for our father. I thought he had taken a sudden dislike to *me*. As a matter of fact, he had been falling off in his attention for some time now. Well, I had a long run. Few people last as long.'

'Oh, Mary,' I said. 'I wish it wasn't so. It is so demeaning.'

'To be the King's mistress! My dear Anne, it is an honour. People vie for it.'

'Why, Mary? Why you? I know most of them feather their nests. They look for honours . . . riches . . . but you . . .'

Mary's eyes were glazed with memories. 'He is a very fine man,' she said.

'Of course he has a beautiful crown.'

'I never think of that. I think he liked me for it. No one has ever lasted as long . . . not even Elizabeth Blount.'

'I cannot understand Will Carey.'

'He is a gentle soul. He would never make trouble. He is happy enough as long as he doesn't know too much about it.'

'He must know . . . all. Everyone knows.'

'There is great discretion at Court. The King does not want people to know. He wants them to think he is a faithful husband . . . and he would be . . . if he could.'

'Most of us would be virtuous if sin was not so enticing,' I said.

'Well, there is the Queen, you know. She behaves to me as though I were just one of her maids of honour. There is never any mention . . . of the fact that I visit him at night. Those in attendance disappear when I slip in and when I come out. And nobody ever says when I return to the maid's apartment, "Where have you been?"'

'But they all *know*!'

'But it is not spoken of . . . and that makes it seem all right.'

I laughed. 'These matters are conducted differently in France.'

'Well, this way is better. It makes it easier for everyone. But I did think it was the end. He sent for me so rarely . . . and the occasions were becoming less and less frequent. They stopped altogether for several months. I thought it was over. And then, suddenly, recently, it started again. He was very affectionate. He seemed to have forgotten that we were the upstart Boleyns and a member of our family had attempted to marry into the House of Northumberland.'

It was impossible not to laugh with Mary, although I deplored her position and would have preferred our father to have done without what I called his ill-gotten gains, because I felt life at Hever was intolerably dull, and I could not help urging Mary to talk of the Court.

When she had gone, it seemed duller than ever.

After a year or so of this quiet country existence, George came home. I was much happier then. George and I had always been two of a kind; the family bond between us was close. Now I had a companion; we rode together; we hawked and hunted; but best of all we talked.

There was an occasion when we had visitors from the Netherlands. George had met them on one of his visits abroad and we entertained them for a few nights at Hever.

I remember that night as we sat round the table after the meal and how we talked long into the night. Our visitors were fascinated by the works of Martin Luther and they talked glowingly of the reforms which were needed in the Church. They talked of the growing anxiety throughout the Catholic world and the attempts to destroy this man. So far they had not succeeded and those who followed him were growing in number. There was going to be a revolution throughout the Church, and the outcome would be that a new doctrine of protesters would be formed . . . a branch of the old religion, but an improved religion with much which was evil in the old removed.

When they departed, with many thanks for our hospitality and in particular for our participation in those interesting discussions, they left with us two books by Martin Luther – one of which was his famous address to *The Christian Nobles of Germany* and the other his treatise on *The Babylonish Captivity of the Church*.

George and I spent many an hour reading them and

discussing them afterwards.

He had received a grant of the Manor of Grimston in Norfolk, for which he was extremely grateful.

'The King has been generous to our family,' he said. 'Our father has done very well out of his daughter. The Boleyns have always found a way to improve their lot. Oddly enough, it has usually been through the women.'

'Sometimes I think I would rather have stayed humble . . . in our London merchant's home. He at least kept his pride and his honour.'

George laughed at me. 'My dear Anne, you have become a simple country maiden with your talk of pride and honour. The King likes Mary . . . very well. Let him honour her family. What always amuses me is that it should be Mary. Do you remember . . . we used to despise her just a little, when we were young. She never saw the point of our conversation. She was never really with us, was she? And now . . . here she is, our charming little benefactress.'

'You've become cynical, George.'

'It's the only way to live at Court.'

'Then perhaps it is better to live away from Court.'

'Oh . . . you like the quiet life, do you?'

'No.' I refused to deceive myself any longer. 'I want to be there. I want to dance and sing and play in the masques. I want to know what is going on in the world . . . and not just to hear it secondhand when a visitor happens to call. I want to have my revenge on the mighty Cardinal.'

George laughed out loud. 'My dear Anne, how will you bring that about?'

'I don't know.'

'Nor would anyone else. He stands high in the King's favour. I'll tell you this: Henry is a Tudor, and Tudors are not sure of their crowns. It's understandable. Henry cannot forget that his father came by his most fortuitously. If the battle of Bosworth had gone differently, as it so well might . . . if Stanley hadn't turned traitor . . . Oh, that would have been another story. The crown sat rather unsteadily on this King's father's head and he never forgets it. Wolsey is one of those who is helping to hold his steady.'

'I know it is foolish. But I do hate the man.'

'You blame him for what happened with Percy.'

'He berated him in a most unseemly manner before so many. And what did he call me? "A foolish girl." I should like to show him that I am not that. I should like to make him suffer as he did me and my poor Henry.'

'It's over and done with, Anne. Nothing will change it. Percy quickly succumbed to family pressure and married Shrewsbury's daughter. I have heard that it is a most unhappy marriage.'

I should have felt some satisfaction at that, but I did not. I was surprised by my feelings for Henry Percy. They had had something motherly in them. I had always wanted to protect him; and although I could not have borne him to be happy with Mary Talbot, at the same time I did not want him to be miserable.

'Such a marriage would be,' I said.

'He should have had more spirit.'

'I think he was heartbroken . . . as I was.'

'My poor Anne! But you were not meant to pine away with a broken heart. I should like to see you at Court. You'd outshine them all.'

After talking with George, I began to think I should like that too.

George could not stay indefinitely. He had his duties in Norfolk. And when he went away, I was desolate.

And then, one day when I rode over to Allington, Thomas Wyatt was there. When he saw me, his eyes lit up with pleasure. He took both my hands in his and kissed me on the cheek.

'Anne . . . it is wonderful to see you,' he said.

'That is how I feel about seeing you.'

'I thought you might have gone back to Court.'

'Oh no. I am banished for ever. I am in disgrace.'

'I heard the story. What a fool Percy was! He should have run away with you.'

'His father came, you know. He was sent for by the King. They were all against us.'

'I can't be too sad about it. I should hate anything that took you away from Hever.'

'Are you staying at Allington long?'

'Only for a while.'

'Then I shall see you now and then.'

'Often, I hope.'

And that was how it was. Every day he was at Hever or I was at Allington. The days passed quickly in such company. He was one of the most handsome men I ever knew. Nature had given Thomas Wyatt almost everything – except perhaps discretion; he never had much of that. He was reckless always. I think he especially enjoyed courting danger. He was tall and excelled in athletic accomplishments; a skilful rider, he shone at the jousts, and that had brought him to the King's notice; he could dance with grace and had a good singing voice; not many were so gifted. But Thomas's chief asset was his scholarship; he could speak several languages fluently; he was a recognized poet; it was rare that such gifts were mingled so that he could be as completely at home in the tiltyard as he was in the most intellectual company. His expression was lively, and his eyes were clear and blue; his blond hair curled about his head; he had a finely chiselled nose and his mouth was sensitive. He had a rare distinction. He was, in all respects, a man who could not fail to charm and attract attention.

The King had soon drawn him into his intimate circle of friends. He liked to hear Thomas's poetry. He considered himself a poet of no small merit, and I was sure his efforts received more acclaim than those of Thomas. This would amuse Thomas but perhaps cause a little uneasiness in the King's mind, for he was – as I was to discover later – by no means of a simple nature. One part of him would know that Thomas was the greater poet, but another part was too vain and childish to admit it. These two sides of his nature were in constant conflict with each other. If he had been a little less intellectual or a little more vain, he would have been more easily understood, and conequently those about him, who depended on his whims, would have been so much more secure.

At this time I knew none of this. I was forgetting that scene in the gardens at Hever and had long told myself that the King could not really have borne resentment towards me because of it, for if he had wished to punish me for my insolence he could have found some means of doing so at the time. No, I assured myself, the break-up of my betrothal had been due to the Cardinal's spite. He was the one whom I must blame.

And now there was Thomas Wyatt, that delightful companion to brighten my days by falling in love with me.

He told me frankly of his feelings for his wife. There was no love lost between them. It had been an arranged marriage and she cared no more for him than he did for her.

Somehow that lulled my conscience.

Often I thought: If Thomas had not married, I might have married him. How different my life would have been if that had been possible! I was not in love with him, but he was the most pleasant companion I knew, and no one – not even George – had helped to soothe my wounds as he had.

He could not stay at Allington for ever, for he had duties at Court. The King, impressed by his performance in the tiltyard, had made him Esquire of the Body, and now he had another post: Clerk of the King's Jewels.

'You see I have pleased His Grace,' explained Thomas. 'I think it is mostly through my verses and the masques I have arranged at Court. The King has complimented me on them. He will be missing me, I dareswear.'

'So you must go back,' I said dolefully.

'I have to tear myself away, Anne. I would you were there. You would open the eyes of some. There would be no one to match you ... nor ever could be in my eyes.'

He looked at me with a burning passion, and I knew he longed to be my lover, but much as I enjoyed his desire for me, I would never succumb to it. I was not one to be carried away, even by this handsome poet.

He used to read his poetry to me; some of it spoke of love and those sentiments were directed towards me. I basked in his admiration. It soothed me. But my temperament was as different from my sister Mary's as it could be. She was as ready as her lovers to reach the climax of such encounters; I was determined they should never arrive.

I suppose I was sexually cold. I had not felt so with Henry Percy; but even with him there could have been no consummation of our love until after marriage. Mary's adventures had had a marked effect on me, and I should never forget the humiliation of her banishment from the French Court.

So I basked in the love of charming Thomas Wyatt with the avowed determination never to give way to his pleas. But those days helped me. I began to feel there was a life other than one of brooding sorrow and loneliness at Hever.

My stepmother was delighted to see the change in me, but at the same time she was a little fearful. She was aware – as all must be – of Thomas's almost irresistible charm, and she knew, of course, how I had suffered. I felt very tender towards her; her disinterested love for me amazed me for it was something I had not had from my natural parents, and it seemed strange that it should come from a stepmother.

'Do not fear for me, dear Mother,' I said to her, for in the closeness of our relationship I had dropped the word 'step'; and I think that, for her, that was a reward for all the kindness she had shown me. 'I have had such example that I shall always know how to take care of myself.'

And I meant that.

When Thomas went back to Court, I was desolate. I

re-read Luther's books but it was frustrating to discover points for discussion and have no one with whom to discuss them. Mary Wyatt was not always at Allington, and much as I loved my stepmother, such matters were beyond her understanding; nor would she have wished to know of them.

There came a time when an even greater honour was bestowed on my father. My stepmother had to go to Court for the ceremony. She was very nervous and wished that I could accompany her; I found myself joining in that wish. But I had been exiled and there had been no invitation for me to return. So I must remain at Hever.

When she returned I heard what had happened.

It had been most impressive. She was so proud of her husband. He was certainly a very great man, she said, and now he had been made Vicount Rochford, a peer of the realm.

The ceremony had taken place in the great hall at Bridewell. Such beautiful tapestries had been hung on the walls, and Thomas had been led up to the dais on which stood the King himself under a canopy of gold.

'Your father is extremely pleased,' she told me. 'He has worked hard for this. He told me that the Emperor Charles is so delighted with his services to his country and ours that he is giving him a pension.'

'Yes,' I said, 'my father has come far. Did you see Mary?'

'Yes. She is very well and happy. All seems to go well with her.'

'I'll swear my father is very grateful to her.'

'Your father has earned his success through his loyal service to the King,' she replied with a hint of reproach; and I did not take the matter further, not wishing to upset her.

She told me later that there had been some gossip about the newly created Duke of Richmond. He was the son of Lady Talboys, who had been Elizabeth Blount, and the people seemed to think it was significant that he had been given the title.

'He is the King's son,' I said.

'Oh yes. There does not seem to be any doubt of that. I heard that the King is very proud of him. There is a great deal of talk about the King's sadness because the Queen cannot get sons.'

'There was always such talk. The boy was called Henry Fitzroy and that is clear enough. The King never denied he was his son. In fact, from what I heard, he seems proud of it. It is a proof that *he* can get sons even if the Queen cannot.'

'Well, he has made him Duke of Richmond, and some seem to think he is going to have a very special place at Court.'

'He is not very old, is he?'

'About six years old, I should say. But there was a great deal of talk about it. They say the Queen was not very happy.'

'I should think not, poor lady. It is like a reproach to her.'

'As if she could be blamed! Such matters are in God's hands.'

'Well, I can see you have enjoyed your little excursion.'

'It was not as bad as I thought it might be. You know how I fret about these things. I was not cut out to be the wife of an important man.'

'I hope he appreciates you,' I said.

And so my father continued in his rise.

We had visitors often at Hever. People came from the Court at my father's invitation. Not that he accompanied them, but if they were travelling in the vicinity of Hever, he told them there would always be a welcome there. I was happy to help my stepmother entertain them. It was a pleasant way of keeping in touch with events for I found it irksome to be shut away in a little backwater, knowing nothing of the world except what I learned through others. I felt that I could not continue in this way of life much longer. I did not, in fact, believe it would be expected of me. It was inevitable that a husband would be found for me ... perhaps some obscure country gentleman who, after my disgrace at Court, would be considered, providing he was wealthy enough to meet my father's demands.

I had heard from these visitors from time to time about the wars in which we were engaged. We were now allies of the Pope and the Emperor. My father's reward from the latter had been due to his services in helping to strengthen the bond between him and King Henry.

I often thought of that time at Ardres and Guines when the two Kings had so falsely made their pact of friendship . . . the jousting, the wrestling . . . all the pomp and show. What a pitiful waste it had been! How much better it might have been if the money had been spent for the good of their countries instead of bolstering up the arrogance and egoism of the sovereigns.

And now they were enemies.

So I was always interested when my father's friends came with news of what was happening.

We were seated at supper, I remember, in the great hall, and my stepmother was flushed with her efforts to provide my father's friends with a meal worthy of his state. As we talked, I could see that her eyes were on the serving men and women, and I guessed that her thoughts were in the kitchen.

And then came the news. 'The King of France is now the Emperor's prisoner.'

'King François!' I cried.

'Exactly, Mistress Anne. He was deserted by the Constable de Bourbon. The papal troops had driven the French out of Italy, and our soldiers, with those of the Emperor, were invading the north of France. The King of France had put up a good fight on all fronts on which he was being attacked and for a while had some success. But in February the Emperor's troops completely routed the French at Pavia and the result is that François is the Emperor's prisoner. He is kept in Madrid.'

I felt very sad when I thought of him . . . his gallantry, his wit, his love of beauty, his self-assurance. A prisoner! Surely not François! 'He will have to give up a good many of his conquests, I doubt not,' I said.

Then I wanted to hear more about the situation. In a way, I regarded France as partly my country since I had been brought up there. These people were not just names to me. I wondered what Louise was feeling now that her Caesar was the Emperor's prisoner; but most of all I was sorry for Marguerite. She would be beside herself with grief.

Later I heard that he had become very ill in his prison and would have died but for the fact that Marguerite had gone to Spain to nurse him. There was something very beautiful about the bond between those two, although people tried to besmirch it and accuse them of incest. I had never believed that. I could understand relationships that did not have a physical nature. Many people could not. I think they were apt to judge what their conduct would be in certain situations and imagine that others would act in exactly the same manner.

I thought about François and Marguerite a great deal and tried to get news of them. But soon after this my own life began to change, and my thoughts were all of my own affairs.

My father came to Hever. He seemed a little more interested in me and was quite affable. Prosperity suited him. Viscount Rochford was even more pleased with life than Sir Thomas Boleyn had been.

He said to me: 'We cannot have you living like a country wench for ever.'

I thought: Now it is coming. I shall be presented with some country gentleman and must be ready to listen to his virtues and how he would make an adequate husband for one who cannot expect better, having disgraced herself at Court.

But this was not so.

'It is possible,' he said, 'that I might find a place for you in the Queen's household.'

Great excitement possessed me. I should be there. Thomas would be there. George would be there. Mary, too . . . and my father.

So I was to go. My sins were forgotten. I was no longer the outcast.

The Pursuit Begins

I was nineteen in that year of 1526 when I returned to Court. I had gleaned some wisdom from my years of exile. I was no longer the guileless girl who had fallen in love with Henry Percy and believed in the easy road to happiness. I was hardened by experience, and I made up my mind never to be hurt like that again.

I should be guilty of false modesty if I denied that my coming to Court created a sensation. From the first moment I appeared, I was noticed. I had a natural flair for dress, and my apprenticeship at the Court of France had enhanced this, for while my gowns called immediate attention to me, there was nothing flamboyant about them. It was the style – and the manner in which I wore them. I favoured the long hanging sleeves – which became known as the Boleyn Sleeves – not out of choice but because they hid that sixth nail. I wore a band of velvet about my neck on which was set a small diamond; this hid the mole which had caused me so much distress. It was not long before the fashion was for long hanging sleeves and a band about the neck, but no one else achieved quite the same effect. I had designed these sleeves for myself and they were mine alone. They never looked quite the same on anyone else. Moreover, those who favoured the neckband forgot that I had a longer and more slender neck than is usual, and the band was most becoming to this. For some reason, though they copied me, they never looked quite like me.

Having been banished from the Court, I felt especial gratification in the effect I had created. George and Thomas Wyatt were constantly at my side. But there were others . . . mostly men, among them Henry Norris, a very attractive man and a great favourite of the King, who had given him honours, as he was accustomed to do with those whom he especially liked. He was married to Mary Fiennes, the daughter of Lord Dacre, and had one son; but his wife was not at Court and it seemed to be a not very happy marriage, for Sir Henry showed little regret for her absence.

Another in our group was young Francis Weston. He had just been made a page and was a great favourite of the King because he excelled at all games. He was the King's tennis partner and they played bowls and dice together. The King was always good humoured when he lost to Weston, and it was said that the boy added greatly to his income through his winnings at games.

Francis used to gaze at me with frank admiration, and I had to admit that I liked that.

It was really very gratifying after being so despised and banished to be received back in this manner. Thomas Wyatt had professed his love for me; Norris's eloquent looks betrayed his feelings for me, and with the youthful devotion of Francis Weston I felt very cherished.

There was always some sort of masque going on at Court, and I, with our little group, was usually at the centre of it. Tom Wyatt was by far the best of the poets, though my brother was quite a good versifier, and Norris was inventive in devising scenes and situations. Since we had been together, the entertainments had become more classical; we introduced themes from the Greeks and moved away from that type which the King had so loved – such as a party of travellers arriving from the East, or somewhere exotic – in splendid costumes and dancing among the company until their identity was betrayed and the tall one turned out to be the King. At first we had thought he might not approve but there was a side to him which loved literature and good music and he had a keen mind so that he could follow allusions; consequently our little pieces became favourites of his.

Mary was a little rueful. She was very frank with me. She

told me that she thought the King was no longer interested in her. Her reign had been long but now it appeared to be over.

'Are there any rewards for long service?' I asked.

'I never wanted rewards, Anne,' she replied seriously.

'No. I expect that is why you lasted so long.'

'You are so cynical now. What makes you so, sister?'

'Long experience of life.'

'You have always been rather bitter about me . . . and the King.'

I turned to her and said: 'I hate to see us humiliated. Why should we be picked up and dropped . . . just as it suits them? We should stand out against it. That is what I feel. And you, Mary, have pandered to it. You have demeaned not only yourself but our sex.'

'I never heard such talk.'

'I don't suppose you have. You have been honoured because your partner in adultery was the King. Suppose it had been one of the stable-men, what then?'

'Anne!'

'The principle is the same. Cannot you see that?'

She shook her head. 'In any case,' she said, 'it is all over now.'

'Are you sure?'

She nodded. 'He is brooding . . . absent-minded. The last time I saw him he was simply not aware of me. I was dismissed before I had had a few words with him. I think there is someone else.'

'Who is she?'

'I don't know.'

'We soon shall, I suppose,' I said. 'These matters have a way of forcing themselves on the public notice. Everyone knew of you, in spite of all the discretion.'

'Yes. It cannot be hidden long.'

'You don't look broken-hearted.'

'Oh . . . I'm sorry. It was great fun . . . but I always knew it would end at some time . . . and Will is so patient.'

'As becomes a complaisant husband.'

'You shouldn't be scornful of me. Our father has not done too badly. George either.'

'No. There is that. Our father can say, "Well done, thou good and faithful daughter." I'm sorry, Mary, but I cannot like it.'

I marvelled at her. She had that kind of temperament which would enable her to sail comfortably through life. She saw no evil, thought no evil, said no evil ... therefore for her, there was no evil. It was the way to live. Perhaps I should have learned from Mary.

I often thought about the Queen. I had noticed a change in her on my return. She had aged considerably. She must long ago have accepted the fact that she could not keep up with her husband. She turned a blind eye on his amorous adventures, just as Claude had with François. But she had not had to face that blatant infidelity as Claude had. At least Henry was, in a manner, discreet; and it was easy for the Queen to make a pretence of not knowing about his *amours*, whereas it would have been farcical for Claude to have done so.

Queen Katharine was gentle and kind to me. I think she was a little sorry for me because my proposed marriage to Henry Percy had been so ruthlessly prevented, but I could understand that she might not feel very friendly towards our family since Mary was a member of it; yet she showed no rancour to me – nor in fact had she to Mary.

I had my duties in her household, but there was plenty of spare time for Court activities. The Queen had, if that were possible, become more devoted to religion than ever and a great deal of her time was spent with her confessor and in prayer. She seemed to be suffering from some lingering illness which brought her pain and exhaustion. Often she would be unable to attend the evening's entertainment, but that did not mean that we, her ladies, could not; our services were often in demand.

I often think of Katharine now. I have to confess I did little then. My great pleasure was in my freedom from her sombre presence.

I was happy at this time because I realized that I had recovered from my disappointment in my love affair and I had discovered that it was not true, as I had once thought, that I should be wretched for ever. In addition I had learned a great deal. I should never be carried away again. I doubted that I should ever love anyone as I had loved Henry Percy; that had been a love which had surprised me for he had been no Adonis, no dashing hero; yet I had loved him for his weakness, and even now I did not blame him, but those who had prevented our marriage. The life I had imagined with him still remained an idealistic dream. I often wondered whether if we had married I should have become that gentle, tender wife – rather like my stepmother – thinking first of him and our children and so going on in peace to the end of my life. Knowing myself, that seemed hardly likely; but sometimes I thought it was not an impossible dream.

And now here I was – experienced, understanding something of human nature, determined never to be hurt again, making sure that always my head should be in command of my heart, perhaps making a brilliant marriage. I was not sure about that. But at last I felt myself no longer vulnerable . . . I was well warned against the blows of misfortune. I could protect myself and the thought exhilarated me.

Moreover, I had discovered something. I could draw men to me in a rather inexplicable way. Mary's attraction was obvious. Someone had said it was Promise. She displayed her delight in sexuality, and that was an immediate magnet. It brought her lovers in plenty – not always constant, but how many lovers were? My brother George was good looking and had a great fondness for the opposite sex. It was natural that he should have considerable success with them. I was quite different. I had a certain aloofness, a disdain for men. I did not crave for a lover; in fact, I was determined that there should be no dallying with me. One would have thought this would act as a deterrrent, as I had seen it did in some others; but in me it was like a magnet. I seemed to challenge them. My looks were unusual. I was not pretty like Mary, nor did I have George's good looks. I was like a changeling. Dark, strange . . . with my Frenchified clothes and manners. But I had learned that what I had drew people to me.

So there I was, no longer suffering from the scars of a broken love affair, surrounded by a group of admirers, excelling in dancing and playing the lute, the centre of attraction.

I revelled in this new situation, and following on my long exile it was particularly alluring. I was going to enjoy it.

And then suddenly I realized what was happening.

It was unlikely that the King would be unaware of one who was often to the fore in the festivities.

In the dance, where partners were exchanged from time to time, I found myself face to face with the King. He dominated the Court, of course, not only on account of his size. He scintillated. He took my hand and said: 'It pleases me to see you at my Court, Mistress Boleyn.'

I bowed my head.

'Your Grace is kind.'

'I like to be kind . . . to those who please me.'

I lowered my eyes. My heart was beating wildly. There was no mistaking that expression. I had seen it before in those little blue eyes in the garden at Hever.

He was holding my hand firmly and smiling at me.

We danced and I was passed on to my next partner. I was very disturbed. I knew what was coming. He had finished with one sister and he would try the next.

'No,' I said to myself. 'Never.'

I did not sleep very much that night. I tried to re-create in my mind that scene in the garden, recalling, as far as I could, every word that had been spoken. He had gone along with the play-acting for a while and then he had grown angry. I had offended him by feigning a headache. 'Tell her she should not linger too long in the rays of the sun.' He had said something like that.

I will never submit, I told myself. And the result? Banishment. Back to life at Hever.

Well, that was better than being taken up for a while and then being discarded, as Mary had been. Was this why she had been given her *congé*? Perhaps he did not want to be engaged with two sisters at the same time.

I had to be prepared. I had to be strong.

It was not long before he made his intentions clear. He did not send for me, which he could easily have done, but he was aware that if it were known that he had summoned me to his presence there would be talk. He always deceived himself that members of the Court did not know of his actions, whereas they were never in doubt. It might be that already someone had interpreted the glances which he had sent my way and they were saying: So Anne Boleyn is to be the next. I imagined the chortles of amusement. Meet and fitting! Off with the elder sister first and then on with the younger.

But it should not be so.

He contrived to come upon me one day when I was alone in a chamber close to the Queen's apartments.

He was smiling, looking at me with those eyes, which seemed too small for his large face, shining so that they glinted like aquamarines, the little mouth which could at times look grim, slack, in a satisfied way.

'Ah,' he said. 'Mistress Boleyn.'

'Your Grace,' I said, bowing.

He came towards me, overpowering, glittering, menacing to my mind.

'I have seen you at Court,' he said, 'and it pleases me.'

'Your Grace is kind.'

'But it is not our first meeting, eh?'

'No, Your Grace.'

He pointed a finger at me in a jocular manner. 'Our first

meeting . . . I remember it well. You played a little trick on me.'

'Your Grace, I was young and foolish . . .'

'And you are so no longer? You are an added glory to our Court. Your voice delights me. I can hardly think of one who plays better on the lute.'

Now was the time to say that none could excel His Grace – but I did not.

I stood there, tense, wondering what I must do.

'Because your singing and playing have pleased me, I should like to show my pleasure. So I have brought this for you.' From his pocket he drew a necklet of diamonds and emeralds. He held it before me, his eyes shining with pleasure . . . his hands ready to clasp it round my neck.

I drew back. I said: 'Your Grace overwhelms me with his kindness.'

' 'Tis but a trifle,' he said. ' 'Tis nothing to what I do for those I care for.'

'My Lord . . . my King . . .' I stammered, for I knew now what rôle I had to take. 'Your bounty overwhelms me, but I cannot accept this gift.'

'Cannot accept it? What mean you?'

'Your Grace . . .' I lifted my eyes to his face fearfully, as well I might. The little eyes were beginning to cloud a little, the mouth was hardening. 'I . . . I am a simple girl . . . I cannot accept such a gift . . . even from Your Highness. I could only take such jewels from the man who would be my husband.'

'This is nonsense.'

'My lord . . . it is what I have always believed. I could not in honour accept such a gift. I trust Your Grace will understand the feelings of a simple girl who has been brought up to respect her honour and preserve it until she shall bring it to her husband.'

He was bewildered. I looked at him in trepidation.

'Then,' he said, 'I have been mistaken.' He thrust the necklet into his pocket and strode out of the room.

I was trembling. What now? I visualized being sent back to Hever. The Court life which I was beginning to enjoy, and which had done so much to lift me out of my melancholy, was over.

Perhaps I had been wrong. My father's advancement and that of George would be over. But I could not help it. I had to let him know that I was not like my sister and I was not prepared to demean myself for any man ... not even the King.

*

I waited for the blow to fall. Nothing happened. I helped Thomas and George to write the masque. I went about my duties in a daze, expecting every day to be told I must leave the Court. Then I began to think that he had forgotten the incident. It had not been of any great importance to him. If only that were true. But I noticed him at the festivities; he would sit, frowning every now and then, and I would find his eyes following me.

Once we were partners in the dance as we had been before. 'You flouted me,' he said. 'It is not the first time.'

'I humbly beg Your Grace's pardon,' I said quietly, 'but I must be true to my principles.'

'I like not those who disregard my wishes.'

I thought then that he was probably thinking of a greater punishment than exile. He was really angry with me.

And still nothing happened.

Then one day he sent for me and I was prepared for the worst. We were alone in a small chamber. His mood had changed. He was no longer angry, merely sorrowful.

'I am the King of the realm, am I not?' he asked.

I lowered my eyes. Such a question was obviously rhetorical.

'I have given my life to the comfort of my people, and yet there is one among them who would cause me great pain.'

I raised my eyes and looked at him in surprise.

'Have done,' he said. 'You know to whom I refer. It is you, Mistress Boleyn. You have plagued me ever since the first moment I set eyes on you.'

'Your Grace, I meant no . . .'

'I know now why I have been so patient. I have been lenient. You have flouted me. In your father's garden you mocked me . . . then you pleaded a headache to avoid my presence. I should have commanded you to appear. I should have confounded you. But what did I do? I said, "She is but a girl. Let be." And I was tender towards you, was I not? And did you show me gratitude? No, you prate of your principles. You could have gone off to the wilds of Ireland, but I stopped that. You might have married that snivelling Percy, but I saved you from that, too. And why? Because I could see that you were different from all others, and where I wanted you to be was at my Court. I could see that you were saucy . . . haughty, too. I like that not in my subjects . . . and I let you go. I said I would forget the feelings you had aroused in me. And now here you are, back in my Court, and I can no longer hide from myself . . . nor from you . . . the true state of my heart. I am in love. By the saints, I never felt this for any other. I want you, and when you are mine I promise you I will forsake all others.'

I was surprised, but I was not unprepared for I had thought often of what I must do if confronted by such a situation. True I had not expected him to be so definite or vehement in his protestations, but I was ready, and I knew what I must do and do it quickly.

I said: 'I think, my noble and worthy King, that you speak these words in mirth, to prove me, without intent of degrading your princely self. Therefore to relieve you of the labour of asking any such question hereafter, I beseech Your Highness most earnestly to desist and take this my answer – which I speak from the depth of my soul – in good part. Most noble King, I would rather lose my life than my virtue, which will be the greatest and best part of the dowry I shall bring my husband.'

He could not believe he was hearing aright. I wondered how many times he had been repulsed. Surely this was the first.

He must be furiously angry to be so rejected. I was really rather surprised to see the softness of his expression. Later I learned of that sentimental streak in his nature which so oddly mingled with the cruelty of which he could be capable. His character was such a mass of contradictions, which was why he was such a dangerous man to deal with. He could respect virtue while he was planning an onslaught upon it.

'Rise,' he said, for I had knelt as I spoke.

I did so, and for a few seconds we stood looking at each other.

Then he said: 'You speak with conviction.'

'I mean every word I have said.'

His mouth hardened. 'I shall continue to hope,' he muttered.

With great daring I replied: 'I understand not, most mighty King, how you should retain hope. Your wife I cannot be in respect of mine own unworthiness and also because you have a queen already. Your mistress I will not be.'

He looked at me as though I had struck him. Then abruptly he left me.

*

I was in a terrible quandary. I could sense danger all round me. I was amazed that I could have spoken so boldly to him, but what else was there for me to do? The only way I could please him was to submit; and there would be the story of Mary Boleyn all over again.

I tried to reason with myself. Was I attaching too much importance to the matter? He had had mistresses before and although he was not as promiscuous as François had been and liked to conduct his affairs with a certain secrecy, it was well known in the Court that he was attracted by women.

It was only my determination not to be one of them which had given me the courage to speak as I had.

Perhaps he would accept my refusal and put me out of his mind. François might have tried some trick if he were really eager; I did not think Henry would. I thought his pride was such that he would dismiss me from his mind. If he would only do that and allow me to continue with my life at Court, I should be greatly relieved.

I decided I must confide in someone, and there was no one I could trust as I did George.

I sought him out as soon as possible.

'You look disturbed, George,' I said when I saw him, as indeed he did.

'As I might well be,' he answered.

'You, too!'

'You mean you are also. What ails you?'

'Tell me your trouble first.'

'It is Jane, of course.'

He was referring to his wife. I knew their marriage was a stormy one. I had never liked Jane Parker and had always thought it was a pity he had married her. So did he. It had been considered a fairly good match – otherwise my father would not have agreed to it. Jane was the daughter of Lord Morley; they were a noble but impoverished family and Lord Morley had been unable to meet my father's demands for the dowry. The King had actually come to the rescue and made up what Morley could not afford. It was a sign of the King's favour towards the Boleyns at that time – and all due of course to Sister Mary. What a pity it had worked out as it had!

Jane was as different from George as one person could be from another. She was dull and stupid; she could not understand his wit and she was very jealous. I think she loved him passionately but, being Jane, did not know how to attract him. Her possessiveness made her repulsive to him, and it was true, of course, that he was not the most faithful of husbands.

'Another of her jealous outbursts?' I asked.

'If only she were not so stupid, it might be worth while reasoning with her. She never understands anything. She gets an idea in her head and goes on repeating it.'

'Has she discovered you in some misdemeanour?'

'She does not need to discover. She invents. She says that I care more for you than for her.'

'For me?'

'Yes, you, sister. She says I am dancing attendance on you like Wyatt and the rest of them, and she reckons I should have married you instead of her.'

I burst out laughing.

'Did you tell her that a man may not marry his sister?'

'You cannot tell Jane anything. Now tell me what is bothering you.'

'It is the King.'

He stared at me.

'He has made a proposition to me.'

'And you?'

'I have told him it is impossible.'

'I knew, of course, that he was interested in you.'

'How?'

'It was obvious. He watches you all the time. Mary has been dismissed. He has not been interested in her for some time. It had to wane, but, being Mary, so easy and always ready to placate, he must have found her soothing. She became rather a habit with him, and the affair dragged on . . . almost like a marriage. She was so undemanding. But since you have been at Court, he has been rather unnaturally abstemious.'

'I can't believe this is because of me.'

'He has a sentimental streak. He has romance in his nature. He has changed quite a lot. He is quieter . . . thoughtful. It seems to me that he must truly be in love.'

'Kings don't fall in love like ordinary mortals. They just

look at the object of their desire and say, Come.'

'And you?'

'I have told him that I will not be his mistress and I cannot be his wife by reason of my lack of royalty – my unworthiness, I called it, and I reminded him that he already has a wife – so the matter is closed.'

'By my troth, you are a bold one.'

'I meant it, George. But I am uneasy.'

'As you might well be.'

'What do you think he will do?'

'It's hard to say. He has done nothing so far. I expect the Boleyns will be out of favour. A pity ... when I was just beginning to make my way.'

'I'm sorry.'

He put his hand over mine. 'I am joking,' he said. 'It is a tricky matter to flout the King.'

'I know. I did it before. That was long ago on our first meeting. I pretended I did not know who he was. I was, apparently, saucy. He forgave that. But did you know that it was he who stopped the Butler marriage?'

He looked at me in amazement.

'Yes ... and my marriage to Henry Percy, too.'

'I wondered about Butler. It was very mysterious. Our father was most put out, but Wolsey warned him not to mention the matter to the King. Piers Butler has been enjoying the estates ever since. So ... that was the explanation!' He looked at me incredulously. 'But it was so long ago. Why has he left it all this time? I'd say he must be very much affected by you.'

'I was exiled to Hever ... He came down soon after. I was at Allington while he was at Hever. But I never heard anything afterwards. That was three years ago. If he was interested, he has a strange way of showing it.'

'It is very strange. I have no doubt that he is greatly taken with you now ... and I can understand it. Nobody at Court could be unaware of you. You are the leading light. You have many admirers, and the King has always liked to be at the head of the chase. And . . . he expects to win. Everyone must stand aside while he claims the victory. It has ever been thus. I can only think that he had some notion about the closeness of your relationship to Mary. I believe it might be considered some sin or other . . . almost as though Mary were his wife. He would have very strong views on matters like that. To tell the truth, Anne, he always has one eye on Heaven, assuring God and the saints that what he is doing is all for the good of his people. He must justify himself. It's strange really. He has power . . . complete power over us all . . . and while he uses it to his own ends, he wants to deceive the heavenly hosts into thinking that he is acting according to his conscience. It has to be stretched sometimes but he is a man who knows how to be lenient with himself . . .'

'What shall I do, George?'

'You will have to wait for him to make the next move.'

'And when he does?'

'It depends on what that move is.'

'If he is annoyed, and I somehow think he will be, for it must be a bitter blow to him that someone refuses him, what do you think he will do?'

George shrugged his shoulders. 'It will be a blow, yes, but you tackled it in the right way . . . all that talk of virtue will touch him. He'd think of the recording angel up there making a few notes, and in his heart he knows that when his time comes he can't take his crown and the power and the glory with him. Wait and see what comes next. He may accept what you say and give you up as the one prey he was unable to catch. On the other hand, when he thinks about your temerity in refusing him, he may trump up some charge and have you dismissed from Court. I think you must be prepared for that. Your presence here would remind him of his failure and I do not think he would like that.'

'I should hate to go, George. It was so dull . . . but now it would be more so.'

'There is an alternative.'

'What?'

'Follow in our sister's footsteps.'

'That I should never do! And you should know better than to suggest it. I have been so ashamed of Mary. It is so humiliating ... that ... and what happened at the French Court.'

'Those French gallants were not so gallant after all, I know.'

'All talking of her in that ribald way!'

'Henry would not do that. He does not discuss the details of his *amours* with anyone. It would be against his image of himself. Besides, I am sure he convinces himself that he is quite faithful to the Queen.'

'I am very uneasy.'

'If anyone can handle this, you can. Be prepared for whichever way the wind blows. I am. And if we are stripped of our honours, we shall have to go back to merchanting in London. At least it would be interesting.'

'George,' I said, 'you are a comfort. I knew you would be.'

'Don't fret. Whatever it is, we'll face it.'

*

Thomas noticed that I was preoccupied.

I had taken to wandering off down to the river – the Court was at Greenwich – and watching the boats sail by. I hardly saw them because I was thinking deeply of all I was going to miss in this life.

It was only a day since the King had spoken to me and I had not seen him since. At any moment I expected to be told that I was to leave. He would not tell me himself. There would be some order, vaguely suggesting that it would be better for me to return to Hever.

Thomas had seen me and came to talk to me.

'Why so sad? Why alone? How have you managed to escape

your admirers?'

'It seems that I have not done so entirely,' I replied.

'This one would find you wherever you were. But tell me, Anne, what is on your mind?'

'It is the King,' I said.

'He has made certain suggestions?'

'You have guessed aright.'

'I thought I saw it coming.'

'It was so obvious to you then?'

'Fairly. He is not one to hide his feelings. I saw his eyes following you with a certain expression. Interest is too mild a word to describe it.'

'I am afraid.'

He nodded.

'You understand that I do not want to be like my sister.'

'I do. You are proud. You would not surrender until you love. Is that so?'

'Yes, it is.'

'Dear Anne, how I wish . . .'

'Life is as we make it, I suppose. It is no use wishing it were different.'

'Where's the harm in wishing?'

'None, I suppose, as long as you remember that it cannot be.'

'I often think of those days at Hever and Allington . . . and in Norfolk. It seems like fate that our families should be together both in Kent and in Norfolk. We should have plighted our troth then.'

'As children?'

'Why not? Was there not always that special feeling between us?'

'If I remember rightly, both you and George despised me for my youth and sex.'

'Put that down to the folly of the young.'

'You and George used to talk of great adventures, how you would go forth and win battles and honours. I do not remember that *I* had any part in them.'

'But I always loved you, Anne.'

'Thomas, I think that, like so many of your sex, love is something apart from the rest of your lives ... a pleasant diversion to return to when the adventures begin to pall.'

'Was that how it was with Percy?'

I shook my head sadly. 'No ... that was where he was different. With him, I should always have been first.'

'So much so that he allowed himself to be married off very quickly to Shrewsbury's daughter.'

'Poor Henry, he just could not stand out against the pressure. You know how fearsome Northumberland could be. Besides, the King insisted. So did Wolsey.'

'They made quite an issue of that affair.'

I shivered and he turned to me. 'Let's get away from Court. Let's defy them all.'

I laughed at him. 'You have been sitting too long in the sun,' I told him, and I remembered that was what the King had said of me.

'You know Elizabeth and I do not live together. Our marriage is a disaster.'

'Most marriages seem to be,' I replied.

'They are usually brought about for the convenience of the family.'

'Is that the reason why they are so unsuccessful?'

'Who knows? Anne, what are you going to do?'

'I deplore the manner in which your sex treats mine. You think of us as playthings for a while, and when that particular toy no longer excites you, you reach for another. Do you think I would ever be submitted to such humiliation?'

'No.'

'Therefore I will be no man's mistress.'

'Not even the King's?'

I shook my head vehemently.

'You're playing a dangerous game, Anne.'

'It was not of my choosing.'

'In a way you are to blame. You have made yourself outstanding at Court.'

'I have been myself. That is all I can be.'

'There is always something to be done. I think you care for me a little. Just suppose they had not married me off . . . just suppose I were free.'

'You are married, Thomas, so there is no point in considering the matter.'

I touched the jewelled tablet which I wore on a chain about my waist. It was a favourite trinket and I was hardly ever without it. It had my initials engraved on it. I was thinking of what might have happened if Thomas had not been married. Perhaps it would have been a match which could have been approved by my father. The Wyatts were old friends. There would doubtless have been haggling over my dowry . . . but Sir Henry would not have been too hard. I was very fond of Thomas . . . but I was not really in love with him. I told myself I never would be in love again.

One of the links in the chain had broken and the tablet slipped off. I turned it over in my hand; it reminded me of Hever and Allington and the old days.

'You give up too easily, Anne,' he said, coming nearer to me. 'Am I going to spend the rest of my days longing for what might have been?'

I smiled at him. I did not believe he was as deeply involved as he made out to be. He was a practised lover and he had always known how to use words effectively: he was the sort of man who would know how to touch the heart of a susceptible girl. But I was not susceptible. And I had no more intention of becoming Thomas Wyatt's mistress than I had the King's.

'Think about it, Anne. Think about us.'

He leaned farther towards me and took the tablet from my hand.

'I remember this trinket well.'

'I have had it for years.'

He held it in his hand and looked at it lovingly.

I stood up and held out my hand for it. He was beside me, laughing, with a mocking glint in his eyes.

'I shall keep it.'

'No. You will give it back.'

'It will be a memento . . . something that has been near you. I shall sleep with it under my pillow in the hope that in my dreams that which you deny me will be mine.'

'You are ridiculous, Thomas. Give me the tablet.'

He took a few paces backwards, laughing at me. He held out his hand. 'Come and get it,' he said.

As I went to get it, he snatched his hand away and ran.

'Give it back,' I shouted.

'It is mine,' he called over his shoulder. 'I shall never let it go.'

He ran and I went after him. He outstripped me. As he turned the corner of the palace, he help up his hand and the trinket glistened in the sun.

Then he was gone.

*

I did not see the King for several days. I thought his attitude was very strange as it had been throughout our acquaintance. I could not understand why there should have been those great efforts to stop my marrying either James Butler or Henry Percy, and then the long silence. And now the passionate avowal and more silence. It was really very odd. I did wonder, having heard from both George and Thomas, who in their positions at Court knew something of the intimate nature of the King's character, whether his conduct was in some way connected with his relationship with Mary.

But it was more likely to be annoyance with me. He was probably indicating how much he resented my refusal to accept his proposal. Or it may have been that he made such declarations to any woman who might interest him momentarily.

Weston had gathered us together. The King wished a masque to be devised which would outshine all others. It was to take place at Greenwich, where the Court would be for the occasion, and it was to honour the departing French ambassadors.

When the King wanted to impress foreigners – and particularly the French – he liked the entertainment to be of special grandeur.

A great deal had happened since that display at Guines and Ardres which had surpassed all with its pointless flamboyance and which had so quickly shown itself to have been of no value whatsoever. There would never, I guessed, be another Field of the Cloth of Gold.

George was particularly interested in what was going on abroad and he often talked about it. The fate of King François was of particular interest to me. In a way I had been fond of him. I knew he was a libertine, untrustworthy, and that the only true loyalty he had was to his sister and mother, but as a lover – in spite of his numerous affairs – he was constant to only one passion in his life and that was Art. He genuinely cared for it, and I had never forgotten his reverence for great artists. Moreover, I had been very fond of Marguerite. I would always remember her as the model I had looked up to in my youth. She had taught me so much; I had wanted to be like her. She had given me an appreciation of literature which I had never lost. So I was always avid for news of what was happening at the French Court.

I had felt quite sad when I had heard that François had been captured at Pavia and was the Emperor's prisoner in Madrid. I tried to imagine his frustration in such circumstances. It seemed inevitable that he should become sick. There had been a pitiful attempt to escape by changing clothes with a Negro servant who delivered the coal. I could not imagine François as a servant in any circumstances and I was not surprised that the attempt failed. Emaciated, failing in health, there could have been no doubt that he would have died if Marguerite had not gone out to nurse him. She brought her zeal, her energy and her efficiency to over-riding all difficulties and to her determination to save her beloved brother.

Having lived so close to them, I could picture, far better than my brother or Thomas could, their feelings in this terrible situation in which they found themselves. When I heard that on her arrival Marguerite found her brother so near to death that he was ready for Extreme Unction and to take his last farewell of the sister who was so dear to him, I felt deeply shocked. But Marguerite would not accept what seemed to others inevitable. She had not overcome such opposition, and travelled so far, just to say farewell to him. I could imagine her discourse with him. She was an eloquent and convincing speaker and she would be practical, too. She would have forced him to keep his grip on life, for without him she would have no wish to continue. I did not doubt she had taken remedies with her, and in spite of the fact that he was on the threshold of death, she nursed him back to life.

He was free now, but Charles's conditions had been harsh. François had had to agree to relinquish the sovereignty of Flanders, Artois and the Duchy of Burgundy; and moreover to restore to the Constable de Bourbon, whom he considered a traitor, all he had taken from him.

Poor Claude had died. I was very sad to hear of her death. She must have been about twenty-five years old and she had always been a weakling. Nevertheless, she had borne François seven children in spite of her infirmities. I supposed it had worn her out. Perhaps I should not have pitied her. She had never really been unhappy, which must have been because she had shut herself off from worldly matters and given herself to good works and religion, and this had brought her a peace and serenity which I found remarkable.

François was now married to Charles's sister Eleanora, as part of the peace terms. But although he was allowed to leave Madrid, which seemed necessary if he was to recover fully, he

213

had to deliver his two sons, the Dauphin and the Duc d'Orléans, as hostages until the treaty was signed. So the two little boys were sent to Madrid and François had returned. Poor François! They said he had left his youth behind in a Madrid prison.

There were other important events taking place in Europe. Pope Leo had died and Clement VII had replaced him. Wolsey's dream of being Pope had not come true. I could not feel sorry for him. I would never forgive him for what he had done to Henry Percy and because he had regarded me as a foolish girl unworthy to mate with the great House of Northumberland. Wolsey's conduct – although it had been instigated by the King – was unforgivable. I was glad Clement had been chosen instead of him. So he had not gained the papal crown and here he was in England, the servant of an unpredictable master. The King was delighted that he had failed to be elected, so George told me. He could not bear the thought of parting with Wolsey.

I said: 'Is he so important to the King, then?'

'Henry could not do without him. Wolsey has genius. One has to admit that.'

It was true. He was involved in many diplomatic negotiations. His name was a by-word on the Continent. When people thought of influencing the King, they first thought of Wolsey.

However, as soon as François was free, he set about inducing Pope Clement to absolve him from his oath. Clement was no Leo. That he was weak, swaying towards whichever side would bring more benefits to him, became more and more obvious to us later.

He absolved François from his oath, which, of course, meant that François would immediately plan to go to war again.

The power of the Emperor had increased enormously. He was now the most powerful man in Europe. Young as he was, he was proving a statesman of stature, and this gave great concern to those who had previously been his allies. The King, with Wolsey behind him, sought to break the alliance with the Emperor and form a new one with France and the Italian states. This was the reason why the French ambassadors were in England.

I supposed that satisfactory conclusion had been reached and this was to be their farewell entertainment.

Thomas had written the masque. There was a certain amount of mime, poetic lines were to be declaimed and some singing. Several of the ladies would be dressed as nymphs and they were to be disturbed by satyrs from whom they ran in terror to be rescued by heroic knights. It was a setting which had been used many times; the difference was in the singing and the dances, which would be more exciting than anything that had been done before.

During the day the great hall was hung with tapestries. These usually depicted some great battle but at Poitiers, Crécy, Agincourt and suchlike the French had been our enemies, so we fell back on the Field of the Cloth of Gold, which seemed one of the few occasions when there had been amity between our two nations.

Some very artistic scenery had been erected and this never failed to win admiration.

The King would naturally take part. He would be the leader of the knights who rescued the maidens from the satyrs.

There was a great deal of laughter as we planned all this. I often thought the planning was more fun than the actual performance. I had given a lot of attention to what I should wear. Water nymphs should be green but I wanted to wear red and I did. My gown was red velvet but it fell open from the waist to the hem to show a green velvet petticoat. The band about my neck was green velvet, as was the lining of my hanging sleeves. It had been difficult to find a green which toned to my satisfaction, but I decided that the contrast was quite effective.

I felt a mingling of apprehension and excitement. If he ignored me tonight, I was sure that I was safe, for if he had intended to banish me, he would surely have done so by now. Yet suppose his ardour had remained, what then?

My gown was becoming. Perhaps I should have made myself drab. That was something I could not do. Clothes had always been so important to me and I did not think I could be entirely happy when they were not becoming – nor could I be completely happy if they lacked charm.

I wanted to remain at Court. I wanted to be the brightest star of the evening. I wanted admiration from them all, including the King. But *I* must be in control of it and never allow any of them to get beyond desiring, and my instinct warned me that they must do so if their desire was satisfied.

So in high excitement I danced and I sang; I fled in terror from the satyrs; and then out came the knights wearing masks of course in a ridiculous pretence of hiding their identity – their leader tall and commanding, a glittering figure.

I made sure I did not run towards him but almost flung myself into the arms of one of the other rescuing knights. But he was thrust aside and Henry was seizing me.

'Mine, I think,' he said, and I was immediately relinquished.

'Thank you, good knight,' I said, rather apprehensively.

'Have no fear, maiden. You are safe now.'

I was one maiden who felt far from safe.

Then there followed the unmasking of the knights and the exclamations of amazement.

He was looking at me with a boyish expression of pleasure. I think he was expecting me to be overcome with surprise to find that the tall, glittering figure was not a humble knight but the King.

I almost liked him then. There was something appealing in his childlike amusement, his love of a game, his boyish indifference to reality.

But my anxiety was acute. I suffered a great many qualms

216

because I knew that the chase was not over; it was only just beginning.

'I trust,' he said, 'that you are grateful for your rescue.'

'Your Grace is indeed a valiant knight.'

'I was just in the nick of time. I did not care to see you carried off by another.'

'Your Grace is very kind,' I said cautiously.

'And would be kinder.'

I pretended not to hear that.

He had taken my hand. They had started to play a galliard.

'I know you dance like an angel,' he said. 'There is no one who dances as you do.'

Now was the cue. The correct answer was: I am clumsy compared with Your Grace. But I said: 'I have never thought of angels dancing. One sees them playing harps. But dancing . . . never.'

He said: 'You like to tease, Mistress Boleyn.' That was a hint of reproof. Be careful. I did not like that little mouth. It was slack and happy at the moment, but I knew it could be cruel.

I said: 'Did not Your Grace think the scene was well done?'

'Yes . . . yes . . . that was Wyatt, I dareswear.'

'And the nymphs . . . they were charming, were they not?'

'I only saw one of them.'

'Your Grace!'

'Have done. You know my heart.'

'I can add nothing to what I told Your Grace at our last meeting.'

'We'll see,' he muttered, his lips tightening – the spoilt boy, I thought, who has been told he may not have another sugar plum.

We gave our attention to the dance. People stood apart from us. I was more than a little uneasy. He had already shown his preference for me by choosing me from among the nymphs. There would be a great deal of talk now. I imagined the sly comment: Off with the elder sister; on with the younger.

No, I told myself vehemently. It shall not be.

But I knew in my heart that this passion of his was something which could not be lightly thrust aside.

I was aware of the Queen. She was watching us and there was an expression of infinite sadness in her eyes. I knew that she took little pleasure in occasions of this nature, but for this one she must put in an appearance.

I was remembering that she had been married to him for many years. Her youth was over; she looked years older than the King. I thought of all she must have suffered through those miscarriages which had failed to produce the longed-for son. And now she saw him pursuing one of her attendants – myself – and at an entertainment given in honour of her nephew's enemies.

From what I knew of her, her heart was still in Spain. When she spoke of her mother, it was with reverence. I knew she thought often of her childhood, which must have been happy in spite of that stern Spanish Court, because of the love she bore her mother. She had suffered because of the madness of her sister Joanna who had been Queen of Spain and had grown madder when her handsome husband had died. He had cared little for her but she had loved him in her wild, mad way to such a degree that she had his dead body put into a glass case and she carried it round with her wherever she went. Then with the ascendancy of her nephew Charles – a man meant to become a great monarch if anyone was – Katharine felt that her fortunes were going as her mother, Queen Isabella, would have wished. And with the betrothal of her daughter Mary to him, she had been content. But how quickly life changed. Friends of today were enemies of tomorrow. Those whom men loved one day they wanted to be rid of the next.

I felt very sorry for the Queen and I wished it were any but myself whom she must watch being pursued by her faithless husband.

I was glad when the dance was over.

The entertainment must not stop. There would be singing and perhaps we would dance again.

I sang a song, the words of which had been written by one of the Court poets and set to music by another. I knew the King's eyes never left my face as I sang.

He led the applause and then declared he would sing.

'Your Grace,' cried someone, it might have been Norris or Weston, I was not sure. 'I crave your pardon, but might I ask a favour?'

The King was all smiles, knowing what was coming. It had happened so often before.

'Could I make the plea that Your Grace will sing one of your own songs?'

Henry appeared to be reluctant. There was a chorus: 'Please, Your Grace . . . on such an occasion.'

'There is a little thing I have recently composed,' he said, smiling happily, and again I felt that twinge of gentleness; his childish vanity seemed so incongruous with all the pomp and ceremony which surrounded him.

He had a pleasant voice and he accompanied himself on the lute which he played with excellence; if we had not had poets at Court like Thomas Wyatt, his verses would have aroused genuine admiration for their skill. Of course they were declared the finest in the Court, but even he must know that it was the aura of royalty which made them so.

I felt again that rush of tenderness. In spite of everything, he looked a little vulnerable, as though pleading with the Court to like his song.

He was singing for me, and the words sent a shiver through me.

Does not the sun dazzle the clearest eyes
And melt the ice and make the frost retire?

The hardest stones are pierced through with tools
The wisest are with Princes made but fools.

The song finished, he laid his lute on his knees and looked ahead of him – his usually rosy cheeks a deeper shade, a special shine in his eyes.

The applause rang out. People were talking all at once.

'A new song, Your Grace. It was beautiful. The music . . .'

'My own,' said the King.

I did not join in the applause. I sat wondering about the intent behind those words.

'The wisest are with Princes made but fools.' What did he mean? That I was a fool to think myself wise enough to resist him? Did he mean that he would force me into the position he had chosen for me? I could not believe that. I was beginning to understand a little of his character. I knew of the boyish vanity and that strong streak of romance. If I clung to my determination, surely he would never threaten me.

Others sang. Thomas gave them one of his latest poems set to music. A love-song which had also been written for me. I wondered if the King knew. He did not look very pleased. Was that because he knew it was for me or because the verses were so much better than his own?

Now there was dancing. The King would be the first to select the lady of his choice, and others would follow.

He was making his way towards me. I closed my eyes and when I opened them I was looking into those blue ones.

My first thought was: God help me. This is serious. He is making his preference known.

He held out his hand. I put mine in his and he held it firmly, smiling at me.

He said: 'This night I shall dance with none other.'

I did not answer.

'I want all the world to know that it is you I honour,' he went on.

'It is gracious of you . . .'

'Oh, Anne,' he said, 'have done with this game. I know you are not like the others. I know you hold yourself dear . . . but not more dear than I do. You have but to ask and whatever it is shall be yours. Only love me as I love you.'

'Your Grace, I cannot. I have explained. I am still of the same mind, and shall remain so.'

'Didst like my song?'

I was silent and he pressed my hand more firmly. 'The company did,' he said, almost pleading with me to compliment him.

'The company will always applaud Your Grace.'

'You did not like it?'

'It scanned well. The rhyming was excellent.'

'Then what?'

I would be bold. It might well be that I should offend him and that he would be done with me forever. Perhaps a return to Hever would be preferable to what he was insisting on.

'I do not think the wise can ever be made fools,' I said.

'And the sun does not dazzle?'

'The sun dazzles but it does not change opinions.'

'You would instruct us then?'

'I crave Your Grace's pardon. I thought you *asked* for my opinion, otherwise I would not have presumed to give it.'

'I am grieved that you did not like my song.'

'There was much that I liked in it.'

'Oh . . . have done. There are matters of which we two must talk. You know for long I have loved you . . . ever since you were a saucy girl in your father's garden, you have plagued me. I find little satisfaction in others. And now there is no peace for me at all, and there will not be until you give me that for which I crave.'

'Your Grace must forgive me. I am only a simple girl.'

'You . . simple! Oh no, Mistress Anne Boleyn, not that. You are wise, are you not? One of those who will not be made fools by princes?'

'Not wise, but I am as I am, and no one could make me other.'

'You are determined to plague me.'

'I would I could please you.'

'Oh Anne, my Anne, it would be so simple.'

'Not for me, Your Grace. I think the Queen needs me. She is looking my way.'

'But *I* need you.'

'I am one of the Queen's ladies, Your Grace.'

'You are *my* subject. Forget not that.'

'It is a truth I cannot forget.'

'Come, come. You have been shy long enough. By God's Holy Mother, I love you. None other will do for me. I want your answer.'

'Your Grace, you have had my answer.'

'That you love me not?'

'That I love my honour and I would rather die than give it up. I will be no man's mistress.'

I could see the anger in his face – the spoilt boy who had rarely been denied what he wanted since he came to kingship, and I was frightened by the intensity of his desire for me.

'Think on it,' he said. 'And do not be deceived. You are mine. I will not let you escape me.'

The dance could not stop until he decided that it should. It had to go on for some time. The whole of the Court, while they could not hear our dialogue, must be aware of its nature.

I stopped in the dance and bowed to him. He led me back to my place. Although I might appear cool, I was trying to control my trembling limbs.

I lay in bed thinking about everything that had been said. The Court was now aware of the King's passion for me. It was unlike him to make such a public display of his *amours*; before he had always been discreet. It was only the case of Elizabeth Blount which had become common knowledge, and that had been the most serious of all his love affairs. And now he had recognized her son as his.

I could imagine the gossip. 'Not since Elizabeth Blount . . .'

What could I do? I was afraid. There was a certain anger in his passion. I must remember that he was all-powerful. He could ruin my family just as quickly as he had built it up. I appeared to be in a position to carry on the tradition of the Boleyn women and bolster up the family fortunes. Mary had done it. The honours which had come to my father and George had clearly been due to the King's affection for her. How much more could I do for them?

I should be once more in disgrace. My father would never forgive me. His lands, his appointments at Court, the King's favour, his rising riches were all very dear to him. He despised Mary for her lack of acquisitiveness and her humble marriage to Will Carey, who was as spineless as she was. But he had not hesitated to take the spoils she had brought to him.

I wondered what the King would do. It was clear that he would not lightly accept my refusal. In fact, I had an idea that my reluctance made his desire more urgent. He was a great hunter. He as indefatigable in the chase. It was said that in a day's hunting he never failed to tire eight or ten horses. The joy of pursuit was great, and that evening he had shown me that my reluctance to give way to his wishes only made him more determined to bend me to them.

I did not know what I should do, and I determined on flight.

The next day I asked for an audience with the Queen.

There was no change in her attitude towards me. This proud daughter of Spanish kings would not betray the fact that she was even aware of her husband's infidelities.

I knelt before her. I said: 'I wish to leave the Court, Your Grace, and return to my father's house for a while.'

There was a faint flicker of interest in her pale, almost expressionless face.

'When do you wish to go?'

'At once, Your Grace.'

She did not ask the reason. She knew and she applauded

my decision. She could not fail to see how hotly the King was pursuing me, and she thought that was the decision of a good and virtuous girl.

'You will take your maid with you?'

'Yes, Your Grace.'

'Then leave when you will.'

'I thank Your Grace.'

She gave me a sad little smile. 'I hope you will find a solution to your problems, Mistress Boleyn.'

'I thank Your Grace.'

I was dismissed.

And so I returned to Hever.

The Secret Matter

My stepmother was amazed to see me. There had been no time to warn her of my coming.

I threw myself into her arms and clung to her.

She said: 'Anne, you should have let me know. How are you? Are you well? My dear, what does this mean?'

'It means that I am home. I will tell you later on.'

She bustled about. My room must be prepared. She must go to the kitchens. I told her I wanted little to eat.

'Something is wrong,' she said. 'I know it.'

Soon I was telling her.

'It is the King,' I said. 'He has cast his eyes on me . . . as he did on Mary . . .'

'My dear . . . *dear* child.'

'I'll not have him,' I said. 'I have told him so.'

'And you have been sent from Court?'

'I left of my own free will.'

'You will be out of favour for it.'

'I hope so, Mother.'

'It is so sad. If only they had let you marry Henry Percy, you would have been happy.'

'Yes,' I said. 'I was determined to be and I should have been . . . just as now I am determined to be no man's mistress.'

'Well, you shall stay here, my child, and we shall be together as we were. And one day perhaps there will be some man whom you can love.'

'Oh, it is good to be with you.'

'You must eat and sleep and then we shall have lots of talk. You shall tell me everything.'

I lay in my bed.

This could be the end of my Court life. Perhaps I could go to France. What was happening there now? Marguerite might help me. She was a widow now but she had never had any great love for her husband. If I wrote to her, I could tell her how I had followed her sorrows and been very sad for her. I wondered what the Court of France would be like now . . . with François no longer the splendid figure of his youth. But Marguerite would be the same. I would be able to talk to her of Henry's passion as I had once talked of that of François. She would understand and help me.

It was like a raft to cling to in a stormy sea.

The next day I talked to my stepmother. I told her of my conversations with the King; she listened intently and sympathized with me. I was glad my father was not there. I knew he would be eager to throw another daughter of his into the arms of the all-powerful dispenser of honours to the families of his mistresses.

I watched her at her sewing and she told me of the trivialities of life at Hever which were so important to her – how the wine had matured, how the herb garden was growing, how one of the servants was with child by a stable-man.

I listened half-heartedly and thought: This is how my life will become.

But it was not to be.

The following day I was in my room when I heard the clatter of horses' hoofs and I thought at once: It is my father sent to upbraid me, or a messenger from Court perhaps.

I looked out of my window. The King, with a few attendants, was riding into the courtyard.

My stepmother, in a state of extreme nervousness, went out to greet him.

I heard his loud booming voice. 'Lady Rochford, good day to you. It does me good to see you in good health. And Mistress Anne, I hope, is in like case.'

I leaned against my door. So he was not going to let me

escape. I would be firm, though. I should need all my skill to withstand him.

My stepmother was coming up to my room to tell me that he was here, commanding me to appear before him.

The door opened. My stepmother stood there, looking frightened.

'Anne . . .' she began.

And he was there behind her. He was smiling, boyish again, proud of his achievement. See, here I am!

He stood looking at me for a moment, his blue eyes tender, yet burning with passion. I flung back the hair from my face for it was loose and unkempt.

He said: 'You may leave us, Lady Rochford.'

My poor stepmother, bewildered, hesitating but overawed, dropped a curtsy and departed.

He came into the room.

'My Anne,' he said.

I said: 'Your Grace, we are unprepared for the honour of this visit.'

'That matters not at all,' he replied. 'This is not a state affair. This is a lover come for his lass.'

'Your Grace, the honour is great, but . . .'

He was beside me. He had taken my hair in his hands and was pulling me towards him.

'Did you think I would let you run away from me?' he said. 'I will never let you leave me.'

'You find me . . . unprepared.'

'I like it,' he said. 'I find you delightful in any guise.'

'I must help my stepmother. She is overwhelmed by this visit.'

'Nay . . . no need. I came for you . . . not a banquet.'

'But my father will be most upset if we do not treat Your Grace with due respect.'

'Treat me as I would be treated, Anne. I ask nothing more.'

'My lord . . . I am in great distress.'

'I would cause you no distress. I would bring you only joy.'

'Then, my lord . . .'

'Don't say it again,' he said. 'I know your mind. I know you love your honour and I respect that in you. Dost think I am some satyr who would force myself upon a reluctant maiden? That is not so. You have been in my thoughts for a long time. I have tried to put you out of them but when you came back to Court, I knew that was impossible. Now we must act. I have much of importance to say to you.'

'Your Grace, I cannot change my mind.'

'I have thought of that. I will speak long with you and tell you what is in my mind.' His eyes lighted with a touch of mischief. 'We will go to that garden. Do you remember, the scene of our first meeting? There I shall tell you what I plan for us. We will go there. Come with me.'

'I must comb my hair . . . make myself worthy of your presence. I must change my gown.'

'It is not your gown I came to see, sweetheart. To me in any guise you are all that I need. But this is serious talk. It can mean so much to us two. How long shall I wait for you in the garden?'

'Ten minutes.'

'It will seem an eternity, but I can deny you nothing.' He took my hand and kissed it lingeringly. 'Know this,' he said seriously, 'I love you well. No one else shall be your rival. Think of that, and it will incline your thoughts towards me.' He smiled and raised a finger. 'No. Do not say it again. I know it well. My mistress you will not be. That will be the purpose of our discourse. Ten minutes then. No more, sweet Anne.'

'I will be there, Your Grace.'

He left me. I took a comb and combed my hair back from my hot face.

My stepmother came into the room.

'Anne,' she said in dismay. 'I know not what to do. We have no special fare in the kitchens.'

'It is of no importance.'

'The King . . . visiting us like this . . . No warning.'

'He has come to talk to me. He is not interested in food.'

'What does it mean?'

'I do not know. Later perhaps I shall.'

I was feeling calmer every second. He wanted to talk. What could he possibly talk about? He was going to try to persuade me by telling me all he could do for me and mine. Some of my fear had left me. Seeing him face to face had given me courage.

The thought came to me: This is no light matter with him. He really does care for me.

And so I went down to the garden.

He was waiting for me and came swiftly towards me, his arms outstretched. I evaded them by bowing.

'Anne,' he said, 'my sweetheart, all will be well ere long and you and I will be together. Come, sit beside me. Sit close to me. Ah, this is what I long for . . . to be close to you . . . to hold you against me . . . like this. Anne, you are a witch.'

'Your Grace, I am just a simple girl.'

'You were never simple. You were born with that witchery. You have put a spell on me.'

I was momentarily alarmed by this talk of witchcraft. I wondered if I were to be accused of that and burned at the stake. But, of course, he meant witchery of another sort.

'You hold yourself aloof,' he said. 'Oh, do not think I do not respect your virtue.' His little mouth was prudish suddenly. 'It is a virtue I most respect in ladies. But I see a way for us, and that is what I will speak of and you will then see how deep is my love for you and that I will have none other. I will sweep away your scruples. You and I shall love as, from the moment we met, we were meant to.'

'My lord, there is no way in which I will become your mistress.'

'Nor shall you be. But . . . you could be my Queen.'

'That is not possible.'

'That word does not exist for kings, Anne. There is a way

and I believe I have found it. Listen to me. When I first saw you in the gardens, I knew that this was no light emotion which you had aroused in me. When I returned to Westminster, I said to Wolsey . . . yes, these were my very words, I remember them well . . . I said: "Thomas, I have been discoursing with a young lady who has the wit of an angel and is worthy of a crown." Now I look back, I see that my words were prophetic. Wolsey said, "It is sufficient if Your Grace finds her worthy of your love," and I answered that I feared she would never condescend in that way. Wolsey replied that great princes, if they choose to play the lover, had in their power that which would mollify a heart of steel. You will say that your virtue is unassailable, so you must remain virtuous. But I cannot give you up. Now listen. For some time past, my conscience has been troubling me. You know that I married my brother's widow. I was young. I was chivalrous. Katharine was alone in this country. Her father and mine were haggling over her dowry. She was sad and lonely and I have a tender heart . . . as you will discover. I married her, letting pity get the better of wisdom, and in doing so I have offended against the laws of God.'

I listened in amazement.

'For some time,' he went on, 'I have been a most unhappy man. My conscience has never let me rest. Now I feel it cannot be silenced, for when my daughter Mary's union with the son of the King of France was in progress, one of the ambassadors raised the point of Mary's legitimacy.'

'This is . . . impossible!' I cried.

'Nay, my love, and I fear it may well be true. There is a verse in Leviticus which clearly says that a man may not marry his brother's wife and such a union would be without the blessing of God and fruitless.'

'Does the Queen know of your fears?'

'Not as yet. But she will. She must. I cannot go on living a life of sin in the eyes of God.'

'But what would be the outcome?'

'The marriage will be declared no marriage.'

'And the Emperor Charles?'

'He will have to look the truth in the face.'

'But the Queen's relationship with him . . .'

'My dearest Anne, you do not understand these matters.'

'But surely he would not care to see his aunt accused of living in a sinful union?'

'If it be proved . . . as it must be . . . he will have to accept it.'

'After all these years . . .'

'That matters not.' He was a little impatient. He had clearly thought I should greet this news with joy. I could not really believe the dazzling proposition he was putting before me. I could not accept for one moment that he would be allowed to discard his wife in spite of the verses in Leviticus. Whatever they were, I did not believe that the great Emperor would allow his aunt to be shipped back to Spain or perhaps put into retirement in England just like a mistress who had ceased to be desirable and is now to be pensioned off. That was not the way of great monarchs. I felt that Henry was being carried away by this idea which had occurred to him, and I suspected that he was using it as a means of dazzling me with the prospect of a crown – a notion which I felt too wild to bear any semblance to reality – so that I should receive him without delay into my bed. And afterwards? Well, it would be seen to be just a wild dream, and the ministers of Spain and England would explain to him how impossible it was.

I was sceptical. The conscience, I knew, existed. But it had taken seventeen years to arouse itself, and I felt it could easily be subdued in a few weeks once his goal had been reached.

He went on: 'I understand so much now. She could not get a son. Again and again there were disappointments. A king *must* have sons. It is part of his duty to his people. He has to think not only of his own reign but the one to come. The dynasty must go on. And what have I? One daughter.'

'The Princess Mary is healthy and very clever.'

'A girl, Anne. I want a son.'

'There is no Salic Law in England.'

He hit his knee with his fist. 'This country wants a king. I have to give England a male heir. And how can I do that while God frowns on my union with the one who, in His eyes, is not my wife? Anne, once I am free . . . and by God and all His saints, I soon shall be . . . you and I will come together. Now this revelation has come to me. The French ambassador has shown me the way. I have marvelled that I . . . full of health and vigour as I am . . . can get no sons . . . from her. With others . . . You know that at one time I thought myself in love with Elizabeth Blount. She was a handsome girl . . . she danced and sang well . . . I thought excellently, but remember I had not seen you . . . nor heard you then. From now on there could be no other. I was young . . . and affectionate, as is my nature. I had begun to feel a reluctance to share Katharine's bed. You must understand these matters, Anne. And I had a son by Elizabeth Blount. It is only from Katharine that I cannot get boys, because God has turned His face away from our union. For a long time He has been telling me that it must end . . . and only now have I seen it.'

I thought how naïve he was, but perhaps that was why he could deceive himself.

'What does Your Grace propose to do?'

'I have spoken to Wolsey.'

I caught my breath.

'He will help in this?' I asked.

'Sweetheart, he is my servant. He will do as I wish. He sees the need for heirs. He is a clever fellow and will devise a plan. We shall be together ere long, Anne. You will be my Queen. I'll swear there will never have been a more beautiful one . . . and one more worthy to wear a crown. You do not speak.'

'I am overwhelmed.'

He laughed, well pleased. 'As well you might be. But it shall come to pass. I am determined on that. Ere long you and I shall be together, and we'll have boys, Anne . . . you and I.

And what boys they will be! We'll have a brood of princes. What say you?'

'I think there would be difficulties.'

'This is my will.'

'But the Queen is the Emperor's aunt.'

'The Emperor is too busy governing his vast empire to think much of that. Moreover, Wolsey is getting to work on it.'

'Does he know your plans for *me*?'

There was a brief hesitation. 'I have not told him yet. He knows, of course, of my feelings for you.'

'But he thinks I should be your mistress while some foreign princess shall be your Queen. What was it . . .? "Princes have the power to mollify steel . . ." '

'Wolsey has his devious ideas. He is . . . at the moment . . . all for stronger ties with France. When I talked of remarriage, he did mention the Princess Renée of France. I did not think it necessary to be more explicit as yet.'

'It would not occur to him that one as unworthy as I could aspire so high. Yet he himself has climbed far. Was he not a butcher's son?'

'I care not for these matters, sweetheart . . . whether a man be a cook's son or a duke's son . . . it matters not to me. I am a king and a king's son, and it is only those of lesser ranks who concern themselves with such things. If I love a person . . . that is enough for me. Thomas Wolsey is my good friend and has been for years. I love the man. He is the best of servants to me . . . as he was to my father before me.'

'Yet I believe he sought election for the Papacy. That would have taken him from Your Grace's service . . . and set him on equal terms with you.'

'He would have worked for me in Rome. Although I should be sad to lose him, it would have pleased me to have someone there working for England. But enough of this. Here I tell you of our great matter and you prate of Wolsey.'

'I think he may well play a big part in it.'

He slapped his thigh. 'That he will, but Anne, what of your

part and mine. I would it were done with. I would we were now joined together in holy union, as one day we shall surely be. What do you say?'

I did not know what to say. My first thought was that it would never happen. There would be too many to work against it. Henry was all-powerful in England, and if the Queen had been anyone but the aunt of the Emperor Charles, it could have been a possibility. The Emperor might be busy with his Empire but he would never allow a member of his house to be degraded. And that was what the King proposed for Katharine.

I thought of her, with her Spanish pride and her piety, her great dignity, her upbringing. What would her reaction be if she were told: You have been living in sin all these years. This is now revealed. So you are no longer Queen of England.

I could not believe what the King was suggesting would ever take place. But the fact that the King could suggest it showed the intensity of his passion for me – for I knew that his conscience had conveniently reared its head at this time, not because of his desire to live in accordance with the rules of the Bible but because he wished to live in passion with me.

He was beaming at the pond in the middle of the garden; he was so pleased with himself because he had thought up this scheme, and I believed, at that moment, he thought I should be so dazzled at the thought of sharing his throne that I would immediately throw aside the principles I had so forcefully expressed, fall into his arms and become his mistress on the spot.

I was wary. Of course, there was a possibility that it *could* come to pass.

His hand was on my knee. I could feel its heat through the stuff of my gown.

'It will soon be,' he said. 'We can trust Wolsey. He will get this in motion. I am sending him to the Pope. Then, my sweetheart, we shall be together.'

He put his arm round me and crushed me against him. His

lips were on my ear. 'What say you, Anne? What say you?'

'What can I say?' I replied. 'You are not yet free.'

'But soon will be.'

'I am unsure.'

'Do you love me?'

'I am unsure,' I repeated.

'Unsure! I ride out here to see you. I offer you a crown . . . and you are unsure!'

'I do not look for a crown from my husband . . . only fidelity and love.'

'But you shall have all three. I swear I'll not look at another. You shall have no rival. Say that you love me.'

'I must think on this.'

'You do not love some other?'

'No longer. I loved Henry Percy, but he was taken from me. When one has suffered in that way once, one is chary of doing so again.'

'You loved that spindle-legged, spineless creature?'

'Yes. I loved him and I lost him; and now he is most unhappy.'

'He would never be anything else. Shrewsbury's girl despises him as any woman of spirit would.'

'But I loved him.'

'Oh come . . . come . . . It would not have done.' He was suspicious suddenly. 'Was he your lover?'

'My principles have always been the same. I never was and never will be any man's mistress.'

'Soon you will be a Queen.'

'I do not know.'

He was bewildered. He was offering me himself, the greatest catch in the kingdom and a crown to go with it . . . and I was hesitating.

He took my hand. 'We will plight our troth. Give me that ring.' It was one which I wore on my middle finger. It had been in the family for a number of years. 'And I shall give *you* a ring. It will be a sign. Come, Anne, give me the ring.'

I shook my head. 'Your Grace must understand that all this has happened so suddenly. I am bewildered. Please understand.'

He was all softness. His moods changed quickly. 'I know. This has dazzled you. You were not expecting such a prospect. Let me be with you tonight and I will show you how it is between us two.'

'No,' I said firmly. 'I could not be happy.'

He turned to me almost angrily. I was certain then that he had thought the project he was opening before me would overwhelm and delight me to such an extent that I would fall into his arms. Now he was the small boy again about to be deprived of a coveted toy. His hot hands burned through my dress. He said roughly: 'You forget to whom you speak. I could command you. I could take you here and now if I wished and snap my fingers at this virgin's talk.'

I stood up and holding my head high, I said: 'That is true. You could do that. But you will not because if you did I should never love you. And being a king you are also a knight and I should be much mistaken if you, powerful as you are, ever forgot the laws of chivalry, which you would most certainly do if you behaved in the way you suggest towards an unprotected woman.'

It was the right note. The lust left his eyes and there was the shining knight, courteous and chivalrous. The thought occurred to me then: It would not be difficult to handle him.

'And now, my lord,' I went on, 'if you will give me leave to retire, I shall do so; and my stepmother and I will endeavour to find hospitality which, though it will not be worthy of you, will be the best we can offer as your arrival was unexpected.'

He stood close to me and taking my hand, he kissed my finger with the ring for which he had asked.

'Anne . . . Anne, I am beside myself with longing for you.'

'If that be so, my lord, you will give me time to ponder on what you have told me.'

'And then I shall have my answer?'

'Yes, then you shall have it.'

'I cannot leave here until I know you will be mine.'

'I will tell you before you leave tomorrow morning.'

'Then I must possess myself in patience.'

He was complacent. He could not believe that even I, who had been so difficult to woo, could refuse a crown.

When I was alone, I felt exhausted.

I found it hard to believe that I had heard correctly. He would rid himself of Katharine and marry me! How could that possibly be? Whatever he said, he was married to Katharine. No one could discard the daughter of kings just because she was no longer desirable.

That was the crux of the matter. I dismissed the conscience as I felt it deserved to be. The fact was he was tired of Katharine and he had been for a long time, and he was obsessed by his desire for me. How I wished I could have consulted Marguerite about the matter. I wondered what she, who was essentially worldly, would say.

What if I refused? How long would he pursue me? I had had little warning signs even now. That expression of impatience in his eyes . . . He was not accustomed to being denied. To give way to him would mean to become his mistress. But was there the faintest possibility that I could become his Queen?

I looked at myself in the mirror and saw the crown on my head. I could not deny that the thought dazzled me. To be the Queen presiding over the Court. All would be my slaves, bowing to my will – including the King. Master Wolsey, who had called me a foolish girl and had destroyed my marriage to the man I had loved disinterestedly, would have to pay homage to me. That would give me great pleasure.

I should have to marry sometime . . . someone my father would choose for me. It would not be a love affair – just a suitable match which my father would want. But what of the most brilliant match of all: Queen of England? Could it be possible? It might just be. He was powerful, so was Wolsey . . .

if they worked for it ... if they could placate the Emperor Charles ... Excitement possessed me. It was a bewildering but exhilarating prospect.

I dressed myself with care – scarlet velvet, hanging sleeves and a red band about my throat with its one solitary diamond. Excitement had added something to my eyes; they looked enormous and very bright, and the faintest colour showed in my cheeks.

I went down to the great hall. My stepmother had performed a miracle. She had set them to work in the kitchens and they had provided an excellent meal. The King sat at the head of the table, my stepmother on one side of him, I on the other.

He was beaming, well content.

He liked my stepmother's awe of him and her anxiety that the food should be well served and to his liking. He kept reassuring her that he had rarely enjoyed a meal so much.

Then he turned to me as though to say that it was my presence that made his pleasure.

Later I sang and played the lute and he and I sang a duet.

It must have been rarely that he spent an evening without all the pomp and ceremony to which he was accustomed; but it was quite clear to everyone that he was pleased and happy.

When I retired to my room, I found sleep impossible. I had a terrible fear that in spite of my comments on chivalry he might come to me. But he did not.

I rose early in the morning. I had expected that by the light of day I should see the absurdity of what he had suggested and realize it was just empty talk to get access to my bed. But instead it seemed to me that there was a faint possibility that it could come to pass. I had made up my mind that I was going to accept him. I would let him know that if he were free I would be his wife.

Now it began to look like an exciting adventure.

He was eagerly waiting to see me.

He looked at me yearningly. Surely he loved me. He could

238

not have been so restrained if he had not. Again I felt that tenderness towards him. I thought I could be quite fond of him; and a woman would be a fool to turn her back on such a glittering proposal.

He said: 'Have you aught to say to me, Anne?'

I took the ring from my finger and gave it to him. I felt happy to see the joy which suffused his face. He closed his eyes as if in an ecstasy. I thought: He really does love me. And I experienced something more than gratification. I felt happy.

The ring was a tight fit on his little finger. Then he took off one of his rings and placed in on the middle finger of my left hand. It was too big for any other.

'Now we have plighted our troth,' he said, 'and I am happy. Soon you and I will be together. I shall lose no time in bringing this about. You will soon come back to Court.'

I said that I was so overwhelmed that I needed a little time in the quiet of the country to think about what had happened.

He kissed me tenderly.

'It shall be as you wish, sweetheart,' he said. 'Now and forever.'

I waved him farewell as he rode away from Hever.

*

I was still bemused. The prospect which had been put before me did seem incredible . . . almost . . . but not entirely so. Why should it not work out as he had said? It was true he had married his brother's wife, and divorces were granted on flimsier pretexts. So much would depend on the new Pope Clement and whom he would consider it more dangerous to offend – the Emperor or the King. And Wolsey? What would he be thinking when he knew of this proposal that a 'foolish girl' was to mate with the King?

It could never happen. There were too many obstacles. I had given him my ring and he had gone away happy and confident. But could it be possible?

I was dreadfully uncertain. I could not talk to my step-mother. I was not sure what her reactions would be. She would certainly be sorry for the Queen who must be set aside if I were to take her place; but perhaps, because she loved me, should would be proud to think of me – Anne, her step-daughter – Queen of England. Would she understand the pitfalls?

I felt as though I had set out to sea in a flimsy craft, and I wanted the King to know that I was aware of the dangerous course. I asked the jeweller to make an ornament of gold and diamonds, depicting a woman in a frail craft on a stormy sea.

I was very pleased when George came to Hever for a few days. He knew that something was afoot. He had noticed the King select me for the dance when the French ambassadors were being entertained and he would naturally presume that I was about to become the King's mistress.

He came straight to the point and said that it seemed to him that the Boleyn fortunes looked bright.

When I told him that the King had hinted at breaking up his marriage to the Queen and setting me in her place, he was astounded.

'Even the King would not dare to do that.'

'That is what I think.'

'If the Queen came from a noble English family . . . well, it would be as good as done. But the Emperor's aunt! He would consider it an insult and would do anything to prevent it.'

'The King says he is determined. He says that his consci-ence is disturbed because he married his brother's widow.'

George raised his eyebrows. 'The King has a conscience, I know. Strictly between ourselves, it is a most accommodating conscience, one of his most loyal subjects and always ready to act at his command.'

I laughed. 'Oh George, you will have to guard your tongue, you know.'

'You mean in the presence of our gracious Queen-to-be?'

'Don't joke. It alarms me. And I cannot believe it will ever come to pass.'

'Miracles happen, and if anyone other than God can create them, it is our powerful King. He would have to get the Pope on his side.'

'Do you think he could do that?'

'Clement is no Leo. He wavers ... unable to make up his mind which way it is wise to jump. So much will depend on which one he fears more ... the King or the Emperor. Popes have, of course, always been ready to give dispensations to monarchs. When you look back, you see so many cases. The King's own sister, Margaret, was divorced from the Earl of Angus on account of a pre-contract. And there was Suffolk ... Not royal it's true but he could not marry his first wife without a dispensation from the Pope ... and now he is the King's brother-in-law. You see, it can be done. The only obstacle, it would seem, is the Queen's relationship with the Emperor.'

'He quotes Leviticus.'

'Yes,' said George. ' "If a man taketh his brother's wife, it is an impurity; he hath uncovered his brother's nakedness; they shall be childless ..." or something like that.'

'It fits,' I said.

'Yes, but the marriage with Arthur was never consummated. Arthur was very young and moreover sickly. He must have been on the point of death when he married.'

'George ... if it should come to pass ...'

'I shall enjoy seeing my sister Queen of England.'

'I cannot believe it could be possible.'

George looked at me quizzically. 'More extraordinary things have happened. And I will say that you are worthy to wear a crown.'

'You think so because I am your sister.'

'I think so because you are yourself.'

I put out my hand and he took it.

'George,' I said, 'whatever happens ... always be there.'

He nodded, and it was like a pact between us.

*

The jeweller had completed the ornament. It was very beautifully wrought and clearly portrayed what I had intended.

I sent it to the King with a note telling him that I was like the storm-tossed lady in the boat.

He wrote immediately, telling me how delighted he was to have such a gift from me. He thought it beautiful and he thanked me cordially. He took it as an expression of my humility because the lady in the boat was meant to be myself. He said he would outdo me in loyalty of heart and the desire to please. He prayed daily that his prayers would be answered and that the time before we could be together would be brief. The letter was 'written by the hand of the one who in heart and body and will is your loyal and most assured servant', and it was signed 'H seeks A.B. no other. R.' And round my initials he had drawn a heart.

I was very uncertain. I wanted to go to Court but I knew my presence there might make difficulties while the delicate procedure was going on.

The King was urging me to go back, so I decided I would, and return if I found the situation becoming difficult to me, which it well might. I did not know how he intended to proceed, but all now knew of his feelings for me. And there was another matter which was imperative. I should have to hold off his importunings, and now that I had given him my ring and sent him the ornament, thereby proclaiming my willingness to accept him, they could become more persistent.

But I could – in desperation – always return to Hever.

*

When I reached the Court, I was aware of the different

attitude towards me. It was difficult for the King to take any action without someone's being aware of it, and it was known that he had visited Hever unannounced. There could be only one reason for that.

Many of them thought I was the King's mistress. They would not have believed that any woman could hold out against him and keep his attention. I often wondered whether I should be able to do this because, although I confess to having been dazzled by the prospect of a crown, I had always realized how difficult it would be to come by; and always at the back of my mind was the thought that it might be better if the whole thing were forgotten; this brought out an indifference in me which enabled me to keep my dignity and helped me to hold back. It was probably that quality in me which had enslaved the King. He had been used to surrenders – as in the case of Mary – and he had come to suspect that in his case the hunt was over almost before it began. That I was not ready to give way, set me apart and made the chase more exciting.

When I returned, a certain feverish excitement gripped me, but while I secretly enjoyed the power my position gave me, I had an uneasy feeling that there was something essentially ephemeral about the entire situation.

I was at the centre of the gaiety of the Court. Already people were gathering round me. My cousin, Surrey, George, of course, Thomas Wyatt, Francis Bryan, Weston . . . all the wits and most lively and interesting of the men. Naturally the King wanted to be with such.

He was amazingly patient and although it was his most urgent desire that I should share his bed, he liked to think of himself as a religious man, and such a one must not only respect my virtue but applaud it. I believe, as much as he desired me, he wanted me to remain virginal because he felt that was right in God's eyes. He was very preoccupied with God during this time, and I felt that helped me to evade the issue for which he so desperately longed. He was really asking God to come to his aid for now he had convinced himself that the Almighty was showing his disapproval of the marriage to Katharine by telling him – in the usual mysterious way – that he would never get sons while he was a partner in an incestuous marriage.

He cherished this thought. It soothed his conscience, and it enabled him to enjoy the entertainments and the company of the band of wits.

Thomas Wyatt caused me certain anxiety. He was jealous of my relationship with the King. Thomas had never been discreet. He was married, it was true, and therefore he could not marry me, but the King was married also. It might have been that, now everyone knew of the King's devotion to me, they could not believe that I was not his mistress. Thomas had ideas that, when my affair with the King was over, I would turn to him.

There was an unfortunate incident which I heard of through Francis Bryan, who hastened to tell me as soon as it took place.

The King had, of course, noticed Thomas Wyatt's feelings for me, and this did not please him. Wyatt was as tall as the King, and very handsome indeed with his blond looks and nonchalant charm. He had a dignity which, at times, I feared might be his undoing, for he often sacrificed subservience to wit. He was too clever to do anything of which the King could complain, but he came very near to it. He would often imply a lack of appreciation for the King's poetry, and there had been occasions when he had come near to giving offence.

But Henry was a strange mixture. He truly loved poetry and therefore appreciated Wyatt's; he liked good-looking people about him and he enjoyed wit. There were two natures battling for supremacy in Henry; I knew that much – even then, but I was to learn more of him later.

On this occasion Henry was playing bowls with Wyatt, the Duke of Suffolk – who was back at Court with his wife, the King's sister, who had once been my mistress – and Sir Francis Bryan.

There arose a little dispute between the King and Wyatt. Any but Wyatt would have glossed over the matter and accepted the King's opinions. The King had said that his bowl had passed that of Wyatt.

Wyatt protested. The King was not annoyed at this stage. He liked to talk in parables and always had done. He was very proud of the ring I had given him, and he probably wanted to stress to Wyatt that he was the successful suitor.

Displaying the ring which I had worn often and which was well known to Thomas, he ostentatiously pointed to the bowl with his hand in such a way as to call attention to the ring.

'I tell thee, Wyatt,' he said, 'it is mine.'

Francis told me that Wyatt looked mildly crestfallen but only for a few seconds. Then he felt in his pocket and brought out the jewelled tablet. 'I knew at once that it was one of yours,' he said. 'I have seen it often. Moreover it had your initials on it.'

'I remember it well,' I said.

'What do you think Wyatt said? "If Your Grace will give me leave, I will measure the cast with this. I have good hopes that it may yet be mine." '

'The fool!' I cried.

'Fool indeed, but you know Wyatt.'

'And what said the King?'

'He was very put out. He could not take his eyes from the tablet. Then he said sharply, "It may be so, but then I am deceived." The players knew not which way to look. I thought Wyatt would be sent to the Tower. He just stood there. Picture him looking pleased with himself, turning the tablet over and over in his hand and gazing at it with fond absorption. The King said, "The game is over." Then he strode away.'

I felt deeply apprehensive. He would not believe that Wyatt was my lover! But he would know that we had seen a good deal of each other all through our lives and that there was a close friendship between the two families. I wondered what action he would take.

It was not long before I discovered. A messenger came to me. The King commanded me to go to him at once. That sounded ominous.

I was taken to him almost like a prisoner. When we were alone, he said: 'Anne, is Wyatt your lover?'

'I believe he has some affection for me.'

He came to me and took me by the shoulders. He shook me. I drew myself up haughtily. 'Your Grace, I do not know what I have done to merit such treatment.'

I saw the fondness come into his eyes, and I marvelled at my power over him.

He told me what had happened on the green. I was glad that Francis had warned me so that I was prepared.

'He had your tablet. I know it was yours. I have seen it about your person. He suggested that you were his.'

'Your Grace, I am no man's.'

'The tablet . . .'

'He snatched it from me when the link of the chain which held it was broken. I demanded that he give it back to me and he refused to do so.'

His mouth slackened. He was believing me. I was touched because I could see that he so desperately wanted to believe.

'And he has never been your lover?'

'I have told Your Grace that I have never been any man's mistress and I never will be.'

'Then all is well, sweetheart. And I am happy.'

He took my hand and kissed it.

'This waiting is intolerable,' he went on. 'But soon now . . . soon.'

The incident was not over.

George told me that the King had suggested that Thomas Wyatt should retire from the Court for a while.

This Wyatt did. I heard that in leaving the Court he had met Sir John Russell, who was an ambassador at the papal Court. Russell was on the point of returning to Rome, and

Wyatt said in a characteristically impulsive manner: 'Suppose I accompanied you? I could get the King's leave, for I do not think he is in the mood to deny it. Can you delay your journey for a few hours?'

Russell was delighted to have such entertaining company, and the King readily gave his permission.

So after that fracas on the green, Thomas Wyatt retired from the Court and went off to Rome with Sir John Russell.

*

Henry had certainly decided there should be no more delay. He told me gleefully that Wolsey believed that, as Papal Legate, he could give the divorce, and all that would be needed would be the Pope's endorsement.

'Therefore, sweetheart,' said Henry, 'you may set your fears at rest. The Emperor will know nothing of what is happening until it is too late for him to do anything about it.'

Then he went on to tell me what he proposed.

'Wolsey is a past master in diplomacy. There are few problems that man cannot solve. And he is giving his full attention to this matter. There is to be a meeting at York Place between myself and the clergy.' He gave a little grin of amusement. 'I ... *I* am to be summoned to appear before them. Wolsey will preside and Warham will be there.'

I eagerly awaited the outcome of that meeting. It was to be conducted with great secrecy insomuch as the people were not to know what was taking place.

The King arrived by barge at the York Place privy steps and with him were Warham, Archbishop of Canterbury, and several lawyers.

I did not greatly fear Warham, for I guessed he would go which way the King wanted him to. He had held his archbishopric since the early years of the century; he was a tired old man and no doubt longing to escape from his duties. Wolsey had, so the King told me, referred to him as 'an old fool'. It seemed likely that he would raise no objections.

There were of course the lawyers and Wolsey himself. But I knew that none of these men would have entertained for a moment the thought that the King could possibly be thinking of marrying me. They would all be of the opinion that it was simply because of Katharine's inability to provide a male heir that she was being replaced, and they would be assuming that, when the divorce was completed, Henry would marry some princess – almost certainly Queen Claude's sister, Renée – as we were on such friendly terms with the French.

If any of them had known that the King wanted a divorce in order to marry me, their reactions would be very different. Of course I was not foolish enough to expect the King to tell them the truth. They must believe that all this had been set in motion because the Bishop of Tarbes had raised the question of Mary's legitimacy, and Henry felt the need to sift the matter in order to get to the truth. So the ecclesiastical court which was to assemble in York Place at the command of Wolsey must not know of the King's infatuation for me and my refusal to be anything but his wife.

As soon as the meeting was over, the King came to me to tell me about it.

'Wolsey was superb,' he said. 'I never saw him more astute. The man is truly marvellous. He sat there at the table surrounded by the clergy and the lawyers and he told the court that the Archbishop had a searching question to put to me. You should have seen poor old Warham. He was trembling in his shoes. And understandably so. He had to stand up and charge me with living illegally for all these years with a woman who was not my wife.'

'Oh yes, I can understand his fear.'

'Wolsey had told him beforehand that it would be no surprise to me and that my conscience had been troubling me on this score for some time, so there was no need to fear that he would offend me. He told him that when I had heard what the Bishop of Tarbes had said and this was conveyed to me by the French ambassador, I knew that I must search my soul and face up to any questions which a court of enquiry might ask me.'

'But to stand before those men and accuse you!'

'Poor fellow, I was quite sorry for him. At one point he faltered, but Wolsey pulled him through. I listened carefully to what he had to say and when he had finished they were all watching me intently. I told them then how grieved I was and how I could understand their concern. I had no hard feelings towards those who had thought it necessary to bring this case.'

'You could not have been expected to have hard feelings against yourself,' I reminded him.

He frowned. That was one thing I had to learn about him. In the midst of the most blatant hypocrisy he could delude himself into believing what he was trying to make others believe. It was extraordinary that a man of his intellect could do that. It showed an unusual dexterity of the mind. It amused me and I could not help referring to it. That was dangerous. I was as impetuous and reckless as Thomas Wyatt.

But he was too excited at that moment to reprove me. He went on as though I had not spoken: 'I think there is only one thing for me to do and that is, however distressing, to submit to an enquiry.' He turned to me, his face alight with joy. 'Anne, it will not be long now. We shall be together. All we have to do is wait for Wolsey. He will go to the Pope and get the whole matter sealed and settled before the Emperor hears a word of it.'

I was beginning to believe that this fantastic future could be mine. The King would submit to an enquiry which Wolsey would see took the right course. The clergy would be convinced that the King's marriage to Katharine was no true marriage; and then Wolsey would declare it invalid. All he would need was the sanction of the Pope as a matter of form, and as a Cardinal he would be in a position to get that.

It did not occur to Henry that the Queen would raise any objection. She had always been gentle and loving; she had pretended not to notice his peccadillos; she was of a dignified, quiet and retiring nature. He said with an air of magnanimity that he would regard her as his sister. She would be well looked after. She should have a household worthy of her, and she could spend her days in meditation and prayer. Perhaps she would like to go into a nunnery? It all seemed very simple.

I was changing. That was inevitable. I excuse myself by stressing my youth. I was only twenty years old and not really as wise as I thought I was. Who is, at twenty? I thought, because I had been brought up in the sophisticated French Court, because I had a ready wit, because I was an accomplished musician, because I could thrust and parry in conversation and join in a discussion with the best of them, that I was wise.

If only I had been, my story might have been different.

Now my reluctance was slipping away from me. I now knew why it was that men risked everything for a crown; through the ages that had been so. They fought for it, sacrificed everything they had for it. I did not pause to think that often, when it came, it had brought only trouble, care and tragedy.

I wanted now, desperately, to be Queen of England; and only now, when the crown seemed to be within my grasp, did I realize how much.

I was sorry for the Queen but I told myself I was more suitable to share Henry's throne. She would have hidden herself completely away if that had been possible. Henry needed someone as lively as he was, someone who could share in the revelries, plan them, sing, dance, look the part of Queen just as he did that of King.

He had urged me to buy what materials I needed – velvets, brocades, cloth of gold and silver. The cost would be taken care of. He wanted to see me outshine them all, which he assured me I could do if I were dressed as a beggar; but that did not mean he wished me to have anything but the finest.

I gave way to my passion for clothes and he supplied the jewellery. Gifts came to me frequently; and they were usually priceless gems.

I was now learning the meaning of ambition.

The Queen was aware that something was very wrong. It was impossible to hide it from her. The King had not yet spoken to her as he intended to. He wanted the ecclesiastical court to have progressed a little farther in its findings. Then he would go to her, and I was sure he would put up a great show of melancholy which would appear all the more genuine since, while he was with her, he would be able to convince himself that he really felt it.

I think she was a very frightened woman.

She knew of his favour towards me, but she was not really concerned, for she did not realize what part I was to play in 'the King's Secret Matter'. I was, she no doubt believed, his mistress as my sister had been before me.

That she would have liked to banish me from Court I was sure, but she would not run the risk of dismissing me any more than she had Mary, for she knew that, if she did, the King would call me back to Court, which would be humiliating for her; she did not want, at this stage, to irritate him.

There were only a few – my brother George, for instance, and my father, both on intimate terms with Henry – who knew of his plans for me. He was very anxious to keep me out of it, and I believe he was determined that Wolsey should not know. Though Wolsey was *his* servant, he was also a Cardinal and owed a certain allegiance to the Pope. I could not guess what Wolsey's reactions would have been had he known. I expected he would have done his best to dissuade the King from that course of action and tell him that the only thing he could do, when he was free of Katharine, was to marry a foreign princess.

Ambassadors were natural spies. I had always known that; and the Spanish ambassador was skilled in the art as much as any, save only the French. They had to be because of the relationships between the countries. I do not know how many people Inigo de Mendoza had working for him in secret –

although we did learn that he knew that Wolsey was promoting the divorce and that the King had assembled bishops and lawyers to prove that the marriage was illegal.

I believed at this time that everything was going well. Wolsey was about to proclaim the marriage invalid and then go to Rome to persuade Clement to give the final word, which would be easy with a sizeable bribe. Only when this had been accomplished did the King wish him to know that he intended to make me his Queen.

We anticipated no trouble, and the end seemed in sight.

Soon, I told myself, I should be going to my coronation.

*

An entertainment of rather special splendour was in progress. Since I had been of such importance at Court, I flattered myself that our masques and playlets were more cultivated, more witty. I was remembering so much of what I had learned in France.

On this occasion we were dancing. I was with the King as usual, and people had fallen away so that we could be almost alone as we danced. This often happened when the King performed. He liked it. It was an indication that when he danced people wanted to look at no others but him . . . and his partner.

I enjoyed it, too. I knew that my dancing was of the highest standard. I liked to be watched and admired – even as he did.

Then there was a clatter beyond the hall. A man appeared in the doorway. The ushers sought to hold him off, but he cried: 'I must see the King. I have news.'

He was travel-stained and muddy and looked as though he had ridden far.

Henry shouted: 'How now. What means this? What news have you brought? Ill it would seem.'

'Your Grace, a most terrible tragedy. Rome has been over-run by the Constable de Bourbon's troops. the Constable has been killed. The troops have sacked Rome, and the Pope has escaped to the Castle of St Angelo, where he is a prisoner.'

There was a deep silence throughout the hall. The King's face had turned ashen and then purple.

I knew what this meant. Bourbon had been an ally of the Emperor, and Clement was in truth the Emperor's prisoner.

What hope was there now of getting the necessary sanction to the divorce which we had so confidently expected?

*

There was no more dancing that night. The King summoned Wolsey and retired with him.

There were several versions of that catastrophic event. It was the work of the Constable de Bourbon who had deserted François and become the Emperor's ally. It was his troops who had captured François at Pavia and handed him over to the Emperor.

Charles had honoured the Constable but some of the Spanish nobles had despised him as a traitor, and there was a story that when he arrived in Madrid and the Emperor had wished to do him great honour for the service he had rendered him, he asked the Marquis of Villena to give up his residence to be used by Bourbon while he was in the town, because it was one of the finest there. The Emperor called him the Hero of Pavia. The Marquis had replied that, since the Emperor asked it, he must indeed obey, but after the Constable had left he would set fire to it with his own hands, for he could not live in rooms which had been occupied by a traitor to his country.

I wondered about the Constable. I did not think he had been a very happy man, although he had been known as one of the greatest soldiers of our day and the Emperor, delighting to have him in his service, had made much of him. But Bourbon had been too proud to be happy serving any man.

Charles had promised him Milan but he had cast covetous eyes on Naples. He had been a brave and audacious leader and had never hesitated to face danger; and the soldiery had been ready to follow him where he led.

He had gathered together a great army which included fifteen thousand *landsknechts* from Germany, many of whom had been deeply affected by the teachings of Martin Luther and regarded the Pope as the enemy of true religion. Bourbon had promised to make them rich from the treasure they would find in Rome. They would corner the Pope in his hideaway; they would help themselves to his riches ... all the great fortune which had been milched from the poor in the sale of indulgences and suchlike anomalies.

They went through Italy past Bologna and Florence, resisting the temptation to plunder these rich cities because the march on Rome was all-important.

Outside the city they camped. The Constable made a moving speech, reminding them that they had come far, travelling through the bad weather of the winter; they had had several encounters with the enemy from which they had emerged at some cost; they had been hungry and thirsty; but now they had arrived at their goal. Now was the time to show their mettle. An astrologer had once told him that he would die in Rome, but he cared not. He knew what he must do. They were to attack in the early morning and if his men followed him they would take the city and be rich.

Clad in white so that his men should always see him, and to show the enemy that he feared them not, he led the assault. It was a foolhardy gesture. As soon as he started to scale the walls of the city, he was identified and hit by an arquebus shot which mortally wounded him.

His dying words were that an enterprise so well begun must be continued. Had he lived, it might have been a different story. He was a great soldier; he would have taken what he wanted from the town and made the Pope his prisoner, and the victory would have been conducted in accordance with the laws of warfare. But now Rome was at the mercy of rough, licentious and fanatical soldiery.

The Sack of Rome would surely be remembered as one of the most horrifying events of the century. Churches were desecrated; priests were murdered and nuns raped on altars. There was no end to the stories of horror, and for weeks people talked of nothing but the terrible events which had taken place in Rome.

But to us it had a special significance. For how could Clement give us the sanction we needed while he was virtually the prisoner of the Queen's nephew?

'This,' said the King, grinding his teeth, 'is going to delay our matter.'

He turned to Wolsey, and afterwards I learned what had taken place at that interview.

'Wolsey says the ecclesiastical court should be closed without delay. No good can come of keeping it open. We can get nowhere until the Pope is free of the Emperor. Wolsey proposes to go to France and get François to work with him. The Pope must be freed. There must be peace throughout Europe. If he could bring that about, with the help of the French, he would consider making a fresh alliance with them against the Emperor. I said to him, "But what of my matter, Thomas?" And he replied, "Your Grace, nothing is closer to my heart, but before we can continue further we must be sure of success. We cannot proceed while the Pope is in captivity. Unfortunately we need his sanction. Allow me to proceed to France and I swear to Your Grace that I will seize every opportunity to conclude Your Grace's matter to Your Grace's satisfaction." '

Henry looked at me and shrugged his shoulders.

I said: 'It seems like fate. Just now . . . at this time . . . the Pope to be taken prisoner and delivered into the Emperor's hands.'

He nodded sombrely. 'You'll see, sweetheart. He'll have the answer. I doubt it not. This unfortunate matter of the

Pope has delayed us, but Wolsey will find the solution. Never fear. He always has and he knows that this matter is of greater importance to me than anything has ever been.'

It was the beginning of July when the Cardinal left for France. Crowds gathered in the streets to see him pass, for he and his entourage were a splendid sight indeed. He was noted for his ostentatious love of ceremony and show, which some unkind observers said was natural since he had begun life in a butcher's shop. I was not sure of that. He did not love such things more than the King who had first seen the light of day in Greenwich Palace and had lived as a prince all his life.

But the Cardinal certainly loved splendour. His palaces – York Place and Hampton Court particularly – were as magnificent as (some said more so than) the royal residences. There was a little rhyme which the people often quoted. It had been written by Shelton, one of the poets of the Court. It ran something like this:

> Why come ye not to Court?
> To which Court?
> The King's Court
> Or to Hampton Court?

Wolsey had certainly made his place at Hampton worthy to be royal, and there was nothing he liked better than to entertain the King there. Henry himself had remarked on its magnificence and, I fancy, was a little envious of it. But he was really fond of Wolsey. It was not only the man's brain – and really he was amazingly astute – but something in Wolsey's personality which charmed Henry; and in spite of all the jealousy and sneering remarks which were directed at the Cardinal, Henry ignored them, or on some occasions showed his displeasure, which was the quickest way of putting a stop to Wolsey's detractors.

Wolsey took with him a large company of attendants. They were all elegant in black velvet with gold chains about their necks. Their servants must be there, and they were distinguished by their tawny livery.

The Cardinal himself was a most impressive figure. He used a mule, but what a mule! It was caparisoned in crimson to match the Cardinal's robes; and, lest anyone should forget his high office, in both Church and State, carried before him was the Great Seal of England and his cardinal's hat.

I do not think he was a very happy man. I was sure that, as far as the treaties he had in mind, he felt confident enough; it was the King's Secret Matter which gave him such concern. I believed in his heart he was against the divorce. Perhaps he thought there was still time to get a son. On the other hand, the King had no brothers, no obvious heirs, and there could be trouble for a country when a monarch died and there might be several claimants to the throne.

Perhaps Wolsey thought it was a matter with which he need not concern himself overmuch. The King was younger than he was, and it was plausible to think that he would be dead long before such a contingency arose.

And so he passed on his ceremonious way to France.

The Court at Blackfriars

Time was passing. Wolsey was making progress in France but he was no nearer to bringing about the freedom of the Pope.

Henry wrote impatiently. I saw the letter. It accused the Cardinal of not giving his full attention to the matter uppermost in the King's mind.

Wolsey replied that he was straining every effort. François was sympathetic and Wolsey believed that he would welcome a union with the Princess Renée.

My father came to see me. He now regarded me in a very different light. He looked at me with some wonder and called me 'dear daughter'.

I was sceptical of his sudden affection for me. Of course I was carrying on the tradition of the Boleyn family, which had forced a few roots into society through the women of the house. I was about to follow the tradition – but in a much more spectacular fashion than any of my predecessors.

I wanted to laugh at him.

'My dear daughter,' he said, 'you look in good health.'

'You too, my lord,' I replied coolly.

'This is a most exciting project we have on our hands. The King has told me of his feelings for you.'

'So I have found favour in your sight, my lord?'

'My dear child. I always knew that you, of all my brood, were the one with special talents.'

'Mary had some excellent talents,' I reminded him.

'Ah, your sister Mary . . . she was always a fool. Well, she reaped her folly. There she is . . . living humbly with Carey. He will never make a name for himself.'

'Except as the husband of the King's one-time mistress.'

He laughed, rather sycophantically, which amused me.

'It is you we have to think of.'

'I can think for myself.'

'I am sure you can. But the King is most put out. He thinks Wolsey is dilatory about this Secret Matter.'

'He has a big task before him.'

'I don't trust Wolsey. At this moment he is trying to make an agreement with the King of France for the Princess Renée. If he knew the King's true mind, I cannot imagine what he would do.'

'Surely he would do as the King commanded him.'

'He is a wily creature. I would not trust him. And the King has a special feeling for him. He has been talking to me. He is very uneasy about his relationship with Mary.'

'That is over.'

'But the King has qualms. He is wondering whether his intimacy with Mary might be an obstacle to his marriage with you . . . due to the fact that you are her sister.'

'You mean . . . the closeness of the relationship?'

'It is natural that His Grace should want everything to be indisputable. He wants to get a dispensation on account of Mary. He has talked of it with George and me. Wolsey has plans for setting up a papal government in Avignon over which he, Wolsey, would have full powers. This is to last just during the Pope's captivity. He could then give sanction to the divorce, but before he could do this he would have to have the agreement of the Pope. He did not think it would be an insuperable task to smuggle a man into the castle of St Angelo to get the Pope's agreement to this scheme. The King does not think it a good idea. It is all too slow. He wants to send an ambassador, and he has chosen Dr Knight. He is going out ostensibly to meet Wolsey and assist him, but in fact he has a secret document with him with which he will ask for a dispensation on account of the King's relationship with Mary.'

Everything seemed to go against us. We discovered later that Wolsey's spies had searched Knight's bags before he joined him and therefore the King's true intentions were revealed to him. This naturally made his position in France untenable. The King had betrayed him to such an extent that he was negotiating with the King of France for a marriage with the Princess Renée when all the time he was determined to marry me.

Wolsey had no alternative but to return home.

I daresay he was a very worried man. For the first time he did not have the King's confidence. The King was working against him, keeping him in the dark, which put Wolsey in an impossible position.

We were at Richmond Palace when he arrived back.

I was with Henry and a few of our special friends – my father, George, Francis Bryan, Weston, Surrey and several others.

One of the Cardinal's servants came into the palace and was brought at once to the King.

'The Cardinal is on his way, Your Grace,' said the man. 'He comes straight from France and would know where Your Grace will receive him.'

I knew that Wolsey wanted to see the King alone. I was very suspicious of Wolsey. I could never forget that he had called me a foolish girl unworthy to mate with Northumberland, and because of that I always felt that I wanted to show him my power.

I said boldly: 'Where should the Cardinal see the King but where the King is?'

There was silence throughout the company. I had been over-bold. But I was sure of myself.

Henry nodded and did not answer.

So Wolsey came to him there ... where we all were, and the look of amazement on his face when he saw how he was received was pitiful indeed.

He seemed to change in that moment. He looked like an old, tired man who had failed in his mission.

I think Henry was aware of his dismay and despair, and he

had a true affection for Wolsey.

He said gently: 'Well, Thomas?'

Wolsey bowed. Then he looked straight at me. I wondered whether he read the triumph in my eyes.

*

They were difficult months to live through. There was frustration at every turn. Wolsey's position was growing more and more uncertain. Henry told me that, when he had confessed to him his true intentions, Wolsey had pleaded with him to abandon me and consider Renée of France.

'I told him that in no circumstances would I.'

'He has always hated me,' I said.

'No, sweetheart. He is a good servant. He is afraid that if it is known that I wish to marry you no one will believe the question of divorce has arisen because of my doubts about the legality of my marriage with Katharine. They will say it is because of my desire for you.'

I felt exasperation rising in me. That *was* the reason . . . but he would not accept it. He wanted his actions to be seen as selfless, a desire to right a wrong. But at least between ourselves surely he could admit the truth? But he could not do that. Sometimes I thought it was impossible to reason with such a man.

When I look back, I see how foolish I was. I should never have allowed my desire to take revenge on Wolsey overcome my common sense. I should have taken more care in my attitude to those about me. I should have remembered Queen Katharine's gentleness, her dignity, her religious life, the fact that she had never wittingly done harm to anyone, which had made her many friends. They closed in round her now that she was in trouble.

One who greatly resented me was the King's sister, Mary, whom I had accompanied to France when I was a little girl. She was at the Court often with her husband, the Duke of

Suffolk. Because of the King's Secret Matter, doubts were being raised all around; and there had been some hints that due to Suffolk's previous marriage to Margaret Mortymer, the widow whose defunct husband had been Suffolk's grandfather's brother, his marriage to the King's sister might not be valid. This may have given Mary a special sympathy with Katharine. However, the two were great friends and Mary showed her resentment that one who had been her maid of honour should now aspire to be Queen of England.

I think she would have spoken out against me had she dared but of course Henry would not have allowed that; and she had changed a little from the fiery young woman I had known. She was now a sober matron completely absorbed by her family and wanted to bring no trouble on them.

My aunt, now the Duchess of Norfolk, did not approve either, although I could not see why she should resent the glory I should bring to the family; and another aunt, Lady Boleyn, out of jealousy I think, would have been critical if she had dared. The fact was that they were all friends of Katharine and they understood – as I did myself – what she was suffering at this time.

They all knew now that the King wanted a divorce from the Queen in order to marry me. They looked upon me as some sort of siren possessed of evil powers which had bewitched him. They attached no blame to him. If I had told them that in the beginning I had tried hard to evade him, they would not have believed me. They would not accept the fact that I had been robbed of the man I loved and had had no wish to be in this situation – but now that I was, I was determined to make the best of it.

Perhaps I flaunted my position too much. Perhaps I enjoyed the power I had over the King. I basked in the admiration of many of the courtiers; the King's passion had added a kind of glamour. I knew this and I revelled in it. I can only say that I was young – and like all the young thought I was wiser than I actually was.

The summer had passed and the winter days had come, with their long evenings. Fires burned in the big rooms of the palaces, and there were dancing and entertainments which continued far into the nights.

I often found the Queen's eyes on me. She knew – as everyone else did – that I was the object of the King's passion and the reason for his wanting to be rid of her. I think that, for all her saintliness, she must have hated me. She would often give me duties to perform which meant that I must be at her side instead of that of the King. There was a brooding tension throughout the palace, and I wondered how much longer we could go on thus.

The Queen liked me to play cards with her. I think this was because the manner in which I was obliged to hold the cards brought my sixth nail into prominence, and even my hanging sleeve could not hide it. I was sure it was whispered that it was a sign of witchcraft, and that only one with special powers could have had such an effect on the King.

I shrugged my shoulders at them all. I cared nothing for their whispering, I told myself. But it was a little disheartening that so many of them should be against me.

I remember one occasion when I was playing cards with the Queen and some others. In the game one had to take a card from the pack, and it was good luck to be dealt a king. This card came to me.

The Queen looked at me very steadily and said: 'The Lady Anne has had the good hap to stop at a king. But she is not like the others. She will have all or none.'

I smiled and continued to play as though I did not understand the bitterness behind her words.

We were to go to Greenwich for the Christmas festivities. I and my little band of wits devised the masques, and each day I waited for the messenger to come from Rome with the good news that the Pope had given the sanction. I knew that Henry was waiting with the same eagerness and that it was not due to sloth on his part that we were making such little headway.

Dr Knight wrote encouragingly and frequently, but we never seemed to make any progress. There were always promises.

A few days before Christmas a messenger came in great haste and demanded to see the King. I was with Henry at the while. It was the most exciting news we had had for a long time. The Pope had made a dramatic escape from his prison. Disguised as a merchant, he had left the Castle of St Angelo, passed through the city undetected by the Emperor's men and found refuge in the bishop's palace there.

He was therefore no longer the Emperor's prisoner.

Henry was delighted. 'It cannot be long now, sweetheart,' he said.

That was a very merry Christmas at Greenwich. The plays were especially witty, the dancing more vivacious than ever. The King was in excellent spirits and was at the centre of everything.

Henry said: 'This is a matter for great rejoicing. The Pope is free. Let the whole country thank God for his delivery.'

The people were always ready for a celebration, and they threw themselves into the rejoicing with vigour. There was dancing in the streets, and the light from the bonfires made night like day.

But no one could have been more delighted than the King and I. Henry said: 'It will be easy now. Clement will have no love for the Emperor. He will want to pay him back for all he has suffered. This time next month you will be my Queen.'

But it did not work out like that.

At first when we read the letter we thought our hopes were realized.

Dr Knight said that Clement had hesitated and prevaricated and that he still feared the Emperor. He wished to please his good friend the King of England and he knew how dear this matter was to his heart. He therefore found himself unable to deny his friend what he so eagerly wished for.

Henry read that aloud and embraced me. 'At last!' he cried. 'At last.'

The dispensation was following. He had had to hold it back for Cardinal Pucci to do a little revision on it, and as soon as it was ready it would be despatched.

At first Henry wanted to celebrate immediately. He wanted to tell Wolsey that he could now hold his court and decide in his favour, for the Pope's dispensation was about to arrive any day now.

And so we waited. The days passed. The King gave orders that any messenger was to be brought to him without delay.

The waiting was hard and the delay seemed long. The King cursed first Clement and then Dr Knight. Clement was a vacillating fool; Knight was slothful and indifferent to his master's needs.

And then it came.

With what joy it was received!

But as the King read it, his face grew scarlet.

'That meddling Pucci,' he cried. But he knew it was not Pucci who had made the thing useless. It was Clement . . . swaying this way and that, afraid of Henry but more afraid of the Emperor.

That which would have given Wolsey the power to pass judgement had been deleted. So the dispensation was useless, and all our efforts had been in vain.

It was clear that the Pope – even now he was free – was unlikely to give us the help which was necessary before the King could marry me.

*

The King was furious. He shouted threats against shilly-shallying Clement, sly Pucci and the bumbling Dr Knight. Poor Dr Knight, he had done his best. It was not his fault that Clement was in fear of the Emperor.

'We should have left it to Wolsey,' he said. 'He is the only man who can outwit them. I know you feel he is no friend to you, sweetheart, but it is not so. He is a friend to me and that means he must be to you. We need Wolsey to set this matter to rights.'

In the meantime he declared war on the Emperor.

I had to forget my animosity towards Wolsey. I must remind myself that it was the King who had prevented my marriage to Henry Percy; Wolsey had merely obeyed instructions. His manner in carrying out those orders, though, had certainly been arrogant and offensive. 'This foolish girl . . .' I would never forget that, nor the humiliation he had meted out to us both. But I *had* to forget it. A master's hand was needed to sort out this business, and Wolsey's was undoubtedly the one.

Wolsey decided to send two men to the Pope – Stephen Gardiner and Edward Fox. Fox was an extremely clever young man, about thirty years of age. He had been educated at Cambridge, where he had astounded his tutors with his brilliance and had been known as the wonder of the university. He was related to Richard Fox, the Bishop of Winchester, who had certainly not been a hindrance to his advancement; but Wolsey said he was a man of immense energy, ability, resource and tact; and he had those qualities which were necessary to bring this matter to a satisfactory conclusion.

Stephen Gardiner was one of Wolsey's private secretaries and like Edward Fox had shown his brilliance. He was older than Fox – I should think by at least ten years; and his birth was somewhat obscure. Some said he was connected with the Rivers family. At Cambridge he was soon noticed. He was a doctor of civil and canon law; he became a lecturer and then tutor to the son of the Duke of Norfolk, and it was Norfolk who had introduced him to Wolsey. Always on the alert for talent which he could use, Wolsey decided to employ Gardiner. And thus he was chosen with Fox for this very delicate task which was going to need the utmost tact and resourcefulness.

So together Fox and Gardiner left England, two ambitious

men, fully aware of how much hung on the succeess of their mission.

Meanwhile there was trouble at home. War with the Emperor meant a cessation of trade with the Netherlands, and the clothiers in Suffolk lost their markets in Flanders. The Flemish too were disgruntled by the interruption the war brought to their trade with England.

Rioting broke out . . . first in Suffolk, and then it began to spread.

Henry had a dread of losing the affection of his people. He had always known that, however powerful a monarch might be, he must never lose the approval of his subjects as a whole. Emperor Charles no more wanted war with England than Henry did with him. A truce was arranged; trade was resumed; and the rioting died down.

Henry had been very anxious to see a friendship between Wolsey and me. He made a point of the three of us supping together. He beamed on us both; he wanted the two people who were closest to his heart to be friends. There was a certain simplicity about him which was at that time endearing. It was hard to recognize in this Henry the cruel person I knew, even then, that he could be.

His affection for Thomas Wolsey showed in his voice when he addressed him. 'Good Thomas,' he would say, putting his arm about the Cardinal's neck in a gesture of affection, 'he will lead us through this maze.' It showed that he was capable of caring for people. I was not sure that his affection was disinterested though. He was no fool. He had been most carefully educated; he was a man of culture; and he knew Wolsey's worth. Perhaps it was for that that he loved him. And myself? Why did he love me? For the excitement I could bring? Were we loved for the pleasure we could bring him? But was that not the source of all loving? So why should I doubt Henry?

During those meetings Wolsey, because it was the King's wish, showed great deference to me and I to him; and it was amazing how some semblance of friendship grew up between us. I do not think it went very deep, but it was there on the surface for the King to see and delight in.

Wolsey had given Gardiner and Fox an account of my virtues to take to the Pope. He had been most flattering; he had also written a masterly treatise on how important it was to get a male heir, and the King's fears as to what would happen on his death if he did not leave a son to follow him. He was young yet . . . young enough to have a son and bring him up as a ruler. If the matter were delayed for a few years, he might no longer be young enough to get a son and give him the necessary guidance.

The spring had come and all through the days we awaited news of the mission with which Gardiner and Fox had been entrusted.

At last it came. They had made some progress, and the Pope now realized the King's predicament. Clement wanted to help, so he was sending Cardinal Lorenzo Campeggio to England, and he, together with Cardinal Wolsey, should try the case.

It was not what he had hoped, but it was something.

The King was eager for the court to be set up immediately, but before this could be done calamity struck us.

The sweating sickness came to England.

*

The dread disease struck terror in everyone. It spread rapidly through the country and into the towns. It was dangerous to be in the company of anyone who had suffered from it because it was so infectious; and one could never be sure where it would strike. If anyone in a household contracted it, it was necessary that no one should leave or enter that house.

I decided that the best thing I could do was go to Hever. Henry was all in favour of this for he was terrified that I should catch the disease. He himself would leave London and travel with a depleted entourage about the country, for the country was always less dangerous than the crowded towns.

So I returned to Hever.

On my first night there, I awoke feeling alternately hot and cold. I touched my face. It was wet. I tried to sit up but I had not the strength to do so. My nightgown clung damply to my skin, and a fearful lassitude had taken possession of my limbs.

I do not remember very much of the days which followed. I saw vague figures in the room and recognized that of my stepmother. Occasionally my thoughts were lucid. Then I said to myself: So this is the end of all my dreams of glory. I shall never be Queen of England. I am to die, as so many have before me, of the sweating sickness. The Queen will be pleased, and the King . . . he will love me forever because I am dead.

They were strange thoughts but I must have been near delirium.

Later – it must have been much later for I had lost count of time – I was lying on my bed aware of my damp sheets and pillows; they changed them frequently but they were always damp. I heard them speaking about the crisis. So they would soon know whether I was to live or die.

In that strange state of being in limbo as though suspended between two worlds, I was not sure which way I wanted to go. I was vaguely aware of a crown for which I was reaching . . . and on the other hand there was a delicious peace which seemed to me infinitely more desirable.

I learned later on that they were all convinced that I would succumb to the sickness as so many had before me. My stepmother called it a miracle that, when the crisis was over, I was still with them.

I was aware of a man standing by my bed. I heard my stepmother's voice. 'The King has sent him, darling. He will make you well.'

So . . . I was not to die. I was too weak to move but no longer affected by the dreaded sweat. I could recover.

My stepmother was ever at hand, bringing me soothing possets from which I turned away until she begged me to take them for love of her.

'The King is beside himself with anxiety, Anne,' she said. 'You must recover for his sake. He has sent his physician, the great Dr Butts. Dr Butts says, if aught happens to you, he would not dare to return and face the King's wrath. So you must try, sweetheart. You must get well for all our sakes.'

Dr Butts commended my stepmother for her care of me. She had nursed me not only tenderly but wisely. Rest was what was needed now – and nourishment. 'The Lady Anne is strong and healthy,' he said. 'We shall soon have her well again and gracing the Court.'

My stepmother told me that the King was still wandering round the country with a small company of courtiers. If there was the slightest hint of the sickness near any place, he avoided it.

'The greatest calamity to the country would be if aught happened to him,' she said.

She read me the letter which he had sent with Dr Butts. It was all that I could have wished for.

The most displeasing news that could occur came to me suddenly at night. On three accounts I must lament it. One to hear of the illness of my mistress, whom I esteem more than all the world, and whose health I desire as I do my own. I would willingly bear half of what you suffer to cure you. The second from the fear that I shall have to endure my wearisome absence much longer, which has hitherto given me all the vexation that was possible. The third because my physician, in whom I have the most confidence, is absent at the very time when he could have given me the greatest pleasure. But I hope by him and his means to obtain one of my chief joys on earth, that is, the cure of my mistress. Yet, from the want of him, I will send you my second and hope that he will soon make you well. I shall then love him more than ever. I beseech you to be guided by his advice in your illness. By your doing this, I hope to see you soon again, which will be to me a greater comfort than all the precious jewels in the world.

Written by that secretary who is, and forever will be, your loyal and most assured servant. H.R.

'What a beautiful letter,' said my stepmother. 'How he loves you! Who would have thought that a King could care so much!'

I put out my hand; she took it and kissed it.

'Thank you,' I said, 'for all you have done for me.'

'My dearest child,' she replied, 'it has given me great joy to be of service. As for what I have done, you must repay me by getting well. I long to see you on your feet again.'

My stepmother had kept disturbing news from me, and I was dismayed to hear that my brother had taken the sickness – so had my father. They had both recovered before I was told. Mary's husband, Will Carey, had not been so fortunate. Mary was now a widow.

She came to Hever in some distress, not knowing where else she could go.

My stepmother welcomed Mary but she clearly had not the same affection for her as she had for me. I think she had been greatly shocked by Mary's behaviour in France. To have been sent home because of her immoral conduct was something which could not be easily forgotten; and then she had blithely entered into a relationship with the King, which was quite different from mine. Until now her misfortunes had sat lightly on her, but this was a bitter blow, because she had lost not only her husband, of whom she was quite fond, but her means of sustenance as well. Will Carey had been ineffectual but he had – owing to his complaisant attitude to his wife's affair with the King – been awarded certain grants which had given him a fair, if not affluent, income on which he and his family could live in comfort. He had been Constable of Plashy Castle and

Steward of the Duchy of Lancaster – both very desirable posts. On his death, of course, there had been no lack of people clamouring to take them up, and the King had bestowed them.

This was to be expected, but what of Mary? She was left penniless.

'I do not know how I shall live,' she told me.

'Have you never saved anything?' I asked.

She shook her head.

'But all the time you were at Court . . .'

'I never asked for anything. Clothes I had, which the King's treasury paid for . . . but there was nothing else. And clothes wear out.'

'What do you propose to do?'

'I thought you could help?'

I raised my eyebrows.

'If the King would listen to anyone it would be to you.'

I felt ashamed that Mary should have been left like this. Of course it was her own fault. She had been feckless – or perhaps I should say over-generous. I felt a shiver of alarm. She had been his mistress – not just casually but over a long period. And here she was . . . cast off, penniless. What a lesson! That should never happen to me.

I said: 'I will speak to the King.'

I wrote to him of her plight.

His reply was another of those love-letters which he sent to me while I was absent from him. I had a number of them, all professing undying devotion. There was hardly a mention of Mary except that I should speak to my father, telling him that it was the King's wish that he should look after his daughter. Of course, it was what my father should do, and it angered me that he should need the King's order to do it.

When I pondered on the matter, it occurred to me that Henry had shown no interest or compassion to one who must have been very close to him at one time. It should have been a lesson to me, but I was heedless of lessons in those days.

Looking back, I can see many that I failed to learn.

I knew that Henry hated any mention of Mary. She troubled his conscience not because of his affair with her and her present need but because he feared her relationship to me might prove a stumbling block in our union.

Henry was single-minded; he had no thought to spare for a discarded mistress who had fallen on evil times.

The tragic summer dragged on.

Cardinal Campeggio had left Rome and was on his way. He had been on his way for weeks. He was so old, so full of gout, that travelling was painful to him. He would travel for a day and rest for two in order to regain his strength.

At home in Hever, I fumed. Sometimes I despaired. I believed that the Pope had decided that the matter should never be settled and that, terrified of the Emperor as he was, he was determined to drag it out – hoping perhaps that Henry would grow tired of me. Perhaps that thought was in my mind too. Mary's affair had not helped to appease it. But I would get those letters of his, pulsating with his desire for me – and my optimism would return. I would beat them all – Katharine, Wolsey, Campeggio . . . every one of them.

My relationship with Wolsey would always be uneasy; no matter how we displayed our new friendship, for the pleasure of the King, the animosity was never far below the surface. I knew that he regarded me as an upstart. Is it not upstarts who are most antagonistic to other upstarts? At least *I* had not been born in a butcher's shop. Wolsey respected me now, but as a formidable enemy. Before, I had been a foolish girl. That was the difference.

Wolsey could see that another – as he would say – had the King's ear. Before my coming, Wolsey had been closer to the King than anyone. The King had, from the first, seen Wolsey's tremendous capabilities and moreover had a deep affection for him. Wolsey had carried him through many a difficult situation, but this matter of the divorce was defeating him. He had been thrust into an almost untenable position.

He was a Cardinal who owed allegiance to the Pope, and it was almost impossible to serve two masters. Many powerful forces were against him. Before, his own power had been so great that he could withstand his enemies; now they were crowding round him, seeing the champion weakening, waiting for the moment to give him the *coup de grâce*.

I was not sorry for him. Mine was not a forgiving nature. I often thought of what my life might have been: the peace of it in Alnwick Castle with my husband who would love me devotedly all our lives, our children sturdily growing up in the clear northern air to be strong men and women. The Northumberlands were the kings of the North. I should have been a queen in a kingdom more congenial to me than that of the Court.

Wolsey had prevented that. No, it was the King who had commanded it because all those years ago I had had a special attraction for him. But why had he let me go for so long? All that time he had been sporting with my sister Mary who now, poor girl, was cast aside and was an embarrassment to him. He simply did not want to know of her; he wanted to forget she had ever existed.

Was that the first warning sign? Perhaps my guardian angel was showing me a signpost on the dangerous road along which I was travelling. But I did not see that then and it was only afterwards that these thoughts came to me.

If only I had had the wisdom to take heed!

Mary stayed at Hever. My father would of course have to provide for her, which he would have done, I suppose, though grudgingly. But now he must do it with a fair grace since the King commanded it.

Perhaps I wasted sympathy on Mary. As soon as she knew that she would be able to live in some comfort, she cast off her dejected looks and was almost her old self. Misfortune sat lightly on her.

My stepmother wanted me to be quite well before I returned to Court. I was nothing loath to remain at Hever during this time. It was becoming increasingly difficult to hold off Henry. He was impatient. He was not going to go on being content with a few caresses. All the time he was urging me to greater intimacy. Instinct told me I must hold back. If I submitted, where would be the incentive to fight for this divorce when he would have what he wanted without? It was a very difficult position for me. I often wondered whether I dared hold out, whether his lack of satisfaction might indeed curb his passion. On the other hand, if I submitted, would he decide to drop this contentious matter of the divorce which so many people seemed determined to prevent?

It was a quandary which hung heavily upon me. This was why I was delighted to stay at Hever and was in no great hurry to end my convalescence.

Mary and I were sitting in that garden where I had had my first encounter with Henry. I always remembered it when I was there, for it was the beginning of all that happened afterwards.

She told me that she had had a letter from her sister-in-law Eleanor Carey, who was a nun.

'The Abbess of Eleanor's convent has recently died,' she was saying. 'That means her place is vacant. Eleanor would dearly love to step into it.'

'Perhaps she will.'

'It needs influence.' Mary looked at me. 'Eleanor asks if you would help.'

'I? What do I know of convents?'

'You don't have to know anything about them. A word from you to the King is all that would be needed.'

'I don't usually meddle in such matters.'

'Oh come, Anne, this is one of the family. Everyone knows that the King dotes on you. You only have to say the word and it is as good as done.'

I must confess that I liked to feel I had influence with the King, so I wrote and mentioned the matter to him.

To my intense annoyance I heard that Wolsey had passed

over Eleanor Carey and given the appointment to one of the other nuns.

Who became Abbess of the convent was of no importance to me, but that my wishes should be slighted was.

As soon as I heard, without waiting to hear any explanations, I wrote angrily to the King. Wolsey had deliberately ignored my request. He had known I wished the appointment to go to Eleanor Carey and because of this he had appointed someone else.

It was characteristic of Henry's devotion to me that he immediately called Wolsey and wanted to know why Eleanor Carey had been passed over when he had mentioned my interest in the matter.

Wolsey had his reply. Before appointing a woman to such a post, he must discover whether she was worthy of it. Under cross-examination, Eleanor Carey had admitted to having not only one illegitimate child but two – and with different fathers. Two priests, in fact, which made it worse. Wolsey had thought there was no need to report such a sordid happening because he was sure that all concerned must agree that such a woman was unfit for the post.

I was young and foolish. If only I had had the wisdom which later events were to force upon me!

I raged. I stormed. I would not let the matter rest. It should have been clear that Eleanor Carey's past made her unfit for the post, but I would not see that issue. All I saw was that I had asked a favour and it had been denied me because Wolsey thought it fit to do so.

I implored the King to give the post to Eleanor Carey.

Henry was torn between us; he hated to offend me and I think he understood the humiliation I had suffered.

He compromised. Neither Eleanor Carey nor Isabel Jordon – the woman whom Wolsey had installed – should have the post.

'But,' he wrote me, 'I would not for all the world clog your conscience or mine, to make Eleanor Carey a ruler of a House of God . . .'

He then went on to say that, as I had especially asked for it, this was the only way his conscience would allow him to act.

Wolsey could be foolish too. Isabel Jordan had already been appointed, he said. There was no way in which she could be cursorily dismissed.

I laughed when I heard it. I said: 'Wolsey is one of the King's subjects who does not have to obey him.'

Henry was getting angry. The whole matter had been blown up to immense proportions. He sent a stern rebuke to Wolsey.

The Cardinal was the perfect diplomat. He put on a show of abject humility.

The epidemic had disrupted his household. He himself had been in a state of poor health. Somehow the matter had gone ahead too quickly.

The King's reply was: 'It is understandable. The Cardinal would never go against my wishes.'

I was dismayed – first at his lenience with Wolsey and secondly that I should be so blatantly outwitted by him.

I knew now that, for all his fine words and show of friendship for me, Wolsey was my enemy.

*

I think of that year as one of frustration and wild optimism, ending in the fear that nothing would ever be accomplished. I dared not think what would happen if the divorce was not granted soon. How long could Henry be kept with this burning desire for me? How long before he was as weary of the matter as I was?

It seemed then that everything worked against us. There was the Queen, who remained aloof with an air of piety which disturbed me more than any outburst of anger would have done. Wolsey was a frightened man, I knew. He feared that this matter of the divorce would be the end of him; he could hear his enemies baying at his heels. How Norfolk, Suffolk and the rest of them would rejoice to see him brought low. I shall never forget how two years before he had calmly handed over Hampton Court to the King. Hampton Court! The pride of his life, with its magnificent architecture and all its treasures which were indeed grander than many of those in the royal palaces.

'Should a subject have a palace more royal than those of his King?' Henry had asked him one day. He had long coveted Hampton Court, and Wolsey, so clever, so astute, knowing that the King's favour was essential to his well-being, had immediately realized his folly in creating such a residence and replied that a subject could build on the perfection of such a place with only one object in view. And that was to present it to his King.

What a masterly stroke! It was sheer genius. And how delightedly the King had accepted the magnificent gift. After that he had loved Wolsey more than ever. Wolsey knew better than to let a canker grow. Cut it right out was his method, however painful the surgery.

But this was something from which Wolsey could not escape. He was a Cardinal. Some would have said his first duty was to the Pope, and Henry would want none about him whose first duty was not to himself.

The Cardinal's power was slipping away from him. Yes, there were certain times when I thought he was a very worried man.

He was not the only one who was worried. That year was one of misfortune. Nothing seemed to go right.

We were still waiting for Campeggio's arrival. When the King made impatient enquiries, the reply was always the same. Cardinal Campeggio was an old man; he was racked with gout; he was making progress as fast as he could.

I was shuttling from Court to Hever. I never stayed long at Court – a fact which pleased me, for it was becoming more and more difficult to hold Henry off. His impatience was growing. He made constant references to the consummation of our love. I greatly feared it. How long would I be able to hold him once I had surrendered? But how long could I keep him at bay? It was a terrible situation to find oneself in. I often wondered at his devotion, which so far had not wavered, and sometimes I thought that all the obstacles which had been raised might have strengthened his purpose, made him more determined to overcome them, but at others I wondered if he would ask himself whether it was all worth while.

We had decided that while Campeggio was presiding over the court it would be better for me to keep out of sight, to give the impression that Henry's desire for a divorce had nothing to do with me.

Although I was not present on so many of those occasions, I heard about them from several sources. Henry kept me informed; so did my brother and my father. They were both working assiduously for the divorce. My father was naturally overjoyed at the prospect of my becoming the Queen; even with his ambition, he had never visualized a daughter of his going so far.

So all through that year we waited.

Everything concerned with the matter seemed to take on an almost farcical note. The King had decided that Campeggio should be given a royal welcome. Indeed, while he was in England, deference must be paid to him; he must be placated; in every way his sympathy was to be won. Therefore he was to have a warm welcome.

The merchants of London with their apprentices brought out the banners of their guilds and their houses were decorated with streamers of cloth of silver and gold. Noble lords and their retinues formed the procession, which was joined by the clergy with all their paraphernalia of office, making a colourful display. And at the head of it rode the Cardinal, more splendid than any, in his rich red robes, his silver crosses and the Great Seal of office borne before him with his cardinal's hat.

This was to be the great occasion – the meeting of two Cardinals both appointed legates of the Pope. Such scenes were rare in London.

It was characteristic that Campeggio, for whom all this pomp and ceremony had been arranged, should fail to appear.

While London was waiting for his great entry, he was in bed, suffering from another attack of the gout. So the crowds who had come out to see him were disappointed of the spectacle to which they had looked forward.

Campeggio came into London by barge the next day, and no one noticed his arrival. As soon as he was there, he had to retire at once to bed.

I had expected that once he was in London the court would be set up and the verdict given quickly.

But no. That was what Wolsey might desire but he could not act without the co-operation of Campeggio, and I began to wonder whether that prelate ever intended to give a judgement, for he showed every reluctance in taking even the first steps.

Henry was in a state of suppressed fury. He wanted to shake them until their teeth rattled. He wanted to threaten to have their heads. But, of course, he was not Campeggio's master – even Wolsey must bow to the wishes of that other beside whom even the King's power was ineffective.

The head of the Church was the Pope of Rome, and this was a Church matter.

But for his difficult position I believe Henry would have stormed at them, threatened them, but he could not do so. He was caught by his own conscience. He must pretend throughout that it was the reason for the enquiry.

I soon realized that Campeggio must have had his instructions from the Pope to delay matters as long as possible, in the hope that most likely the King's passion for me would burn out – and they could play a waiting game until that happened, when the entire dangerous business could be forgotten.

This was all due to the powerful Emperor, who was clearly a man not to be trifled with. The Pope's position was very insecure. The Emperor had made great progress in Italy; and while the Pope sought to placate Henry, he could not offend the Emperor. My future depended on the politics of Europe.

After he had arrived in London, Campeggio lay in bed for two weeks, unable to move. Henry was getting frantic and Wolsey had to make some move, so he visited Campeggio and pleaded with him to help bring the matter to a conclusion. The court must be opened.

Campeggio was not feigning illness. He really was in great pain. The devious Pope must have sent such a man because he knew his very incapacity could help to bring about delay.

Then Henry had an unsatisfactory meeting with the legate; he explained to him how much his conscience troubled him. Henry could be very eloquent where his conscience was concerned. But he nearly lost his temper – which he realized he must not do – when Campeggio suggested that the Pope might be ready to give him a dispensation so that he need have no more qualms about his marriage to Katharine.

Henry was adamant. He could not reconcile his conscience to that. He had had God's warning in his inability to get sons.

God had made it clear to him that He was displeased with the marriage. He quoted Leviticus. No, Henry must divorce Katharine and marry again speedily for the sake of the heirs his country needed. He was acting as a monarch should – thinking solely of his country.

When Campeggio suggested that Katharine might go into a nunnery, Henry was delighted. He almost clapped the poor old man on the back, which would have had a disastrous effect on his bones. It was the answer. Why, there had been an example across the water only a short time ago. Louis XII's Jeanne had retired to a convent and the King of France had married Anne of Brittany. Yes, that was indeed an excellent idea.

Campeggio was sure the Emperor would not object to that.

'The Queen is a lady of great virtue and deeply religious,' said Henry. 'I am sure that she would feel great happiness in a convent. She shall have her own. She shall live just as she chooses. It is the answer.'

Full of optimistic hopes that the end of this contentious matter was in sight, Campeggio and Wolsey presented themselves to Katharine.

The Queen never forgot that she was the daughter of the great Isabella. Her health was not good but her determination was strong. Her devotion to her daughter was unswerving. I think she would willingly have sacrificed her life for her daughter's sake. Now she was going to fight for her daughter. Mary at this time was heiress to the throne and would remain so until the King begat a son. Katharine knew that *she* would never bear that son. Henry was her husband, she maintained, and therefore the crown must in time be Mary's. She would fight for her daughter as she never would have fought for herself. If she allowed her marriage to be branded invalid, then her daughter would have no right to the throne. I was sure that was the one thing which was uppermost in her mind. Strictly religious, adhering to the rules of the Church of Rome, she was not going to lie about her marriage because the King was besotted with one of her maids of honour who was ambitious enough to demand marriage in return for her favours. She told Campeggio and Wolsey that, although she had been married to Prince Arthur, the marriage had never been consummated and she had come as a virgin to Henry. She was not going to tell or act a lie before God; nor would she live a lie by allowing herself to be sent to a convent, which would be tantamount to admitting that she had never been married to the King and had been living in sin all those years. The answer was No.

How Henry fumed! How Wolsey trembled! Campeggio retired to bed; he had no desire, it seemed, except to rest his painful body.

Anxiously we watched events on the Continent. The

successful Emperor made an offer of peace to Clement which would be of advantage to him. Clement, in a difficult position, wavered. There was Henry thundering on one side and Charles menacing on the other; and Clement had more to fear from Charles than he had from Henry. What could he do? The peace with the Emperor was still being considered; Clement dared not offend on that front; on the other hand he needed Henry's friendship. He was an unlucky man. On other occasions when his predecessors had been asked to help kings out of unfortunate marriages, there had not been these complications. It had simply been a matter of placating the powerful monarch or accepting a bribe. Rarely had a man been in such a position – and a man such as himself who asked only for a peaceful life!

Campeggio was holding back – just in case affairs with the Emperor did not go as promised, for then, if Henry was offended, where would Clement be . . . without friends and allies?

To Wolsey the Pope wrote with feeling that if it were merely a matter of his own personal safety he would have given the King what he wanted; but it was more than that. If only the lady concerned did not have such powerful relations, it would have been easy. But he, Clement, could not risk what action might be taken by the Emperor if he considered his aunt had been unjustly treated, even by a monarch so great as King Henry.

Wolsey had his network of spies, and most correspondence which came back and forth was scrutinized by him.

He knew that the Pope was telling Campeggio to prolong the matter in the hope that the King might change his mind, for what he asked could not be granted without peril and scandal.

Wolsey knew also that Clement had no intention of granting the divorce and that Campeggio was using his gouty condition to enable him to prevaricate with some semblance of plausibility.

I was so frustrated. Sometimes I was quite hysterical. I did not know what the outcome would be. The King seemed as deeply enamoured of me as ever; but he was in a nervous state too. It had not occurred to him that when he asked for a divorce he would not get it. He could cite so many examples of monarchs in his position. 'Why, oh why,' he demanded, 'should I be the one to be denied?'

The answer was easy: Because his wife was the aunt of the Emperor Charles.

We saw each other now and then. I would chafe against the delay and he assured me that Wolsey was doing his best. I doubted this.

'Your Grace is bemused by that man,' I said incautiously.

Henry replied: 'Nay, sweetheart, I know him well. No one knows him better. He has always worked well for me and he will continue to do so.'

'Cannot you see that he is working for his master, the Pope?'

'Wolsey is *my* man.'

'*Cardinal* Wolsey?'

I withdrew myself from his embrace. He was amazed. No one contradicted the King. No one but myself denied him what he wanted.

He left soon after that, his expression bleak.

When he had gone, I asked myself what I had done. I was letting my nervous tension get the better of my common sense. He had never looked like that before. He was frustrated beyond endurance and instead of soothing him I had irritated him.

I thought of writing to him. No, that would not do. I must not show weakness. There might be a reconciliation, which could very well have the ending which I was so desperately trying to hold off. On the other hand criticism was something that he would not take from anyone . . . not even from me.

What should I do? I spent a sleepless night. If only this dreadful waiting was over! In the end I wrote a note to him in which I told him I was sorry for my outburst. I was so weary with the waiting.

His reply was instant.

What a joy it was to understand my reasonableness and he was delighted that I was suppressing my fantasies.

'Good sweetheart,' he went on, 'continue the same not only in this but in all your doing hereafter, for thereby shall come to both you and me the greatest quietness that may be in the world ...' He ended: 'Written with the hand which fain would be yours, and so is the heart. H.R.'

Perhaps the most disturbing element of all came from the people. They knew of Campeggio's presence in London and they had heard of the King's Secret Matter. They knew that he wanted to put away Queen Katharine and set me up in her place.

Katharine had always been popular, though not as the King had, of course. They loved their large glittering monarch who gave such splendid entertainments at his court, which they were sometimes able to see. He was always cheerful, smiling and approachable ... to them, for the ordinary people found him much more affable than his courtiers did. His father – though he had made the country prosperous – had never enjoyed the popularity which had come to his son. The people wanted someone who looked like a king – and Henry certainly did that.

They did not like what they heard, so they had to have a scapegoat. The King was too popular to take that rôle, so who should it fall to but myself?

Little did they know that in the first place I had been brought reluctantly into this. If only I had married Henry Percy, they would have known nothing of me; I should have lived my life in obscure and peaceful happiness as the Countess of Northumberland.

Now I was called Sorceress. I had a sixth finger which had been given to me by the Devil. By spells I had seduced the King from the path of virtue. The Devil and I had concocted a scheme to break up the King's marriage, that I might take the Queen's place.

They gathered about the palace. They cheered Katharine whenever she appeared, which I think she did more frequently than in the past, revelling in their sympathy. Who could blame her? She was fighting for her position, for her child's right to the throne. I saw that clearly . . . much as I wanted her out of my way.

They greeted the King with silence. It was the first time in his life that he had lacked the vociferous appreciation of the crowd and he did not like it. It worried him considerably. He must be remembering that his father had come by a devious way to the throne.

'We'll have no Nan Bullen,' they shouted at the King.

Angrily he gave orders that crowds were not to be allowed to gather near the palaces.

They talked about my low birth. This was amusing coming from the apprentices, the seamstresses and the watermen. They passed over the fact that I was of Howard blood – one of the highest families in the land. I was of tradesmen's stock, they said. It had always been amazing to me that the lower orders hate to see someone rise in life. Though humbly born themselves, they cannot bear to see one whom they consider to be of their own kind rise to greatness. It was the same with Wolsey. One would have thought they would have been delighted, and see in such a rise a chance for themselves.

So the demonstrations grew and I could not go to London. It was depressing to be so hated.

Henry wrote that I must stay away for if I were there he would fear for my safety.

I had heard that he had appeared before the Mayor of London and the Aldermen because he wished the City of London to understand what was actually happening.

He spoke eloquently of that which always aroused a passionate fluency in him – his conscience. He was thinking of his people. As men of intelligence, they would know that one of the most important safeguards to a country's security was the succession. If only he could be shown that his marriage was legal, nothing would please him more. The Queen had so many good qualities which he had good reason to know, and in birth she was incomparable. If he had to make a choice now, he would choose her above all women.

When such words were reported to me, I was filled with fury; but I grew calmer. Hypocrisy was second nature to Henry and he used it so well because he believed it when he said it. But could he even for a moment have believed that he would have chosen Katharine now if he had a choice? It was not a matter of choice. He only had to stop proceedings and Katharine could remain his wife; and I did not suppose for a moment that anyone would question the matter.

How could one trust a man who could talk so convincingly and so untruthfully?

Was that another signpost which I ignored? Should I have asked myself at that time more searchingly what dangers lay ahead in union with him?

It was decided that I should spend Christmas at Court. I should go to Greenwich.

How many weary months ago had I thought that by this time I should be crowned Queen of England?

*

No sooner had I arrived in Greenwich than I realized it had been a mistake to come.

The Queen was naturally there and, as the King's Secret Matter was secret no longer, all knew that his desire for a divorce was because he wished to marry me. That put me in a very difficult position. There were those who flattered me because of the favours I should be able to bestow on them when I became Queen; on the other hand there were those who thought I never would be, that Katharine's obstinacy and piety would prevail, and to her they wished to show their fidelity. There were some, I knew, who had a genuine affection for Katharine and would rally round her no matter what happened.

I had one or two faithful friends. There was my cousin Madge Shelton, my brother, Mary Wyatt, my dear step-mother, who was torn between pride and fear. There were plenty to flutter round me: Norris, Bryan, Brereton, Weston. They were all in love with me, or professed to be. I think the King's desire for me must have given me a special aura.

However, in spite of these people, I felt alone that Christmas.

The Queen, of course, could not be expected to receive me, so I had my own apartments at Greenwich, and Henry had seen that they were very splendid. In fact they had every aspect of royalty. At times it seemed as though I were already the Queen.

I was determined to hide my apprehension, and whatever the feelings against me, it was in my apartments that the lively and witty courtiers assembled; most people wanted to be there, including the King. I am sure Katharine's domain must have been very sombre compared with mine. But, of course, for the traditional Christmas ceremonies, Henry must be with her, for instance at the church services and the state banquet when people crowded into the hall and helped themselves from the tables in accordance with custom. They would except to see the King with the Queen, not with the Concubine – as they called me.

But it was gratifying that, whenever he could, he escaped to my quarters, and there we danced and sang and enjoyed all the entertainments which I and my friends had devised.

That was a great success but I had a heavy heart at these festivities. There is nothing so frustrating as to have one's hopes rise only to be dashed down again and again after months of planning and joyful anticipation, and to realize that there had been no move from the position one was in this time last year.

I was growing more and more suspicious of Wolsey. I began to believe he was in collusion with Campeggio and received his instructions from the Pope no less than the Italian did. Of course, his first obedience *was* to the Pope, but Henry was too bemused to see this.

During my stays in the country I felt time weighing heavily, and in order to pass it pleasantly I was studying the new religion which was beginning to take a hold on people. Ever since Martin Luther had pinned his theses on that church door in Wittenberg, something had been stirring.

I found that very exciting. I was drawn to the new ideas. I liked what I read. Perhaps it was because I felt a certain antipathy to the Pope that I was fascinated by the idea of curbing his power. The sale of indulgences, which had been Martin Luther's first complaint, was definitely wrong. How could forgiveness be bought in Heaven by giving money to a priest?

Since the King had written his book and become Defender of the Faith, he had been fierce against heretics. He had no fondness for Martin Luther. He had been ready to adhere to the Church of Rome, but I was not sure what his feelings would be now that the Pope was hesitating so long about giving him what he wanted.

Heretics were imprisoned. One sometimes saw them on their way to penance, carrying a faggot – though there was not enough fierce feeling against them to burn them at the stake. On the whole, we English are not a fanatical people. When I dwell on the horrors of the Inquisition in Spain, I feel a sense of pride because we never had it in England – apart from that one occasion when we had been obliged to in the case of the Templars. In almost every other country it had flourished – except ours. I think that says something for our national character. We are inclined to use religion as a crutch to help us along when we need it, not, as particularly is the case in Spain, to be dominated by it. I often marvel how people who claim to have special piety and virtue could calmly look on at the torture of others because they did not share the same faith. I preferred to be a little less religious if this helped me to regard others with tolerance. Moreover, if they had ideas, I wanted to hear them. I would not close my mind and shout: Heretic. For these reasons it seemed to me that our country was a good breeding ground for the new religion.

A man called William Tyndale had written a book which he had entitled: *The Obedience of a Christian Man and How Christ's Rulers Ought to Govern*. I was very interested in this man because he was one of Luther's followers. Most of his time was spent translating. He had lived in England for a while, where he was translating the Bible, and he had gathered together a group of friends who were interested in Luther's doctrines, but after a while he left the country to go to Wittenberg. He had also written *Parable of the Wicked Mammon* which I had read. It was not easy to get these books, for they were forbidden entry into the country, and the King, at Wolsey's suggestion, had had a strict watch kept at seaports to prevent their being smuggled in.

Of course copies did get through and that was how this one had come into my possession. I found it quite fascinating.

I was reading *The Obedience of a Christian Man* one day when I was called away and I carelessly left the book lying on the window seat.

I forgot about it for several days. Then I asked one of my attendants, Mistress Gaynsford, a young and very pretty girl who was being pursued by a certain George Zouch, one of the gentlemen of the household, if she had seen it.

She blushed hotly and said she had.

'Come,' I said, 'where is the book? Bring it to me.'

She stammered that she had been glancing through it when someone had come upon her and, in fun, snatched it away.

'Well, where is it now?'

'He . . . he kept it . . . to tease me.'

'Was it George Zouch?'

She admitted it was.

'Well then, go to George Zouch and tell him I want my book and he is to return it at once.'

It was not as simple as that. Mistress Gaynsford came back without the book, and when I asked where it was, she said that George Zouch wished to speak to me.

He was clearly very embarrassed. 'I took the book to tease Mistress Gaynsford,' he said, 'and I was just about to go on duty in the King's chapel, and during the service I glanced into it, and to tell the truth I became so absorbed that I was reading it when the service was over. The Dean saw me and wanted to know what I was reading.'

'Yes . . . yes . . . Where is the book?'

'He . . . he took it from me. He was displeased. He wanted to know how I had come by it. I had to tell him that I had it from Mistress Gaynsford and that it was your book.'

'Why did he not give it back to you then?'

'He . . . said . . . he was going to take it to a higher authority. He . . . he mentioned the Cardinal.'

I confess I was dismayed. The book was forbidden. It had been smuggled into the country. There was a penalty for possessing it. It had been written in direct defiance of the Church.

So Wolsey had my book! I knew what he would do. He would take it to the King. He was trying to brand me as a heretic. Did he want to see me in prison? Walking barefooted in humiliation, carrying a faggot?

So it had come to a conflict between us. I was furious. I said to Zouch, who, poor young man, was in a state of abject terror at what he had done: 'This will be the dearest book that either the Dean or the Cardinal took away.'

I thought it best to go to Henry, if possible before Wolsey reached him.

The Cardinal had just left him when I arrived, and Henry had the book in his hands.

I went to him and knelt, taking his hand. There was

puzzlement in his face, but he was very soft and tender seeing me thus.

'Is it the book?' he said.

'You must understand.'

'Come, darling,' he said, taking my hands and helping me to rise. He looked into my face and added: 'Wolsey has brought me this.'

I said: 'It behoves those who love you to know what is going on.'

The words were well chosen, Henry was enchanted to hear that I was one of those who loved him.

'Sweetheart,' he said, 'this book is forbidden to the country.'

'I know it well. But I must know what is being written. How could I tell you of it if I did not know? It might be setting out some treachery against you.'

He laughed.

'Come, sit down, sweetheart. Tell me more of this book.'

So I sat beside him exultantly. What had I to fear? It mattered not what I did, what rules I broke, as long as I was his darling. Rules didn't apply to me.

I said: 'Henry, it is a most interesting book. I want to talk to you of it.'

So I told him and he showed interest – whether it was feigned to please me or whether he felt it, I was not sure; but he was a man to whom new ideas had always appealed, and he was a great lover of literature.

'Promise me one thing.'

'Anything you ask of me.'

'You will read this book and judge it for yourself. Then we can talk of it together. That is what I like . . . interesting discussion.'

He looked happier than he had for some time.

'I promise to read the book,' he said. 'And then we will sit thus . . . close, and talk of it.'

I was very pleased by the way in which the matter had evolved.

But, Master Wolsey, I thought, I have no doubts now that you are my enemy. And you will find a good adversary in me.

*

The King came to me in a state of great excitement.

'News, sweetheart,' he cried. 'I think this may well be the beginning of the end of our little matter. Clement is ill ... nigh unto death, they say.'

'And you think his successors will be kinder to you?'

'If the right man succeeds him, without doubt, yes. Anne, it could be the Papacy for Wolsey.'

I caught his excitement. What an answer to our problem! Wolsey ... Pope. And why not? It had been his lifelong ambition. He would grasp at the chance, not only because he longed to wear the papal crown but because he would escape from a situation which was becoming very dangerous to him.

'Do you think he has a chance?'

'The best chances. I shall support him. François will support him, I believe.'

'And the Emperor?'

'The Cardinals will vote. Will they regard the Emperor's candidate with any favour, think you? They had some rough handling not so long ago. It will take them a long time to forget the sack of Rome. Yes, Wolsey could be the man, and I will remind him that his first task is to grant my wish.'

'He will no longer be your man, Henry. He will be head of the Church.'

'He will obey me. Nay, sweetheart, this is our chance. It will not be long now.'

Our hopes were raised. It seemed Wolsey had a fair chance. He was like a man reprieved from a death sentence. I did not see clearly then what great danger he was in. He had set the divorce proceedings in motion, and now he could not stop them; if Clement did not give what Henry wanted, it could mean the fall of Wolsey. He had made promises to the King; he had assured him that the Pope could be persuaded to comply; and so far he had been wrong. Wolsey would see more clearly than anyone that, if he failed to give the King what he wanted, it would be the end of his power; and because he had risen so high, the greater would be his fall.

It was small wonder that he clutched at this hope. From a fearful apprehension he would leap to the very heights of his lifelong ambition; from the servant of a despotic king he would rise to a position as powerful as – perhaps more so than – that of the King himself.

Wolsey was going to put every effort into achieving that ambition.

We waited. Everyone believed Wolsey's chances were high, and the result seemed almost inevitable. He was very rich, and money was important to the Sacred College. His three bishoprics and his abbey would bring untold wealth to the Holy See. He was Archbishop of York, Bishop of Winchester and Abbot of St Albans – and he had just been given Durham.

A glorious prospect for him. The King would lose Wolsey – but not entirely so. He was certain that he would have him working for him in the Vatican. A good English Pope – and there had not been one since Nicholas Breakspear.

It might have worked, for throughout Europe Wolsey was considered to be the favourite.

Alas for Wolsey, Clement, who had wavered between the Emperor and Henry, now wavered between life and death – and finally life won. Clement lived on; there was no papal election; and the matter of the divorce dragged on.

Soon after that, Mendoza was recalled. I think he was glad to go. Everyone involved in this affair wished to be free of it.

Henry told me that before Mendoza had left he had had an interview with him in which the ambassador had said that the Emperor was obliged to defend his aunt because he regarded her plight as a private affair which touched his family's honour.

'I replied,' said Henry, 'that he had no right to interfere. This was a matter of state affecting the succession. "I do not meddle in the state affairs of other princes," I told him. So we must needs press on.'

That was the state of affairs when in June the court was opened in the Dominican priory at Blackfriars.

Both Henry and Katharine were cited to appear. Henry's case was that he feared for the validity of his marriage, and he wanted the matter to be resolved. Katharine made a very dignified impression as the wife who had been set aside after twenty years. She had not believed that the case would be tried in England and had wished it to be in Rome. She pointed out that Wolsey was an English subject and Campeggio held an English bishopric. Therefore they could not be impartial.

She demanded that the court be held in Rome. The King declared that he would certainly not plead in any court over which the Emperor had control.

After this the court adjourned for three days. Then both Henry and the Queen were summoned to appear.

Henry stated his case, reiterating that for some time he had feared that, since his marriage to his brother's widow, he had been living in mortal sin; and he wanted judgement on this.

When it was Katharine's turn, she made a deep impression on all who saw her. I had feared this. The people were already on her side. They said it was a case of a man wishing to be rid of his lawful wife because she was getting old and his fancy had turned to a younger woman. It was something which aroused indignation, particularly in the women. If this became a precedent, many of them could be set aside after twenty years of marriage. As for the men, they understood the King's desires, but they thought the matter should have been handled with discretion; I should have been Henry's mistress and put an end to the controversy.

But since I would not accept such a position and Henry was so determined not to lose me, the whole country – no, the whole of Europe – must be disturbed because I refused to become the King's mistress.

Katharine had great dignity. It was as though she was reminding all that she was the daughter of the great monarchs of Spain. Slowly she walked across the floor to the chair on which Henry sat. She knelt before him and raised her eyes to his face. I could imagine how she would unnerve him, he who liked his own actions to be seen always as right and honourable.

She said in a loud clear voice that she wanted justice. He must let her have justice for the sake of the love which had once been between them.

I could picture his embarrassment when I was told of this scene. I could see him, wretched, turning his eyes away from her supplicating figure. She was a stranger in this land, she said; and for that reason the court was against her.

Her words were remembered and repeated to me. I could never forget them. It was as though they had been engraved on my mind.

'I take all the world to witness that I have been a true, humble and obedient wife, ever conformable to your will and pleasure.'

It was true, of course. She had always tried to please him. She had made no protest when he had left her bed to share those of his mistresses; Elizabeth Blount, for instance, whose son he had honoured; my sister Mary, who had been his mistress over several years. She had accepted Mary at Court and had been a kind mistress to her. And myself . . . true, she had shown a little rancour where I was concerned. But I understood that – and so must Henry.

'I loved those whom you loved, only for your sake, whether they were my friends or enemies . . .'

Tolerated, would have been a better word in the cases of Mary and Elizabeth Blount; but he could not complain of her behaviour even to them.

'These twenty years I have been your true wife and by me you have had children, although it has pleased God to call them out of this world.'

He would be growing angry and steeling himself not to show it. If these children had lived – and there had been boys among them – he would not have been trying to rid himself of her. He could not have done so . . . even for me.

Then came the crux of the matter.

'And when you met me at first, I take God to be my judge, I was a true maid, without the touch of man.'

The court was silent. A woman so deeply religious would not swear before God unless she was telling the truth.

'Whether this be true or not, I put it to your conscience.'

A masterly touch. His conscience was a source of great embarrassment to him. She, who knew him well, would be aware of this. She was telling him that he knew as well as she did that when they had married she had been a virgin. She was calling on him to search his conscience.

But it was his conscience which was his great ally in this matter. Had he not schooled that conscience to plague him to such an extent that he had no alternative but to bring this case?

'If you will not favour me,' she went on, 'I commit my cause to God.'

With that she walked out of the room.

Although they called her back, she took no heed of them; and when she left the hall, the crowd which had gathered outside – consisting mainly of women – cheered her wildly. Their shouts of 'Long live our Queen Katharine' were heard in the hall.

During those hot June days I could not believe that the court would go against the King's wishes. Henry was optimistic, he was glad Katharine had walked out of the court and refused to return. It was much easier without her mournful, resolute figure to inspire admiration and pity.

There was only one who dared raise his voice against the King's wishes and that was John Fisher, the Bishop of Rochester, who stood up in court and said that his only intention was to have justice done and relieve himself of a scruple of conscience.

These consciences, how they bedevilled us! The King's conscience was well known to me; now here was Fisher's. He could not risk the damnation of his soul by failing to declare his opinion. He believed that the marriage of the King could not be dissolved by any power, human or divine; and he was prepared to encounter any peril for the truth.

Henry was furious. If he could, he would have had Fisher transported to the Tower on the spot. Wolsey came to see Henry, who berated him for allowing the bishop to stand up and make such a statement. Wolsey – torn as he was between Pope and King, disappointed of the Papacy – was showing signs of breaking up. His supreme confidence had left him. Being so much more shrewd and clever than most of us, he could see farther ahead and the danger towards which he was being hurried. He implored the King to believe him when he said that Fisher had given him no indication of his intentions.

'He'll be sorry for this,' growled Henry. 'I'll not be plagued by these traitorous bishops.'

News of what was happening in the court always seeped out, and now the Bishop of Rochester was receiving acclaim from the people, which was a further source of irritation to the King.

'But fear not,' he said to me. 'This matter must end soon and it can only go one way. I shall make those who act against me feel my wrath.'

But there were some who embrace martyrdom as joyfully as a bridegroom does his bride. I had a notion that Fisher was one of those.

*

The news from the Continent was not very encouraging. Charles had had a decisive victory over François in Italy; and worse than ever, the Emperor was making peace terms with the French and Clement at Cambrai. This was a greater blow than Fisher's outburst. Henry might deal with his own subject's waywardness; the great obstacle had always been the mighty Emperor.

And so the days passed.

My father, Norfolk and Suffolk were all working hard to have the matter settled. I felt I had powerful friends. It mattered not to me that both the Duchesses of Norfolk and Suffolk were haughtily cool to me. It was their husbands who could do me most good; and they were too firmly behind the King to be influenced by their wives.

It was well into July before the final judgement was to be given. I was beside myself with excitement. I was visualizing my coronation. Queen of England – with the King my slave. We had passed through some difficult times. For four years the King's courtship of me had persisted. Such fidelity could mean only one thing: his devotion was complete.

What a brilliant future lay ahead of me! I was already paying back old scores on Wolsey. Poor old man, he would not last long when I came to power.

I would teach him – and all men through him – what it meant to insult Anne Boleyn, to take from her the only man she had ever loved, to ruin their lives . . . well, Northumberland's had been ruined. As for myself, I looked upon my brilliant future as a kind of consolation prize. I had lost what I had most desired, and in place of love I had ambition. I could not be Henry Percy's wife – which in my heart I believed would have brought me the greater happiness – so I would be the Queen of England.

Fisher's outburst had caused a great deal of anxiety at the time, but Henry had decided to dismiss the man as a hotheaded fanatic. There were others to give evidence more to his liking, particularly those who had been with Prince

Arthur on the morning after his wedding to Katharine, and who stated that the Prince had staggered out of the bridal chamber exhausted, declaring to them all that 'that night he had been in the midst of Spain'. It was hard to believe in Arthur, a weakling who was not far from death and was of an especially retiring nature, making such a statement. But it was good evidence ... or would have been but for the effect Katharine had had when she had called on God to be her witness with such obvious piety and dignity. Moreover, during the court proceedings the shouting of the crowds outside could often be heard in the hall ... like a threatening chorus in a tragic drama.

All the same he was optimistic. The King could not believe that, as he had made his wishes so clear, his desire would be denied him in his own capital.

How wrong he was!

At last the day for which we had all been waiting arrived, and the judgement was to be given.

I was waiting impatiently for the verdict and in spite of certain misgivings my hopes ran high.

The King went into the gallery in the company of his brother-in-law, the Duke of Suffolk. He was certain of the verdict. The bishopric of Durham would be Campeggio's when the case was favourably settled and that would assure him of great riches. The man would not be such a fool as to turn his back on that, reasoned the King.

Perhaps he had forgotten that, when men are old and sickly and death does not seem to be so very far away, they are not so easily bribed by wordly goods. Campeggio's illness, which had served him so well in his efforts to play delaying tactics, was genuine. He did indeed suffer from excruciatingly painful gout. His one desire was obviously to leave our damp climate to get away to peace and perhaps a little comfort for his aching limbs.

He stood up and with the King's eyes on him declared: 'I will not for favour of any mighty prince do that which should be against the law of God. I am a sick old man looking daily for death.'

He went on to say that he would not put his soul in danger by incurring God's displeasure. He had only one God before his eyes and the honour of the Holy See . . . He was giving no judgement. He was referring the matter to Rome.

I could well imagine Henry's fury. Suffolk was beside him. He muttered through his teeth: 'It was never merry in England whilst we have Cardinals among us.'

It was a direct shaft at Wolsey.

Wolsey had promised the King that the matter would be dealt with speedily and as the King wished.

Wolsey had failed him.

The Cardinal Departs

That was a time of great tension and anxiety for me. After all that had happened, we were just where we had started. Wolsey was in disgrace, and it angered me that Henry still could not bring himself to dismiss him. Had I been wiser, I should have welcomed that degree of fidelity in the King. He had relied on Wolsey ever since his accession and he really loved the man. It was only in this matter of the divorce – this conflict between Rome and the Crown of England – that Wolsey had failed him ... and through no fault of his own. Had he had his way, Campeggio would have declared the marriage invalid and all would have been simple.

I was foolhardy. Looking back, I see my mistakes clearly – those impetuous steps which I had taken unheedingly all the way through to my dismal climax.

And so I was angered by the softness of the King's feeling for the Cardinal.

I was aided and abetted by Norfolk and Suffolk, whom I thought to be my friends. How misguided I was! Their aim was to dishonour and ruin Wolsey and they saw, through me, a way of doing it. I was young ... twenty-three years old. What can an impetuous, vain, foolish girl know at that age?

We were fully aware of what would happen if the case were tried in Rome. The Pope would never dare give the verdict against Katharine. The Emperor would insist on that. To try the case in Rome was tantamount to saying that the verdict would be given against the King.

During the summer the Court made its journeys through the country. It was necessary for the King to show himself to the people, and these peregrinations had become a custom. Of course the Queen must be beside him to accompany him

302

to all state ceremonies, and as a member of the Court I was there, too.

As we rode along, I wondered how much the people knew of what was no longer the King's Secret Matter. I was certain that the Queen would receive the sympathy and acclaim of the people wherever we went. And what of me? I was angry and frustrated. Again and again I raged within because I had not sought this in the beginning. It had been forced upon me. And yet I was held to blame.

The King was as devoted to me as ever, and spent as much time as possible with me. He had sent his emissaries to Rome but he was in no hurry for the case to be tried there, since the outcome would be inevitable. He wanted it delayed. He was ready to prevaricate with the Pope as the Pope had with him.

My character was such that when I was most anxious I gave way to an excess of gaiety. Perhaps there was an element of hysteria in my attitude. I used to wake up in the night from muddled dreams in which the fear that the King had abandoned me was prominent. That fear hung over me even when I woke up, and it could only be dispersed by his obvious passion for me. I heard it said that he was bewitched and seemed fit to go to any lengths to make me his Queen. Then my dreams seemed foolish, just shadows of the night; but the thought must have been in my mind to make me dream of it.

When the Court came to Tittenhanger, Henry actually went to Wolsey's place to visit him. When I heard, I was furious. And I let the King see my annoyance.

He said: 'He is an old man, sweetheart. It was pitiful to see what good a little show of affection from me brought him.'

'He is no friend of mine,' I retorted. 'He has ever worked against me.'

Henry said patiently: 'The Emperor was the stumbling block. Wolsey would have freed me if it had been in his power to do so. But we were in conflict with the Emperor, and the Pope has about as much willpower as a frightened chicken. Yes, Wolsey would have brought the matter to a satisfactory conclusion if it had been in his power.'

Mayhap, I thought – that the King might marry the Princess of France. Wolsey was determined to destroy me. I did not forget the incident of the book which George Zouch had stolen. He had hoped to deflate me in the eyes of the King and might have done me great harm if Henry had not been so besotted with me.

When were were at Grafton, a message came from Wolsey begging the King to receive him. He proposed to come with Cardinal Campeggio, who wished to take his leave of the King before departing.

It was from Suffolk that I had the news that the King had agreed to receive both Cardinals.

'It is a marvel to me,' said Suffolk, 'that Wolsey dare show his face . . . Campeggio either. And a greater marvel that the King has sent word that he will receive them.'

I was angry, for the King had said nothing to me of the matter.

'I am going to teach both of them a lesson,' went on Suffolk. 'I never liked Cardinals.'

'Nor I,' I answered.

'Wolsey will come to Court here at Grafton and he will discover that there is no apartment prepared for him. He will have to find his own lodgings.'

'That will be a great insult to his dignity.'

'As I intend,' said the Duke with a smile.

'And the other?'

'Master Campeggio? We must needs lodge him, I dare-swear. But I have ordered that before he leaves this country his baggage shall be searched, for it would not surprise me if we should find there what does not belong to him.'

'That would be an even greater insult than Wolsey's.'

'I find a great delight in insulting Cardinals.'

I laughed with him. It was at the time when I thought he was my friend.

Wolsey arrived in somewhat humble state compared with

the grandeur in which he had indulged previously. When I had talked to the King about my dislike and distrust of him, he had listened gravely and nodded. Suffolk and Norfolk believed that when the King saw him he would not speak to him and they were all looking forward to seeing the Cardinal's humiliation.

However, it was quite different from what they had imagined.

There were so many stories about Wolsey's villainies in circulation. It was true that he had amassed great riches. He was a perfect example of all the evils which Martin Luther had set out to condemn. He had lived in as great splendour as most monarchs. He had accumulated benefice after benefice. In addition to three bishoprics he held the most wealthy of the abbeys; as legate and chancellor he disposed of the entire patronage of the country. Any member of the Church – the richest abbot or the most needy priest – if he needed a licence, had to pay Wolsey for it. Fees from wills and marriages were paid to him. He received pensions from abroad, for all knew his influence with the King. His wealth was enormous but, while he accumulated it, he posed as a man of God, in the service of the Master who had lived all His life in poverty and in the service of mankind. Wolsey served one master: Mammon, and Mammon was Wolsey.

I had reminded the King of all this and he appeared to listen. He had commented that Wolsey was richer than any subject ought to be.

With the others I was waiting for the Cardinal's reception by the King, who, I was sure now, was in a state of indignation against him.

I could scarcely believe my eyes. No sooner had the man come in – looking strained and ill – no sooner had he knelt before the King than Henry laid a hand on his shoulder and bade him rise.

'You look frail, Thomas,' I heard him say.

They looked at each other, and in the Cardinal's face there

was a great joy because of the gentleness of the King's tone; Henry noticed this, and the soft and sentimental look came into his eyes and all the cruelty was gone from his little mouth, leaving it slack, as it had been so many times for me.

They talked together and I could see that the Cardinal's hopes were rising. He believed that if he could get past his enemies he could regain the King's favour.

The King received Campeggio somewhat coldly. He let him see that there was nothing for which he had to thank him.

Later, when I sat beside the King at dinner, I showed my displeasure at his treatment of Wolsey.

I reminded him of all that had come through the Cardinal's actions. He gave me that indulgent smile. I think he was not particularly interested in my words.

'How so, sweetheart?' he said idly.

I mentioned Wolsey's failure in the matter which was so important to us both.

'He was of the opinion that we could come to a satisfactory conclusion with ease. It is no blame to him that we did not.' I should have been warned – but I did not see warnings in those days – because he added: '*I* know this matter better than you or any.'

But I could not stop. 'If any nobleman had done half of what he has done, he would be worthy to lose his head,' I said. 'If my father, my lords Norfolk and Suffolk or any other noble person had done much less than he has, they would have lost their heads ere this.'

There was a certain coolness in his manner as he drew away from me. 'I perceive,' he said, 'that you are not the Cardinal's friend.'

He was showing clearly that the discourse displeased him and that I had forgotten that he was the King and I but a subject. It was he, though, who had made me forget that.

I added: 'I have no cause, nor has any other that loves Your Grace, to be his friend . . . if you consider well his doings.'

His lips were pursed. The meal was over and he indicated

that he wished to leave the table; after that he sent for Wolsey. They went into the King's privy chamber and there they talked for a long while.

I was very annoyed but there was nothing I could do.

Suffolk had kept his word, and there was no lodging available for Wolsey. Then I heard that Henry Norris had taken pity on him and given up his rooms that the Cardinal might have somewhere to sleep.

The King kept Wolsey with him and when he left told him they would continue their discussion the following morning.

I was filled with rage. It was clear to me that Henry had only to see the man to be beguiled by him. He was really concerned about his health. A few hours listening to him, I thought, and Wolsey would have regained his old ascendancy over the King.

It must not be.

Henry had talked to me about a deer park he wished to install in this area. We had looked at it on the previous day and he had said that before we left Grafton he would like to take a closer look at it.

That gave me an opportunity. Very early the following morning I went to him, full of excitement. I told him I had arranged an excursion with his pleasure in mind. We should ride out with a few of our very special friends and we should go to the site planned for the deer park. We should have a picnic there. It would be a very merry occasion.

The King was delighted. He very much enjoyed my making such arrangements and he could always be sure that the entertainment I devised would be amusing, for I gathered round me the people whose company most pleased him – my brother, Weston, Norris, Suffolk and the rest.

'There is one thing we must do,' I said, taking his arm and smiling up at him. 'We shall have to leave very early or we shall not get there and back in the day. I insist that Your Grace is ready to leave within the hour.'

It worked. We assembled in the courtyard and were all

ready to start when Wolsey arrived, so there was no time for anything but a brief exchange of words between him and the King.

The Cardinal knew, of course, that this was of my arranging. But there was now no point in disguising the fact that he and I were the bitterest of enemies.

*

In spite of that brief respite for Wolsey, it was clear that his days of greatness were numbered. His enemies rallied round – as enemies will – like hunting dogs at the kill, all eager to take a part in his destruction.

Perhaps there were some who acted from motives other than envy and the desire for revenge on one who had risen higher than they, for all their advantages, were able to do.

Lord Dacre of Templehurst was an ardent Catholic and one of Katharine's most faithful friends. He had fought with her father, Ferdinand, during the conquest of Granada and he was against Wolsey as he wished for a closer alliance with the Emperor, which Wolsey had opposed. Dacre pointed out that Wolsey had extracted sums of money from bishops, deans and all members of the clergy for benefits and had taken for himself the plate and riches of the abbeys. There was a long list of his sins but the most significant of all Dacre's charges against Wolsey was that of *praemunire*, which meant that he had resorted to a foreign jurisdiction in matters which should be settled in an English court. This was a serious charge, because it meant that Wolsey was accused of serving the Pope against the interests of his master the King.

The penalty for this offence was that the guilty man must relinquish all his lands and goods.

Wolsey, by this time, was so sick and ill that I imagine all he wished for was peace. He knew his great career was over and was too feeble to want to fight; moreover his enemies were too numerous. I believe he thought I was the greatest of them and he blamed me for his fall. He referred to me as 'that night crow who hath the King's ear'. He knew very well what the King's feelings were for me; he probably looked back and saw his mistakes. If he had placated me in the beginning, if he had worked for me and not against me, this would not have come to pass. With me he could have withstood those bitter enemies – Norfolk, Suffolk and the rest who could not bear to see a man so low rise so high above them. If Wolsey had had a little more insight into human nature . . . But even he had failed in that.

So Wolsey resigned the Great Seal and left his beloved York Place for ever – as he had earlier left Hampton Court.

Poor Wolsey! I feel pity for him now – and then, in my heedless way, I rejoiced in his fall.

As soon as he had left York Place, the King and I went together to inspect it. We were overcome with amazement by the treasures he had accumulated.

Henry's eyes glistened with acquisitive pleasure, and I remembered how he had taken possession of Hampton Court.

'How did the man gather together so much riches?' he demanded.

'Lord Dacre has an answer to that,' I retorted.

Henry nodded. This time he did not defend Wolsey, and together we went through the rooms gloating over the treasure which was now the King's.

*

But in spite of Wolsey's decline we were no nearer our goal. We continued to be alternately frustrated and hopeful.

Eustace Chapuys had arrived in England to take the place vacated by Mendoza. Like most ambassadors he was a spy for his master. He was clearly very astute and had no doubt been selected with care by the Emperor as a man with those very special qualities needed in a situation such as that which persisted at the Court of England.

Wolsey's loss of power meant a reshuffle of important positions. Wolsey had been in sole command. Now the King was his own First Minister, the Duke of Norfolk President of the Council, with Suffolk Vice-President, and Sir Thomas More Lord Chancellor. The King announced that *he* intended to rule with Parliament to advise him.

It was turning out in the way which the Dukes of Norfolk and Suffolk had wished, though they would have preferred to impeach Wolsey and send him to trial for High Treason. The Commons were less vindictive, largely because of a certain Thomas Cromwell who was vehement in his support of the Cardinal.

I think that was the first time the King noticed Cromwell. He was a man of very humble beginnings, the son of a blacksmith who must have been a very energetic man as he was also a fuller and a shearer of sheep, besides keeping a hostelry and a brewhouse. Thomas Cromwell was to play a big part in our story, and I learned a good deal about him later.

He had been wild in his youth and had even spent a time in prison – though I did not know this at the time. It is only when people attain power that there is an interest in their origins, and if they are in any way disreptuable, this fact is triumphantly brought to light and even exaggerated. After serving his sentence he went abroad and was in the French army for a while. Then he returned to England and married the daughter of a shearman determined, some said, to remind everyone of his beginnings. He became a successful businessman and moneylender; he was clever, shrewd, quick-witted and witty, and in due course he was noticed by Wolsey, who liked to recruit clever people to his service. There was no doubt of Cromwell's cleverness, and Wolsey was quick to make use of it, rewarding him and teaching him a great deal – for which Cromwell was grateful.

He became – doubtless through Wolsey's influence –

member of Parliament for Taunton; thus, when Wolsey's case was brought forward, he was present in the House and he defended his old master with courage and determination to prove him innocent and avoid the accusation of traitor.

Whether he saw his own ambitions – which depended so much on Wolsey's favour – fading, or whether he acted out of loyalty to his old patron, I was not sure. But with everyone ready to attack the fallen man, his action was a brave one.

The King noticed it and approved. I think Henry had decided he was going to pardon Wolsey whatever verdict was reached. But it was Cromwell's speech which decided the Commons' vote against impeachment.

So there was Wolsey – a broken man, robbed of almost all his vast possessions, but still free.

In spite of the fact that he had been my enemy and was no longer in a position to harm me, the situation had changed little.

It was true that I was at Court, where I lived in great state. I had my dressmakers working for me; I had the most exquisite materials sent to me by the leading mercers; my clothes, designed by myself, were a legend; but I had to keep changing the fashion because I was imitated to such an extent that, if I appeared in a new style of gown, a week later most of the ladies at Court would be wearing a similar one.

People paid homage to me. I was the acknowledged queen of the Court. But I was not Queen of England, and Katharine was there, a shadowy third to spoil my pleasure.

Moreover the strain of holding Henry off was great. I was in a state of bitter uncertainty as to whether or not it would be better to give way, fearful that if I did he might come to the conclusion that Anne Boleyn was just like any other woman in the dark, and if I did not, would he grow tired of waiting? How long could I keep him at bay? I allowed certain intimate caresses. I was torn between my love of adulation and my fear of losing it. Of course I knew that those who flattered me today would be the first to attack me if I were brought low. I should have looked upon Wolsey's case as an example, but I am afraid I did not think of him very much now that he was out of my way. Most of the time I was too sure of myself, possessed as I was of that mysterious allure, the essence of which was my aloofness – so different from my sister Mary. I was a heedless girl in those days – but all the same I was becoming aware of the passing of time.

Another year was almost over and I was no nearer to becoming Queen in reality than I had been four years ago.

I had always been of a quick temper. My stepmother had constantly told me to guard it – especially in my precarious position. But when it flared up, I could not restrain it; and I was at this time under great pressure.

Henry had for some time given up sleeping in Katharine's bed. He had declared that, as he believed he was not really married to her, cohabitation must cease. His conscience would not allow him to continue to sleep with her, as it would be committing a sin. For some time they had occupied the big state bed, she at one end, he at the other – so he told me – but now he thought it wise that they should not share that bed.

I remember that November day – a dreary day with a heavy mist which seeped into the room and somehow added to my depression and the feeling that this matter would not be resolved.

Royalty is rarely ever alone, and there is always someone in attendance to report what is done and said. Only in bed at night do they have any sort of privacy, and then there are servants who, though they are not actually present, are aware of what is going on.

Henry had dined with Katharine and came to me afterwards. He was looking glum and I asked him what ailed him.

'Katharine!' he said. 'How that woman plagues me! Now she is reproaching me because I do not share her bed.'

'So . . . she misses you,' I said.

'By God's Holy Mother, she thinks of what she calls her rights. I told her that I was not her legal husband and therefore I cannot share her bed.'

'And she, being such a pious lady, doubtless agreed with you.'

'She would not leave it at that. She accused me of not daring to have the case tried before an unprejudiced court. She said that, for every one I could find to decide in my favour, she would find a thousand to declare that our marriage was a good one and indissoluble.'

I was amazed and apprehensive that he had allowed the discussion to go so far with her. I thought: We shall never defeat that woman. She will always win. And how could he allow her to speak to him thus? It showed that in spite of everything he was still in awe of her.

'I can see,' I said, 'that she will always better you in argument. One day you will listen to her reasoning and cast me off.'

'Never,' he declared vehemently.

'I have waited for so long,' I said. 'I might have been married by now. I might have had children, which is the greatest consolation in the world. But alas, farewell to my time and my youth . . . spent to no purpose.'

I stood up then and left.

Unfortunately one of Chapuys' spies overheard the scene between us and reported it to that cynical man, who in turn at once sent an account of it to his master.

I believe at that time they all thought that Henry would soon grow weary of the matter – as I so clearly was.

My words had had a particular effect on Henry, especially my reference to marriage. He knew that there were many men at Court who wanted to marry me. In fact, I thought sometimes that the King's unswerving devotion to me was fostered by the effect he saw I had on other men at Court. He was terrified of losing me. The desire for the divorce had become a passion with him – whether entirely due to his desire for me or because of that obstinacy in his nature which

313

would not be denied, I was not sure. But his determination was fierce.

To placate me, he gave my father the title of Earl of Wiltshire. Thus George became Lord Rochford, and I was the Lady Anne Rochford. It increased our status considerably.

This was a settlement of that old matter concerning Piers Butler which was to have had been brought about by my marriage to James Butler and which had so suddenly – seemingly without reason – been broken off. As a result, for years there had been a dispute about the earldom between Piers Butler and my father. Henry had kept the matter in abeyance. He did not want to offend me by disappointing my father of his hopes; but on the other hand Piers Butler was very useful to him in Ireland. Now Henry made the sudden decision that my father should have the title. Butler was given certain lands in Ireland to console him; and the matter was peacefully settled, for over in remote Ireland Piers Butler would know how important the Boleyns had become to the King.

Looking back over that year, I had to admit I had my triumphs – the chief of which had been the downfall of Wolsey. Campeggio had left, but before he went he had been submitted to the indignity of having his luggage searched, which upset him greatly, though nothing was found in his bags which should not lawfully be there. He complained bitterly to the King that this was a violation of his privilege as an ambassador. The King retorted sharply that there was no breach of etiquette on our part. The Cardinal had ceased to be a legate when he had revoked the case. However, he did think it wise to send an apology, which placated Campeggio.

*

Another uneasy year had started.

In January my father was created Lord Privy Seal. The

King said to me: 'I think it would be a good idea to send your father to the Emperor. None knows the case better than he, and he has been a very successful ambassador on other occasions.'

I agreed. We must have been foolish to have acted in such a way. My father was the last person we should have sent. Perhaps we were getting so frantic that we did not pay enough attention to our actions.

However, we soon learned our mistake.

Sly Chapuys came to see the King. I was present, as I often was, for I saw no reason why I should leave the King when something so vital to me was being discussed.

Chapuys said he had had a special message from the Emperor. Very soon the Earl of Wiltshire would be returning. The Emperor was surprised that His Grace has sent one to plead a cause of which he was an interested party.

'It is my master's view that the matter should be tried in Rome, without delay.'

Henry was furious; he dismissed Chapuys, who went away with a secret, smug smile on his face which I loathed.

My father returned. He said that, before he had time to deliver his prepared speech, the Emperor had cut him short and declined to listen to 'one who had a personal interest in the outcome'.

'So I heard from that snake Chapuys,' cried Henry. 'The Emperor is determined to flout me. He wants the case tried in Rome, and we all know what that means.'

The next day there was a communication from the Pope. When Henry read it his face was scarlet, and his eyes blazed with wrath.

'Look at this. I . . . I am summoned to appear before the Rota in Rome. How dare they! Do they forget who I am?'

'He does it to degrade you,' I said.

Henry read on, his eyes narrowing.

'A pox take the fellow! Do you see what he hints here? I

must return to Katharine or run the risk of excommunication.'

I do not think my spirits had ever been so low as they were on that occasion. I saw the fear in Henry's face. He was still sufficiently under the influence of Rome to dread that threat.

'He would not dare,' I said.

'He has the Emperor behind him.'

'He has always had the Emperor behind him. That is the reason why we are as we are.'

'Excommunication,' murmured Henry. I knew what he was thinking. There had been one occasion when a King of England had suffered this at the hands of a Pope. It had plunged the country into tumult; indeed, it had been one of the most disastrous periods of King John's disastrous reign. Although the new religion which had been started by men like Martin Luther and William Tyndale was being discussed with interest throughout the country, there were still many who regarded the Pope as the Vicar of Christ and who might well turn against the King if that dreaded sentence were carried out.

I feared that even for me the King would not lay himself open to a threat of excommunication.

I said boldly: 'So the Pope is still your master.'

He clenched his fist: 'Marry, God forbid it,' he said. 'I'll not endure this. There must be a way out, Anne. I swear I'll find it.'

I put my arms about his neck and held him closely to me. 'Yes,' I said, 'we'll find a way. You'll ignore this threat?'

He nodded. 'They must come up with an answer soon.'

Would they? I wondered. Was there an answer? My uneasiness was increasing hourly.

For a time no more was said of the possibility of excommunication. It may have been that the Pope's agents, who were everywhere and would have a good idea of the state of affairs throughout Europe, realized that, if the King were cut off from Rome through excommunication, he might turn to

Lutherism. These ideas were spreading with a speed which must have seemed alarming. Books might be banned but that did not prevent their being smuggled into various countries. Although the King had always supported the religion of Rome – was he not Defender of the Faith? – he was adamant about this matter of the divorce, and excommunication in the circumstances could be a double-edged weapon.

As an act of defiance he took me everywhere with him. Sometimes I rode beside him, my horse caparisoned in royal fashion; I even rode pillion with him.

I shall always remember riding through the sullen crowds as we came into London. The people did not cheer him, because I was with him. A man shouted an insult to me and the King ordered his arrest.

He had always enjoyed the people's acclaim and never lost sight of its importance; he had always gone to great lengths to seek popularity; but at the same time they must know who was master; and if he wanted to ride into his capital with me sharing his horse he would do so.

But he did not like it; nor did I . . . perhaps less than he did. It struck fear into my heart. He might wake up to the fact that it was I who was turning his people's love away from him. The years were passing. I was getting older. How long? I continually asked myself. How long?

Wolsey was still a source of anxiety. I could quite well imagine his returning to power. If the King were to repudiate me . . . then everything would be as it had been before . . . friendship with the Pope and the Emperor. And the divorce – for Henry was bent on that? As well as his obsession with me was that of getting a male child, which he believed he could never do with Katharine. Then Wolsey would negotiate marriage with some foreign princess, and Anne Boleyn could fend for herself. That was a continual nightmare, even though the King showed no sign of swerving from his devotion to me; but it was there, a niggling thought at the back of my mind even when I was riding in pomp beside him.

317

I knew that Henry thought of Wolsey often, and he was well aware how I hated and distrusted the Cardinal; but Sir Henry Norris, who was my very good friend, told me that, when Norfolk and Suffolk had taken the Great Seal from Wolsey and found much pleasure in doing so, Wolsey had been ordered to Esher.

He took his barge to Putney, from where he would go by mule to Esher; and thinking of him, the King was overcome with pity, for he knew that Wolsey's enemies would be assembled to jeer at him on his way.

So the King called Norris to him and gave him a ring which contained a rich ruby. Wolsey would know the ring well, for he had seen it on the King's finger. Norris was to give the ring to Wolsey and tell him to be of good cheer, and wear it for love of the King.

Norris, telling me, said: 'It was a most affecting scene. Wolsey was like a man reprieved from the scaffold. I shall never forget his face when he saw the King's ring. I do believe he thought that his troubles were over. He believed that, if only he could get to the King, talk to him, explain so much to him, tell him that all his wealth had been accumulated that he might leave it to the King, all would be well.'

Norris went on: 'He took a chain and cross from his neck and gave it to me. "Take this from my hand, good Norris," he said. I was deeply touched, as any man must be to see this once-great man now brought low, and hope come flowing back because of the kindness of the King. The King truly loved Wolsey. So did Comus, Wolsey's Fool. Comus was one of the best of Fools. One could be sure Wolsey would have the best of everything. He said to me then, "Take my Fool and give him into the King's care. Tell him I loved the man and mayhap that will endear him to the Fool." Then he said to Comus, "Come here, Fool. You are to have a place at Court." And do you know, the man begged Wolsey not to send him. He wanted to stay with his master. He wanted no other ... not even the King.'

'You speak most affectingly of him, Sir Henry,' I said.

'It was a scene never to be forgotten. The Fool would not go and Wolsey called several yeomen to drag him away. I felt I was taking away a man in chains. And I said farewell to Wolsey and he went on to Esher.'

'Where I believe he found no warm welcome waiting for him.'

'A cold house without furniture . . . or plate or goblets. Poor Wolsey! How are the mighty fallen!'

And, I thought, so must he remain.

That Christmas the Cardinal was very ill.

I remember the news being brought to Henry when I was with him. Norris told him and I saw the concern in the King's face. Perhaps he felt a twinge of that conscience which was ever ready to be aroused – though usually at his bidding. However, this was a genuine twinge.

'How sick is he, Norris?' he asked.

'They say sick unto death.'

'I will send Dr Butts to him without delay.'

This he did, and when Dr Butts returned, he summoned him and wanted to know how the Cardinal fared.

'Tell me,' he said, 'have you seen yonder man?'

'I have, Your Grace.'

'And how do you like him?'

'Your Grace, if you will have him dead, I warrant you that he will be dead in four days if he does not receive comfort from you.'

'Marry, God forbid that he should die,' cried Henry. 'I would not lose him for £20,000.'

'Then must Your Grace send him some comforting message.'

'That I will do by you, good Butts.' He took a ring from his finger. 'He will know this ring,' he went on, 'for he gave it to me. Tell him that I am not offended with him in my heart for anything and bid him be of good cheer.'

'That will I do, Your Grace, and great good will it do him.'

Dr Butts looked at me significantly. Wolsey had probably told him that I was his enemy and that it was due to me that he had been brought low.

Henry intercepted the glance and understood it. 'Good sweetheart,' he said. 'As you love me, send the Cardinal a token at my request, and so doing you shall deserve our thanks.'

There was nothing I could do but obey when the King was in such a mood, so I unlinked a gold tablet which I wore at my waist and gave it to Dr Butts and asked him to convey my wishes to the Cardinal for a speedy recovery.

The King's eyes were glistening with sentiment. He took my hand and kissed it.

And Dr Butts went back to Wolsey with the tokens.

They were evidently effective, for within a few days Wolsey had left his bed.

*

I could see no way out of the maze in which we were caught up. Things grew worse instead of better.

Clement and the Emperor were now on good terms. Peace had been reached; the Pope was back in Rome; and Charles had received the crown of the Holy Roman Empire which was a symbol of unity between the Church and the States of Europe.

It was clear to me that we were never going to get papal approval for the divorce.

Then came a glimmer of hope from an unexpected quarter.

Henry's two chief agents who had been working assiduously for a settlement – his secretary Gardiner and his almoner Fox – happened to be staying at the house of a certain Mr Cressy at Waltham Abbey. Mr Cressy had two sons, both scholars who had been at the university with a certain Thomas Cranmer, and this Cranmer happened to be staying at the Cressys' house, on a visit to his friends.

Cranmer was a man of about forty. We learned that he was a brilliant scholar who had taken degrees of BA and MA with great distinction and had become a fellow of Jesus College. He married, and this could have called a halt to his career at the college, but so that this should not be unduly interrupted, he sent his wife to live at an inn in Cambridge which was run by a relative of hers. There he used to go to see her until, about a year after the marriage, she died in childbirth. He was then re-elected to a fellowship. So, unencumbered, his career progressed and he was at this time one of the university's public examiners in Theology. It was only to be expected that, on the arrival of Gardiner and Fox, there should be a great deal of lively conversation and the topic which was uppermost in the minds of most people at this time was the divorce.

Few men knew as much about this intricate matter as Gardiner and Fox, and Cranmer listened intently to what they had to say.

'There will be a very long delay if the King pursues this matter through the courts of Rome,' said Cranmer.

I could imagine the scene. The two men who had travelled extensively and talked endlessly in this search for a solution, to be confronted by a fellow who could not know very much about the affair.

'What the King needs,' went on Cranmer, 'is sufficient assurance that his marriage is invalid – notwithstanding the dispensation. He then might take the responsibility of marrying again at once. He ought therefore to take the opinions of the divines of the universities and act accordingly.'

The two agents looked at him incredulously.

'To act against the Emperor!'

'As I see it,' said Cranmer, 'the King does not need Rome. He just needs the assurance of the divines that his marriage is invalid.'

'You take a simple view of a complicated matter,' said Fox.

'The solution to most matters is found to be simple when one knows what it is,' replied Cranmer with a smile.

Then the matter was apparently dropped, but both Gardiner and Fox pondered on what Cranmer had said and when they were next in the company of the King they mentioned it to him.

I was present at the time, so I saw what effect those words had on the King.

He was quiet for a second or two; then he crashed his fist down on the table. 'By God,' he cried, 'that man hath the right sow by the ear!' He turned to Fox and Gardiner. 'Where is he? Bring him to me. I would see him without delay.'

Within hours Thomas Cranmer was at Greenwich.

The King talked for a long time with him and his mood changed. He saw hope through Thomas Cranmer.

Cranmer was made much of and taken into my father's household, where he was given a very comfortable apartment. He was to write a treatise on the matter and then to return to Cambridge to give a lecture in which he would persuade the learned divines to give their vote in the King's favour.

There followed months of preparations. It was necessary that the divines, not only in England but in the whole of Europe, should give the right answer. This involved a great deal of money for the expenses of journeys and also for bribes and promises of favours to come.

All through those months Henry laboured. He was sure that we were working in the right direction now. If he could get the approval of the divines, he would dispense with that of the Pope.

Finally he had all the information he needed. He summoned the clergy and the nobles; he wanted their seal on the document he was sending to the Pope. It was amazing that some of them had the courage to refuse. There was Bishop Fisher and Sir Thomas More among the leaders of the opposition. If the King married without the approval of the Pope, they pointed out, the succession would be in danger.

If they did not agree, thundered Henry, he would find some other form of redress.

They were uneasy. I knew what the King had in mind. There was that man who had recently come into prominence – a very clever and artful fellow – a man of the people whom the King heartily disliked personally but who, he had to admit, had clever ideas. This was, of course, Thomas Cromwell – said to be the son of a blacksmith, who had risen high through his cunning. He had made an extraordinary suggestion which Henry could not forget. Since the Pope would not grant what the King wanted, why did not Henry make himself Head of the Church of England, which would mean that he could have his own way in the matter of the divorce – besides bringing many other advantages with it. Why this adherence to the Pope, a foreigner? It was obvious that the Pope regarded himself as the King's master. Had he not recently summoned him to Rome?

Henry had been obsessed with the idea ever since he heard it.

And now he was incensed because some members of the clergy and the nobility hesitated to sign his petition to the Pope.

They wanted discussion on the matter, they said.

'Delay, delay,' cried Henry. 'Procrastination. By God's Holy Mother, I have had enough of it.'

He knew that their talk of discussion was just another example of those delaying tactics which was the method of all who feared to bring the matter to a conclusion.

He sent commissioners to the houses of all those who hesitated over giving their signatures, and it was made known to these dilatory men that if they did not sign they would lose the King's favour.

In time this method produced the required result, and the petition was despatched to Rome, where it lay neglected for some time.

I could not see why Henry and I should not be married as the divines had declared the marriage to Katharine invalid. Why should we wait for the sanction of the Pope? Was not the reason for this that we should act without him?

But Henry's fear was not so much of the Pope as of the Emperor Charles. If he were faced with war through this matter, he would have lost the love of his people.

He was torn between his inclinations as a man and a king.

So the weary waiting went on.

I was getting very tired of it all, and sometimes I thought with yearning of Hever. But how long would the peace of the countryside keep me happy? I had tasted power. I wanted power. I wanted adulation, grandeur and all the accoutrements of royalty. It was to be my consolation for losing the love and marriage which I had planned. Looking back now, I believe I romanticized my relationship with Henry Percy. I had made it into an ideal. Would our marriage – if it had taken place – have been like that? Should I have tired of that windswept castle? Would I have found Percy's gentleness insipid? On the other hand, here before me was grandeur such as, in those days, I could never have imagined would be mine. The King adored me; he would set me up beside him. I was different from all the other women at Court; and because of this I should be the Queen of England.

How foolish to dream of the green fields of Hever! What I wanted was the cloth of gold, the diamonds, the rubies, the homage, given to the power behind the throne.

I was so young and heedless. I had thought because Norfolk and Suffolk had supported me and, with my father and brother, had been my strongest adherents, they were truly my friends.

How could I have been so foolish, how so simple!

What they had planned for – I know now – was the downfall of Wolsey, and they had seen that I could be of help in this. Now that Wolsey could not rise again, my usefulness to them was over.

The King was in a sullen mood; he was studying me speculatively and I could see that he was suppressing some secret emotion.

I felt a twinge of fear. I had so often thought that the day might come when he would be tired of waiting. It would be understandable, for indeed this patient fidelity of his had amazed me in a man of his sexual appetites. There was something miraculous about it. Sorcery, on my part, thought some; true love, a respect for purity, thought others. I sometimes wondered whether it was because he had passed his first youth. He was thirty-nine years of age. But always in my thoughts had been the fear that I could not hold him off forever.

Now he was seriously disturbed and displeased ... with me.

I asked: 'Is Your Grace not feeling well?'

His answer was: 'I never forget Wyatt and that tablet of yours.'

Wyatt! But Wyatt had been away from Court for a long time. I had rarely seen him since he departed after the affair of the tablet. He had been having an adventurous time and I only heard news of him through his sister Mary. He had left the Papal Court to which he had travelled with Sir John Russell and had wandered through Italy to Ferrara, Bologna and Florence, and to Venice where he had been engaged in some diplomatic work in conjunction with Russell. Travelling from Venice to Rome, he had been captured by the Emperor's troops, and a ransom had been demanded. The adventurous Wyatt, however, escaped, after which he came back to England but only briefly. Henry did not wish him to remain and he was given the post of High Marshal of Calais, where he spent most of his time.

'But I explained to you that he snatched the tablet from me and refused to give it back,' I said.

'He must have been on friendly terms with you to do such a thing,' retorted Henry coldly.

'What nonsense is all this!' I was frightened so I went into the attack, dispensing with that ceremony with which even I was expected to address him. 'The Wyatts were my family's neighbours, in both Kent and Norfolk. We have known each other since we were children.'

'All the more reason . . .'

'All the more reason for what?'

He took me by the shoulders and looked into my face. 'Wyatt was your lover,' he said.

'He declared himself in love with me, if that is what you mean. Many have declared themselves to be so. Why pick on Wyatt?'

'Tell me the truth.'

'The truth is that no one has been my lover in the sense that you imply; nor shall any man be. My virtue is for my husband.' I could see that slack look coming back into his face, so I whipped up my anger. 'I see that you have some doubt. Mayhap you have been listening to those who would slander me. I will not remain here to be so treated. I shall go home at once. I will not stay where my word is doubted.'

'Anne . . . Anne . . . you are so impetuous . . . so quick to anger . . .'

'And so would you be, my lord, if you were doubted by the one in whom you had placed the most trust.'

He said: 'The waiting is too long. It unnerves me.'

'I know, I know. But we have the remedy. The divines have supported you. Cromwell believes you can do without the Pope. Yet you continue to bow the knee to him and at the same time you believe calumnies about me. And that is something I will not endure.'

'It was false . . . that story of Wyatt? But he is an attractive fellow and I have seen you two together.'

'What would you have me do? Say to him, "Go away, old friend and neighbour. The King has forbidden me to speak to you." No . . . no . . . I see that this waiting is wearying you and you must seek excuses to be rid of me. There is no need, my lord. If I am not wanted, I am ready to go.'

He held me close to him. Inwardly I was exultant, while I assumed anger. I could command him. His love for me was not to be destroyed by scandals which my enemies sought to circulate about me.

'I believe you,' he said. 'I would always believe you. It is sometimes hard to accept the fact that one so beautiful . . . so different from the rest . . .'

'You must believe me, Henry,' I said firmly. 'If you do not, I must go.'

'Never even speak of it.'

'I must . . . if you wish to be rid of me.'

'By God's Holy Mother, did you ever believe that?'

'Sometimes I do not know what to believe. The divines have declared your marriage invalid, yet you hold back. You are afraid of Katharine.'

'Her nephew is the most powerful man in Europe. I cannot risk offending him. The Pope!' He snapped his fingers. 'Vacillating Clement . . . swaying in the wind . . . I will, I won't . . . What do I care for him?'

'The new religion sets out the wrongs of the Church of Rome.'

'I do not question the Church itself – only its leaders.'

'But the leaders *are* the Church.'

'Nay,' said the King. 'I am as fervent a Christian as any man.'

'So can you be without adhering to the Church of Rome. What did Cromwell say: "Why should you not be head of your Church . . . the Church of England?" '

'These are weighty matters, Anne, and I, at the moment, am most concerned about what I heard of you and Wyatt.'

'I would know who has whispered this slander to you.'

'I should not tell you.'

'But you will, Henry. I must know who it is who spreads lies about me.'

'I should not have troubled you. Suffice it that I believe the rumour to be false.'

'It does not suffice for me. I must know the names of those who have said this of me.'

'I do not believe the man.'

'So it was a man.'

'Let it be, Anne. It is you I believe. It is you I love. It is you whom I will make my Queen.'

'This can never be if you do not trust me, and if you refuse to tell me the name of my slanderer, I shall know you do not.'

'Anne, if it had not been someone close to me, one whom I love as a brother, I should have cuffed him and threatened him with my displeasure.'

So it was someone close to him! My heart was beating fast. It was not just something which had been whispered in the streets. Someone in a high place had actually come to him and told him this.

It was imperative that I knew who.

'But you believed him . . .'

'Only until you assured me. Oh, Anne, how I longed for that reassurance.'

'Henry,' I said seriously, 'it cannot be as it was between us if you do not trust me. Who was it?'

He hesitated for a moment. Then he said: 'It was Suffolk.'

Suffolk! The Duke who, with Norfolk and my father, had appeared to be my strongest adherent. His wife had come to hate me, although she had been friendly towards me long ago in France. She could not forget that once I had been her maid of honour and would – if all went well – soon take precedence over her. She was only the King's sister; I should be his Queen. She, at least, had been open in her resentment; he, the traitor, the sly schemer, had feigned support just until I had helped to bring about the fall of Wolsey, and now he was seeking to bring me to mine.

'Suffolk!' I cried. 'Then I must indeed leave Court.'

'Assuredly not. You cannot go.'

'The Duke of Suffolk is your brother-in-law and one of Your Grace's greatest friends. I know how you enjoy his company. I cannot ask you to deprive yourself of it; but that means you must be deprived of mine.'

'Anne, I'll speak to Suffolk. I'll tell him he was wrong. An apology . . . he shall apologize.'

I shook my head. 'I do not trust him. He is a liar. He thinks as his wife, your sister, and resents my presence here. It is better for me to go. Let us have an end of this matter.'

'An end! What do you say, Anne?'

'I say that we have the approval of the divines; we have Cromwell's solution; but still we remain in this state. And you listen to the lies of your *dear* friend . . . your brother-in-law, whom I now know to be my enemy and who will not cease to pour poison in your ear concerning me. I cannot remain at Court while Suffolk is here.'

He sought to pacify me. I felt my power over him then. I had to show Suffolk that I would not allow him to go unpunished. As the King embraced me, I held aloof.

'I must leave,' I said.

'Nay, nay sweetheart. Suffolk shall go. He shall be banished from Court.'

'When?' I asked.

'This very day.'

This was victory. Suffolk would learn his lesson.

I was triumphant, but I felt exhausted and very uneasy.

*

I was surrounded by enemies. Norfolk had never really been appreciative of the fact that I was bringing great glory to the family. It seemed ironical that the Boleyns, whom the Norfolks had always resented, should be the ones to find such favour with the King. My father must now be one of the richest men in the country; George was rising; Mary remained in obscurity, but then that was Mary's own fault and probably her desire; she was unlike the rest of us, completely without ambition. The Suffolks were now my declared enemies. Perhaps I should have been more wary of them than I was. After all, Charles Brandon had always been, from the early days, a great favourite with the King, and there was no doubt that Henry loved his sister. So they were very powerful enemies.

It was impossible to keep news from seeping out. The whole country knew about the verdict of the ecclesiastical courts, and there were even whispers that there might be a break with Rome. People had been used to the old ways for centuries. Many did not like change but there were some who were becoming imbued with the new ideas. This was something quite different. The proposal was not that the religion should change in any way, only that the head of the Church in England should be the King and not the Pope.

Garbled versions of what was actually happening circulated. I was at the centre of the controversy, it was said. This was true in a way, for but for me the matter would never had been raised, or would it? Partly it was due to the King's obsession with me and the fact that I would not become his mistress and held out for marriage; but on the other hand he desperately needed a male heir and it was clear that Katharine could not give him that. His continual complaint was: I need an heir. The country needs an heir . . . and that heir must be male.

If his wife had been anyone but aunt of the Emperor, the matter would have been settled long ago.

And now there was this mighty controversy for which I was blamed. I was a witch. I was a sorceress. I was an emissary of the Devil.

If only I could tell them that I had been drawn into this affair unwillingly at first. I had been robbed of my chance of happiness and because of that I had become ambitious.

Yet, I was the scapegoat. It could be terrifying at times. I was afraid to ride through the streets. They shouted after me. They called me lewd names.

Once, when I was supping with the King, a messenger came in haste to say that a crowd of people were assembled at the stairs waiting for me to leave.

'Your Grace, they look murderous to me,' said the servant.

Henry was angry. He hated little so much as these displays of the people.

I had to leave in haste by a side door and not take the barge. It was disconcerting.

I heard everywhere: 'We'll not have Nan Bullen.'

I thought: We cannot go on like this. Something must happen soon.

I had my family and a few good friends like Norris, Weston, Brereton. George was the one I could truly trust. My father was growing uneasy. He was aware of the storms about me. He had so much relished the promotion and the way in which the money was rolling into his coffers. He was not particularly grateful to me; it was the Boleyn tradition, he believed, that the daughters should build up the family fortunes. I was only following along that road in a more spectacular way than my predecessors.

I read a good deal and was getting more and more interested in the new ideas. I always had a book near me so that, if I had any spare time, I could pass it in reading.

One day I found a book on the table which I had not seen before. It was a kind of almanac, a book of prophecies. I was always amused to leaf through such books. I even remembered some of the prophecies and took an interest in seeing whether they came true. I opened the book. There was a picture of the King. He was standing, and, kneeling at his feet, was the Queen. She was wringing her hands. It was clearly meant to portray the recent trial.

I turned a page and caught my breath in horror. There was a picture of a woman, and I knew at a glance whom it was meant to depict. There were the hanging sleeves; the sixth nail was visible, though it looked like an extra finger. The woman had no head on her shoulders. The head – unmistakably mine – was lying on the floor; the hair was like black snakes, and on it was a crown.

This was meant to be a prophecy, and after the manner of

such was told in pictures. What it meant was that, if ever I attained the crown, I should have to pay for it with my head.

I was shaken. I knew of the enmity which surrounded me, of course, but that anyone should have gone so far as this was a great shock.

I sat back in my chair. One of my attendants came in. She was a pleasant girl named Nan Saville.

I called her. 'Nan,' I said, 'did you put this book here?'

She stared at it in astonishment. 'No, my lady, I have never seen it before.'

'It is a book of prophecies,' I told her.

'Oh, I know the sort of thing, my lady.'

'I don't think you know this. Just look. Here is the King and here the Queen wringing her hands.'

' 'Tis a fair likeness, my lady.'

I turned the page. 'And this?'

Nan gave a little scream and put her hand over her mouth to suppress it.

'You know who this is, Nan.'

'My . . . my lady. It . . . it is . . . horrible.'

'Yes, it is, is it not? It is meant to warn me.'

'Oh, my lady, if ever I thought that was to come to pass, I would not have him though he were an emperor.'

'It is only a book. Take it away. Burn it. Don't show it to anyone. It is just a bauble. Nan, I am resolved to have him that my issue shall be royal.'

'But, my lady . . .' She touched her neck.

'Whatever becomes of me, Nan, I shall be Queen of England.'

I think I disguised my disquiet from Nan Saville. She took the book away and I never saw it again.

I did not mention the book to the King. I wondered if anyone had shown it to him. That was hardly likely. He would have had enquiries made, and the publisher and printer would have been brought to trial and probably lost their right hands for producing such a book.

Then one day I saw that Suffolk had returned to Court. He had been forgiven. The King was lenient with those who amused him. Suffolk had been his companion for so long; they were alike in many ways.

I was about to protest but a flash of caution came to me. The King hated to be without Suffolk, and he could not remain for long on unfriendly terms with his sister. So I said nothing.

I was cool to Suffolk and ignored his attempts to behave as though nothing had happened.

My uneasiness was increasing.

*

The Cardinal was still on our minds. I knew that on the least pretext Henry would reinstate him. He would never have his old power, nor would he regain his possessions – the King loved York Place and Hampton Court too much to part with them – but Henry's affection for the Cardinal had gone deep and he did not forget it.

Although at times Henry appeared to be childish – as in those disguising games which he loved to play and in deceiving himself that what he wanted to believe was the truth – as I have said he was a man of conflicting characteristics. He was romantic and sentimental; he was something of a scholar. He had governed his kingdom with a shrewdness which had aroused the envy of François, who, at the time of the Field of the Cloth of Gold, had been inclined to have a certain contempt for his naïvety. Henry was complex, and I had to remember that he was all-powerful and could, if he so wished, exert that power over his subjects. True, he had to consider the will of other rulers and that was galling for him. But he was our monarch and I must not forget that he had complete power over us.

He was fair enough to accept that what had happened over the divorce negotiations was not Wolsey's fault. Wolsey had wanted the divorce but marriage into France; and that was reasonable. It was the Pope and the Emperor who were the reason for Henry's frustration, not Wolsey. I was sure that Henry was remembering the past and all the good Wolsey had done for him and the country.

So the situation with Wolsey was fraught with danger. If he came back, if he ever had the King's confidence again, he would remember his enemies.

So it was necessary for Wolsey's fall to be complete. We had all expected him to die early in the year, and so he would have but for the King's leniency which had given him so much comfort; and Henry's physician had supplied physical help.

So ... the years of frustration continued and Wolsey was still with us.

Neither Norfolk nor Suffolk would allow matters to stand still. They sought evidence against Wolsey.

Norfolk claimed to have wrung an admission from Wolsey's Italian physician, Dr Augustine, that at the time the Cardinal was persuading François to write to the Pope asking him to favour the divorce, he was urging the Pope to excommunicate the King if he married Anne Boleyn.

This was outright treachery. Norfolk pretended to be deeply shocked by Augustine's revelation; he had the doctor brought to London in a most humiliating fashion – with his legs tied under his horse, as prisoners were carried.

However, when Augustine arrived at the Duke's residence, he was given spacious quarters and lived there in some comfort.

During the year Wolsey had been travelling north, and it was discomfiting to hear how the people came out to cheer him. It was ironical that during the days of his prosperity they had loathed him, called him 'the butcher's cur' and blamed him for the taxes they had to pay, and for the ills of the country; but now in his misery he had become the Great Cardinal.

Wolsey did not encourage the people, for he knew that

would not help his cause, and he did try to travel as lightly as possible.

But the end was near and he must have known it, particularly when the revelations of Dr Augustine were brought to light.

There was only one course open to Henry then: Wolsey would have to stand trial for treason.

He was at Cawood near York and from there he was to be brought to the Tower of London. Henry was very upset but the suggestion that he should be excommunicated angered him.

I had an idea. Someone had to arrest him, and he was in the North. How ironical if the man to do the task should be the Earl of Northumberland who, some years before, Wolsey had humiliated and castigated because he had had the temerity to fall in love with a 'foolish girl'.

I said: 'I wish the Earl of Northumberland to make the arrest.' And the King did not raise any objection.

I wondered what Henry Percy would think when he was confronted with the task. I thought of him often, wondering how much he had changed. Had he remained the same gentle, rather ineffectual boy whom I had known?

I heard the story afterwards. Northumberland did not relish the task and wished he had not been chosen for it. He was not as vindictive as I. Perhaps he did not care so much that our romance had been blighted. But I did know that his marriage was unhappy. We had blamed Wolsey – yet it had not been Wolsey's wish to separate us, but the King's, I reminded myself over and over again. However the fact remained that Wolsey had acted in a most offensive manner.

I could imagine the scene. It was described to me by Walter Walsh, a gentleman of the Privy Chamber who had been sent north to accompany Northumberland on this mission.

The Cardinal had been dining in Cawood Castle, and when the Earl of Northumberland and Walter Walsh were announced, I could picture his astonishment.

The visitors were taken into the dining-room, and Wolsey reproached them for not warning him of their intended arrival that he might prepare to honour them. Northumberland appeared to be tongue-tied. I supposed he could not find it in himself to say the necessary words. He had always been in awe of Wolsey.

Wolsey said he remembered Northumberland well. 'You were an impetuous boy,' he said; to which Northumberland replied that he remembered the Cardinal well.

How had Northumberland felt then, faced with the man who had ruined his life? He must remember me; he would scarcely have been able to forget me, for talk of what was happening at Court would have reached even the remote North. It may have been that he had dreamed romantic dreams. He was more likely to have done so than I was.

However, he seemed impassive, so Walsh told me, when he approached the Cardinal and said: 'My lord, I arrest you on a charge of High Treason, and you must travel to London as soon as possible.'

Wolsey must have been in great fear, for he knew he would be taken to the Tower of London – and it was few who entered by the Traitor's Gate who ever came out free men. Usually the only time they left the Tower was to make the short journey to Tower Hill, where they laid their head on the block.

The Cardinal's legs were bound to the stirrups of the mule he rode. He was the King's prisoner for all to see.

The people came out to cheer him as he passed along. How they loved a fallen man – even though they had hated him bitterly in the days of his affluence.

So he rode into Leicester.

During the journey his health deteriorated rapidly and he found difficulty in sitting his mule. Perhaps he prayed that he might never reach his dreaded destination. If he did, that prayer was answered.

When he came to Leicester Abbey, he was failing so fast

that, when the people crowded round him, he said: 'I am come here to leave my bones among you.'

He was immediately taken to a bed. It was November and the mist hung heavy in his chamber, but nothing could have been so heavy as the Cardinal's heart.

His life was over. All his greatness was gone. I wondered if he thought of himself riding in that proud procession as he so often had, in his glorious scarlet garments, his hat and the great Seal carried before him, an orange stuffed with cloves in his hand that he might not smell the offensive odour of the populace.

His days of glory were gone forever.

He arrived at Leicester on the 26th November. His stay there was brief, for on the morning of the 29th he passed away.

Sir William Kingston was with him at the time and he told me how Wolsey had feared the axe – not for the pain it would bring his body, but because it would mean the end of his hopes and greatness. He had risen high and because of this his fall was the greater.

His last words to Kingston were: 'I see this matter against me. I see how it has been framed. But if I had served God as diligently as I have done the King, He would not have given me over in my grey hairs.'

And having spoken those words, he died.

When his death was reported to the King, and Henry was told of his last words, he went into his chamber and shut himself away. He would not see anyone.

I think he was filled with remorse. Oh yes, Henry had truly loved Wolsey.

The Consummation

Wolsey was dead, and so began another year. Could there be any end to our problem? Were we going on like this for ever? We could not. We had to succeed soon or fail altogether.

Cranmer, together with Cromwell, had brought us new hope, and it was to Cromwell I looked. He was a man with a single idea; that idea was entirely his, and he could see – and so could I – that on the success of that idea hung his entire future; it could be the foundation of his fortunes.

It was so simple. The Church of England should have as its natural head the King of England.

It was a daring idea, and I do not believe it would have occurred even to Cromwell but for the growth of those ideas, begun by Martin Luther, in parts of the Continent of Europe for a reformation of the old religion, which would mean breaking away from the influence of Rome. Cromwell did not, however, suggest a change of religion in England – only a change of Head, the King in place of the Pope. Wolsey had been a brilliant statesman; he had guided the King through many troubled waters; he had encouraged education in the country; his foreign policy had been successful and won respect – and pensions for him with it – from royalty other than his own; but he had become a Cardinal and kept England bound to the Vatican.

The King spend a good deal of time with Cromwell, but he could not like him. Cromwell had a natural coarseness which his elevation could not overcome; he had great ugly hands; but if his uncouth manners offended the King, Henry liked his ideas. He could snap at Cromwell and Cromwell remained imperviously servile. Cromwell was pursuing one goal: he was going to break with Rome and set the King up as

Head of the Church of England.

Henry could be all powerful at home, he pointed out, free of the domination of the Church through Rome. No more fear of giving offence and of threats of excommunication. What would the Head of the Church feel for the vague threats of one who was of no importance in his country? Such an act would make England great, and, moreover, it would be a simple matter for the King to marry where he pleased. Already the authority of the Pope was being questioned in Germany and Switzerland. A new form of the old religion would come about. It would not be subservient to Rome. The King would be leading the way. Others would follow.

But Henry could not forget that he bore the title of Defender of the Faith and he had to wrestle with his conscience.

'Would Clement have denied the divorce if Queen Katharine had not been the Emperor's aunt?' he asked.

The answer was, of course, he would not. But for that relationship, the matter would have been settled four years ago.

Still the months passed in indecision and I was chafing more and more against the delay. Why could not Henry follow Cromwell's suggestion? Cromwell had the answer. Why should the King bow down to Rome?

Henry declared that it was not a simple matter. There was so much to be considered. He must have the people behind him.

'The people?' I cried. 'What do the people know?'

'There would be those who would adhere to Rome and they would create a danger. Why, even all my ministers are not with me.'

'That old fool Fisher!'

'The man is no fool, Anne. There is Warham, too . . . and More is against it.'

'How dare they oppose the King.'

'Oh, Anne,' he said, 'I do not know which way to go.'

My father was as frantic as I was. He feared that the King might be swayed and turn from me. The price of my queenship was too high. Warham was an old man, his protests would not mean much. Still, he stood for the old ways. There was Fisher. He was a man who did not care what trouble he brought on himself; he would stand up and say what he believed to be the truth.

One day there was a disaster at Fisher's dining-table. Twelve members of his household died. There was one woman beggar who was also affected, for the Bishop's palaces were always open to the hungry at midday; they came into the dining-room and sat there at a table on trestles which had been set up especially for them.

The Bishop was unharmed. He had been in deep discourse with a friend and had left his soup untasted.

It was soon discovered that an attempt had been made to poison him.

Henry was enraged. This was not the way. Fisher would have to be coerced, threatened perhaps, but any attempt to poison him – and such a clumsy one – would not be tolerated.

He passed a law immediately. Poisoners should be boiled alive.

The soup was tested. Richard Rouse, the cook, was taken for questioning and immediately confessed to the deed. He could not say who it was who paid him well for what he did; it was a stranger and he knew not whence he came.

Suspicion was, of course, directed against me and my family, although we knew nothing of the matter.

Crowds gathered in Smithfield to see the sentence carried out. I was told that the screams of the victim were bloodcurdling.

The King was annoyed and sullen. He was clearly disturbed but he was thinking more and more of the possibility of a break with Rome. Strict laws were enforced against the clergy; and he stated publicly that some priests were only half Englishmen because they had taken an oath to the Pope. But still the months were passing without any action being taken.

Henry was disturbed further when Sir Thomas More resigned the Great Seal. He asked this through Norfolk, pleading ill health. I think he saw which way we were moving and he was a deeply religious man. Henry wanted the support of such a man who was highly respected; he had simple tastes, living happily in the heart of his devoted family. I heard that Norfolk had found him on one occasion in the chapel of his home in Chelsea, singing in the family choir. Norfolk had reproved him, saying that he dishonoured the King and his office by parading as a parish clerk. More's reply had been disconcerting. He said he was serving God, the King's master. Ominous words, as it happened later.

It was just at this time that he resigned the Great Seal, and it was a clear indication of his thought.

At last there came a turn in our affairs.

What had irritated me most was to be in the palace with the King and to be made constantly aware of the Queen's presence, for, in spite of the relationship between them, Henry kept up appearances in public, and wherever he went on ceremonial occasions, the Queen was with him. This had stressed the fact that Katharine was still the Queen and that put me in the position of concubine. It was something I found intolerable and, I think, was largely responsible for my outbursts of temper.

Henry was becoming more and more anxious to be rid of her. If he were absent for a few days, she would write to him, behaving just as though there was no rift between them. Her attitude was one of tolerance, implying that he was momentarily straying but like a good and patient wife she would forgive him and in due course he would realize his mistake and return to her.

He would endure no more of this, he said. He had been patient too long. He was going to ask her to retire from Windsor Castle. There was a place which had come to him from Wolsey. The Moor in Hertfordshire. She should take up her residence there. It was a command and she could not disobey his instructions; and now, with Katharine gone, I was in the position of Queen. Her apartments became mine. The people in the streets might cry their insults; it was different in Court circles. There, people must pay homage to me, for this move of Henry's was significant. It showed that his determination was as strong as ever.

He said to me: 'We should wait no longer.'

I knew what that meant and I had to make a quick decision. I had always known that this moment must come. I had fought long enough. He had made his gesture by turning Katharine away from Court, which was tantamount to declaring that she was no longer the Queen, and if I was to be, how could I deny the King that which he had been passionately seeking for so long?

I was tortured by the decision I had to make. I was not a sensual woman and I did not look forward to the consummation with any pleasure. Perhaps it was due to my upbringing at the Court of France, when I was in the midst of such promiscuity that I acquired a distaste for it. My virginity had been my strength. What would happen if I lost it? Suppose I had relented all those years ago in the rose garden at Hever, where should I have been now? Cast off like my sister Mary, spoken of as *una grandissima ribalda*, as François had referred to her? So I had become well versed in the art of evasion. Heaven knew, I had had long enough practice with Henry, and even before that at the Court of France. I was avid for admiration; I knew that I had special attractions and I liked them to be appreciated. I liked to know that I was desired, and in that was the pleasure for me.

But I had come to the point when there could be no more hesitation. Since Henry had removed Katharine from Court, I was the Queen in all but fact; and if I were to attain that glittering rôle I must not take one false step now.

One fear haunted me. What if I submitted and he found the result not as satisfactory as he had hoped? For years he had longed for me – me only. Was I so much different from other women he had known? Oh, I knew I was in daylight . . . my clothes, my manners, my sudden moods, my intense delight in the joys of the moment, my ability to devise clever entertainments. Yes, I was different. But in sexual encounter how should I fare . . . I, a novice with no great enthusiasm for the game compared with doyennes of the art like my sister Mary. Experience made perfect and in this matter I was completely without that. He had dreamed so long of possessing me. What if I did not match his fantasies?

There was another possibility. Suppose I became pregnant? That could be a two-edged sword. I could say to him, 'You must marry me at once or our child will be born out of wedlock.' That would never do for the heir to the throne. On the other hand, suppose I was barren? Well, a woman cannot expect to conceive immediately – though it was a possibility.

The matter was constantly on my mind; and then I decided that I could afford to wait no longer. The opposition was crumbling. Cromwell and Cranmer had 'the right sows by the ears'. Henry was prepared to snap his fingers at the Pope and the Emperor and at the same time to break with the Church of Rome.

If ever there was a time, this must be it.

I must prepare for the occasion. As always at such times, I considered what I should wear. This would be one of the testing occasions of my life, and a great deal depended on my clothes. Clothes had always had an effect on me; they changed my moods. I often thought that whatever tragedy was about to befall I could never be completely unhappy if I were wearing a gown which lifted my spirits, and however pleased I was with life, I could not be completely so in a drab and ill-fitting garment.

So therefore, on this occasion, clothes would be all-important.

My nightgown should be made of black satin, lined with black taffeta, and this should be stiffened with buckram and lined with black velvet. I enjoyed designing it. I showed sketches to Henry. He was now so happy – like a bridegroom. He was affable to everyone. I said, 'You must not give away our secret,' and we laughed together.

We even talked about my coronation.

'This Cromwell is a man of ideas,' he said. 'I welcome him. I wish I could like him better. I always want to cuff him . . . then I remember his uses.'

But he did not want to talk of Cromwell for long. We were like two lovers planning our honeymoon. Henry thought we should pay a visit to François. 'He has been our good friend over this matter,' he said.

I knew that François wanted to woo Henry from the Emperor. It was all part of the power struggle. And I should like to see the French Court again.

The nightdress was very costly. The price was £10.15s.8d., and there was a cloak with it edged with velvet and lined with Bruges satin which was almost as costly as the gown, being over £9.

An extravagant garment. But it was for a very important occasion, and the bills were settled by the Treasury, together with many more, for if I were going to France, I should need a new wardrobe and, knowing the French, it must be of very special elegance.

So I tried not to think of the night and gave myself to the joys of discussions with the seamstress and being fitted and making suggestions . . . while I waited with trepidation.

We were to sup together.

I wore the black nightdress and the cloak that went with it. I had chosen wisely, although I had hesitated to wear black because of my darkness – red being the colour which set it off to perfection. But the low-cut bodice, exposing so much white flesh, was alluring.

His eyes never left me. They shone with something more than lust. He was at his most attractive that night. He was almost humble, a quality which sat oddly on him. He looked younger, for the last years had taken a certain toll of him. This was how he must have looked when he came to the throne. I felt an affection for him. I realized, too, that I was different. I had made up my mind. I was no longer tortured by the fearsome question of Dare I? I had given way because I fancied I could see the goal in sight, and this was the way to it.

It was a discreet supper *à deux*; we were waited on by two silent-footed servants. There was no ceremony. We might not have been the King and the one who aspired to be his Queen. He glowed as he talked to me of his love for me, how it had changed his life. Indeed it had – and the course of the country's history perhaps. But he was modest, which made him almost like a stranger. He was so pleased because my choice had fallen on him and that I had saved myself for him.

I did not reply to that. In truth, my choice had fallen on a crown and on him because he could supply it. I had previously chosen Henry Percy, he must remember; and it was he who had snatched me away from that young man.

But on such a night we did not wish to talk of such things; and to see him thus – so different from the arrogant King whose wrath, Warham had once said, 'was death' – to see him thus, for my sake, endeared him to me.

I almost loved him on that night.

I should have liked to linger over supper but he was impatient and we were alone. I emerged from my black satin and went to him.

I had prepared myself for the onslaught of passion which I knew must come – all the pent-up feelings of the years of waiting. He was incoherent, murmuring words of love. I responded, as well as I could, fearful all of the time of my inadequacy – which was a new rôle for me, as the humble lover was for him.

It seemed to me that on that night we were both playing parts to which our natures had made us unaccustomed.

We lay in the darkness. There was silence between us. I asked myself: What is he thinking? Why all this fuss? Is not one woman very like another? Mary had held him for a long time. Mary had special powers. She was born to play bedtime games. I had not been.

'Anne.' His voice came to me in the darkness.

'Yes . . . Henry?' I whispered fearfully.

He said: 'Methinks I am the happiest man on Earth.'

Waves of joy swept over me. Then I had not failed.

I replied: 'Then must I be the happiest of women.'

'There was never love like this,' he said.

No, I thought, never love that would rock the foundations of the Church.

*

The weeks which followed were happy for both Henry and me. I had made the decision; there was no going back, and I was no longer plagued by that eternal question. Henry was delighted; he looked years younger, and everyone noticed the change in him. He was no longer frustrated. Katharine was out of sight and he ceased to think of her. I was there beside him; in fact, he hated me to be out of his sight. I was immensely relieved. I had submitted and I still held him – perhaps even more firmly than before.

He took a delight in my extravagance. I bought yards and yards of red velvet – the colour which became me most. The dressmakers were busy. I was beside him at the Court functions. It was tantamount to being Queen. People began to treat me as such; they brought petitions to me, asking me to intercede for this and that with the King. All knew that what I asked would be mine. Enthusiasm was second nature to Henry. When he wanted something, he wanted it fiercely. Tenacity was another of his qualities. I was not sure of fidelity; but I was determined to keep him as he was now.

He wanted me always beside him. Even when I was alone, I rode in state. He had given me special harness for my horses and my saddle was in the French style – black velvet fringed with gold. But he liked it best when I rode pillion with him, sitting on a down-stuffed pillow.

I was Queen in all but name, but that was not good enough.

The precariousness of my position was brought home to me by the people.

How they hated me! The common people – and not only they – hate to see others rise, particularly if that rise is spectacular. I shall never forget the hatred which was directed against Wolsey when he was at the height of his greatness, and the sympathy which came to him when he was down. The sympathy suggested good nature but the hatred betrayed the truth of the matter, and I came to the conclusion that envy is the greatest of the seven deadly sins, and from it spring all others; the sympathy offered to such as Wolsey when they were brought low is at heart pleasure because of their downfall.

Now I was to taste that hatred.

'We'll have no Nan Bullen,' they cried, attempting to give my name a plebeian note. How I hated them, with their sly, envious faces and their petty minds. This was not sympathy for Katharine; it was not indignation against my position. It was plain envy.

I would have snapped my fingers at them if it were not for the disturbing effect they had on the King.

Cromwell said he would suppress it.

He had his spies everywhere. If they heard an adverse comment directed against me, the person who made it would find himself or herself in chains. This did not prevent a good many people risking imprisonment.

The most disturbing of all were the priests. They were different from the people in the streets. Their great anxiety must have been for their position in the Church. There was one, Friar Peto, who actually preached at Greenwich. He was one of those headstrong monks who see themselves in the rôle of martyr as a way to eternal joy and saving themselves from the flames of hell by one magnificent gesture at the end. He was attached to the Franciscan convent and was emphatic in his denunciation of the divorce. The King had been ill advised, he said. He would be like Ahab, and when he died the dogs would lick his blood.

And this in the presence of the King!

Henry's leniency was amazing. Cromwell would have had the man in the Tower and soon taking the short walk to Tower Hill, but the King was in a mellow mood. The Friar had at least spoken out to his face and had not made traitorous remarks behind his back as he feared so many did. So Friar Peto was sent to France to join a Franciscan order there. Such leniency was not really wise, for he came back later and continued preaching, so that there was no alternative but to imprison him.

But this was nothing compared with the case of Rice ap Griffiths. What made this more unusual was that Griffiths was a distant relative; he had married one of my mother's sisters. Criticism from my own family always surprised me. One would have thought we should have clung together. But the resentment the Howards had always felt towards the Boleyns was constantly flaring up. Griffiths was arrested and put in the Tower. He never left it, except to walk out to Tower Hill and lay his head on the block.

This was an example to others, and it did have some effect, but I knew that the people were ready to revolt against me, and the clergy against the new laws which were to be imposed.

At the Court, where I sat beside the King, few dared show resentment, for it was those close to the King who had the most to fear. It was true that Mary, Duchess of Suffolk, had left Court on account of me but I did not greatly care. It seemed amazing to me that she could behave so. After all, she herself had married a commoner. When I thought of that bright young girl and her passion for Charles Brandon, I could scarcely believe that she could behave thus towards me. She had been quite fond of me in a patronizing kind of way. She had let the little Boleyn into her confidence as she had no other. Of course, she had been a friend of Katharine, so perhaps that was behind her dislike of me.

I doubted that anyone in England had more enemies than I at that time. Vaguely I was aware of the antipathy, but I tried not to let it bother me. If I had been older and wiser, I should have been deeply shocked and horrified and certainly alarmed by the rancour I engendered.

One day the Duke of Norfolk asked to see me. I wondered why he had come. I was very wary of him. I suspected that he, like Suffolk, had used me to help discredit Wolsey; and I suspected they would work against me with the King if they had a chance.

Norfolk said that he had been handed a note which had been written by the Countess of Northumberland and sent to her father, the Earl of Shrewsbury. The Earl had brought it to the Duke, who thought I ought to see it.

I took it, wondering what Henry Percy's wife should have to say to her father which could be of interest to me.

I opened it and, when I read it, I was trembling with dismay.

Here was one of my enemies who could do me harm if she wished – and she clearly did wish. She had written to her father to say that her husband, Henry Percy, had admitted to her that, while he was in the service of Cardinal Wolsey and I was a maid of honour to Queen Katharine, he had had a pre-contract with me.

I stared from the paper to Norfolk. He was smiling sardonically, fully aware of the contents of the letter.

'I thought, Lady Anne,' he said, 'that you would wish to give some thought to the matter.'

'It is of no importance,' I lied. 'But it shall be shown to the King.'

He bowed and retired.

I sat there reading and re-reading the letter. How she must have hated me! Her marriage had been a failure from the start. Henry Percy would have been a faithful husband to me.

I wondered if he still thought of me, and I was sure he did. Mary Talbot's vindictiveness was evident in that note. How reluctantly he had married her – and she knew it.

Now she would have heard of the brilliant marriage which lay ahead of me. Henry Percy would know, too. And what was he thinking now? Of what might have been, I dareswear, with a certain longing, as I did now and then when I was particularly frustrated and thought that nothing would ever come of my attachment to the King.

Now she saw a chance of revenge – this petty Mary Talbot who had had the misfortune to marry a man who was deeply in love with someone else.

But she had a point. That was the frightening aspect. One always thought of precedents when such occasions arose. Not so long ago Richard II had declared himself to be King because of his brother's pre-contract with Eleanor Butler before marrying Elizabeth Woodville, thus rendering illegitimate those two little Princes who had died so mysteriously in the Tower. If this pre-contract with Henry Percy was proved to be valid, my offspring with the King could be declared to be a bastard.

There was only one thing to do: I must lay the matter before Henry without more delay.

I went to him. His face lit up at the sight of me. Then he saw that I was disturbed.

I said: 'Norfolk has just handed this to me.'

He took it, read it and cried: 'My God, this must not be.'

He looked at me questioningly.

I said: 'There was no signed contract of marriage. You know full well that when I was at Court I knew Northumberland and that there was talk of marriage between ourselves. It never went further than that. It was you who arranged with Wolsey to separate us.'

'Thank God,' he cried. 'Then there was no pre-contract.'

'Once we thought that we would marry, which we might well have done if it had not been prevented.'

'I will give this to Cromwell at once. We cannot let it pass. Norfolk knows of it . . . and Shrewsbury, of course.'

'You think this will prevent our marriage.'

Henry smiled. 'Sweetheart, nothing on God's earth is going to prevent our marriage. That rogue Cromwell will sort it out.'

And Cromwell did.

Percy was summoned to appear before the Archbishop of Canterbury and the Privy Council.

I knew that I could rely on him. He had loved me deeply; I think he had never forgotten me. He would know that I wished to marry the King, that I must marry the King after all that had passed between us. He was loyal as I had known he would be. He admitted that he and I had known each other at Court and there had been an attraction between us, but there had never been a pre-contract.

Whether he had been threatened by Cromwell, I did not know, but I liked to believe that he said what he did out of love for me.

So that was another defeat for my enemies. The King – as he was determined to – believed Northumberland was speaking the truth and the rest of the Council must also.

That little matter was settled and need not bother us further.

*

Henry was relieved that the question of my alliance with Henry Percy had been satisfactorily settled and he could talk of little else but our coming visit to France.

François had been a good friend to us throughout the troubled negotiations with the divorce. I wondered why. Was it because he was romantic at heart? Hardly that. He wanted an alliance against the Emperor. That was the answer. But he could not afford to ignore such a powerful ally.

François was eager for the visit, and as Henry and I should

be together, and I should be travelling with him as his Queen to a man who was prepared to accept me as such, it should be a most enjoyable occasion.

'There is one point,' said Henry. 'You are merely the Lady Anne Rochford. It is not a very high rank for the exalted position you will occupy. Therefore I have decided to make a change.'

I looked at him expectantly and he kissed me.

'I am going to make you a peeress.'

I felt dizzy with pleasure.

'I have thought out the matter and it is all settled. You are to be the Marquess of Pembroke. It is a title which I must esteem because it was last borne by my uncle, Jasper Tudor. It links you with my family.'

'Do you think that will be approved by the nobles?'

He spoke almost haughtily. 'It is my wish.' Of course I was delighted. It was a great honour. It would set me above those who had resented having to pay respect to me.

Marquess of Pembroke! A title – and such a title – in my own right! I had clearly taken the right course.

Henry announced that his reason for bestowing this honour was because a monarch ought to surround his throne with the worthiest of both sexes, and so, by the consent of the nobility of the kingdom (he did not add that none of them dared withhold his consent), he was creating his cousin Anne Rochford, the daughter of his well-beloved cousin the Earl of Wiltshire, to be Marquess of Pembroke. Then he added a most important point: by putting on the mantle and the coronet, he was investing the name and title to the male heirs.

This was a precaution. If by some evil chance it should happen that my marriage to the King was prevented – although he had sworn nothing should – and I were to give birth to a child, that child could be assured of a grand title.

It was plain that the King wished to do great honour to me and to show all that I was the most cherished being at his

Court, for this was the first example of a woman's being created a peer.

Everything seemed mellow on that lovely September morning – summery, yet with a touch of autumn in the air. Henry was seated in the Presence Chamber at Windsor Castle surrounded by many of the peers, including Norfolk, Suffolk, my father and the French ambassador.

I had been dressed in a surcoat made of crimson velvet and lined with ermine; it had short sleeves for I was to wear the mantle over it. I wore my hair as it suited me best, loose about my shoulders, and I was led in by a company of lords and ladies, at the head of whom was Garter-king-at-arms. My cousin Mary Howard, daughter of the Duke of Norfolk, carried the robe of state and the golden coronet. Slowly I approached the King, between the Countesses of Rutland and Sussex, and knelt.

Gardiner read the Charter, and the King took the robe from Mary, which he caressingly laid about my shoulders. Then he placed the coronet on my head.

I was ennobled. Marquess of Pembroke. It was a moment of great triumph.

Henry presented me with another charter which ensured me £1,000 a year during my lifetime.

I was very happy as the trumpets heralded my departure from the Presence Chamber.

In my apartment were gifts from Henry – some exquisite miniatures, the work of his favourite painter, Holbein; these were made more valuable by the jewels in which they were set. They were beautiful and could be worn as pendants. Henry was determined that all should know of his love for me. He showered gifts on me. I now had a train-bearer and maids of honour – all noble ladies – just as though I were already the Queen. The cost of my clothes alone for the ceremony had been more than £30 – all cheerfully paid for from the privy purse.

I had nothing to fear.

Then we were planning the journey to France.

François had been most cordial and he delighted us both by suggesting that we married while we were in France. This was an exciting prospect because if we did so it would proclaim to the world that the King of France was on our side. He had always shown a great deal of sympathy and understanding, and I was vain enough to suspect that it might be because of a fondness for me. He had certainly cast rather lustful eyes upon me when I was at his Court, and I imagine he thought of me with some respect because I had refused him. Therefore this coming visit was of very special importance to Henry and me, for we planned to take François's advice and then, when we returned to England, the marriage would be a *fait accompli*.

So there I was at the peak of my dreams, soon to have done with this anomalous position in which I had stood so long – Queen of England.

I was delighted for the time being with my new eminence; but soon I should be in that place to which I had aspired for so long. Perhaps I became a little haughty, assuming airs of royalty. Henry did not object to my doing so – in fact, he rather encouraged it. I felt now that I could command all . . . even him.

I was preparing a wardrobe for the French visit. Velvets and silks were brought to me and I planned with the utmost pleasure.

I was really happy during that time. I had ceased to look back nostalgically to the past and what might have been. There never could have been for me a more glorious future than that which confronted me now.

There were one or two minor irritations. Henry demanded that Katharine should give up her jewels. Although as Queen of England she had been wearing them for years, they did not belong to her but were the property of the Crown. Henry said that, now God had shown him that theirs was no true marriage, the jewels must be returned.

The fact was that he wanted me to wear them during the

French visit and after my marriage they would be in my possession.

Katharine indignantly refused to return them. She would not give up such jewels to adorn the person who was the scandal of Christendom, she declared, and whose very presence at Court brought ignominy to the Crown.

Katharine could be very bold, and always there was the shadow of the Emperor beside her. For that reason, although she might be insulted, even the King would not dare harm her physically.

But the Emperor was far away and the King was supreme in England and promising to be even more so than he had been before.

He now commanded her to deliver up the jewels, and messengers were sent to collect them.

It was wonderful to have them but I did regret that they had had to be forced from Katharine.

Then there was the Duchess of Suffolk. As the ex-Queen of France she would renew many old acquaintances, for Henry wished her to accompany us. She had always been stubborn, and she had, of course, special privileges with the King. He always thought of her as his little sister Mary. She had married Suffolk and overcome his displeasure. And now she resolutely refused to come to France with us.

This was, of course, because I was going. Had Katharine been in my place, Mary would have been happy to join the party.

I did not know what I wished for – whether he should command her to come, which would have been most unpleasant for she would have been very disagreeable, I was sure, or whether he should give way and accept her refusal, which was an insult to me. In either case it was not very pleasant, but really, as I said, just a minor irritation.

Then there was Suffolk himself. Henry was really angry with him. Because of his longstanding friendship with Henry and his close relationship to him through marriage, he had

had the temerity to suggest that the idea for the trip was not a good one.

I guessed what his comments were. Henry was taking a woman not his wife, and flaunting her as his Queen on a visit to another state. It was a mistake, even though François had sent messages expressing his pleasure.

Henry had been furious.

As a result Suffolk had been sent from Court – not to remain in exile but to prepare without delay for the journey. As this was going to be very costly, Suffolk was far from pleased; and his wife insisted on staying at home.

Even though François had welcomed the plan so enthusiastically, the visit had its less pleasant side. He was to meet us at Boulogne, but none of the ladies of the French Court would accompany him.

Of course, the important person was François.

'We'll do better without the ladies,' said Henry, but it naturally meant there would be occasions when I could not be present.

I had to remind myself that it was probably the first time a King had taken with him a woman who was not his wife on what must be a state visit.

'In any case,' he added, 'I would not wish to meet the Queen of France.' She was Eleanora of Austria, sister of Charles, and therefore Katharine's niece. 'I'd rather meet the devil than a lady in Spanish dress,' added Henry.

*

In spite of all these setbacks, plans went ahead. There was a certain amount of misgiving of which I could not fail to be aware. It was a daring thing to do to take me away with him on such an occasion before there had been a marriage ceremony. True, I was now a peeress with one of the highest titles in the land, but I was more unpopular than ever with the people.

Nevertheless I was happy, and so was Henry. He could not

356

bear to leave my side; he sent the company ahead to Dover so that we could be alone – or almost – together. We stayed at the house of Thomas Cheyney – always a good friend to me – and Henry insisted that there should be no fuss and we would live simply for a few days. This we did – riding together . . . eating alone . . . and living away from people . . . privately. I was surprised how much we both enjoyed it. Perhaps I was beginning to love him. It is difficult for a woman of my nature not to be fond of one who shows such care for her.

Love changed Henry; he was both ardent and grateful; it made a different man of him; and I liked that man better than the mighty King; or it may be that I enjoyed seeing the mighty King reduced to a humble lover. It was difficult to think of Henry without his royalty. It was so much a part of him; and to think that he could cast it aside was very endearing.

He said he had never been so happy in his life as during those days we spent away from the rest of the company, and what joy it gave him to contemplate that in a very short time we should be married.

We could not live in our sylvan paradise forever. We had to go on to Dover.

As we rode along, I noticed the looks of the people; they were more sullen than vituperative. They did not approve of the French visit – well, perhaps it was not the visit, but the fact that I was accompanying the King.

There was plague in some of the hamlets along the south-east route. A sign, said the people. There were all sorts of omens. People had dreams. Some saw a sign in the sky – a comet perhaps. But it was more likely to have been conjured out of someone's imagination. Someone else had seen a strange creature in the sea. It looked like a fish, but it was not. It had the face of a man. What its purpose was supposed to be, I had no idea – except that it was some dire warning because of our evil ways. And all these signs meant that God was not pleased with a king who put away his wife and flaunted his concubine – even before the eyes of the King of France.

In due course we embarked for Calais. We had a fair crossing in spite of the dire prophecies. A great welcome had been arranged for us. The town was *en fête*. The townspeople were gathered to cheer us as we went first to the church of St Nicholas, where Mass was celebrated and we gave thanks for our safe crossing. After that we were taken to the lodgings which had been prepared for us. Henry's huge bed and furniture which we had brought with us had gone on before and were already installed.

They were wonderful days. Henry and I were together most of the time. He took great pleasure in riding round the town with me. I was cheered by the people there. How different from the reception I had from the people at home! Perhaps the news had not reached Calais or perhaps they were so glad to have us there, with our ceremonies to enliven their days, that they accepted me as part of it.

It was wonderful to see Thomas Wyatt again. He was as handsome as ever and delighted to see me in such good spirits.

'Do you remember those days at Hever still?' he asked me.

'They will never be forgotten, Thomas,' I answered.

'I rejoice in your good fortune, but it is bad fortune for me.'

'How so?'

'Because you are lost to me forever.'

'Thomas,' I said seriously, 'there must be no such talk.'

'Indeed not. Look what it cost me before! I still have the tablet.'

'Then do not let it be seen.'

'It was such a cause for royal jealousy.'

'Thomas, there must be no more.'

'Anne! Queen Anne! Well, you were made for distinction.'

'You too, Thomas.'

'You will be remembered as the Queen. I perhaps . . . perhaps not . . . as a poet.'

He wrote a charming poem at that time which was for me. I always remembered it.

Forget not yet the tried intent
Of such a truth as I have meant,
My great travail so gladly spent
   Forget not yet.

Forget not, oh! forget not this
How long hath been and is
The love that never meant amiss
   Forget not yet.

Forget not now thine own approved
The which so constant hath thee loved
Whose steadfast faith hath never moved
   Forget not yet.

It could not help but please me that a man such as Wyatt had loved me for so long. Yet I was a little fearful of him. He was very impetuous. But perhaps he had grown wiser now. He knew what it meant to offend the King.

Henry seemed to have forgotten the affair of the tablet and the slander which Suffolk had spoken against Wyatt and me. Now that we were lovers he was satisfied. I had managed to convince him that my passion for him matched his for me; and if I was less sexually ecstatic than someone like my sister Mary, he would regard that as evidence of my finer nature.

I was perfect to him in those days. Moreover, with François's approval we should soon be married. Then his conscience would be at ease, for Cromwell and Cranmer were working assiduously to prove that Henry's marriage to Katharine was no marriage, and soon he and I would be together without having to endure the occasional – very occasional now – twinges of that infuriating conscience.

After a week in Calais, during which preparations were made to welcome the French King there, Henry rode off to meet François at Boulogne. It had been decided, after a great deal of consideration, that it would be better if I did not accompany him, as we had been warned that the ladies of the French Court would not be coming with François. I did not like this, but I understood it. Until I was actually married to Henry, I could not be treated on ceremonial occaisons as his Queen; and like Henry, I had no wish to meet the French Queen since she was Katharine's niece. It would have made a very awkward situation; but all this would soon be at an end, for Henry had decided that our marriage should take place in a week's time; and if François was a guest at the ceremony, that would mean a great deal to us.

Meanwhile I remained in Calais. I had devised several masques which I wanted to be considered witty, amusing and elegant, even to French tastes. Wyatt was present and he would write some of his verses, and everyone must admit that he was a poet of quality.

Henry had spared no expense in fitting out the castle's banqueting chamber, and it was hung with tissue of silver and gold, the seams of the material studded with glittering stones and pearls. The plate was all gold. It was going to be very elaborate and worthy of our guest, the King of France.

I was impatiently awaiting their return. Then the all-important ceremony would take place, and my fears would be at an end. I should go back to England as Queen.

The meeting of the two Kings had been, I heard, a glittering occasion. I wondered if they had both been re-minded of that other meeting at Guines and Ardres. They embraced warmly, as though there had never been any enmity between them. François had arranged entertainments for Henry at Boulogne; but I knew he would be impatient to return to me; and I thought it was a pity the ladies of the French Court had not come, for then I could have been present. I tried to convince myself that it was really due to the fact that the Queen of France was so closely related to Katharine, and the last person she would want to see was Henry, who had just cast off her aunt.

So I supposed it was a wise decision, although a little

galling, and it would give them the impression that they had not come because I was not Henry's wife.

I consoled myself that that would soon be remedied.

In due course the two Kings arrived in Calais.

I was received with the utmost graciousness by François. He soon dispensed with ceremony and told me that I had become even more beautiful than he remembered. I could hardly say the same of him with truth. A great deal had happened to François since those days of his early kingship. Those years of imprisonment in Madrid, where he had almost lost his life, had taken their toll of him. He looked debauched, which was not surprising after the life he had led; but François had an innate charm, and his graceful manners and general elegance could not fail to please.

There was to be a banquet in the splendidly decorated hall, but before that I had an opportunity of being with Henry alone.

He kissed me with passion and said the separation had seemed long, but I noticed that he was deeply concerned about something. As our wedding was to take place so soon, I felt a tremor of alarm.

And well I might.

It was not long before he was telling me all about it.

The wedding ceremony which we had planned could not take place. François, who had urged us to marry in France and return home with the deed already done, was now of a different opinion.

The Emperor Charles had defeated the Turks, so they were no longer a threat to him. This meant he would be free to turn his attention elsewhere. We could guess that that could mean France.

In the circumstances, François could not appear to give his public approval to our marriage, although he hoped we would continue to regard him as our very good friend.

'So,' I gasped, 'there is to be no marriage.'

'Not here. We shall have to postpone it . . . but only for a short while.'

I was angry. Once more I was faced with frustration. I had been so certain that all would be well, and I should have security within a few days, and now to have it snatched away from me, just as I was about to reach out and take it, was more than I could bear.

'How dare he!' I cried.

'Sweetheart, he has good reason. It is true that, if he gave his outward blessing to us, the Emperor would take his revenge. We must see his side, my dearest.'

'He has tricked us.'

'No . . . no. It is the King of France of whom you speak.'

'I care not for kings.'

He raised his eyebrows and looked grave. He said, slightly coolly: 'I trust there is one King you care about . . .'

I threw myself into his arms. He was very patient with me. I often marvelled at that afterwards. He stroked my hair. 'You must not be distressed,' he said. 'It is a bitter disappointment . . . but it is not the first we have had, eh? We'll get over it. Mayhap it would be better to be married at home. Doubtless there would be some to question its legality . . . if it took place here.'

There was some truth in that and I allowed myself to be subdued.

I had to forget my rancour and prepare for the entertainment we were to offer.

I had arranged, with the help of Wyatt and a few others, a splendid masque; and Henry was right, I must not show my animosity towards François. Henry gently reminded me that I was now dealing with a powerful man. I should have to be particularly gracious to him. So I must subdue my irritation – which he felt no less than I did, for by God and all his saints I could not long for my marriage more than he did.

So there was the grand banquet in that splendidly decorated hall. The food was served in a unique manner – in the

French fashion for François and in the English for Henry. There were three courses; in the first, forty dishes were served, in the second sixty and in the third seventy. François declared himself to be amazed.

I and my ladies were not present at the dinner. This was because the ladies of the French Court had not accompanied François. Perhaps this should have made me doubt his sincerity, for he could have commanded them to come. I had thought that Marguerite might have been with him. She was now Queen of Navarre, having married again; she had always been so forward-thinking that I was surprised she should have found it impossible to meet me just because I was not yet married to the King. I tried to convince myself that it was for some other reason that she had not joined the expedition.

We came into the hall when the meal was over. We were all masked and our dresses were of a strange exotic style meant to imply that we had come from some far-off land. The gowns were made of cloth of gold slashed with crimson tinsel thread and laced with gold. They were very effective, I had made sure of that. Each of us was to select one of the French guests for the dance; and, of course, I was to choose François.

We would then dance together, and it would be assumed that the French did not know with whom they danced until that moment when Henry came to the ladies in turn and removed their masks. They would all express surprise – a gambit which had delighted Henry from those long-ago days when he had just come to the throne and had turned the sombre Court of his father into one of merriment and laughter.

Through my mask I watched the King of France. He was not as handsome as Henry, for Henry was still a very good-looking man and had been particularly so in his youth. Some ten years ago the Venetian ambassador had described him as 'more handsome than any sovereign in Christendom – much more handsome than the King of France – very fair and admirably proportioned. His beard looks like gold and he is an accomplished musician, good horseman, speaks French, Latin and Spanish, is very religious and hears Mass three times daily when he hunts and five on other days.'

That had been said before his obsession with me. I wondered what the Venetian ambassador's opinion would be now.

Still, if time had wrought some havoc on his looks, he was still a fine figure of a man – so tall and commanding, and above all he carried that aura of royalty which set him above other men.

François though had an incomparable charm of manner; he was highly intellectual; he had an air of almost weary worldliness, but his mind was alert; he was cynical, whereas Henry could at times be almost childishly simple.

One could scarcely imagine two men more different; and I decided that I was fortunate to have Henry.

François was studying me lasciviously.

'How fortunate I am to be chosen by you,' he said. 'As soon as I saw you enter the hall, I thought, though I may not know the lady's name until unmasking time, I see she stands high above all others in charm and beauty. I was praying that she would select me.'

'The King of France would be the choice any lady would hope for.'

I spoke in French which I could do with as much ease as I spoke English.

'Then let us rejoice that you chose me, and if the choice had been with me, I should have chosen you.' He then complimented me on my rendering of his language. 'You might be one of us,' he added, 'but for the so slight difference which makes your speech entirely delightful.'

In spite of my anger against him, I could not be unaware of his charm. My mind went back to the days of my youth when those lascivious eyes of his were turned on me. I had heard stories of his conquests. He was ruthless in his pursuit. No matter whom he sought, he would employ any methods to satisfy his desire. There had been whisperings of girls who had been kidnapped and brought to him because he had seen them in the streets . . . in church . . . anywhere. I had heard that the daughter of an innkeeper had thrown acid into her own beautiful face because she feared that her soul would be damned if he forced her to be his mistress.

We continued with that light banter which was completely false.

'Would not Your Grace have been a little rash in choosing a woman whose face he could not see?'

'Some instinct tells me that her face will be as beautiful as that which I can perceive and which so delights me.'

'And the King of France, as all know, is a connoisseur of beauty.'

'I would hope that is so.'

'It amazes me that, with all the beauties of France ready to fall at his feet, he should be so ecstatic about one masked Englishwoman.'

'But such an Englishwoman! The Lady Anne is here tonight. I'll swear she could not match with the lady who had the goodness to select me for her partner.'

'She would not be pleased to hear you talk thus.'

'I had the pleasure of being acquainted with the lady . . . once.'

'That must have been a long time ago. And still you remember her?'

'She is making history now.'

'That surprises you?'

'It is not given to all to do that. She was an entrancing creature in those days. Such eyes! I remember them well. Black eyes . . . a witch's eyes.'

'You think she has bewitched the King?'

'Not I alone. The whole world knows she has bewitched the King. I long to see this face which has so enchanted my brother of England.' He leaned towards me, smiling that lazy, sensual smile which I remembered from the past, his eyes boring through me, through my mask, through my gold and tinsel.

'Do you know, mysterious lady, I'd wager that the Lady Anne is no more beautiful than you.'

'The King of England might be hurt to hear you say that.'

'The King of England would never deny the truth.' I heard the irony in his voice, I imagined how he must have laughed – probably with Marguerite – at Henry's declarations concerning the gnawing of his conscience.

'I see none of the ladies of your Court here tonight, Your Grace. That is unusual is it not?'

'Oh, they dared not face the competition of the English ladies . . . particularly the Lady Anne.'

'Are they so lacking in confidence then?'

'They have heard so much of her charms. The jealousy of your sex! It seems they would rather remain in ignorance than be so out-classed.'

'So you did not command them to come?'

'Oh, it is not my practice to command ladies.'

I was amazed that he could indulge in such frivolous conversation. Of course, it was all part of the masque that he should pretend not to know who I was. He would, of course, understand that in the traditional manner I would choose the King of France. I wondered what he remembered of me from the past; although he had aged considerably, I should have known him in any guise.

Henry was watching us, and I could see that he was beginning to be irritated. François's manner was distinctly flirtatious and he knew that the King of France could not be in the company of any attractive woman without attempting to seduce her.

Henry decided that it was time the deception ended, so he started to remove the visors, coming to me first. His face was a little flushed. It reminded me of that long-ago occasion when the rivalry between the two Kings could not be disguised for all the cloth of gold settings and protestations of friendship. Henry, a brilliant figure in velvet cloth of gold, about his neck a collar of rubies, diamonds and pearls as large as any I have seen, as usual looked a trifle flamboyant beside the elegant, more soberly clad François about whose person diamonds discreetly sparkled as he moved.

'Your Grace has been dancing with the Marquess of Pembroke,' he announced to François.

François, in the approved manner, declared himself astonished, gratified and delighted, his sly smile indicating to me that of course he had known all the time.

Henry passed on to unmask the other ladies.

Francois looked at me, still smiling.

'Of course,' I said, speaking to him now as one on equal terms, for though he was King of France, very soon I must be Queen of England, 'you knew all the time.'

'How could I fail to know that one so full of grace and charm must be the incomparable Lady Anne? I will tell you something: I should have known you anywhere . . . masked or otherwise. I could see those black sparkling eyes through the slits in your mask. There is only one pair of eyes like that in the whole world.'

'You were teasing me.'

'Forgive,' he said pleadingly.

'The King of France asks forgiveness of a mere Marquess!'

'So soon to be the Queen . . . as she already is in the heart of the King of England and that of the King of France.'

I had had enough of this frivolous talk, and I asked about Marguerite.

'You and my dear sister were good friends, I remember. She follows your fortunes with great interest. She sends her good wishes to you. She says that she always knew you were meant for a distinguished career.'

'I am sorry not to see her.'

'She is now the Queen of Navarre.'

'I see that the King of Navarre is of your company.'

'He leaves Marguerite in charge of his kingdom.'

I did not believe that. I knew very well that the ladies had not come because I was not married to Henry. It was hurtful to my pride but understandable to my logic.

'She has a daughter – Jeanne – a bright child.'

'That must give her much pleasure. And her writing?'

'She will always have time for that.'

'I remember the stories of the *Heptameron* so well. My happiest times in France were with her.'

'I will convey your kind words to her.'

The King had called a halt to the dancing and François conducted me to Henry.

*

Whether François was genuinely sorry that he had not been able to give us his support and consequently we were still not married, I was not sure. One could never be entirely sure with François. But he seemed to be sincerely eager to do something to help.

Henry and I talked with him alone. He was very attentive to me and treated me with the utmost respect. He had sent me a gift of some magnificent diamonds and, apart from the fact that he had not brought the female members of his Court with him, he had behaved as though I were already Queen of England.

Frankly we discussed the divorce with him. The Pope was on the point of giving his verdict and we knew, in view of the relationship now existing between him and the Emperor, that it must be in Katharine's favour. Once that decision had been given, it would be difficult to act against it. It could only result in excommunication for Henry and myself if we went ahead with the marriage after that.

'I suggest that I send two of our cardinals to Clement,' said François. 'I will tell him that I have seen you in person and that you have agreed that the court shall be held here in France and when the verdict is given you will accept it.'

'But I will not accept it,' cried Henry hotly.

'Ah, but the whole point is the delay this will entail. It will give you time to conclude the measures you need to get the divorce declared in England, and for you to marry in the meantime. Then, whatever the decision of the court here, it will not affect you. You will already have obtained the divorce and married.'

'It seems feasible,' agreed Henry.

'We know Clement. He will seize on anything that will enable him to delay. He trembles because he fears that whatever decision is come to, he will suffer. He is afraid of you . . . but the Emperor is nearer at hand. He dare not offend Charles – but at the same time he does not want to offend you. You should be thankful that you have such a man to deal with.'

'There could be something in that,' Henry admitted.

We sat for a long time discussing the plan and we were both of the opinion that – for whatever reasons – François wanted to help us.

The following day there were tournaments and wrestling matches, but this time the two Kings did not attempt to wrestle with each other. They were not as agile as they had been thirteen years ago.

On the 30th of the month Henry left Calais with François. He escorted him to that point where the English dominions ended and they dismounted on French soil. They embraced like brothers – Henry told me afterwards – and they vowed eternal friendship before they parted, François for Paris, Henry to join me in Calais.

We were not altogether displeased, although we had hoped to be married by now. But there was a good deal in Henry's point that the people would not have liked a marriage which had taken place in Calais. It was not fitting for a King of England to marry there. And this plan which François had put forward seemed feasible. So it had not been a wasted journey.

We now turned our faces towards home but the weather

was against us. The gales had started and each day when we expected to sail we were advised not to.

We were nothing loath. We were together and there was plenty to do in Calais. In the evenings we played cards and dice. Henry lost a great deal of money to me, which seemed to amuse him. He liked me to win – and I liked winning, so we were both satisfied.

We played Pope Julius, a game which was now very fashionable at home. It was topical because of the divorce; and the various points in the game were matrimony, intrigue and pope – so it was significant and caused a great deal of amusement.

They were very pleasant days which we spent at Calais waiting for the weather to improve; and although I had not yet the legal right to call myself Queen, I felt I was in every other way.

I had rarely seen Henry so happy.

It was not until 14 November, about a fortnight after we had said goodbye to François, that we landed at Dover.

*

Christmas which had been celebrated with the customary festivities had passed and January had come. I had made a momentous discovery. I was pregnant.

I could scarcely wait to convey the news to Henry. He was overcome with joy. I sometimes wondered whether his desire for a son surpassed that for me. The two ran very close.

'I knew it must come,' he said. 'When, sweetheart? When?'

'In September, I think.'

'It is a long time to wait.'

It was the usual period, I reminded him. 'And in those months there is much to be done . . . unless you wish your son to be born a bastard.'

He was sober at once.

'A pox on Clement,' he said. 'This matter would have been

370

settled long ere now but for him.'

I agreed.

His brow was furrowed. I understood our predicament as well as he did.

Warham had, most conveniently, died during the previous August, and Cranmer was to take his place, but until he was actually installed as Archbishop of Canterbury he could not declare Henry's marriage to Katharine invalid; and until this was done we could not marry. If the Pope's court decided that Henry was indeed married to Katharine, *our* marriage would be invalid.

But with the child on the way, something had to be done.

Henry was torn by different emotions. Immense joy at the prospect of the child was uppermost; but he knew what effect excommunication could have and he could visualize the country rising against him – men like Fisher and More who had no fear of consequences.

But the child was on the way.

*

It was early morning of a day I shall never forget – 25 January in the year 1533. I was told I must be in the west turret with Nan Saville in attendance.

The King was there with William Norris and my father and brother.

As soon as I entered, I saw that the King was talking earnestly to one of his chaplains, Dr Rowland Lee, who, Henry told me afterwards, had come in the belief that he was to celebrate Mass. When he was told that he was to perform a marriage ceremony, he was overcome with fear. He had to obey the King but he was in terror of offending the Pope, which he would most certainly do if he officiated at this ceremony.

Henry was exasperated but managed to control his wrath for he needed the man's help, and he was afraid he might be one of those martyrs who were ready to face any consequences rather than go against the Pope.

In order that the ceremony should go on, Henry was forced to tell him that the Pope had declared his marriage to Katharine invalid.

So, with great trepidation, and obvious uneasiness, Dr Rowland Lee complied.

Henry and I stood hand in hand. Then he solemnly kissed me. I was Queen of England in very truth.

*

I was exultant. At last I had reached my goal. Once my son was born, I should be secure in my power, but for the time we must act cautiously. The wedding was a secret. Only those present knew of it. Even Cranmer was kept in the dark.

I wish I had been wiser. I wish I had been able to look ahead. I was surrounded by ill-wishers and I snapped my fingers at them. How the Queen and her daughter Mary must hate me! I had usurped Katharine's place, and through me Mary had lost her birthright. What did that proud Princess feel to be branded illegitimate?

But I did not stop to think. I was overwhelmed by the power which was in my hands. I had seen the fall of the great Cardinal – once the most powerful man in the land – and his fall was in part due to me. *I* had toppled him from power – that 'foolish girl' at whom he had sneered.

I saw no obstacles now to my progress. Henry was my slave; and all these important men must bow to my wishes.

At last Cranmer was installed as Archbishop of Canterbury. Before taking office he had made a declaration that the oath which he was about to take in obedience to the Pope, was a matter of form, and could not bind him to act against the King or prevent his reforming anything that was amiss in the Church of England.

The matter was now getting urgent. April had come. I was

four months pregnant. We had to move fast, I reminded the King – not that he needed reminding – if our child was to be acknowledged as legitimate.

Cranmer was entirely the King's man. He opened a court and gave sentence; the marriage to Katharine was invalid and the King was, in fact, married to me.

That was the signal. Now I could really come into my own. I arranged my household. I lived in the state of a Queen – although to some extent I had done this before. Now all must recognize me as such.

Moreover, it was time for my coronation.

May was a beautiful month – a momentous month for me, as it was to be not so very long afterwards.

I was to be crowned at Whitsun. The people loved these ceremonies even though this one was for someone of whom they could scarcely be said to approve. Still, they were determined to have their fun.

Everyone who could find a craft seemed to be on the river that day. The city merchants were out in their decorated barges, and dressed in scarlet, their heavy gold chains about their necks, they made a fine sight. The Lord Mayor, splendid in his ceremonial robes, was followed by fifty barges filled with the leading men of the city . . . all rowing down to Greenwich. In the leading barge – the Lord Mayor's – was a dragon which, to the amusement of the crowds on the bank, capered as the barge passed along and spat out fire – a most ingenious feat. The people laughed and cheered. The vessel I liked best was the one decorated with my device and in which were seated young girls singing sweetly of my beauty and virtues; in the midst of them sat a white falcon surrounded by red and white roses. At the foot of this was written my motto, 'Me and Mine'. The white falcon was henceforth to be my device. It was taken from the Butler crest, and of course the roses indicated that my offspring would bind even closer the Houses of York and Lancaster.

I came out from Greenwich Palace at three in the afternoon, dressed in cloth of gold, and as I stepped into my barge, the trumpets sounded. This was indeed triumph.

We went up the river towards the Tower – my barge followed by members of the nobility, my father in the lead. As I approached the Tower, the guns began to sound. I alighted and was conducted to the postern gate, where Henry was waiting to greet me.

He kissed my hand, his eyes alight with pride. I was doubly dear to him because of the child I carried.

Nan Saville had wondered whether the ordeal of the coronation would be bad for me in my condition, but I told her no. I had waited years for this and I was determined to enjoy every moment.

I was to stay in the Tower for several days. There Henry knighted several people in honour of the occasion, and through those days the river was alive with craft; the sound of music was everywhere; there was singing and revelry and the streets were crowded. For these few days the people were ready to forget their animosity towards me. I might have been Nan Bullen, the King's concubine, yesterday but today I was Anne, Queen of England, and this was my coronation. These were great days for them as well as for me: a holiday with feasting, sporting, dancing, singing and general rejoicing. So therefore just for today it was 'God bless Queen Anne'.

There had never been a more splendid occasion. Henry was determined that it should be so. It was more than a coronation. It was an act of defiance against the Pope. No one should gainsay Henry. He was King in his country, and his will should be law.

I was to ride through the city from the Tower to Westminster Abbey. Rails had been set up in the streets to protect the people from the horses. The Lord Mayor, Sir Stephen Peacock, received me at the Tower gate. Then came the French ambassador, the judges, the nobility and the Archbishop of Canterbury with the bishops. Suffolk was there as Lord High Constable of England. I wondered what he

374

would be feeling to see me here as Queen. He had tried to destroy me and had worked hard to try to prevent me reaching this position; his wife, my one-time mistress, had refused to accept me. Poor woman, there would be no question of that now, for I had heard that she was very ill – sick unto death, they said – and even if she had wished to leave her home at Westhorpe to come to my coronation, she could not have done so.

It was strange, thinking back over all those years – but such thoughts will come on these occasions – to those days when as a little girl I had accompanied the proud beauty to France. Now I was a Queen and she was a dying woman.

I stepped into my litter. My surcoat was of silver tissue and my cloak was of the same material lined with ermine. I wore my hair flowing about my shoulders, and on my head was a circlet of rubies. My litter was made of cloth of gold, and my two palfreys, which drew it, were in white damask. They were led by sumptuously clad footmen, and the company stretched out behind me.

There were wonderful pageants on the way; we stopped to marvel at their ingenuity and to listen to the speeches of praise. One of these represented Mount Parnassus, from which sprang jets of Rhenish wine. Of course, the white falcon figured in these scenes. One was particularly effective – the falcon uncrowned in the midst of red and white roses; as I approached, an angel appeared and placed a golden crown on the falcon's head. In Cheapside the wine flowed freely – white in the conduit on one side, red on the other.

And so we progressed through the city to Westminster, where I was to spend the night with the King.

I went to bed that night exhausted, but deeply content. I reminded myself that I was not only the Queen but the idol of the people. Well . . . perhaps for a day or so. The joy was so exquisite that I must savour it to the full. This was no time for analysing my thoughts and finding uneasy portents there. It was a time for absolute rejoicing, and I gave myself up to it.

The morning dawned . . . that day for which I had waited through the years. The first day of June. In four months time my joy would be complete. Then I would hold my son in my arms and I would have the King's gratitude for ever. People would no longer revile me. They would realize that I, Anne Boleyn, had won the love of the King so that he had discovered his first marriage had not found favour in the sight of God. So he had married me and I was giving them their new King, thereby saving the country from split loyalites and perhaps civil war. Henry was not yet old – forty-two years of age. He had time to bring up a son to be a good King to follow him. Had it not been for this marriage and my production of the heir, what would have happened on Henry's death? The old wars of the roses might well have broken out. Any country which has endured civil war would go to any great lengths to prevent that happening again.

I was up early, ready for the great day. My ladies helped me to dress in surcoat and mantle of purple velvet lined with ermine. Then came the walk from Westminster Hall to the Abbey. The barons of the Cinque Ports held the canopy over me; the Bishops of London and Winchester walked beside me; and the ladies, led by the Duchess of Norfolk, carried my train.

I sat in a chair between the choir and the altar, and then I went to the high altar where Cranmer was waiting for me. Finally the crown of St Edward was set on my head, and the Te Deum was sung.

The ceremony continued and afterwards we left the Abbey for Westminster Hall where a banquet was being prepared. Then we sat at a table which had been decorated in a most splendid manner; we were served with twenty-seven dishes and ate to the accompaniment of music.

The King was not present. This was my occasion. He watched, he told me afterwards, through a window, for he wanted to see the whole company do honour to me. I was to be the most important person at the table; and had he been there, of course, that honour would have fallen to him.

The meal went on until six o'clock, and when I had drunk from the golden cup which had been brought to me by the Mayor, I presented him with the cup as a reward for his services. I gave the canopy, with its golden bells, to the Barons of the Cinque Ports as payment for their services in accordance with custom. Then I thanked them all for what they had done for me.

Very tired, but deeply contented, I left the hall.

The great day had come to an end and I was Queen of England.

Into Danger

I had thought that when I reached the pinnacle of my ambition I should be completely happy. Here I was, Queen of England, soon to bear the heir. My tribulations were over. Whatever the Pope did could not harm me now. Cranmer was the King's man and he had declared the King's first marriage invalid; and if there was any difficulty from Rome, Cromwell had his solution. Oh, I knew it was a drastic one and that the King was nervous of putting it into practice; but we were married now. This was the culmination of all our efforts for seven years.

But it was not quite perfection. Perhaps there is a reaction after such a conclusion is reached. Perhaps the continual plans, the upheavals, even the setbacks gave a zest to the days. I wondered if the King felt as I did. The excitement of our encounters had waned a little. Perhaps it was because the excitement of doing what was forbidden was removed. There is a spiciness in sinning which acting virtuously lacks. It was now perfectly legitimate for us to share the same bed. We were almost like a long-married couple; and there was I, no longer alluring, for how could a woman heavy with child be that?

The King was very tender towards me, very solicitous that I should take great care. But I began to ask myself whether that was really for the sake of the child.

I was surrounded by all the ceremony which is a Queen's natural right; I was the most talked-of person in the country. Soothsayers and astrologers were making prophecies about my child. They all declared it would be a boy. They would have received little thanks from Henry for a girl.

I was learning more about my husband. When I thought of

all the warning signs I had had during the last years, I marvelled at my lack of perception. I had been adored so long that I thought that was going on for ever. I had come to believe that I was possessed of some special powers to draw men to me. I should have looked more closely at men's motives – more than that, I should have looked to myself. I had been the most attractive woman at Court, and I had been convinced that this was due to some special quality I possessed. Now I perceived that, although I was not without attractions, it was the ardent desire of the King which had enhanced my allure. There must be something very exciting about a woman for whom a man would do so much. That was what they told themselves, and they promptly fell in love with me. I should have seen that Henry was tired of Katharine and that his mixture of piety and sensuality made it necessary for him to indulge his desires while placating his conscience. He had never taken mistresses to the extent that François had. He wanted a regular union because he thought that was pleasing in the eyes of God, and Henry sought favour in that direction – just as his courtiers did with him. Thus there had been a combination of events: boredom with Katharine and the need to remove her but in a manner which could be seen to be righteous; desire for me, who had stood out against anything but marriage; the obstinacy of his nature which could not bear to be baulked; and above all the overriding need and desire for a son. That was what had motivated Henry, and I had deluded myself into believing that it was entirely due to his passion for me.

My brother George had been my main supporter through all my triumphs and tribulations. He was closer to me than any other person. I loved him dearly and I knew he was the only one whom I could trust absolutely. My father, for whom I had some natural feeling of affection, was, first and foremost before he was a father, an ambitious man. He saw me not so much as a daughter but as the Queen of England, who had made the grandest marriage of all those obliging Boleyn ladies. I knew that he would always think first of the fortunes of the family. George would think first of my wellbeing.

I saw my stepmother from time to time, for, because of my father's rising power, there were occasionally times when she must be beside him at Court functions. I knew she came most reluctantly from Hever and much preferred to be in her still-room or herb gardens. She was overawed to see me. I laughed at her and embracing her assured her that I was the same Anne in spite of my crown. She began to fuss about my condition and the baby, giving me all sorts of hints as to what I should do. It was a great pleasure always to see her.

George's married life was far from happy. He was a very attractive man; he had good looks and was extremely witty and cultured. He had travelled widely for the King had employed him on many missions abroad. He was a poet – not quite up to Wyatt's standards, but Wyatt was reckoned – correctly I think – to be the greatest poet at Court.

It was because of George that I took his wife, Jane, into my household. Perhaps that was another of my mistakes for I did not like her in the least and she presumed on the relationship. I often thought what a pity it was that George had married her. So did he. He had been relieved when, in the course of his duties, he had had to spend much time abroad. It gave him some respite from Jane.

What was so difficult for him to endure was her jealousy. She was desperately in love with him. Perhaps she might have been a different person altogether if he had returned that love. How could he? Jane was a stupid woman, a blundering woman; she had a habit of making remarks showing clearly that she had not followed a discussion; yet instead of keeping quiet, she would insist on speaking; she would offer opinions that were trite; she could not match George's intellect. She irritated me in the extreme; but at least I could see little of her. She was a foolish woman but if she had been meek and gentle I could have put up with her more easily.

I began to notice that Henry's attitude was changing

towards me. He was no longer quite so respectful as he had been; he was careless; and when I lost my temper, which I am afraid I did with increasing frequency, he did not attempt to placate me as he had in the old days.

He was often out of my company and seemed to seek that of his friends. I, of course, was now unable to join in the dancing and frivolities which were so much a part of Court life. Before our marriage he would have wished to spend the time with me; we would have read together or played cards; I would have listened to his latest musical composition; we would have discussed topics of the day, very likely the reforming of the old Church laws, a subject which was very much in most people's minds these days.

But he spent little time with me. We slept together in the royal bed and he was always talking about our child, what should be prepared for him on his arrival, even getting as far as his education. He was already making plans for his christening. But he had changed.

He was making me feel that now I had become Queen I had to remember constantly that he was the King, so that after my coronation, ironically, I had become less important than I had been before. Then I had been so essential to his happiness; my outbursts of temper had been painful to him, and his great desire had always been to bring me back to a sweeter mood. Now he would walk out and leave me and later make no reference to the matter and still behave in a somewhat lordly way as though saying: I have made you my Queen, but I am the King and you are still my subject.

He did not actually say this, but he was not a man to cloak his feelings, and one could often read from the expressions which flitted across his face; his little eyes would harden, his little mouth grow cruel; and the colour in his big face would deepen to a rich purple. These were the signs which could terrify his subjects. I had never allowed them to frighten me but in the past they had rarely been directed against me.

I was in my eighth month – longing for the time to pass.

Pregnancy in August is even more trying than in the cooler months. I was beginning to think of the child – not so much as a future King but as my baby. Sometimes for hours I would talk of little else. I gathered women about me who had shared the fearsome but exhilarating experience of childbearing. I made them talk to me. I enjoyed the discourse.

I longed for September. I would hold my son in my arms, and Henry would be as he was before. He would be so grateful that I should be assured of his devotion for ever; and it would not be long before I regained my ascendancy over him.

It was Jane Rochford who planted distrust and suspicion in my mind.

I think she delighted in it. In spite of the fact that she was my sister-in-law and a member of that family to which I was bringing great good fortune, she hated me. Envy was the key to her character. Most people have a sprinkling of it in their natures, and it had always seemed to me the most deadly of all the deadly sins and the one from which most others erupt; but with Jane it was the theme of her life. She was envious of George while loving him passionately. I did not realize then how deeply she hated me and that it was mainly because of my brother's love for me.

So she delighted to whisper this secret to me.

She began by gazing at me in perplexity, beginning to speak and then stopping. 'Perhaps I shouldn't . . . Only I thought . . . and after all . . . we are sisters . . . and if anyone should . . . perhaps I should be the one . . .'

I cried impatiently: 'What are you trying to say?'

'Please don't ask me to go on. And you in your condition . . . This month has been so trying. I thank God it will soon be over. September is almost here.'

'Jane,' I said firmly, 'tell me what you are trying to say. I command you.'

She hung her head as though suddenly aware of my exalted position, but I noticed the satisfied turn of her lips.

I took her by the shoulders and shook her.

'Well ... then ... since you insist. The King is seeing a great deal of a certain lady. They are saying he is seeking her out. And she is giving herself airs.'

'Who told you this?'

'Your Grace, the whole Court is whispering of it.'

'I don't believe it.'

'No, no,' she said soothingly. 'It can't be true ... and you just on the point of giving birth to the heir.'

'There are always those who will gossip in the Court and see what does not exist outside their evil imaginations.'

'Oh, 'tis true, 'tis true. But I just thought ... I thought you would want to know what people are saying.'

I said: 'Thank you, Jane, for telling me. It's nonsense but one should know what is being said.'

I dismissed her then. I wanted to be alone to think. So it was true. He was seeing someone else. All during those waiting years I believed he had been faithful to me; now that we were together, as soon as we had reached the desired state, he had already begun to stray.

I could not believe it. Not so soon! And in a week or so my child was due.

Was Jane lying? I did not think she would dare. She was sly and delighted to plant uneasiness in my mind, but I did not think she would dare lie in such a matter.

My anger against Henry grew with every minute.

I was always impetuous and perhaps more so than ever now. My fury seemed to be choking me; the only way I could keep a little calm was by thinking of the baby.

A little later I saw Henry. He was not alone, though only one or two of his friends were with him. I could not wait. He came over to me leaving them in a corner of the room. He asked after my health and I burst out: 'And you, sir, how is it with you and your mistress?'

He looked at me in astonishment, his little eyes narrow. I should have been warned. But I had many lessons to learn and I had not yet mastered one of them.

'Do not feign innocence,' I cried. 'It is all over the Court. I will not endure such conduct. Here I am ... in this condition ...'

'Madam,' he said coolly, 'you forget to whom you speak.'

'I speak to my husband,' I retorted, 'who should have more concern for me and our child ... than to chase my servants.'

I had never seen him look like that before. His face was pale for a moment before the colour flamed into it. Then he spoke. 'You will close your eyes as your betters did before you.'

I was stunned. I had expected him to deny the accusation. I would not have believed him, but I would have accepted his assurances of eternal fidelity and told myself that this would be a warning to him. That I had not expected such a reaction showed how little I knew him or understood the situation to which I had been brought.

He seemed to have forgotten the listening courtiers – as I had temporarily – but I remembered afterwards.

He then said something which sent a shiver through me. He had taken a step towards me, and his expression was almost threatening. 'You ought to know that it is in my power in a single instant to lower you further than I have raised you up.'

And with that he turned and went from the room, his companions following him.

I went to my apartments in a daze and sank onto my bed.

It was like a nightmare. Was this the tender lover who had always sought to placate me during my outbursts of temper, the man who had sworn eternal fidelity and worked with such determination – and world-shattering consequences – for seven long years to make me his Queen? And in less than seven months he was tired of me!

I lay looking up at the ornate canopy. I had never been so bewildered in my life.

Then I thought of the child stirring within me. He could do me no harm ... not while I carried the heir. This child was what he wanted more than anything . . . more than he wanted me or the simpering maid of honour he was pursuing.

His words would be reported all over the Court. I could imagine the sniggers of my enemies.

But I carried the heir. I would be the mother of the future King.

I had never loved Henry. But I was already loving the child I carried. The child would be my salvation.

*

I did not see Henry for three days afer that incident. I was glad. I was very uncertain how I should behave towards him. I could not forget the ominous threat behind those words. During those few days I thought more often of Katharine than I ever had before and with different emotions. I had considered her an obstinate woman who refused to make life easier for us all because she would not go into a convent. What anguish had she suffered when he had made it clear to her that he wished to cast her aside? He could not have spoken to her as he had to me. He had not 'raised her up' – not the daughter of Queen Isabella and the mighty Ferdinand; she was of nobler birth than he with his dubious ancestry. He could not lower the daughter of kings; it was different for one whose great grandfather had been a mere merchant in the city of London. Katharine had had powerful relations to guard her; and yet she had been thrust aside by the power of the King.

These, I told myself, were foolish thoughts. I must try to be rational. He was merely having a little sport while I was incapacitated, to while away the time until I was myself again. Jane, with her sly comments, had aroused my anger and without thinking I had flared up – which I was afraid was not uncommon with me.

All would be well when the child was born.

*

September had come – the month for which we had all been waiting. The birthplace of the child was to be Greenwich Palace, and great preparations were being made.

When I arrived in my barge, people lined the banks to watch me. The cheers were half-hearted but at least there were no hostile manifestations. I suppose even my enemies had some respect for a pregnant woman.

The chamber I was to use for my confinement had been hung the tapestries depicting the history of the Holy Virgin. Here I should bring forth this most important child; in it was a very fine bed which Henry had given me some weeks before. It was ornate and exquisitely decorated and had belonged to a French Duke; I think it came into Henry's possession as the spoils of war. It was the finest I had ever seen. In this chamber was another bed over which was a crimson canopy. This was where I should receive those who came to see me and the infant after the birth.

Heavy and elaborate drapes were drawn across the windows to shut out all light; they gave the room, in spite of its luxurious fittings, a somewhat sombre look.

When I arrived at Greenwich, I was taken by a large company of courtiers including my ladies to my chamber where I took communion. Then I was conducted to my lying-in chamber. It was all very ceremonial, for everything must be done in accordance with tradition.

Notices had already been prepared announcing the birth of a Prince. This might seem premature but the soothsayers and prophets had, almost without exception, proclaimed that the child would be a boy. There was only one man who had dared say it would be a girl, and he was so unpopular and had incurred the King's wrath to such a degree that no one else dared mention that disastrous possibility.

The King had come to see me just before I went to Greenwich. There had been a certain restraint between us and if I had expected some humility from him I was disappointed. He had made his point. He would act as he wished, and it was my duty to remember that he was the King and all my honours had come through him.

He kissed me coolly on the cheek and said: 'You must not excite yourself. You must remember the child.'

'I think of nothing else,' I replied.

'Then that is well. I have been considering a name. It shall be Henry . . . Henry IX. That sounds well to me . . . but that is in the future . . . far in the future. He has to grow up first. Or Edward. That is a King's name. I have not yet decided.'

I had expected him to ask my opinion, but he did not do so, and this was a further indication of the changing relationship between us.

But at this time I could think only of my journey to Greenwich and what awaited me there.

*

There I lay in that darkened chamber. My pains had begun. It was a long labour but during the exquisite agony of childbirth my spirits were upheld by what this child would mean to me. Nothing could alter the fact that I should be the mother of the King. Henry's infidelities would be hard to bear, but I should be safe . . . secure; and once I had my son I would make sure that I regained my ascendancy over him.

At last I heard the child's cry. My baby was born.

I lay back exhausted. It was over. I had attained the very peak of my desire. I was drifting off into an exhausted sleep.

I opened my eyes. A woman was standing by my bed. It was the midwife.

'The child . . .' I said.

'Your Grace, the child is strong and lusty.'

'Oh, praise be to God. I want to see him.'

'Your Grace has given birth to a fair lady.'

'No,' I cried. 'It must be a boy.'

'A beautiful child,' went on the midwife. 'A strong and healthy little girl.'

'No, no,' I cried. 'No, no, no.'

'I will bring her to you. She is a little love.'

I shook my head. I could not bear it. A girl! Katharine had had a girl and much trouble she was causing.

'It's a mistake,' I said.

The midwife was silent.

I lay there. But the prophets ... the soothsayers ... they had merely said what the King wanted them to say. They had dared say no other. I had failed. Already he was tired of me. And all I had done, after all that trouble, was to produce a girl. Katharine had done that before me.

I felt the tears on my cheeks.

Henry came into the apartment.

What was he feeling? What would he do now? Would he upbraid me for failing? I was too tired to fight.

He looked at me.

'A girl,' he said, with some contempt.

I did not answer. I just lay there with the tears running down my face.

Then I looked at him, so big, so glittering, so powerful. 'I have failed you,' I said. 'I believed I could give you a son. God is against me. Everyone is against me. I am hated and reviled. There is no one to care for me. It would have been better if I had died in the ordeal.'

There was a strong streak of sentiment in Henry. He had never before seen me like this ... humble, broken and desperately unhappy.

He came closer and took me in his arms.

He said gently: 'This is a blow to us both. They had promised me a son. But be of good cheer. There is time, Anne. We'll get our son yet. The child is strong and healthy, and God has shown us that we can get healthy children. He does this to test us. He will give me a son, I know.'

I said again: 'I have failed. I was so sure that I could please you.'

'How now,' he said. 'All is well between us two.'

I said: 'No ... no more ...'

There were tears in his eyes. They were glazed with memories.

'All shall be well,' he said. 'I would rather beg from door to door than forsake you.'

This was balm to me.

My spirits recovered. It was only a setback. Heaven knew we had had those in plenty.

I felt my spirits rising. I, who had overcome so much, would overcome this.

*

As soon as he had gone, I ordered that the child be brought to me. When I held her in my arms I loved her, and in my heart I wanted her no different from what she was. She was perfect.

I said to the ladies who crowded round my bed marvelling at the perfections of my daughter: 'They may now with reason call this room the Chamber of Virgins, for a virgin is now born in it on the vigil of that auspicious day on which the Church commemorates the nativity of the Holy Virgin.'

I was happy. It was true my moods had always changed quickly, but this was a complete reversal – from despair to great happiness.

Henry had declared his continuing love for me; and I had the most adorable daughter.

Life was good again.

*

The disappointment was forgotten. Preparations for the child's christening were going ahead. The notices which were being sent out had to be altered by adding 'ss' to the word Prince.

This ceremony was to take place on the tenth of the month – four days after the birth.

It was wonderful to hear of all the splendour which was being made ready to honour my daughter – exactly the same which would have heralded the arrival of a son.

She was to be named Elizabeth, which seemed appropriate because it was the name of both my mother and Henry's. She was to be christened at Grey Friars Church, which was close to the palace. The church was hung with arras, and sweet-scented herbs were strewn all along the way to it. All the highest in the land were present; and Mary Howard, who was betrothed to the Duke of Richmond, Henry's illegitimate son by Elizabeth Blount, carried the pearl-and-jewel-studded chrisom. The Dowager Duchess of Norfolk carried the baby, and over them was a canopy held by my brother George, two of the Howards and another recently ennobled member of our family, Lord Hussey.

I wished that I could have been there. I wished I could have seen the Bishop of London performing the ceremony with all the rites of the Church of Rome. Cranmer was her godfather, and the Duchess of Norfolk and the Marchioness of Dorset her godmothers. I should have been so proud to hear Garter-king-at-arms crying out: 'God, of his infinite wisdom send a prosperous life and long to the high and mighty Princess Elizabeth.'

The procession from the church to the palace was lighted by five hundred torches, but round my baby walked gentlemen carrying flambeaux, and thus they came to my chamber.

I held out my arms to receive my little one, that high and mighty Princess Elizabeth.

And I rejoiced in her. I could not have cared more for a son.

*

I wanted to keep her with me to be a mother to her, and for a few days I did so. I loved her more every day. She was a beautiful child – perfect in every way. The ladies said that, in truth, they had never seen a more lovely girl.

Henry regarded her with interest, in which there was only just a faint resentment because she was not a boy; even he was not immune to her charms; and I could see that he was beginning to be fond of her.

He had changed since that occasion when he had made it clear to me that his feelings for me had altered. I heard no more of the woman he had been pursuing. It had been whispered that she was the wife of Nicholas Carew, a very attractive woman, not averse to a little flirtation, and her husband might well not object if he were looking for favours. However, it had blown over and I could tell myself that it was, after all, forgivable. We had suffered a great deal of stress, and I, far gone in pregnancy, had not been a very bright companion. If that were all, I had little of which to complain.

He was now attentive, visiting me often, talking of the future and the brother our delightful daughter would have.

Those who had thought the King's love for me was dead now had to change their views.

He was looking forward to my return to normal life. He had been lonely, he said, without me. It was as near to an excuse as he could bring himself to make for that temporary infidelity, and having suffered a big fright, I did have sense enough to accept it.

I was feeling stronger each day. I had my baby beside me; I had the attention of the King. All was well. The next child would certainly be a boy; and then all would be perfect.

As I lay in bed, I often thought of the injustice done to my sex. Why should not the child sleeping in the cradle be as great a monarch as any man? She could not, of course, lead her armies in war – but wars were folly in any case and rarely brought good to either side; and perhaps if there were more women rulers, then there would be less of that foolishness.

I had attained my ambition to win a crown; now I had something else to work for: my child.

She must be proclaimed Princess of England – a title which had hitherto belonged to the Princess Mary.

I anticipated trouble from that quarter. The girl was devoted to her mother, which was natural, of course; for so long she had thought of herself as heiress to the throne, and no doubt she had been thinking she would be Queen from the time when it seemed unlikely that her mother would have another child. Now she was about to be set aside that another girl might take her place.

At this moment that little baby, the Princess Elizabeth, was heiress to the throne for there was no Salic law in England as in France, and a girl had a chance of reaching the throne unless a boy was born to take it from her. That always filled me with irritation.

I had never realized before that I had strong maternal instincts. How different one becomes when one is a mother! I wanted to be to her all that a mother should. I did not want to hand her over to nurses. She was mine.

In a new confidence inspired by Henry's devotion, I declared I would feed her myself, and I started to do so.

Henry was annoyed. It meant of course that I had Elizabeth in the royal chamber, for she might require attention at any time and I must be at hand to give it. I saw a return of that cold anger which I had glimpsed not so very long ago.

'I never heard the like,' he said. 'A Queen to make herself a nursemaid!'

'This is my daughter . . . *our* daughter.'

'The child shall be with her nurses.'

'But I wish . . .'

'*I* wish her to go to her nurses.'

'*I* want her with me.'

'You forget your state,' he said. 'You have risen too high. You do not understand the ways of royalty.'

'You speak as though I am some kitchen slut.'

'Then pray do not behave like one.'

'Is it sluttish for a mother to love her daughter?'

'It is the duty of the Queen to remember her state.'

I wanted to scream: Very well, you do not want my daughter here. In that case I shall go with her. But I had had one example of his cold anger. Now and then would come to me the memory of those cruel eyes and the words: 'I have raised you up. I could so easily lower you.' And I felt a tremor of fear.

I heard myself say in a quiet voice: 'Very well, she must go to her nurses.'

' 'Tis the best place for her,' he said; he came to me and put an arm about my shoulders. I smiled at him, returning his kisses; but my heart was filled with misgivings.

In spite of his refusal to have her in our bedchamber, Henry gave a great deal of attention to Elizabeth's household. He approved as her nurse the wife of a gentleman named Hokart; he said the Dowager Duchess of Norfolk should be her state governess, which gave the old lady a very fine residence and 6,000 crowns a year. This seemed a good choice as I was a connection of the Howards. Another concession to me was the selection of Lady Bryan, whose husband was a kinsman of the Boleyns, to be her governess. I was delighted, for I knew Lady Bryan was a good woman. She had, as a matter of fact, been governess to the Princess Mary, so she was accustomed to the position.

I was very sad though when, at the age of two months, Elizabeth was sent to Hatfield, which was to be her home; with her went those people whom the King had selected.

I had to reconcile myself to her departure and promise myself that, whenever possible, I should be with my child.

In the meantime there was trouble with Mary.

She must now renounce her title that Elizabeth might have it.

She was a pale girl – delicate-looking – so that her boldness was amazing. She was defiant and seemed to care nothing for the wrath of the King.

I was determined she should submit. I had my Elizabeth to fight for; and it was an undisputed fact that, if Elizabeth were to have her rights, Mary must first give them up.

This the rebellious girl refused to do, and when members of the Privy Council went to her and told her she must resign her title, she refused to see them until she had assembled her entire household – and all those people who had looked after her for the last years, from officials of the household to the humblest kitchen maids. Then, before them all, she had the temerity to announce that she could not give up a title which had been bestowed on her by God and her parents. She was a Princess; she was the daughter of a King and Queen; and she had more right to her title than had the daughter of Madam Pembroke. She was the Princess of England and could not order her household to address her in any other way.

I was very angry when I heard this. By referring to Elizabeth as Madam Pembroke's daughter, she was implying that she was illegitimate. This I could not allow.

I sent orders that she was to lose her royal privileges; she was not to eat alone when she wished to; the custom of having her food tasted before she took it was to be stopped; and she was to have no communication with her mother. Perhaps this last was harsh; but I had begun to see that in Mary I had as formidable an enemy as I had had in Katharine; and I was incensed by her implications directed at my daughter.

Later I regretted the last injunction. Mary loved her mother with an almost fanatical devotion. Looking back, I can imagine what they must have meant to each other in those years when Katharine was fighting for her position and her daughter's; and indeed I think now, having a greater understanding of human nature, that each suffered more on account of the other than for themselves.

It was decided that Mary should be sent to Hatfield. I realized that she would consider this an added insult, for she would be in an inferior position in the household of the

Princess Elizabeth who, she would consider, had usurped her place.

I thought it would be just punishment for I was smarting under the insult to me in daring to refer to the Queen of England as Madam Pembroke, with the implication that I was not the King's wife but his mistress.

Christmas was upon us, and this had to be a Christmas to outdo all others. It was my first as Queen. I surrounded myself with the wits of the Court – Weston, Bryan, Brereton, Norris, my brother and Wyatt. We laughed; we were very frivolous; we made amusing entertainments, and the King liked to be with us better than any others. With us he could forget certain anxieties which weighed heavily on him at times. Clement had now given the verdict, which was that the marriage between Henry and Katharine was valid, which meant, of course, that ours was not.

Henry had snapped his fingers at the Pope's verdict, obviously given under the orders of the Emperor Charles; but it put him in a dilemma. Excommunication would follow if he continued to live with me as his Queen, and it was not easy to defy such an edict. At least it might be for Henry himself but there were the people to consider. Many of them were staunch Catholics, and if Henry were excommunicated, that would entail the entire country. He had no alternative but to break with Rome; but this did not mean a rejection of the old religion: it was merely changing the Head of the Church. Everything could be as before – the same rituals, the same ceremonies – but the Church of Rome would now be the Church of England, and Henry would be the Head of that Church instead of the Pope.

It had been Cromwell's idea, and it seemed to Henry the only solution.

But it gave great cause for anxiety because of the reactions of the people.

There were already murmurings.

So therefore it must be a very merry Chrsitmas. It was my

nature to be able to assume an excess of gaiety when the future might be fraught with danger. There had always been an element of recklessness in me. Now it was close to hysteria. I laughed – perhaps a little wildly – and although at this time I did not realize what great danger threatened me, warnings kept flashing into my mind. I knew that I was on a hazardous course for I should never feel quite secure after that scene when Henry had pointed out his power to destroy me.

So that Christmas we danced and masqued and were very merry.

*

The facts could not be ignored. Henry had defied the Pope. There was only one course open to him if he were to withstand the disasters and the discord in the land which excommunication would bring about, and Henry had taken it.

In the new year he declared himself Head of the Church of England. He had broken with Rome. He made it clear that he had no wish to change the religion. In fact, he opposed Martin Luther's teaching; he was not in favour of doctrinal reform. The only difference was that the rights of the Pope now belonged to the Crown.

He was not alone in this departure for many of the German states who were firm adherents of Martin Luther had already done so. There was to be a translation of the Bible into English, which would be wonderful. Many people would be able to read it who had not done so before. Surely they would see the advantage of that.

That was a troubled year. Everything seemed to go wrong.

I was pregnant again. The King was delighted and his old tenderness returned. This time he was sure we would have a boy. Desperately I longed for that boy. He would be my security as my little Elizabeth could not. I saw her when I could. She was enchanting and, I was sure, far brighter than other children of her age. She was more like her father than me in looks. Her blue eyes were bright and enquiring, her hair shone like gold. She was a beautiful child.

When I went to Hatfield to see her, there was of course the unpleasantness of Mary's presence. She was insolent, that girl. When she was told that Queen Anne had come she said: 'Queen Anne? I know of no Queen by that name. There is only one Queen of England and that is Queen Katharine.'

What could one do with such a girl? Beat her? Little good that would do. I loathed her. I did not see her when I was at Hatfield. I could have forced her to be present but I did not want to do that.

I told them that they must be sterner with her and not endure her tantrums.

Henry was going to Hatfield to see Elizabeth. That pleased me. I did not go with him because I was not riding now. I was taking every possible precaution. Nothing must go wrong with this child. Once I had a son, I was secure. It was a wonderful relief that I need no longer fear the Pope. He had lost his power over England.

Oh yes, I assured myself, once I had my son all would be well.

Of course there were the people. They seemed as if they would never like me whatever happened.

There was unrest throughout the country. For years the Pope had been almost like God to them. They had obeyed him without question. To those ignorant people he was not a man but a deity.

And the King had defied him – and all because of a black-eyed witch.

I was blamed for everything. The King had been led by me and I had the powers given to me by the Devil.

All through that year there was grumbling among the people. I was blamed for any misfortune. If it rained too much, it was God's displeasure because of the havoc brought to the Church by a witch.

At Hatfield, when Mary appeared, they cheered her as they

did Katharine at the Moor. People were talking freely of the disasters which were coming to England; and Cranmer and Cromwell decided that something would have to be done about it.

There was one woman who was causing a great deal of trouble, and there could not have been anyone in the kingdom who had not heard of the Nun of Kent. Her name was Elizabeth Barton and she was a woman of some eloquence and persuasive powers. She had in fact been a servant in the house of a certain Thomas Cobb, who had been a steward of one of Archbishop Warham's estates – that was her connection with the Church. It turned out later that, at the age of about twenty, she had suffered from some obscure disease which had left her a religious maniac. She began to have visions and was obsessed by Sin. Thus she began to get a reputation for holiness, and people believed that she really was inspired by the Holy Ghost.

I had always known that Warham was an old fool. Fortunately he had died and so enabled Cranmer to come in with his cool common sense. Warham had subscribed to the belief that Elizabeth Barton was divinely inspired, and he had sent messages to her in which he had told her she must not hide goodness and the words of God which were imparted to her during her trances. About this time she had ceased to be a servant in the Cobb household and was living as a member of the family.

The woman went on prophesying, and the Prior of Christchurch, Canterbury, took her into his charge. She was given instruction in the ways of the Church and the legends of the saints. It was believed that the Virgin Mary spoke through her. I suspected many of these priests of seeking ways of upholding the declining condition of the Church. When Martin Luther had nailed his theses to that church door, he had started something of great importance which must have given many a priest some uneasy moments.

Elizabeth Barton was supposed to have performed miracles. The Virgin Mary, according to Elizabeth Barton, commanded her to leave Aldington and make her home in Canterbury. No one cared to disobey the orders of the Virgin Mary, so the woman was given a cell in St Sepulchre's Priory.

All knew of the Nun of Kent; Warham had supported her; he had collected her pronouncements and presented them to the King. Henry dismissed them as the wanderings of a simple-minded woman, guided by churchmen who led her where they wanted her to go. The King showed them to Sir Thomas More, who shared his opinion.

Sir Thomas More had written a book about a similar case. It concerned a twelve-year-old girl named Anne Wentworth, and although later she withdrew her belief in her own prophecies, Thomas More had written of her as though she were genuinely inspired, and as he was a man of high reputation throughout the country, this helped to enhance Elizabeth Barton's fame.

The King's divorce was naturally something which would be eminently suitable for prophecy, and Elizabeth Barton seized on it and in the name of God forbade it.

That a simple countrywoman should dare tell him what to do enraged Henry, but Elizabeth Barton appeared to be fearless. She went on to say that she had been told by Heaven – whether the Virgin Mary or God himself she did not indicate – that if the King wronged Queen Katharine he should no longer be King of the Realm and would die a villain's death.

She was making a great nuisance of herself. People listened to her and, as she had the support of the Church, they were ready to believe her. Great men interested themselves in her – Fisher for one and Sir Thomas More visited her and made no attempt to treat her as the charlatan she was.

She began to be invited to the houses of the nobility that she might prophesy for them. The Holy Nun had become a fashionable fortune-teller. Her fame grew and grew, and she had a big following in all classes of society.

It was rather amusing that she had prophesied that if Henry married me he would die within a month. It was certainly awkward for her that he was still alive and in good health months later.

She was not completely witless. She said that the prophecy had been rather obscurely worded; she had meant he would be no longer King, and people had construed this as meaning that he would die. But what she had implied was that he would no longer be King in the sight of Heaven; and he was not.

Cromwell had talked very seriously to the King about this woman. She was no longer to be regarded as a simpleton; she was doing great harm to the King and the country; too many influential people were her friends. Therefore she must be arrested.

With his usual efficiency Cromwell soon had the Nun of Kent under lock and key.

He could be trusted to deal with the matter in a subtle way to cause as little trouble to the nation as possible. He did not immediately pass sentence, which he might have done. He kept her in prison and put her through examinations. Questions were fired at her. She was not tortured. He thought that was unnecessary and would bring the usual cry that she had confessed under torture. He could have said that surely, in her case, her friends God and the Virgin Mary might have come to her aid, but he was more crafty than that.

She was after all a simple woman. What education she had was of Church matters, and without her mentors beside her she broke down under Cromwell's expert questioning. He drew a confession from her that she had never had any visitations from Heaven and what she had said came from her own imagination to satisfy those who had looked after her and her own desire for worldly praise.

'That is what we need,' said Cromwell in delight. He had taken the precaution of arresting the two monks who had taught her, and before long he had confessions from them.

'By God's Holy Mother,' cried the King, 'that fellow Cromwell has a way of getting to the heart of a matter. Clever fellow. I wish I could like him better. He deserves it for his brains. I wish the rest of him pleased me as well.'

There was a trial in the Star Chamber – where all confessed and were declared traitors. Lord Audley, the Lord Chancellor, proclaimed that Elizabeth Barton had plotted for the King's dethronement, and the punishment for that was death.

They were taken back to prison. Cromwell thought there should be enquiries about those who had supported the woman; and at the beginning of that momentous year she was still in prison awaiting her sentence.

Meanwhile those who had known her and declared she was indeed a messenger of Heaven, were now in a very precarious position.

Several were attainted, among them Fisher and More. Many were assuring Cromwell that, although they had listened to the prophecies, they had never believed in them. They had been testing the Nun. They wanted to assure the King that never in their lives had they entertained a traitorous thought towards him. Fisher and More admitted that they had seen the Nun and talked with her, but this was only to test her. Fisher's support had been strong and he was not released. Sir Thomas More, however, did prove that he had warned her not to meddle in politics, and he firmly denied that he had ever said she had prophetic powers.

The King had a great fondness for More. He liked to visit the house in Chelsea where More lived, surrounded by his family, rather more simply than a man in his position usually did. This domestic felicity pleased the King, and More was of course a brilliant man – perhaps the most brilliant man in the kingdom – and his conversation was witty, so at More's house the King was entertained as he liked to be.

So he was pleased when More's explanation was accepted. That was the state of affairs at the beginning of that momentous year.

The Nun of Kent was in prison awaiting death; and many of those who had been ready to question the King's action, had now realized that it would be unwise to do so.

*

There was a rumbling throughout the country. Monks and priests were boldly preaching against the break with Rome; people congregated in the streets and talked of the doom which would come to England. Cromwell wanted stricter laws to be enforced. There must be harsh punishment to quell rising revolt, he said.

Sentence was passed on the Nun of Kent and she was burned at the stake. It was an example of what would be done to those who spoke against the King.

Then a terrible thing happened to me. There was no reason for it. I lost the child I was carrying; and it would have been a son.

I could not understand it. I was healthy and capable of bearing strong children. There was nothing wrong with Elizabeth except that she was a girl.

And here we were, conforming to the old pattern which had set itself for Katharine. This was my first miscarriage . . . and a boy. How often had that happened to Katharine? Too many times to remember.

I was heartbroken and the King was bitterly disappointed.

'We'll have our boy yet,' he said; and I had to be comforted because he did not blame me as he had blamed Katharine. I did not want the people to know of my misfortune. If they did, there would be murmurs about the wrath of Heaven.

I was tense and worried.

But Henry was still in love with me. There had been no repetition of the alarming affair just before Elizabeth had been born.

I was very quickly pregnant again. This time, I told myself, it must come right. Nothing shall go wrong this time.

England had changed. Fearful of the murmuring of the people and the great controversy which had arisen out of the break with Rome, Cromwell had thought it necessary to introduce new laws. In the past, if a man stood against the King, that was treason and might well bring the death sentence. Now it was a crime even to speak against the King.

People had to watch their words, and that made for a very uneasy state of affairs, for how easy it was for an enemy to report a traitorous remark spoken by one he wished to harm.

For the first time in his life the King was really unpopular. He resented it. It was he who had insisted on the divorce and the break with Rome, but I was learning something of Henry's character. When something went wrong, he looked round for someone to blame; and there were times when I caught him looking at me with a calculating expression. I did not comment on it. I was afraid to. I thought it might bring forth a tirade of recriminations to which I might make some pointed and unforgivable comments.

Still I was once more pregnant, and that softened Henry towards me.

Then again I lost the child.

This was frightening. I began to suspect it was Henry who could not get healthy children. Of all the pregnancies Katharine had had, she had produced only one girl – Mary; and Mary was scarcely the picture of health. He had one son by Elizabeth Blount; but there was an ethereal quality about the young Duke of Richmond as though he might not be long for this life. And myself . . . healthy in every way – and I had lost two boys. True I had produced my Elizabeth, who was full of vitality, but I had lost the boys. There seemed to be some significance in it somewhere.

Henry was bitterly disappointed. 'Two boys lost,' he said, looking at me as though it were due to some fault of mine.

I had dismissed those niggling fears before, but I could not very easily now.

He was less tender, ready to contradict as though he enjoyed disagreeing with me.

It was Jane Rochford who conveyed to me the fact that he had renewed his attentions to the lady he had sought during my pregnancy with Elizabeth.

'Are you going to endure it, Anne?' she asked. 'At your Court. You are the Queen.'

'I will not endure it,' I said.

'Then what will you do about it?'

'I will speak to the King.'

'Would that be wise?'

'What do you mean?'

'He might be angry.'

I could see that the state of affairs between us was known. I should have seen it too. But I was ever one to act first and think after.

I did say to him: 'It is disturbing to me that the whole Court is aware that you have a mistress.'

His eyes narrowed. 'Then, Madam,' he said, 'you must, I fear, remain disturbed.'

'You dare to flaunt her . . . here at Court. Surely you might have the discretion to attempt to hide the fact that you are an unfaithful husband.'

'You should show more gratitude for what I have done for you.'

'And become your long-suffering wife?' I cried. 'Like Katharine . . . you think . . . to stand aside and watch your affairs with other women. Do you think I would ever endure that?'

'You must needs endure what is given you,' he said.

'I will not.'

He lifted his shoulders and turned from me.

I said: 'Henry . . . have you forgotten . . .'

He turned to me and there was a frightening coldness in his eyes. 'I forget not what I have done for you. I brought you up . . . and I tell you I can cast you down. There are many who urge me to do this. You should remember . . . I picked you up from nothing . . .'

'Nothing!' I cried. 'Do you call a member of the Howard family nothing? There are some . . .' I stopped in time. I was about to say that some thought the Howards more royal than the upstart Tudors. I had to keep a hold on my emotions. I must be careful, I must remember the great power of this man. He was right when he said he could cast me down. He could and God help me . . . in that moment I believed he would.

He was looking at me and I saw hatred in his eyes.

'I have done much for you,' he said slowly, 'and because of it you give yourself airs. And what do you give me? Where are the sons you promised me?'

'It is no fault of mine that we have no son.'

The pious look crept into his face. 'I cannot see why God should so punish *me*.'

So he implied that God was punishing me. When things went wrong it must never be Henry's fault. There must always be others to take the blame.

'Perhaps if you were to give up your philandering and paid more attention to your wife . . .'

He turned to me, his eyes narrowed, colour flaming into his face once more. 'You should be content with what I have done for you,' he said. 'I tell you this: I would not do it again.'

With that he strode out.

I was trembling with rage. It was hard to believe he could have changed so quickly. When I thought of how he had pursued me, how he had put up with my tantrums – and I admit there had been some very unreasonable ones – and how tender he had been, how humble . . . I could not understand what had happened. Was he realizing the great price he had paid for me – and there was no doubt that he was regretting it!

Jane Rochford came in. I believe she listened at doors. She was a foolish, reckless woman; she would be caught one day. If she eavesdropped on the King and he discovered her, I could imagine his fury. The Boleyn clan was not in very high favour even though one of its members was the Queen.

'That woman is a serpent,' she said. 'I have heard that she is poisoning his mind against you. You know how it is . . . at night . . . sharing a pillow.' Her eyes were sly. I knew she was trying to hurt me under cover of sympathizing. She should be sent away from Court before she could do real harm.

I said: 'I am tired, Jane. I want to rest.'

'Of course you are tired. Who wouldn't be! You're worried, aren't you, Anne? It is terrible for you. I do sympathize.'

'Thank you,' I said. 'Good night.'

'I shall be thinking of you. I'm going to do all I can to help. People feel depressed after miscarriages. I know just how you are feeling. But it will be all right. I am going to think of something.'

I wished she would leave. She was sly and stupid. George often said so. I knew that she had no fondness for me and was jealous because of George's affection for me.

I had been a fool to let her come to Court. Yet it is difficult to refuse one's own sister-in-law.

But it did seem that she was trying to help in her clumsy way.

She picked a quarrel with Henry's mistress and they were quite abusive to each other. The matter was talked of: the Queen's sister-in-law and the King's mistress. An interesting combination.

It was an opportunity for me. I sent for the woman.

I said: 'I will not have brawling in my Court. You will leave immediately.'

I was foolish. But then I did act foolishly. My path was strewn with foolish acts. In my mind I was still living in the days when Henry had adored me to such an extent that I could act rashly and no harm come of it.

I was the Queen, I kept telling myself. I was the most powerful person at Court . . . under Henry.

The woman did as I knew she would do. She went to Henry.

Of course he would not allow her to be dismissed from Court. She must have told him of the quarrel with Jane Rochford, and being Jane, I was sure it had been provoked in the most heavy-handed manner.

It was not Henry's favourite who was to leave Court. It was Jane. Jane had always been stupid, and not long ago, when her hatred of me had been so strong, she could not contain it and had talked of her loyalty to Katharine – indiscreetly, of course. This was now brought against her and, as a result of her scheming, Jane was sent to the Tower.

*

Discontent was growing. It was hardly likely that a monarch, even one as powerful as Henry, could make such drastic changes to the religion of the country without repercussions.

People were afraid of Henry. The bluff, genial man they had known in his youth was changing. They had seen how determined he could be when something was denied him. Surely no other sovereign in Europe would have the temerity to break with Rome?

But not all the nobles would bow to his will; this was particularly so with those in the North, who were a law unto themselves and, I knew from Henry Percy, considered themselves the rulers of the North. They were too far away to be so much in awe of the King as those who spent their lives close to him and therefore had to fawn on him and tremble at his frowns.

One of these was Lord Dacre of Naworth. He had always been one of Katharine's most staunch supporters. He was a firm Catholic, and Chapuys, the Spanish ambassador, who was on the alert for some means of getting rid of me and reinstating Katharine, was a friend of his.

Chapuys and he had been in close communication

apparently. Dacre in his border territory had been dealing with the Scots, and he, with Chapuys and others, planned to persuade the Scots to invade England when men such as Dacre would join them and force the King to give me up, take Katharine back and return to Rome.

Cromwell had his spies everywhere and by means of intercepting letters learned what was going on. Dacre was forthwith arrested, charged with treason and sent to the Tower to await trial.

The case looked black against him. He was tried before his peers. It was an indication of how the King's popularity had fallen when Dacre was not condemned.

There were some members of the peerage who regarded Cromwell as a common creature who was worming his way into the King's confidence. It was Cromwell's zeal which had brought Dacre to face his judges. Dacre had spoken so strongly against me that they believed – and correctly – that I would wish to see an end of him. Dacre was a clever man; he addressed the court and spoke for seven hours in such a manner as to carry the peers along with him. He thought that some of inferior blood – meaning Cromwell and myself – were seeking to rule the country, with what results had been seen. He was no traitor. He was a loyal Englishman aghast at the way in which his country was going.

To the amazement of all, and the fury of the King and Cromwell, Dacre was acquitted.

It was an indication of the danger into which we were heading.

There was worse to come. When news of the acquittal was released, the people of London came out into the streets to light bonfires, to dance and sing; they wanted to show their delight that a man who had dared to speak his mind and say what so many of them were feeling was found not guilty.

There was a rumour going about that Cromwell had said that it would be easier if Queen Katharine would pass away and take her daughter with her. This was construed as a threat to their lives, and as usual the blame was laid at my door.

No one in the country had more enemies than I; everything that could be brought against me, was. My slightest remarks were misconstrued.

It was now freely said that I was planning to have Katharine poisoned. I knew I was surrounded by spies. Jane Rochford had been released from the Tower; her sojourn there had been just to frighten her and punish her for daring to attempt to get the King's mistress banished from Court. One would have thought she would have become wiser through such an experience, but that was hoping for too much from Jane.

I was growing more and more nervous; my temper could be easily provoked at the slightest upset; this did not endear me to those around me. I had few friends – and I did know then how much I needed friends.

Here I was at the pinnacle of my ambition, and what an uneasy place it was proving to be! My only real pleasure was in my daughter, whom I could visit only at intervals, and when I was with her I had to be under the same roof as Mary, who showed clearly her contempt for me. I noticed, too, how the conduct of those who accompanied me was changing. Many of them slipped away to pay their respects to Mary. This could mean only one thing: my power was waning and they knew it. What was in the future they could only guess; but they wished to show Mary that they respected her ... just in case she should be of importance later on.

The King had been fond of Mary. She had been for so long his only child. It was only when she had stood so resolutely beside her mother and refused to obey him that he had turned against her.

News came to Court that she was ill. I could not help being pleased, and people noticed it. Naturally I should feel much more secure if Mary died. While she lived, she was a threat to Elizabeth, and one of my greatest desires was for Elizabeth – if I could get no sons – to be the heir to the throne. Perhaps in an impetuous moment I said this. Katharine was dropsical, and her health was precarious. Well, the situation would ease considerably if neither she nor her daughter was there.

This was logical, and many people must agree with it.

What was so disturbing was the King's concern when he heard of his daughter's sickness. He immediately sent his physicians to her.

Jane Rochford told me she had overheard Cromwell say that the King loved the Princess Mary a hundred times more than he did his latest born.

'I don't believe it!' I cried.

'It was what Cromwell said. But of course it isn't true.'

I knew it was true. Elizabeth was too young to interest him. Moreover, she was my child – and he was fast becoming tired of me.

Henry certainly showed a great deal of solicitude for Mary; he said that if he heard of any showing harsh treatment towards her they would have to answer to him.

I could see that his conscience was beginning to worry him, and that boded no good for me.

Clement died. There was no cause for rejoicing in this. Pope Paul III who was elected to follow him was quite different from his vacillating predecessor. He was firm in his resolution to bring Henry back to Rome and showed a certain friendliness towards him. This might have been a good thing if there had not been a shift in the attitude of France towards us. François had been a good friend during the divorce controversy and had helped us considerably to the marriage. I liked to believe that he was kindly disposed towards me because of memories from the past. But, of course, rulers feel no such sentiments, and their actions are invariably dictated by experience.

He now offered to renew negotiations for a marriage between Mary and the Dauphin. This shattered me. It was tantamount to saying that Mary was legitimate – and if she were, what of my position? What of Elizabeth's?

Admiral Chabot be Brion arrived in England to discuss the possibility of the match. I was very tense. I felt so much hung on the decision. The fact that François could suggest it was significant. What was going on behind my back? I was so nervous I felt ready to burst into tears at any moment. There were times, though, when the humour of the situation forced itself upon me. Throughout all those years I had been so passionately sought and had eluded capture. Suppose I had relented early in the chase, would I have been dismissed long ago? When I thought of it, I wanted to laugh ... not the laughter of happiness but something near hysteria.

I had to be careful. I had to control myself.

But if François was seeking the hand of Mary for the Dauphin, it must mean that he considered her legitimate. There was no other answer to that.

I thought I might have an opportunity of speaking with the Admiral. He had been an admirer of mine in the old days at the French Court. He had flirted pleasantly and he had expressed a great admiration for me. I felt I could ask him to enlighten me as to François's motives. But he did not seek a meeting with me, which was strange; in fact, it was not very good manners, on which the French so prided themselves.

I could, therefore, discover nothing of the negotiations, and Henry made it quite clear that he had no intention of telling me anything. My behaviour to his daughter Mary had been such that I was the last person with whom he would want to discuss her future.

So I did not know what had been decided.

The Admiral was to leave for France and we gave a banquet on his departure. I was seated at the table on the dais with him on my right hand. The talk had been formal. Henry seemed a little more affable. I could still look more attractive than most women, in spite of my anxieties, and when I noticed his rather covert looks of approval, my spirits rose a little.

We talked of the Admiral's departure, and Henry asked me if I had said farewell to Gontier, the Admiral's chief secretary.

When I replied that I had not, he said: 'I will go and fetch him.'

For Henry to go and fetch a secretary was most surprising. I could not understand, for the moment, why he did not send someone in search of him. Then I saw him leave the hall, and almost immediately his mistress slipped out after him.

I could not help it. The tension seemed to snap. He had gone out to be with her. I thought of how he used to pursue me, and suddenly I began to laugh. It was terrible laughter but I could not stop it.

The Admiral looked very annoyed, for people were glancing our way.

Then he said in a very cold voice: 'Do you mock me, Madam?'

'Oh no, no,' I cried. 'It is nothing to do with you, Admiral. I was laughing because the King has just met a lady, and the thought of everything else has gone out of his head.'

Still, I could not stop laughing. The Admiral stared coldly in front of him.

I was trying very hard to fight down the hysterical laughter. I was terrified that it would turn to tears.

I saw Henry later. I asked him if he had passed a pleasant time with his mistress.

'You should look to your tongue, Madam,' he said.

How right he was! But I could not restrain myself. I knew I was being foolish but I went on being so. If only I could have faced the situation for what it was and planned calmly.

'Your treatment of the Admiral was not very well received,' I said. 'It was a pity your passion made you forget your duty to your guest.'

He turned to me and I saw the hatred clearly in his eyes. I thought: He feels towards me as he did towards Katharine.

How could it have happened so soon?

There were plans in his eyes. How well I knew him! That pursed-up mouth which could be so pious-looking when he was planning acts of cruelty. The little eyes gazing to Heaven

412

making his case so that it would win divine approval.

Instinctively I knew that he was planning to be rid of me as surely as he had planned to be rid of Katharine.

I was trembling with fear.

I said ironically: 'Have I Your Grace's leave to retire?'

'It is most gladly given,' he growled.

*

My spirits were lifted a little when I heard that François's request for Mary's hand was refused by Henry on the grounds that she was illegitimate; instead he had offered Elizabeth for the Duc d'Angoulême, a younger son of François.

I saw George a great deal at this time. He was my true friend. My father's attitude towards me had grown quite cold. Norfolk had never shown much warmth. They were turning against me since I was falling from favour. Mary, of course, was her old self but she had always been ineffectual. Still, it was nice to have sisterly affection. She had come to Court some little time before, and occasionally I saw my stepmother and she was as loving as ever. I liked to have my family about me.

I had my admirers still. They were faithful. Brereton, Norris, Wyatt were constantly in my company, all expressing devotion to me. It was such a comfort in this changing climate.

George was with us, but he and I talked alone whenever we could. He could be a little sombre sometimes for he was well aware of the King's changing attitude towards me.

'You will have to walk very warily,' he warned me. 'For so long he has been behaving like a besotted lover. It is different now. The tame pet can become a wild beast. Anger and resentment are smouldering there . . . ready to burst out.'

'I know it,' I replied.

'No one would dare speak to you as I do, Anne. It worries me. You could be in danger.'

'I know he is unfaithful. He has become tired of me. How could it happen so quickly, George?'

George was thoughtful. Then he said: 'There must be utter frankness between us two. He has worked himself into a dangerous position. It was a bold move to break with Rome.'

'François, who seemed to support us, seems to be turning right round. The French have been so affable to me. Now they are aloof.'

'You do not put your trust in monarchs, Anne. They go whichever way is most beneficial to them. It suited François to stand for Henry because that was against Charles. But this is different. This is standing against the Roman Catholic world.'

'He did that for love of me.'

George looked at me sadly. 'He desired you greatly, that's true. But he wanted to make sure of the succession.'

'There is Elizabeth. There is Mary.'

'Girls! He wanted a son ... who would be like him ... riding round the country, bluff, hearty, winning the love of the people.'

'Could not a woman do that?'

'Leading the troops in battle?'

'When has Henry last gone to war? When he did, his efforts were not marked with success.'

'Do not tell him that. You are too outspoken ... too frank.'

'I know I am. But what am I going to do, George?'

'Get a son. He would never discard the mother of his son.'

'I see little of him. He has his mistress now. Oh God, George, do you think he will be with her as he was with me?'

'Anne,' he said, 'you are the most fascinating woman at Court. You have a special allure. You must think of that. You *must* get a son. There is something I have to tell you. He has hinted to Cromwell that he wants a divorce.'

'From me!'

George lifted his shoulders. 'Who else?'

'No, George!'

'Why not? He rid himself of Katharine ... at what cost! It

would be simpler with you. The Boleyns are not the Emperor Charles. The Pope would not stand out against it.'

'Then I am doomed.'

He shook his head. 'There is Cromwell. Cromwell has told him that he could divorce you easily . . . by declaring that his marriage to you was no true one. But that would entail one thing: he would have to take Katharine back. That he will never do.'

'Presumably I am the lesser evil.'

'Presumably. Don't worry. Cromwell is a clever fellow. He won't allow it to happen. If Henry went back to Katharine, he would soon be returning to Rome, and that would be the end of Cromwell. He has based his career on the break with Rome. Cromwell – for his own reasons – is your friend. Rejoice in that.'

'Sometimes, George, I am very frightened.'

'You'll come through if you can get a son. Then you would be safe. But you will have to accept his infidelities . . . just as Katharine did.'

'I am beginning to realize the patience of that woman.'

'She is the daughter of Isabella. Remember that. She has stood firm . . . unafraid. She is indeed a brave woman. In spite of everything, she has disconcerted Henry, and there are many throughout the country who support her. Anne, get a son. You *must* get a son. Therein lies your salvation.'

'These miscarriages . . . they were boys.'

'Perhaps you have been over-anxious.'

'It may be.'

'Get him back somehow. Get a son. When you are pregnant, live more quietly. Give up this wild gaiety. You give an impression of indifference to the King's rising animosity. You flirt too much with men about you. It is noticed, and the King does not like it.'

'Even though he is no longer interested in me?'

'Even so. But he watches you sometimes and there is a glint in his eyes. He knows you are outstanding in the Court. You must find a way, Anne . . . soon. It is imperative!'

'I know. But at least he told François that Mary is illegitimate.'

'Yes, and offered Elizabeth to the younger son. That is only because she is so young and the Dauphin needs a bride soon.'

'Do you think François will accept Elizabeth?'

'I hope so. I pray so. Much will depend on it. If François refuses it will be tantamount to saying that he does not believe in her legitimacy. A great deal will depend on François's answer.'

'It is frightening.'

'I know. But we must face the truth, Anne. That is the only way we can continue to exist.'

'Thank you, George, you do me so much good.'

'Curb your temper. Remember when you are about to let it fly that you are dealing with a man who is very powerful and probably the most ruthless in the world. You have to forget the tender lover. He is not that any more. You must stop thinking of him as the man who pursued you and was ready to grant your every whim. He has changed, and not only to you. There was a time when he was a kind and courteous husband to Katharine; he loved Mary; true he strayed now and then, but no more than was to be expected. He had certain codes; religion and morals meant something to him. People do change. Events change them. And there have been some notable events in the life of this King. They brutalize. Think of his conduct to Queen Katharine and the Princess Mary.'

'I have said he was too soft with them.'

'You are thinking only of what you want. Consider a husband who has tired of a wife who has done nothing but good. Her only fault is that she is older than he is and is no longer attractive to him. You come on the scene; you refuse to be his mistress, so he schemes and plots and juggles with his conscience. He would get rid of that wife of all those years, repudiate her, and when she refuses to go into a convent she lives like a prisoner under house arrest. What anguish he has caused. And his daughter Mary – a girl brought up to believe herself Princess of England, now deprived of all her rights and separated from her mother . . .'

'They would have plotted against us. Chapuys is ready to foment a revolt.'

'Think of it, Anne. That's all I ask. If he can act so to one, he will to another. We will see what François's response is to this suggestion for Elizabeth and little Angoulême. So much will depend upon it. In the meantime, Anne, you must get a son.'

I said: 'It is good to talk to you, George. I thank God for you.'

His words kept hammering in my brain. A son. A son. I must get a son.

I had a healthy daughter – so why should I not get a son?

*

There was trouble from an unexpected quarter.

Jane Rochford came to me one day, her eyes shining with that excitement which they displayed when she had disturbing news to impart.

'Mary fainted this morning. She was quite ill. And when we revived her it was clear that . . .'

I looked at Jane, hating her.

I said: 'Send Mary to me.'

'We were amazed . . .'

'Never mind,' I said imperiously. 'Send her to me. I want to see her at once.'

Mary came. She was very apprehensive.

I said: 'Are you with child?'

'How . . . how did you know?' she stammered.

'That snake, Jane Rochford, told me.'

'Yes . . . she was there. I saw her when I came to.'

'Trust Jane to be there. This is a disgrace. You know I was thinking of a good match for you. And now like the silly little

417

wanton you are, you have made it impossible.'

'I don't want a grand match, Anne.'

'You are the Queen's sister. Your marriage should be a matter for the King and me to decide.'

'The King is no longer interested in me. He will be glad to see me out of the way. He rarely looks my way and, if by chance his eyes fall on me, he feigns not to see me. It was different once. But that is his way. When things are over, he wants to forget they ever existed.'

Her words struck me like a funeral knell. How right she was.

'In any case,' she went on, 'I only want William.'

'William? William who?'

'William Stafford.'

'William Stafford! But is he not only a knight . . . of no importance!'

'He is of importance to me.'

'As you are ready to proclaim to the world, it seems.'

'Yes, I am.'

'I don't know what the King will say.'

'Nothing . . . precisely nothing. He is not interested.'

'And our father?'

'Our father has always despised me. I don't know how I happened to be his daughter.'

I looked with envy at the slight swelling below Mary's waist. She had children . . . healthy children who loved her and whom she loved. Why should they be denied to me?

For a few seconds I felt envious of my simple-minded sister who thought love was more important than ambition, and for a fleeting moment I would have changed places with her. But the moment passed.

I said: 'And what do you think is going to happen now?'

'We shall be married.'

'You will leave the Court.'

'It is what we want,' she said, smiling contentedly.

So Mary was banished from Court and married Sir William

418

Stafford. In due course she gave birth to a son.

How cruel fate was! Why give a son to Mary and deny one to me?

*

There was a ray of hope. François had agreed to consider a marriage between his son the Duc d'Angoulême and Elizabeth.

I was delighted. François had not deserted me after all. If he thought of my daughter as a possible wife for his son, she must be legitimate in his eyes, and that meant he considered my marriage with Henry valid.

This was particularly comforting because George had discovered that the matter of a pre-contract between myself and Northumberland had been revived. The King wanted the matter looked into closely. That was very ominous.

But this action of François's was significant.

I realized afterwards that François had no intention of allowing the marriage; he made such outrageous demands as part of the betrothal agreement that they could only be rejected by the Council.

François would have known all along that they would be. But still he had offered to negotiate, which was the important thing, and I still clung to the hope that he had done it out of kindness to me, for I could be sure he was aware of the state of affairs at the English Court.

I kept thinking of George's words. I must act quickly. I must make the King reasonably friendly towards me so that we could occasionally share a bed. Otherwise how was I going to get a son?

He was deeply involved with his mistress. I had to break that somehow for I had discovered that she was a fervent advocate of Katharine and Mary. It might well be that she had been put in the King's path with instructions to become his mistress that she might further the cause of these two. There

419

were all sorts of schemes afoot; there were spies everywhere. Chapuys was a very energetic man, and he had not yet despaired of getting me ousted and Katharine's and Mary's rights restored to them.

An idea occurred to me which I admit was wild, but I was getting desperate.

My cousin Madge Shelton had come to Court. She was an exceptionally pretty girl. Her mother was my father's sister. I had always liked her, perhaps because she had shown a great admiration for me. She used to copy my clothes, my manner, the way I walked; it always amused me. She was delighted to come to Court and I think it was partly because she could be near me.

Naturally such admiration delighted me. She was such a gentle girl, constantly trying to do something which would please me; and not for her own gain either – just to hear me say Thank You and smile at her.

Now that I was Queen, she thought I was wonderful. Little did she know of my inward disquiet. She saw me at Court surrounded by admirers, many of them men behaving, as they always had, as though they were in love with me.

There was a faint family resemblance and, as she rather slavishly copied the fashion I had set, I think she looked more like me than any girl at Court.

The idea came to me one evening. I was sitting with the King on the dais, for on certain occasions we had to make a show of being together, when Madge appeared. She was dancing and looked particularly pretty. I saw the King's eyes come to rest on her, and there was in them that glazed expression which I remembered had been directed towards me so often in the past.

His mistress then came close in the dance, and his eyes were all for her. But I had seen the look he gave Madge.

I dismissed the idea. It was preposterous; but at the same time there was an urgent message hammering in my brain. I must get a son.

I decided to speak to Madge.

'I want to talk to you very privately,' I said. 'And what I say must be between us two.'

Her lovely eyes opened very wide and she looked at me with something like idolatry.

'We have been very good friends, cousin,' I said.

'Yes,' she answered breathlessly.

'Right from the time when we were both very young. I fancied even then that you had a liking for me.'

'Oh, Madam . . . yes,' she said.

'I need your help.'

She looked startled; but I could see that she wanted above everything to please me.

'I hope you will feel you can give it to me.'

'But *you* have done so much for us all . . . the whole family . . .'

I laid my hand on her arm. 'This is something very special. I am going to be very frank. You must have heard that the King and I are not on very good terms of friendship at the moment.'

She did not answer. Of course she had heard. The whole Court was talking about it.

'It is on account of a certain woman. She is his mistress. She has taken him away from me. She is my enemy.'

Madge looked suitably shocked.

'Yes,' I said, 'she is continually talking of the virtues of Katharine and Mary. The King listens to her. And she speaks ill of me. I cannot have that.'

'She should be punished.'

'That is what I intend to do.'

'But how can *I* help?'

'I think the King likes you.'

'He has scarcely seen me.'

'Oh yes, he has. I have seen him look at you, and I know well his ways.'

She was amazed.

'Cousin,' I went on. 'I know not what will become of me if this woman continues to pour her poison into the King's ears.'

'How can you stop her?'

'By supplanting her.'

'But you are the Queen. For you the King has done so much.'

'Men are strangely fickle, cousin. Their loves do not last.'

'But the King loved you for many years. For you he has broken with Rome.'

'The King loved the chase. He wanted a son. He could not get one with Katharine. He wanted me, too. I think it was in that order. You see how I trust you, cousin. I am talking to you very frankly, and what I say does not go beyond these four walls. I believe you love me and would do a great deal for me.'

She nodded.

'May Heaven bless you! This is a big thing I am going to ask of you.'

Her eyes were shining with purpose. She would do it, I knew, for me.

'I want you to lure the King from his mistress.'

'I?'

'Yes, you. You have a freshness and charm and he has already noticed you. Be in his way. Smile . . . nervously. Seem overwhelmed when he looks at you. Let him see that you think he is the most handsome, powerful, god-like being on Earth. He will respect your judgement and immediately fall in love with you, because you are indeed very attractive.'

'But I don't think . . . '

'Try, Madge. My future could depend on it. I want you in her place. I want no more talk of how good and wonderful Katharine and Mary are; I want you instead to talk of me, to tell him of my incomparable charms, my looks, my brains and above all my great fondness for him. Tell him that I am desolate because he has turned from me. Make him believe that, although I may not show this to him, it is because I am uncommonly proud and of a somewhat inflammable nature.

Tell him that I admire him . . . as you do . . . and all women of discernment must.'

'And do you?'

I laughed loudly and checked myself. No hysteria. The plan was so wild it might not succeed. But I was desperate and it was worth a try.

'Madge,' I went on earnestly, 'for my sake I want you to take the King away from his mistress. It is time he began to be tired of her. It is very important to me that he ceases to soften towards Katharine and Mary. It is of even greater importance that I get a son.'

'But surely you only have to tell him this . . .'

I shook my head. 'That would not be the way. This might be. Cousin, I am asking too much. Forgive me. But I thought you would do a great deal for me.'

'I would,' she replied earnestly. 'I would do anything.'

I saw the excitement begin to dawn in her eyes. The King was the King. He was still handsome, and power sets a mighty aura about a man. Most girls would be flattered to be noticed by him. She would have to perform her part well, and he could be courteous and charming enough when he was attempting seduction.

'You will win my eternal gratitude,' I said. 'Do you want to think about it?'

She nodded.

'Then please do. And remember: this is between us two.'

'I swear it shall go no further,' she said.

*

Jane Rochford was very excited.

'The King is no longer seeing his mistress so frequently.'

'Oh, is he not?' I asked languidly.

'There is another.' She looked at me with satisfaction.

'Oh yes, I suppose there would be.'

'You would never guess who.'

'Tell me.'

'It is really rather funny. Who would have thought it? She seemed so quiet. The King is in hot pursuit. It is our cousin, Madge Shelton.'

'Well, she is a very attractive girl.'

'Don't you mind? To think that a member of our family . . .'

'It has to be someone, I suppose.'

'You take it calmly.'

'How else could I take it?'

'George was with you a long time last night.'

'We were talking.'

'I was on the point of coming in.'

'You would not do that unless invited.'

'I knew I shouldn't be invited. I'm not clever enough. George always implies that.'

I did not answer. I was thinking of Madge.

I saw her later. She had changed. She was now the King's mistress. I marvelled at a devotion which had made her go so far. It had seemed such a wild plan and yet it was working.

'Does he talk much . . . of affairs of Court?' I asked.

'He talked about Katharine and Mary.'

'They are much on his mind.'

'He says they have caused him grievous suffering.'

'I hope you were sympathetic.'

'Oh yes. I said it was wrong that any should harm the King. He has so much to think of . . . affairs of state . . . matters of the Court. Everyone should do their best to give him peace.'

'As you do.'

'Yes, as I do. I said I thought it was wrong of Katharine and Mary to be in such close touch with Chapuys. He said he supposed I heard gossip about the Court. I told him I did and he asked me one or two things. I don't think he likes Katharine and Mary quite as much as he did.'

'And did he mention me?'

She nodded, smiling. 'I told him how much I loved you and how kind you had always been to me, how wonderful you were, and that I was afraid I imitated you in so many ways. And he said, "Well, there is no one like the Queen." He looked soft for a while and then he went on: "She has a sharp tongue." I replied that it was really because you were so honest. You did not stop to think what advantage would come to you for saying this and that. You spoke freely and you were quick tempered, but you were so merry quickly afterwards and how much more exciting it was to be with people when you did not know exactly what to expect from them. Then he said: "You are a staunch advocate of the Queen," and I said, "So would Your Grace be if . . ." Then I clapped my hands to my mouth and I said, "Forgive me, sire, I spoke without thinking." He laughed and said: "Like her, eh?" And he seemed to speak of you with some fondness.'

Oh dear little cousin Madge, I thought. It could work. It was not a crazy scheme afer all.

*

It did not take the King long to tire of Madge, but so well had she done her work that even before her time was over he was looking towards me. I think he had come to regard her as a pale shadow of myself.

When we went hawking, he was close to me. He spoke a few words in a most pleasant manner and when I replied gently he seemed pleased.

We progressed from there, and within a week or so my old enemies were looking glum. Some of them obviously thought they had been a little premature.

One day he said to me: 'There is none like you. No matter who . . . I would always find myself coming back . . . to Anne.'

In the old days such a comment would have enraged me. I should have replied that I was not waiting on his pleasure. Now, I smiled as though contented. I had to get a son.

So we were together again, and it was almost as it had been in the first days of our marriage.

Although that was not so very long ago, I had grown up a good deal since then. I had begun to understand him better. He was completely selfish and could be very cruel indeed, and it was odd that his cruelty grew out of his assumed piety. I often compared him with François. François's lasciviousness and his determination to satisfy his carnal desires had stood in his way of becoming a great king. With Henry his actions had to be justified; he had his conscience to consider. It had to be placated, and this could only be done by putting himself right in the eyes of Heaven; that often meant treating those about him with complete ruthlessness. If he wanted to rid himself of me, as he had Katharine, he would not admit to himself that he was tired of me, and I had not, after all the trouble, brought him the desired son, which was the truth; it would have to be a concern of his conscience because of a possible pre-contract with the Earl of Northumberland. He wanted to say, I was not truly married to her. It was a mistake. But any solution which meant taking back Katharine was out of the question for him. Perhaps, as George had pointed out, I owed something to Katharine.

In the past I had been confident of my power to lure him to me, and I now believed that, in spite of the fact that I had grown thinner and older and had suffered disappointment in childbed, that power was still mine.

And it seemed so, for he had come back.

It was not long before I could tell him the joyful news. I was pregnant. I was wildly happy. This time it must be a son.

Now he was the devoted husband, solicitous of me, talking constantly of the arrival of the Boy.

I was very interested in the new religion which was being taken up in Germany and the Low Countries, and I was reading all I could about it. I interested him in it and we would spend enjoyable hours discussing it together. I would read something and hurry to tell him about it. He enjoyed this, for he had an alert mind.

I was full of confidence. Once I had my son, I could feel safe.

That was a year of tragedy.

It seemed I was not to have my child. I was following in the steps of Katharine. I was filled with melancholy when I miscarried.

'Why? Why?' I demanded. I had taken the utmost care. I had so desperately wanted ... so desperately *needed* this child.

The King was bitterly disappointed. He could see that I was useless to him.

But something seemed to touch him. He could be sentimental at times, and that softened him.

'We'll have boys yet,' he said, and nothing could have comforted me more at that time.

It was a disastrous year.

People talked of nothing but the Oath of Supremacy which had to be accepted by all. Those who did not accept it, did so at their peril.

At the end of the previous year, Parliament had conferred on Henry the title of Supreme Head of the Church, and it was declared to be High Treason to deny the title.

It was too much to hope that there would not be some who rebelled.

The King's fury was intense. Fisher and More were in the Tower. The King sent Cromwell to ask for More's opinion of the new statutes. More was a lawyer, and his opinion would be worth having, for if he agreed with them he would carry many with him. More was perhaps the most respected man in England. Learned, deeply religious, a good and moral man, he was above bribery and corruption. If he would be prepared to give his approval to the statutes, it was certain that many would do the same. The King must get that approval.

'Were they not lawful?' demanded Cromwell of him.

More's reply was that he was a loyal subject of the King and he could say no more than that.

When Cromwell returned to the King, Henry abused him. He was like that with Cromwell. But Cromwell stood by, patiently humble, smiling, waiting for the abuse to cease and letting the insults pass over his head.

He tried More again, with the same results.

The King cried out in a pained voice: 'I have given my friendship to that man, and now he refuses this little I ask.'

More's reply was that he was the King's servant, but God's first.

What could one do with such a man? He disturbed Henry, making it difficult for him to reconcile his conscience, which was one of the greatest offences a man or woman could commit.

On the Continent affairs in England were closely watched. Henry was isolating himself, and that made him uneasy.

The Pope had sent word that Fisher had been made a Cardinal. This was clearly meant to aggravate Henry, for Fisher was in the Tower. Like More, he had refused to accept the Oath of Supremacy.

'A Cardinal!' spluttered Henry. 'Tell the Pope I'll send his head to Rome to receive his Cardinal's Hat.'

Such outbursts were of little use.

He was most disturbed by Thomas More. The strong sentimental streak in Henry was uppermost in his feelings for More, and he was at times capable of affection. He admired More almost as much as he had Wolsey. The lively brain, the witty conversation, the clear view of life which comes to most of us too late and to some not at all, that innate knowledge of what is of true importance in life, often seeming to the worldly simple – that was More. A man greatly beloved by his family and his friends, one of whom had been the King. Henry used to visit the house at Chelsea now and then. He knew the family well, and he had at times been a little envious that so much felicity should come to a man who lacked what he, Henry, had – royalty, power, good looks.

And now More was in the Tower. He was going to refuse

to sign the Oath of Supremacy because he was a man of strong will and high principles. This refusal would brand him a traitor, and the punishment for traitors was death.

Henry had to face that. How could he sign a death warrant? This was a man he loved – in spite of his obstinacy. He raged. Why was More such a fool? Why was he ready to give up everything he had – and by God, that man had a great deal! – just for the sake of signing his name!

Fisher was such another. 'Obstinate old fool,' grumbled Henry.

June had come – hot and sultry.

Henry was stubborn. He had to go ahead. Several Carthusian monks and twenty-four other people were cruelly executed for denying the King was Supreme Head of the Church – carried on hurdles to the place of execution, then hanged and cut open while they were alive and their intestines burned.

Fisher's execution followed.

The King sent a command that no one was to preach about Fisher's treason. And they were not to mention Sir Thomas More.

I know that Henry suffered over More. He tried to put off the trial. He was sullen. I found him glaring at me as though I were to blame, for after all, if I had given way in the beginning, there might not have been this break with Rome, and More might, at this time, be living happily with his family at Chelsea.

But he could delay no longer. On the first day of July, More faced his judges in Westminster Hall.

My father was among those judges; so were Norfolk, Suffolk and Cromwell. More was charged with infringing the Act of Supremacy and maliciously opposing the King's second marriage. He answered that he had not advised Fisher to disobey the Oath; he had not described it as a two-edged sword, approval of which would ruin the soul. All the same, a verdict of Guilty was pronounced and he was sentenced to be hanged at Tyburn.

Henry was most distressed. He could not allow his old friend to be hanged like a common felon; he immediately changed the sentence to a more dignified form of execution; More was to be beheaded.

Everyone was talking of More. He was a man much loved by the people. Henry should never have agreed to his execution. But he could not turn back now. He had gone too far.

More had faced his accusers with courage and almost indifference, which was expected of such a man. He had few enemies, which was rare for a man in his position. He loved his daughter, Margaret, especially. People talked of her terrible grief and how she had run to him when he left Westminster Hall with the axe turned towards him and thrown her arms about his neck. Only then did he show signs of breaking his control. He had begged her not to unman him; and the poor girl had fallen fainting to the ground while he was forced to go on . . . a prisoner.

There was one thing which he had said, and this had made a great impression on me. It was reported to me by those who pretended to be my friends and kept me informed of what was going on. Usually it brought disquiet, but I had to know. More's daughter Margaret had raged against the dancing and feasting which was going on at Court while her father suffered imprisonment; and of course she talked of me with hatred, for like everyone else, she blamed me for all the ills which had befallen us.

'Poor Anne Boleyn,' Sir Thomas More was reported to have said. 'It pitieth me to consider what misery, poor soul, she will shortly come to. These dances of hers will prove such dances that she will spurn our heads off like footballs, but it will not be long ere her head will dance the same dance.'

I shivered when I heard that. It was not completely implausible. Oh, if only I could get a son . . .

On that sad July day Sir Thomas More was taken out to

430

Tower Hill. There was a silence throughout the Court. It seemed that everyone was there in spirit to witness that grisly scene.

He was jesting when he died, having approached the scaffold with the utmost composure. He said to the executioner: 'I pray you see me safely up, and for my coming down let me shift for myself.' He told the watching crowd that he died in the faith of the Catholic Church, and he prayed God to send the King good counsel.

Then the axe fell.

The King was playing cards with me when the news was brought that Sir Thomas was dead. He turned pale; his lips tightened. For a moment he looked a frightened man. I knew he was thinking that he had ordered the death of a saint. I saw a quiver run through his plump cheeks; then his eyes fell on me.

He was afraid of what he had done. He feared Heaven's wrath; and in case God had forgotten he had to remind Him of the real culprit.

There was cold hatred in his eyes as they surveyed me. 'You are the cause of this man's death,' he said, and left the table.

I felt death very close then. I saw him more clearly than I ever had . . . this man who could be so ruthless and had the power to work his will on us all.

*

Thomas More's body was buried in the church of St Peter in the Tower, but his head, as was the custom with traitor's heads, was placed on a pole and set up on London Bridge, that all who passed beneath it could reflect on the fate of traitors.

A shiver ran through the Court when news came that the head had disappeared. It seemed like Divine interference. Henry was in a state of great nervousness. He had always thought of himself as being on good terms with Heaven; and now this looked like a sign of disapproval.

It was not his fault that More had been executed, he reiterated. He had been forced to sign the death warrant. Others were to blame. The Parliament had conferred the title of Supreme Head on him and ordered that those who did not accept this were traitors and should be dealt with accordingly. He had loved More; he had suffered when the sentence had been passed on him. He had merely taken the advice of his ministers.

There was great relief when it was discovered that More's daughter Margaret had taken down her father's head. The King declared that she must be allowed to do what she would with it. He would hear no more. The whole affair had been a great sorrow to him.

Strangely enough, he turned to me for comfort and, stranger still, I was able to subdue my feelings of contempt and give him what he sought.

'He was a traitor, Anne.'

I took his hand and said: 'As all who disobey you must be.'

'He was a good man . . .'

'It seems good men can sometimes act traitorously.'

'He was not against *me* . . . only the Act. At the end he thought of me.'

'You had been good to him, Henry.'

His expression lightened. That was the right note. He said: 'Yes, I would go to Chelsea . . . would sit at his humble table. I asked for no ceremony. I walked in his gardens with him and watched his children feed the peacocks.'

'You did him great honour.'

I soothed him; and we were together again.

The Lady in the Tower

We had to be merry . . . outwardly. There was a great outcry on the Continent about the death of Sir Thomas More. Rome was shocked by the death of Fisher. He had recently been made a Cardinal, and no Cardinal had ever been executed in England before. This was further defiance of Rome. Henry was called the Monster of England. The Emperor Charles said that the execution of Sir Thomas More was an act of folly. 'Had we been master of such a servant,' he was reputed to have commented, 'we would rather have lost the fairest city in our domain than such a counsellor.'

Henry's anger was intense. There should be no weakness. Those who opposed the King should face the penalty.

There were more deaths. Monks must acknowledge the King as Supreme Head of the Church, and for those who would not there was death. There were some who preferred it.

Death was not easy for them. There was no quick stroke of the axe. They died as had the Carthusian monks, dragged through the city on hurdles, hanged, taken down alive and cut open, that their entrails might be burned. People congregated to watch these grisly spectacles in fascinated horror.

They said it was all due to the goggle-eyed whore.

The most disturbing news was that Pope Paul – no vacillating Clement – was so outraged by the deaths of Fisher and More and the monks that he was contemplating waging a holy war against England. The Emperor would lead the army of invasion with the help and blessing of the Pope. They were seeking an alliance with France.

Oddly enough, I had ceased to be as worried as I had been. This was a threat against Henry. Before, I alone had been in danger. It is easier to accept a universal danger than a personal one.

I tried to shut myself away from events by taking an even greater interest in the new religion. There were several Protestant bishops in the Church now – chief of them Cranmer, Archbishop of Canterbury, and Hugh Latimer, Bishop of Worcester. They were strong men and my friends, because I was known to support the new ideas.

Henry was still at my side. I told him that he was right in what he had done. Those who thought otherwise were ill advised. The Catholic Church had many faults. It had diverged from the teachings of Christ. I believed I was beginning to make him see that his escape from the bondage of Rome was the best thing that could have happened to him. Providence had set me in his path that it might be achieved. He only had to consider the wealth of the monasteries, much of which had found its way to Rome. Now it was his. He was no man's slave. When he considered all, he would see that he was the richest Prince in Christendom. Through him the Church was to be reformed. He had done a great service to himself and all Englishmen.

He listened and was comforted.

And once again I was pregnant. This time all must go well. I must have my son who would make me safe forever.

*

During the last months of that year England stood alone, fearing that at any time we might be invaded. I knew from what I gleaned from the spies, that Katharine's hopes were high. I heard there was a plot to oust Henry from the throne, set Mary up in his place and marry her into France so that England would become a vassal of that country.

I pointed out to Henry that I had been right to recognize Katharine and Mary as enemies. It was true that they had never deceived him in their attitude; they had remained staunchly Catholic and had never accepted me as the Queen. That was understandable; but nevertheless they were a danger and a threat to the throne and were plotting against him. He was turning over in his mind some way of ridding himself of them.

All through the autumn we waited for some attack from Rome. It did not come. Katharine was ill and frustrated. We understood that the Pope could not act without the Emperor, and the Emperor was at this time heavily engaged in Africa, where he was achieving some resounding victories.

Meanwhile Henry had instructed Cromwell to have an examination made of the monasteries; and according to Cromwell they were stews of iniquity. Rumours were circulating through the country concerning the life that went on behind monastery walls – orgies in which naked nuns danced before depraved priests. We heard of illegitimate children buried in monastic grounds, and obscenities of every kind.

The whole country was talking about the secret life of the nuns and monks.

Cromwell was eager for war to be avoided and was worried that if hostilities broke out this would have a disastrous effect on trade. The people would not tolerate that, and there would be insurrections.

Moreover, the autumn was particularly wet and that resulted in a bad harvest.

It seemed that everything was going against us.

Then our luck turned. Sforza, the Duke of Milan, died childless; and Milan had always been a matter of contention between François and the Emperor. While the Duke lived, their dispute had been suspended. Now he was dead, the question of who should succeed him in Milan had arisen again.

Whether François had ever intended to make war on England was questionable; but it would have suited him if the Emperor had, for then he could have given himself over to the conquest of Milan without interference. François made a complete turnabout. He needed Henry's support, so cynically he ceased to be concerned about the schism in the Church and sought England's friendship.

The Pope could do little without the joint help of François and the Emperor, and although Charles might have been ready to invade England, he was not going to leave himself open to attack by François, which would have meant having a war on two fronts. The Pope had to content himself with thundering out threats against Henry. He cursed him and all those who aided him. When he died, he was to be unburied and his soul lie in hell forever. He ordered the King's subjects to renounce their allegiance to Henry; they were to fall under the interdict of excommunication if they continued to obey him. No true son of the Church was to hold intercourse or alliance with him on pain of sharing his damnation. The princes and people of Europe must, as they owed allegiance to the Holy See, drive him from his throne.

The Pope's ranting made less impression on Henry now that François was seeking his friendship and the Emperor was showing less inclination to go to war with England. He beleived that, providing he showed his strength to his people, they would obey him. The executions and the terrible and humiliating sufferings of those who refused to obey him must bring the people to obedience. It was only saints and martyrs who risked a death like that.

Henry would have his way and trample on all those who tried to prevent him – no matter how close to him they had once been.

It should have been a warning to me that he could even contemplate murdering Katharine and Mary, for during those months I came to believe that he would have done this if he could without dire results harmful to himself. But he had come too close to war to take such a risk.

That Christmas of the year 1535 must be a merry one. We must show the country and the world that we were unperturbed by the threats from the Continent. We stood in isolation, which made us greater than we had ever been. Henry, King of England, would bow to no one.

My kinsman Francis Bryan came to see me some weeks before Christmas. Francis was a close friend of the King. He was one of those witty lively young men whom Henry liked to gather around him. Francis was clever, something of a poet; he had wild ideas and he could be quite outrageous. Henry was amused by him. Cromwell had dubbed him 'the Vicar of Hell'.

He told me that a week or so ago, when the King had been hunting, he had been a member of the party and they had stayed a night in Wiltshire at Wolf Hall, the home of Sir John Seymour. Sir John had a daughter – a quiet, unassuming girl, and he was eager for her to have a place at Court.

'I promised,' said Francis, 'that I would speak to you and ask if you would allow her to join your household.'

'But of course,' I said. 'What is she like?'

'I would not presume to ask Your Grace if she were not a good and virtuous girl. As a matter of fact, she is rather shy and retiring. Her father thinks it would do her good to come out into the world.'

'Let her come then,' I said.

So she came. I took very little notice of her at first. She was rather insignificant – fair-haired, neither short nor tall, with eyes a nondescript shade of water which took their colour from whatever she was wearing. When I addressed her, she spoke almost in a whisper.

For some days I forgot all about her. Then one evening, when we were dining, I realized that the King was watching her. I saw her meet his glance, blush and lower her eyes.

No, I thought, he cannot be interested in such an ... insect!

I was alert though. And yes, he was interested in her. How strange! She was not the type I should have thought to attract him. Elizabeth Blount, Madge Shelton ... they had all been exceptionally beautiful. But this girl looked dull; she was colourless, with hardly a word to say for herself.

I suppose he just wants a change, I thought. She is, I suppose, just about as different from me as a woman could be.

I did not expect the matter to go farther, but as the weeks passed he was still watching her. Then it occurred to me that he might have asked Francis Bryan to see that she was brought to Court. He had gone to Wolf Hall when out hunting. He must have noticed her then.

I laughed contemptuously. I had little to fear from her, I thought.

*

Christmas came. I tried to make it a merry one. Norris, Brereton, Wyatt, George, we all put our heads together to devise entertainments, and there were feasting and festivities as grand as any that had gone before.

I ceased to worry. I was pregnant. I felt sure that I could not be disappointed again. I was more like my old self. I looked attractive, I knew; I detected that serenity in my face which comes to some women when they are pregnant. I felt that we had come through the worst. I would have to accept Henry's infidelities. But did I care? If I had a son, he and Elizabeth would be the main care of my life. It would not matter much what Henry did as long as I and my children were safe. It was not as if I loved him. I knew him too well for that – though sometimes I felt a kind of contemptuous affection for him. He was such a strange man that one could not help marvelling at him. It was that cruelty and selfishness alongside the sentimentality, the conscience which did in truth plague him, even though he manipulated it and set it going in the direction best suited to his needs. I feared him, yes. I knew how ruthless he could be. When I considered how passionately he had pursued me I could now only think that his persistence had been due largely to his need to prove to himself that he was omnipotent. I had been mistaken in thinking it was love for me. One could not love such a man; but one could live with him. I could accept his philandering. I had never had great sexual desires myself, and at this time they were non-existent. That was why I could adopt a flirtatious manner towards the men about me, for I knew there could be no culmination. I merely liked to have them about me, admiring me.

I had a very talented musician in my household, Mark Smeaton, a pleasant young man who still could not believe in his good fortune in being employed at the Court. He was very good-looking and would have made a wonderful subject for one of our painters, with his small oval face, large dark eyes, and hair which curled about his head. He was delicate-looking, with the most beautiful hands and long, white, tapering fingers. He could dance gracefully. He was a charming boy.

I talked to him about music, and at first he was overcome by shyness because I had noticed him. That endeared him to me, and I told him he must not be shy for I admired his playing very much. Sometimes, when I felt depressed and uneasy, I would make him play for me.

I encouraged him to talk about himself, about his humble home where he had lived with his parents. His father had been a carpenter, and people had brought their chairs for him to mend. Mark had helped him but his heart was in music. Being exceptional, he was noticed by the local squire, who had quickly discovered his musical talents and had brought him into his house to teach music to his daughters. When the daughters married and went away, a visitor to the house, who had been impressed by Mark's playing on the virginals, brought him to Court; and as I liked to gather the best musicians about me, he was soon in my household.

He could never grow accustomed to his good fortune, and he had a feeling for me which I can only call adoration.

When I complimented him on his playing, he would almost swoon with delight. I found him amusing. His clothes were shabby, so I ordered them to make some velvet suits for him. Then I gave him a ruby ring to wear with them. He was overcome with joy.

I was something of a musician myself. Very few people played the virginals better, and I had always had a good singing voice; so Mark and I had a good deal in common.

Such adoration was balm to me in those days when I had to accept the fact that Henry had a mistress – so Mark had become a great favourite. He was a good boy and never gave himself airs. He was always incredibly humble, constantly implying his worship for one so far above him.

The others laughed at him sometimes.

'Yet another admirer,' said Henry Norris. 'Your Grace attracts them like bees to the lavender blooms.'

Norris was often in my party. Now a widower, he was supposed to be courting Madge Shelton, but the courtship did not progress very quickly. I really believed it was because he was in love with me.

So that Christmas was a merry one. I looked forward to the New Year. How fortunate it is that we cannot see into the future! And when that Christmas I anticipated the coming year with such pleasure, I did not know it was to be the most disastrous one of my life.

I would have a son. I had come to terms with my relationship with the King. I would pretend not to see his infidelities. I would accept what I had – which was a good deal, and be thankful for it. I would devote myself to promoting my children.

I had suffered certain qualms of conscience over Mary. I had a daughter myself now and knew a mother's feelings. Katharine was heartbroken; not only was she a repudiated wife but she was deprived of her daughter's company. But Katharine was obstinate; she would have removed me if she could, and I doubted whether she would have been over-nice in the method. She was a strong woman determined to hold on to her rights; but Mary was not so very old, not so very knowledgeable in worldly matters. One should have been more tolerant with her.

So I had written to her, telling her that if she would stop being obstinate and be a good daughter to her father, I would be her good friend. She could come to Court and I should not insist that she should bear my train. She should walk by my side.

I had gone as far as that, and I would have kept my word.

But Mary would not give way. She replied that she wished for nothing more than to be her father's good daughter, but she could not forswear the principles for which Bishop Fisher and Sir Thomas More had died.

It was hopeless to try to get Mary to see good sense, but having done what I could, I did feel a little better.

Christmas passed and the New Year was with us.

News came from Kimbolton where Katharine had been sent, that she was very ill indeed. We heard this through Eustace Chapuys, which infuriated the King. He sent for Cromwell. Poor Cromwell, he seemed to be blamed for everything, and yet the King knew that he could not do without him.

'Why is it that I first hear news of what is going on in my castles from foreigners?' he demanded.

Cromwell humbly said he would take Sir Edmund Bedingfeld, who was in charge of Katharine's household, to task.

He came back with Bedingfeld's report, which was that, because he was the King's servant, the Dowager Princess Katharine concealed everything from him. He had known she was ill but not how dangerously ill.

Katharine begged Henry to let her see Mary.

I watched his mouth tighten. They had plotted to bring in the Emperor's armies, to oust him and set Mary up on his throne. That was something he would not forget or forgive.

'There shall be no meeting between those two,' he said. 'How do we know that this illness is not feigned, and they are not meeting to plot treason?'

A few days later a letter arrived for him from Katharine. I read the letter with him.

My lord and dear husband, I commend me unto you. The hour of my death draweth fast on, and my case being such, the tender love I owe you forceth me, in a few words, to put you in remembrance of the health and safeguard of your soul, which you ought to prefer before all worldly matters and before the care and tendering of your own body, for the which you have cast me into many miseries and yourself into many cares. For my part, I do pardon you all, yea, I do wish and devoutly pray God that He will pardon you.

For the rest, I commend unto you Mary, our daughter, beseeching you to be a good father unto her, as I heretofore desired. I entreat you also on behalf of my maids to give them marriage portions, which is not much, there being but three. For all my servants I solicit a year's pay more than their due, lest they should be unprovided for.

Lastly, do I vow that mine eyes desire you above all things.

It was the letter of a dying woman. Henry was disturbed on reading it, but he could not bring himself to go and see her. He sent for Chapuys and told him to go at once to Katharine at Kimbolton and give her his good wishes.

'Let Lady Willoughby go to her,' he said. Maria de Salinas, who had come with Katharine from Spain and had married Lord Willoughby, had been Katharine's dearest friend throughout her years in England. So although she was denied the presence of her daughter, she did see her friend.

On 7 January she died in the presence of Lady Willoughby and Chapuys.

So it had happened at last, and I am afraid I was impetuous enough to say in the hearing of several people: 'Now I am indeed the Queen.'

I was washing my hands when the news was brought to me, and so relieved was I that I gave the messenger the bowl and cover. He was delighted, for it was a costly bowl.

In spite of his conscience, which had been aroused by Katharine's letter, Henry was elated.

'Praise be to God,' he said. 'We are delivered of all fear of war. Now I can handle the French. I can keep them wondering whether I will join forces with them or the Emperor. This is a day to praise God indeed. It is His way of showing He will look after me.'

I wondered if Katharine could hear those words in Heaven. They were so typical of him. He did not see why God should not remove Katharine to show Henry how much He cherished him.

He dressed in yellow that night. Why should he go into mourning? he asked. Katharine was never his wife.

There was no absence of festivities. In sumptuous yellow – as I was, too – a white plume in his cap, he sent for Elizabeth. She came, my little one – just past two years now, very bright, eager to learn about what was going on around her. I was proud as I watched her being carried by her great glittering yellow-clad father.

It was a good omen, I told myself. This was going to be a happy year.

*

Jane Rochford whispered to me that the King seemed mightily taken with Mistress Jane Seymour.

'It must be a passing fancy,' I said. 'She's such a mouse. I feel sure she could not interest him for long.'

'She is not his mistress, you know,' Jane went on. 'She is holding out against him . . . just like . . .'

'How can you know so much?'

'I keep my eyes open. I think it is important to the family.'

443

I was angry. I hated gossiping with Jane. But I did want to know what was going on.

'They say he sent her a letter and a purse full of sovereigns. You can imagine what was in the letter. She sent the sovereigns back saying that her honour was her fortune and she could receive money only from the man she married.'

Oh God! Familiar talk! Had she learned it from me? That silly little creature! One would never have thought she could learn anything.

Still, I did not worry unduly.

I was sitting with my ladies. We did a great deal of sewing for the poor. I was changing, finding less pleasure in the excitement of the Court. I thought often of the needy, and I wanted to better their lot. I think that had been inspired by my interest in the new religion.

A tournament was taking place, and the King was riding that day. I had not attended. I should have to be there, of course, for the presentation of the prizes but that was not until tomorrow.

Norfolk came bursting into the apartment.

'The King has fallen,' he said. 'His horse has thrown him.'

I stood up. I felt the child move within me and I fainted.

When I opened my eyes, Norfolk had gone and I was surrounded by my women who were pushing hartshorn under my nose.

'What . . . happened?'

'The Duke of Norfolk came and you fainted.'

'Oh . . . I remember. The King . . .'

'They have brought him in.'

'Is he . . . '

'We don't know, Your Grace. But I think he is all right.'

'I must go to him.'

'Your Grace should rest. You have had a shock. Lie down and rest awhile. As soon as there is news, it will be brought to you.'

I felt dizzy. I lay on my couch and closed my eyes. What

would happen to us if he were dead? What would happen to the realm? Who would be sovereign? Could it be . . . Mary? And then what of me? She would not tolerate me. She hated me as the one who was responsible for all the ills which had befallen her mother. And if not Mary . . . Elizabeth? A baby. They would prefer Mary.

I was very frightened.

I need not have been. Henry was soon up. The fall had been nothing, he said. No horse could get the better of him. All his life he had been an expert horseman.

I felt I should rest for a little as the shock could not have been good for the child.

And as I lay, my thoughts went to Jane Seymour, who had refused the sovereigns and talked of her honour.

It was a familiar pattern which had worked so well in my case. What if it worked for Jane Seymour?

How could it? I had been alert, clever, and Jane was a fool. She would never be able to plan as I did to hold him off.

I had many enemies at Court, and they would, of course, know of his feelings for Jane. They had always sought a way of being rid of me. What if they saw the answer in Jane? It suddenly struck me. She had two very ambitious brothers. I wanted to find out, if I could, all about those Seymour men.

I discovered that they claimed descent from a companion of William the Conqueror who took his name from St Maur-sur-Loire in Touraine. The St Maur had become Seymour. The two brothers, Edward the elder – he must have been about my age – and Thomas, a little younger, were eager to make their way at Court. I had no doubt that they had noted the spectacular rise of the Boleyns at Court – in a small way through Mary's liaison with the King and a much greater way through his marriage with me.

It must be that they were seeking advancement through their sister Jane.

The idea seemed quite preposterous, because she was such an insignificant little creature.

I did not think a great deal of the matter then, for I was now very preoccupied with my coming child.

Then came the day when I found them together. I had come into the room suddenly and there they were. She was seated on his knee; she was simpering and he was looking at her fondly. I saw that glazed expression which I remembered so well as it had been so frequently directed at me.

Jane Seymour sitting there on the King's knee! Where was the virginal young lady who had to guard her honour? She did not seem to be so very concerned with that at this moment.

I just stood for some seconds staring at them.

Jane Seymour saw me. She leaped to her feet. The King looked full at me, and there was anger in his eyes. He was caught, and he hated to be caught. He always looked then to blame someone else. He would blame me, of course. But I would not be humiliated before Jane Seymour.

I turned abruptly, and departed.

I felt sick and ill. How far had it gone? Was he trying to repeat what had happened to us? Who was behind her? Edward and Thomas Seymour, the ambitious brothers? Who else? How many enemies had I at Court? Too many to be counted.

I went to my chamber.

Nan Saville ran to me in alarm. 'Your Grace . . . you are not well.'

'I think I will lie down.'

She helped me to my bed. That night my pains started. I was in agony. It was far too soon. I could not bear to be disappointed of my one great hope now.

They sent for the midwife and the doctors. I could imagine how the news was spreading round the palace.

'The Queen is in labour. But it is too soon.'

'Oh God,' I prayed. 'You know how much I want this child. My future depends on it . . . perhaps my very life.'

But God did not answer my prayers. My child – a son – was born dead.

Henry came into my room. He looked down at me. I saw his clenched fists, his glittering eyes, his cruel mouth.

His disappointment was as bitter as my own.

'You cannot give me sons,' he said. 'You are no better than that other.'

I hated him. If I had married Henry Percy, I thought now, I might have been a happy woman. But he had chosen to guide my life. He had robbed me of my lover and offered me a crown . . . and now he was threatening to snatch it away from me. I hated him – and I did not care that he knew it. I was finished. I knew that, as sure as I knew anything. I understood Katharine's feelings as never before. She had served him well for twenty years . . . I not yet three . . . but it was long enough for him to tire of me and want to be rid of me.

I said: 'It is you who have done this. It is your infidelities . . . that have upset me so that our child is born dead. I saw you with that silly slut on your knee.' I laughed. 'You might have chosen someone more worthy.'

He was furious. He hated me for having caught him in such a position.

He roared: 'I see God does not wish to give me male children. And you . . . you will have no more sons by me.'

He was blaming me. I was speechless with indignation.

He murmured: 'When you are on your feet, I will speak with you.'

Then he left me.

I lay numb with misery and fear. I had lost my last chance. I wondered what would happen to me now.

*

I did not see him for several days.

I knew there was no way of luring him back to me for the time being. He seemed to be completely obsessed by Jane Seymour. His affair with her was common knowledge. But how far it had gone, I did not know.

He went on one of his journeys through the country. I did not accompany him. It was given out that I needed to rest to recover from my miscarriage.

I was in a precarious position.

I turned to George – the only one I felt I could trust.

I was resting in my bed when he came to me. It was a good place to talk because we could be quite alone.

He sat by the bed, looking grave.

He said: 'I am worried about the Seymours.'

'You think they are plotting?'

'I know they are. There are not two more ambitious men at Court than Edward and Thomas Seymour. They look for great things through their sister Jane.'

'They profit from our example, George, I'm afraid.'

'You must try to get back to Henry.'

'He hates me, I believe.'

'Love and hate are said to be very close.'

'He has said I shall have no more boys from him.'

'When did he say this?'

'When I was lying exhausted after I lost my child because I was so upset when I came upon him with Jane Seymour on his knee.'

'He knows you saw him?'

'Yes, of course.'

'That would make him angry. He hates to be caught.'

I laughed bitterly. 'There is little you can tell me about him, George.'

'You must get a boy. It is imperative.'

'A thought has come to me. Katharine had many miscarriages, did she not? And now . . . look at me. We have both had girls . . . but always if the child is a boy it miscarries. Why should that be?'

'Perhaps boys are more difficult to come by.'

'That does not seem to be the case. There are many of them about.'

'What are you thinking, Anne?'

'That it is due to something in Henry. I begin to believe he will never have a healthy boy.'

'He had Elizabeth Blount's boy.'

'Yes . . . but that was long ago. And have you noticed young Richmond? There is a delicate look about him. I do not think he will live long.'

'But at least he was born.'

'Mary is delicate, but she lives. But she was born to Katharine after several miscarriages. Elizabeth was my first-born and she is very healthy, but I think she gets that from me. I have these misgivings, George. And if I am right, it means that Henry will never beget a healthy boy.'

The horror of this dawned on him.

Then he said: 'What hope is there then?'

'None. The more I consider it, the more I believe that the fault lies with him.'

'He would kill anyone who suggested it.'

'I know. Perhaps sometime I shall say it to him.'

'Anne, for God's sake have a care. Is there anything that might make you think . . .'

'That I am right? There is a sore on his leg which does not heal well. I wonder about it.'

'*That* sort of disease?'

I nodded. 'Sometimes I believe it makes men and women unable to bear healthy children.'

'But there is Elizabeth.'

'I was fresh. I was healthy. And she is a girl.'

'I cannot believe you are right when you say the King is incapable of having healthy children.'

We did not notice that the door had opened and Jane Rochford stood there.

'Oh, Anne,' she cried, 'I came to see how you were. Is there anything I could do . . .'

She looked at George eagerly, but he turned away.

I was thinking: How long has she been standing there? She moved so silently and came upon one unexpectedly. That

449

could be disconcerting.

I said: 'I want nothing, thank you.'

'And are you feeling better?'

'Thank you, yes.'

'The King will be pleased.' There was a touch of malice in her sly face. She hated to see George sitting close to me, deep in conversation.

George kissed me lightly. 'I should rest a little longer,' he said and, taking Jane by the arm, he drew her from the room.

*

All through that terrible winter the sense of doom was with me.

I had so few friends and apart from George I was not sure whom I could trust. It seemed to me sometimes as though they were all watching . . . waiting for my fate to overtake me. Perhaps they were not entirely certain what it would be. On more than one occasion I had recovered a certain power over the King after having appeared to have lost it for ever. Could I do it again? My rival was by no means the most attractive woman at Court. But it might be that she was not so simple as she appeared to be. She had managed so far to preserve her virtue, to cling to her 'honour' and imply 'A crown or nothing'.

It was a complete imitation of the method which I had used with him. I had blazed the trail, given the example, and they were following it slavishly. She was backed by her ambitious brothers – and she was winning.

Once again Henry was being challenged.

I found great relief from tension in my reading. It was mostly religion, and I was growing more and more interested in the new ideas. I read everything the reformers were writing that I could find. I could forget my troubles when I did that. My other source of comfort was my daughter. She was such a bright and intelligent child. I was often with her. I enjoyed going through her wardrobe, discussing it and planning it with Lady Bryan. I thought that surely such an attractive child must be a delight to her father.

As the weeks were passing, I grew more desperate. I tried to make him notice her, for naturally when he turned from me he turned from my daughter also. How could any father be so indifferent to such a child?

I was at that time overcome with melancholy, and after these bouts such was my nature that I would give myself up to wild gaiety.

I still had my admirers. They must have been genuinely attracted by me for my declining fortunes made no difference to their devotion. I wanted their company, their compliments, their looks of admiration; they made my spirits rise and gave me fresh hopes. I even looked for admiration from young Mark Smeaton. He was completely devoted to me. My ladies said that he never played so exquisitely as when I was present, and it was then that he played for me. He now looked very handsome in the new clothes which I had provided for him.

I told him that he must not expect too much attention from me, and he replied soulfully: 'No, Madam. A look will suffice.'

Such complete and abject adoration, even from a humble musician, was balm to me at such a time.

I had some good friends among my ladies. Madge Shelton was as friendly as ever. Our little adventure with Henry had not changed us; rather it had bound us together, and she did not take it amiss that Henry Norris, who was supposed to be courting her, gave his attention to me. There was Margaret Lee, who served me well; and Mary Wyatt had always been close to me.

My sister Mary had come to Court. She had a great capacity for happiness. For the first time in my life I was envious of Mary, with her children and her happy marriage; she was serene and secure. She declared that Will Stafford was the perfect husband; he had made up for the loss of dear

Will Carey. It seemed to me that Mary had found the right way to live. Perhaps I could have learned from her if it had not been too late.

It was part of my tempestuous nature that I could at times be hilariously merry. I still had the wits of the Court about me to help me construct amusing entertainments. I would sing, dance, indulge in flirtations with my admirers; and then afterwards, alone, I would sink into melancholy.

I said to Mary Wyatt: 'The King plans to be rid of me as he rid himself of Katharine. He thinks he will get sons by Jane Seymour. But I think the King will never get a son ... because he cannot.'

Mary warned me that it was unwise to say such things.

Dear, calm, wise Mary. How right she was!

There were times when I knew such despair that I tried every means to touch his heart. Once I took Elizabeth and, with her, waited before the windows of his apartments for him to appear. After a long time he did. I made the child lift her hand and wave to him. He just stared at us stonily for a few moments and turned away.

I knew there was no moving him then. I saw that we had gone too far for him ever to turn back to me. My enemies were all watching, waiting for the moment when they could give vent to their hatred. They were unsure as yet ... waiting for the King.

I knew that George was very worried. He saw what was happening, perhaps more clearly than I did.

A rumour was started about the Court that the King was lacking in the power to get children and that he was all but impotent.

This would madden Henry when it reached his ears. He would blame me as the one best qualified to set about such a rumour. Enemies everywhere. And so few friends.

When we heard that there was to be an alliance with the Emperor and that he had mentioned he was sending an ambassador to talk with the King and Queen, George's spirits rose.

He came to me that we might talk in private in my chamber.

'He has mentioned you,' he said. 'That means he is accepting you as the Queen. It is a great step forward.'

I saw his point. Henry was wavering, but my fate did not rest on Henry's own subjects but those two powerful states of Europe – by necessity enemies of each other, and who were grappling for power. It was so important for France to accept me as Queen; and if the Emperor did also, I might be safe.

'The attitude has changed now that Katharine is dead,' said George. 'He could condemn your marriage only while she lived. Now it seems he is letting his political needs override his family feeling. He needs Henry as an ally against François.'

'François has been a good friend to us for most of the time while the divorce was pending.'

'He has shown himself to be completely unreliable. The Emperor would be more stable. Moreover, he is a great general. He is the wisest ruler in Europe and he would be a better ally.'

'Then there is a glimmer of hope?'

George nodded. 'I cannot believe that the King wants to go through all the trouble of divorce again.'

'He will have to, if he wants to marry Jane Seymour.'

'He must tire of her soon. If only the silly little thing would sleep with him, it would be over in a matter of weeks.'

'She's set on a crown.'

'You mean her brothers are for her. She is of a nature to be pushed this way and that.'

'So different from me. I think he looks for change.'

'It may be. But we have to stop it, Anne. And if the Emperor shows he is ready to accept you, it might well be that the King would forget Jane Seymour.'

'What of the Pope? What of the break with Rome? The Emperor will never accept that.'

'Emperors and Kings accept whatever is expedient. I think the Emperor wants an alliance with England. Religion is used by rulers. That is why there is often conflict between Church and State.'

And so we hoped.

My spirits rose – as they could so easily. We prepared entertainments for the emissaries. I even became friendly with Chapuys. I think, as usual, I reacted too vehemently, and I have no doubt now that my actions were regarded with cynicism by that wily spy.

Then our spirits drooped, for when Charles's mission arrived, Henry made it clear that I was not to be included in the discussions. Moreover, they failed. Presumably Henry would not accept Charles's terms.

Gloom returned and I felt as though I were waiting for a terrible disaster to overtake me.

George was disturbed. 'But,' he said, 'there is one fact that must make us rejoice. Cromwell is the most powerful man in England. He is another Wolsey, which is understandable since he was taught by the great man. It is Cromwell who will decide foreign policy; and Cromwell brought about the divorce and the break with Rome. He must support you. He cannot give way. If he does, the foundations on which he has built his fortunes will collapse.'

That was a comforting thought. Our hopes were based on Cromwell.

Cromwell was indeed a clever man. He was very busy with the monasteries. A new Act had been brought in to dissolve all those which had not a revenue of £200 a year, and to grant their possessions to the King. Cromwell, under the King's orders, was selling them to the gentry, which, according to Cromwell, was a way of involving them in the operation. Those who had come by reasonably priced land and buildings would regard the Dissolution of the Monasteries as a very worthy act.

Wolsey had fallen through the King's desire to be rid of

Katharine and marry me. Cromwell could fall through my removal in favour of Jane Seymour.

I remembered how incensed Henry had been with Wolsey because he could not procure the divorce from Katharine. Would he be equally angry with Cromwell because he could not devise a plan to be rid of me?

I could imagine Henry's irritation. He had always had an affection for Wolsey and never had for Cromwell. I was sure Cromwell had to face some humiliating moments with his master at this time.

But I saw the man as my saviour. He could not desert me. My fate was too closely entwined with his.

How determined was the King to marry Jane Seymour? That was the vital question. I, who understood him well, guessed that it was not that he desired Jane intensely. There were far more attractive women at Court with whom he could have found satisfaction and who would have been only too ready to please him. It was the basic desire for a son which I had failed to give him. It was his determination, his lust for power rather than for the female body. When he became set on a purpose, it must be carried through, for if it were not, it was a denial of his strength.

That was what alarmed me. But I thought: While Cromwell is in charge, I am safe.

How wrong I was, I was to learn later.

Henry was badgering Cromwell. He must bring out some plan for ridding him of me, that he might marry Jane Seymour. They had already tried a pre-contract with Northumberland. When they had brought it up before, Henry had been determined to quash it, for then he had been desperately anxious to marry me. Could it be brought up again? Possibly. But they would need something stronger than that. I guessed Henry wished it had not been brought forward before. It would have been easier to have made it important now if it had not already been examined and dismissed.

Cromwell had to find a way.

Having been on several diplomatic missions during his life, George was well aware of what was going on politically and the manner in which diplomats worked. He now understood that Cromwell wanted an alliance with the Emperor.

George heard that the emissaries had left and that Henry had rejected their terms. Cromwell had had a heated discussion with the King. The King was against an alliance with the Emperor. The man was Katharine's nephew and he had been responsible for much of the anguish which Henry had suffered during those waiting years. Cromwell wanted to put aside all good allies. The Emperor wanted the alliance; he was a strong man. We should understand each other better than we ever could the French.

Henry hated to be contradicted; he stormed at Cromwell. Cromwell did nothing for him. He had saddled him with the Queen and he could find no release for him. He wanted a son. He had to have a son. And so on . . .

Cromwell staged a coughing fit and called for wine. He said he had a fever. The King dismissed him and he retired to Stepney.

There he remained in bed for a whole week. Whether he really had a fever or was weighing up the position, we did not know. George thought the latter, for when he had emerged he had clearly made up his mind.

I was soon to learn with what disastrous effect on me, for Cromwell was no longer my friend. He had become my bitterest enemy – purely as a matter of necessity, for Cromwell's actions were not dictated by personal feelings.

He had learned that he could not keep the King's favour while I was Queen of England; he could not bring about the treaty of friendship with the Emperor, for, as I learned later, Charles had made it clear that he would not treat with Henry while I was accepted as his wife.

Cromwell would do anything – however ruthless – to save his own skin and keep that power which he was building up for himself.

The year was advancing. It would soon be May – a lovely month, with the flowers bursting forth – buttercups and dandelions in the fields, ladies-smocks and cuckoo flowers on the river banks. One's spirits must rise with the May sunshine.

The first hint of alarm had come when May was almost on us and I noticed that Mark Smeaton was missing. I asked one of the women where he was. She replied that she did not know. She had seen him the previous day and he had seemed rather excited.

'Some secret,' I said. 'Do you think he has a mistress?'

'Mark has no eyes for any but you, Madam,' was the reply.

I shrugged my shoulders. 'That is just because I have favoured him.'

'He has a romantic heart. He is Your Grace's slave.'

'Tell him when he returns that I want to know the reason for his absence.'

Mark did not return.

It was another of the women who gave me the news; and I began to feel a faint alarm.

'He was very proud yesterday, Madam. He had an invitation to dine.'

'To dine? With whom?'

'With Master Cromwell, Madam.'

I was astounded. The great Cromwell inviting a humble musician to dine!

What could it mean? Mark should have told me. I wanted to see George at once to tell him what had happened.

*

It was the first of May – two days after the disappearance of Mark Smeaton. He had not returned to the Court and I was full of misgiving.

But this was May Day – a very special occasion, a Court festival which had always been observed with a spectacular show of jousting.

I had not been able to talk to George or tell him of Mark's disappearance but I should see him today, for he would be one of the chief challengers in the tournament; and Norris was to lead the defenders.

I was still the Queen and must be at the ceremony beside the King, so I took my place in the loge. As Henry was coming into the tiltyard, I saw Cromwell approach him and for some time they were in close conversation.

Henry was frowning deeply, so I guessed it was not good news Cromwell was imparting. I wanted to speak to Cromwell, to ask him why he had invited Mark Smeaton to dinner, and why it was we had not seen Mark since.

Henry took his place beside me. I turned to smile at him but he did not meet my gaze; he was staring straight ahead, his mouth tight and as cruel as I had ever seen it; his eyes were cold but there was a hot colour in his cheeks.

Even when the jousting began, he continued to glower and I guessed he was thinking of the days when he had been the champion. He was too corpulent now. He still rode and hunted, priding himself on the number of horses he could tire out; but he was ageing fast. I knew his leg troubled him. The ulcer would not heal and it could be painful. If he had entered a joust, it would have been difficult for his challenger to stage a defeat for himself. Perhaps Henry knew that, and it was why he sat there glowering.

But there was something else which angered him.

I could not concentrate on the joust. I was wondering about Mark . . . and I wished I knew what Henry was thinking.

George performed with skill. So did Norris. They looked extremely handsome, both of them. The King watched them sourly. I was suddenly overwhelmed by the heat and the desire to get away. It was more than the rays of the sun; I was filled with a premonition that evil was hovering very near me.

I took out my handkerchief to wipe my brow. My hand trembled and it fluttered to the ground. Norris happened to be just below. He picked up the handkerchief on the point of his lance and held it out to me. I took it smiling while Norris bowed.

The King was watching us. I turned to him. He looked as though he were about to choke.

I said: 'Are you unwell?'

He did not answer. He stood up. There seemed to be a long silence, but it could have lasted for only a few seconds. Then abruptly he left the loge.

It was the signal for the jousting to end.

There was a certain amount of confusion – a kind of stunned silence. Then the voices broke out. No one knew what was wrong.

There was nothing for me to do but leave.

I went back to my apartments in Greenwich Palace.

*

The brooding silence continued . . . a silence full of meaning. The storm was about to break and I knew that I was at the heart of it.

Norris did not appear.

I sent for Madge. 'Madge,' I said, 'where is Norris?'

'I have not seen him since the joust.'

'It ended so suddenly.'

'The King was tired of it, they said.'

'He was irritated because he can no longer compete with men like Norris and my brother.'

Madge did not answer. I guessed she was thinking that I said the most dangerous things.

'And there is Mark. What can have happened to Mark?'

Madge shook her head.

'There are wild rumours,' she said.

'What rumours?'

'That Norris was arrested and taken to the Tower.'

'Norris! For what reason?'

'He had offended the King.'

'Surely not? The King is very fond of Norris. He was very close to him.'

'Perhaps it is merely rumours,' said Madge.

'How could such rumours come about?'

'They say it was when he was leaving the tiltyard. Norris was with the King. They were riding side by side. The King accused him of something ... and then he called for his arrest.'

'I don't believe it. On what charge?'

Madge shook her head.

'But they say he is in the Tower.'

'What is going on?' I demanded. 'Norris arrested! Mark missing! What does it mean?'

No one could be sure. Or perhaps they were afraid to tell me. Was there something they were holding back?

I wanted to talk to someone. Where was George? I sent someone to find him, but he was not to be found.

I dreaded the night. I knew I should not sleep.

How right I was! I lay in bed, turning from one side to another, constantly asking myself: What does all this mean?

At length the long night was over. I rose. There seemed to be a silence everywhere. I fancied my attendants did not want to meet my eyes. They were all afraid of something.

In the early morning I had visitors. I was surprised to see members of the Council led by the Duke of Norfolk.

I rose as they entered my apartment, for they came unbidden and should have asked for an audience.

I demanded: 'What are you doing here?'

'We are here on the King's business,' replied Norfolk.

'What business?'

'Your music man is a prisoner in the Tower.'

'Mark, a prisoner! He is only a simple boy. On what charge?'

'Of adultery.'

'Adultery! With whom?'

Norfolk looked at me, smiling. 'With you, Madam.'

'Mark! A humble musician! What nonsense is this?'

'He has admitted it.'

'Oh, my God!' I cried. And I thought: Dining with Cromwell. For what purpose would Cromwell invite a mere musician to his house? To bribe him? No, Mark would never take bribes. If it were true that he had said that, they must have tortured him to make him do so. What implacable enemies I was up against. Poor Mark! His slender body . . . those delicate hands . . . What had happened to Mark? What would happen to me?

'How dare you make such vile accusations?' I demanded.

Norfolk used that favourite expression of his which had always irritated me. 'Tut, tut, tut,' he said, as though I were a wilful child. He added: 'Norris is in the Tower . . . another of your lovers.'

'What wicked lies.'

'And now, Madam, we are come to conduct you to the Tower.'

'I will not go.'

'It is the order of the King.'

'I must see the King. I must speak to him.'

'His Grace does not wish to see you. It is his order that you are to be taken to the Tower.'

I felt suddenly calm. The blow had fallen. Perhaps I had been waiting for it for so long that it was almost a relief that it had come at last.

I was in the hands of ruthless men who would stop at nothing to get what they wanted . . . and the most ruthless of them all was my husband, the King.

Lies were being told about me. Had Smeaton spoken against me? If he had, his 'confession' must have been wrung from him with the greatest cruelty. And Norris? Norris was an honourable gentleman. But could he withstand the rack?

I entered the barge, and I felt doom all about me. It seemed such a short time ago that I had come down the river in glory.

Norfolk sat opposite me. There was a smile of triumph on

his face. He had never liked me. In spite of the fact that he was a kinsman, I really believed he was delighted to see me thus. I realized I had been proud and overbearing. I had been haughty, thoughtless, quick to anger. I had not exactly endeared people to me. But I had a few faithful friends and on them I could rely completely.

He said to me almost complacently: 'Your paramours have confessed their guilt.'

'My paramours?'

'Norris, Brereton, Weston ... and of course the music boy.'

'I do not believe it.'

He lifted his shoulders to imply that what I believed was of no importance.

They were taking me to the Traitor's Gate.

In my wildest nightmares I had not thought of this. That he might be seeking means of getting rid of me, yes, but not this way.

I was told roughly to get out of the barge. I did so. I suddenly felt the need of prayer. I sank to my knees and prayed aloud. 'Oh Lord God, help me. Thou knowest I am guiltless of that whereof I am accused.'

Sir William Kingston, the Lieutenant of the Tower, came out to receive me.

'Master Kingston,' I said, 'do I go to a dungeon?'

'No, Madam,' he answered kindly. 'To your lodging where you lay at your coronation.'

The irony of the situation came upon me afresh. Was it only three years ago? I thought of myself sitting proudly in my barge with my device of the white falcon and the red and white roses of York and Lancaster. I was then pregnant ... never dreaming that I should not have boys. I laughed wildly and there were tears on my cheeks.

'Wherefore am I here, Master Kingston?' I asked.

He did not reply but there was compassion in his face, and that brought me a shred of comfort.

As I was taken to my chamber, I heard the clock striking five, and each stroke was like a funeral knell.

Norfolk with his company came with me into the chamber and, having seen me installed there, were ready to depart.

'I am innocent,' I said to them again. 'I entreat you to beseech the King to be a good lord unto me.'

They bowed and left and I was alone with Kingston, who pitied me, I think.

'Do you know why I am here?' I asked again.

'Nay,' he replied.

'When did you last see the King?'

'I have not seen him since I saw him in the tiltyard.'

'Where is Lord Rochford?' I asked, dreading the answer.

'He was in the tiltyard also.'

A terrible fear came to me. I said to myself more than to him: 'Oh, where is my sweet brother?'

'I saw him last at York Place.'

I covered my face with my hands.

'I hear say that I shall be accused with three men, and I can say no more than . . . nay. Oh Norris, has thou accused me? Thou art in the Tower and thou and I shall die together.' I thought of my stepmother; her grief would be terrible. I murmured, 'Oh, my mother, thou wilt die of sorrow. Master Kingston, do you think I shall die without justice?'

'Oh, Madam, the poorest subject of the King has that,' he said.

That set me laughing wildly. I could not shut out of my mind memories of that large face with the hard little eyes and the cruellest mouth in the world.

I threw myself onto my bed and laughed and wept until I was exhausted.

*

I had lost count of the days. I did not know how I lived through them. They were determined to discountenance me, to rob me of comfort.

If only they would let me have my friends about me, that would have helped me. Was it too much to ask? If I could only talk with Mary Wyatt, Margaret Lee, Madge or my sister Mary – that would have helped me through the dismal days. They had given me those who hated me. They sent my aunt, Lady Boleyn, wife of my father's brother Edward, who had always been jealous of me, and although in days past she had been afraid to speak against me, I had always been aware of her venom. Perhaps they chose her because they knew she hated me. And she brought with her a certain Mrs Cosyns – a spy if ever there was one. Those two were certain, I was sure, that I was guilty of all which I was accused.

They tried to trap me into saying something which they could report against me. They were there all the time; they never left me. They slept on pallets at the foot of my bed. Sometimes I would wake from a nightmare shouting. They were alert, listening, noting everything that I said, attaching great importance to anything that might be used against me.

They treated me with a studied lack of respect. I was not the Queen now, they were telling me.

Sometimes they would pretend to be sympathetic and try to get me to confide in them. They asked questions and they phrased them in a way designed to trap me.

'Oh, you were ever so beautiful in the Court. You were the brightest star. Everyone seemed commonplace beside you. It was small wonder that all those men were in love with you.'

The stupid women! Did they not understand that I saw through their probing?

'Norris was said to be courting Madge Shelton, but he came to see you. You were the one. It was obvious . . .'

'And Weston . . . he loved you better than he loved his wife. Well, it was understandable.'

I turned from them. I could live through these days only by ignoring them.

My moods changed. There were times when I just wanted

to die and have done with the wearisome business of living; at others my anger overcame my sorrow.

I wanted to live and take my revenge on those people who had plotted against me and brought me to where I was.

It was a great joy to me when I was allowed to have two more ladies to be with me, and that these two should be my cousin Madge and my dear friend Mary Wyatt.

Lady Boleyn and Mrs Cosyns were still there, but that was more bearable now that I had my friends as well.

Mary was very worried about her brother. He had not been arrested as everyone expected him to be, for he had been known as a great friend of mine and he had never hidden his love for me. Many of his poems had been written for me.

I would contrive to be alone with Mary so that we could talk, and she comforted me a great deal.

'It is only Smeaton who has lied about you,' she told me, 'and that was under torture. Cromwell tortured him at the dinner table. His bullies put a rope round the poor creature's head and they tightened it so that he was fainting with the pain; then they made him say how you had favoured him, given him fine clothes and a ring because he was your lover. He withstood the agony for a long time. Then they took him to the Tower and racked him most piteously. It was only then that he broke down and lied.'

'Poor Mark,' I said. 'He is a tender boy . . . little more than a child. Always so gentle. He told me once that when beggars came to his father's door he wept for them; and when he came across a man hanging on a gibbet which others were looking at, he ran away, for he could not face violence of any kind. He loved beauty . . . And to come to this . . .'

'It was only at the end that he lied,' insisted Mary. 'It was only when those wicked men tortured him beyond endurance. The others would not give way. There is not one, Anne, who has spoken against you . . . only poor Mark, and that under torture.'

'They know it is false.'

'They know ... but they are determined to believe it.'

'Mary, what will become of me?'

She shook her head. Her tears unnerved me more than the brutal treatment of Norfolk had been able to, or the spying of my aunt and her familiar.

'Why is George in the Tower?'

Mary shook her head.

'And my father?'

'He has not been arrested.'

We could not go on talking because my jailors – those two hateful women – would not leave us alone for long.

The nights seemed endless. I would lie staring into the darkness.

He would be rid of me so that he could marry Jane Seymour, just as once he had wished to be rid of Katharine that he might marry me. Silly little Jane Seymour. How long did she think she would last? Who would be the next? He would cast off wives as he did a garment he was tired of.

There were two counts on which I had thought he might be rid of me. One was of course his relationship with my sister Mary which would have made a close bond between us. He had thought of this before for there had been a time when he had sent to Rome for a dispensation. He would not have had to send to the Pope for that now. Obliging Cranmer would have done what was necessary. But he did not wish to stir up old scandals from which he would not emerge too well. I had dismissed Mary as a possible method. There was one other – my pre-contract with Northumberland. That I had thought was very possible. It could be said that I had been pre-contracted to Henry Percy and therefore my marriage to the King was no true one.

That would have been the most likely method if it had not been raised before and he had most definitely quashed it. Then he had wanted me passionately – now he wanted to be rid of me with equal passion.

I would not have believed he would have considered . . . death.

And yet why should he not? That would have been Katharine's fate but for her royal relations. I had no such assets. My relations held the power they did through me . . . and some from Mary, too, of course.

So, if it was not to be Mary or Northumberland, there was only one alternative.

I had sometimes wondered how people felt when Death looked them in the face. Sir Thomas More? Fisher? Those monks who had refused to take the Oath of Supremacy. 'She will spurn our heads off like footballs, but 'twill not be long ere her head will dance the like dance.' More had said that. He was prophetic.

He had known the King as well as I knew him. He knew that mean, selfish nature, that determination to have his way, that ruthless destruction of all those who stood to prevent it. He knew of the conscience which worried Henry when he wished to be worried. It was worrying him now. He had been bewitched by a sorceress; he had discarded his first wife – he could safely regard her with affection now as there was no fear of having to take her back – and all because he had been the victim of a witch . . . as any man might be through no fault of his own. But God had opened his eyes now. He saw the way clear ahead. God had put Jane Seymour in his path to tell him that, if he escaped from the spell which had been put upon him and married this gentle, simple girl, Heaven would smile. He would have a succession of boys. God was showing him the way, and, as once before, God's instrument was Cromwell, who had prised the truth from the boy musician, and now it was known that the Queen had sinned against him with those whom he had called his friends.

I could well imagine how he would prepare his defence with God. What amazed me was that he thought he could deceive the Almighty as he thought he did his courtiers. They had to feign belief; God did not.

When I arose, I wrote him a letter, signing myself 'The Lady in the Tower'.

'. . . if you have already determined of me, and that not only my death but an infamous slander must bring you to the joy of your desired happiness, then I desire of God that He will pardon your great sin . . .'

How I laughed. I could imagine his pallor as he read that. I hoped it would make him shiver. I hoped I would set that despised conscience of his on a course independent of its owner's control.

How did he think of me? I was sure he thought of me often. Did he think of the garden at Hever; that night when I had come to him in my black satin nightdress; of my coronation?

Or did he think of me as 'The Lady in the Tower'?

*

It was 10 May – only eight days after I had been arrested. It seemed like years.

The Grand Jury at Westminster had issued an indictment against 'Lady Anne, Queen of England, George Boleyn, Viscount Rochford, Sir Henry Norris, Groom of the Stole, and Sir Francis Weston and William Brereton, Gentlemen of the Privy Chamber, and Mark Smeaton, a performer on musical instruments, a person of low degree, promoted on account of his skill to be a Groom of the Chamber.'

George and I were to be tried on 16 May; the others on the 12th.

I waited for the verdict . . . I knew that Henry wanted to be rid of me, but surely he must have some compassion for his friends. He must know they were innocent. Or was he so determined to be rid of me that he would take any life which helped him to achieve that end?

The result of that trial was horrifying, although it was what I had expected. They had tried hard to make them all admit their guilt. None of them would, except Mark. In spite of the fact that he had lied to save himself and to destroy me, I could forgive him. I knew of his delicacy, his weakness. I could imagine how he had collapsed under extreme torture. His body had been broken and his mind distracted and when they told him that, if he signed a confession he would be free, the boy signed. Poor foolish Mark! He had bartered his honour, his pride, for the hope of saving his life. He was not wise enough to know that he would never have been allowed to live; he had perjured his soul for nothing. He was condemned to be hanged. What a sad end for a young man who had music in his soul and because of it believed that he had escaped from poverty to a pleasant life – when all he had escaped to was Death.

I wanted to see him, to comfort him, to make him look at me and see if then he would persist in his lies. Of course that would not be allowed. Mark would have broken down and told the truth when confronted by me – and they knew it.

What a sad end for a young man.

Norris, Weston and Brereton, though urged to confess, stoutly maintained their innocence. Henry had been very attached to Norris, and he sent word to him that if he would confess to adultery with me, he would be granted his life.

Norris's reply was that he would rather die a thousand deaths than accuse the Queen of that which he believed, in his conscience, she was innocent.

Mary Wyatt told me that when the King heard this he was so angry that his great friend had turned away from the hand stretched out to rescue him, he cried out in rage: 'Hang him up then. Hang him up.'

Poor Mary Wyatt was in a state of anxiety. Thomas had remained in the background. He was expecting at any moment to join Norris and the rest in the Tower. His name had not been mentioned in connection with the charge – but it was in everyone's mind.

On the 16th George and I were brought to trial, and for this purpose a court had been set up in the great hall of the Tower.

George was the first to appear. I waited in trepidation, but after the result of the previous trial I was prepared for the worst.

George defended himself so well that, for a time, those who sat in judgement on him must have feared it was going to be difficult for them to bring in the sentence the King wished for.

I think even our greatest enemies must have been shocked when Jane Rochford came forward to give evidence against her husband. How she must have hated me! I knew she had loved George passionately, but his indifference to her had turned that love to hatred; and her hatred was especially for me because she knew of the close and loving relationship between my brother and me.

Her accusation of incest was so ridiculous that she could not in any reasonable way substantiate it . . . except to say that we were over-affectionate towards each other, and my brother sought every opportunity to be in my company. She had found him in my bedroom on one occasion. I was at the time in bed. He had leaned over the bed and kissed me – which she had seen as she came into the room.

They must have despised her; but they had not the courage to defy the King. He wanted me vilified as much as possible; and if it could be believed that my brother, as well as those other men, had been my lover, he could then feel completely justified in putting me from him in the most speedy and reliable way. It would ease his conscience considerably if I could be proved worthy of my intended fate; and the King's conscience must be eased, no matter at what cost. They knew this – and their future depended on the King's favour.

So George was found guilty.

As soon as he left the hall, I was taken there with my ladies in attendance, including Lady Kingston. Sir William conducted me to the bar.

I surprised myself by my calm. I felt rather as though I were outside this scene looking on. I knew that I should be condemned, because I knew Henry. Had I not been beside him during the years when he wished to rid himself of Katharine? So the outcome was clear. It was a waste of time to have a trial when the verdict was a foregone conclusion.

I pleaded Not Guilty to the charges and sat down in the chair which had been provided for me.

I listened to the evidence; the words I was alleged to have spoken. It was all so trivial, so obviously contrived. I answered these charges, which was not difficult because they were all so blatantly false. I could see some of the peers beginning to look uneasy. They believed me. In fact, there was little else they could logically have done.

From the fifty-three peers of England, twenty-six had been selected. These were the Lord Triers, with the Duke of Norfolk at their head. I was sure that he and my old enemy, the Duke of Suffolk, would make sure that the King had the verdict he required.

Northumberland, as one of the foremost peers of the country, would most certainly be there. I wondered what it would be like to see him after all these years. I had heard that he had changed a good deal. His disastrous marriage and his unhappy life must have had an effect on him. And now he would be one of those who had come to judge me. How strange it would be to see him there and to think back to those years when he and I had had those stolen moments together, when he came to Court in Wolsey's entourage and I slipped away from my duties with the Queen to be with him.

But I did not see him among the peers.

I said to Kingston: 'Is not my lord of Northumberland here?'

Kingston murmured: 'He came . . . but was taken ill. He has been forced to retire.'

I smiled. So he could not face it. He could not stand there and condemn me. Dear Henry Percy! What did he think of me now? At least he remembered enough to refuse to sit in judgement on me.

The coolness which had descended on me – that strange aloofness – was good for me. It enabled me to answer their questions with precision and to give them the answers which they found difficult to refute. They had, no doubt, expected me to be hysterical, which would have made their task much easier, and they were discountenanced to find me there aloof, so very calm.

Had it been a fair court, they would not have condemned me, though they did not have to have a unanimous vote; all they needed was a majority. All those accused with me – save Mark – had emphatically denied the charges. Could they condemn me on the evidence of a poor, racked boy?

Norfolk and Suffolk saw that they did.

Norfolk then pronounced the sentence. I was condemned to be burned or beheaded at the King's pleasure.

The numbness remained with me.

I clasped my hands together and, raising my eyes, I said: 'Oh Father, O Creator, Thou who art the way, the life and the truth knowest whether I have deserved this death.'

I faced my judges. 'My lords,' I said, 'I will not say that your sentence is unjust, nor presume that my reasons can prevail against your convictions. I am willing to believe that you have sufficient reasons for what you have done, but they must be other than those which have been produced in this court, for I am clear of all the offences which you have laid at my charge . . .'

I could see that many of them were ashamed and that my words would not be easily forgotten by some.

I went on to say that I had never been unfaithful to the King, though I admitted that I had not always shown him the humility which, as one who had been raised so high, I owed him. I said I was not afraid to die. I had faith in God, and He would show me the way. I added that I knew these words would avail me nothing, but I spoke them for the justification of my chastity and honour.

'As for my brother and those who are unjustly condemned, I would willingly suffer many deaths to deliver them, but since I see it so pleases the King, I shall willingly accompany them in death, with this assurance, that I shall lead an endless life with them in peace.'

Having spoken I turned and left them.

*

Cranmer came to see me. The King had sent him to receive my confession.

I was greatly comforted by his visit.

He begged me not to despair. It might well be that the sentence of death would be lifted. He implied that I might be expected to leave the country. Perhaps I should be sent to Antwerp, where I could live out my life in peace. I had given myself up to the study of religion and I had an interest in matters of the mind: reading, music and a growing understanding of the new religion of the reformation of the Church.

I should never regret leaving the Court. The emptiness of life there was very clear to me now. I never wanted to see Henry again. But there was one of whom I thought constantly: my daughter. What would become of her now? Who would care for her? Her mother disgraced, burned or beheaded, branded a harlot. What of my little baby?

Did she know of this? She would wonder why I had not been to see her. She was bright, full of questions. I could trust Lady Bryan. She loved the child and was a good, sensible woman. Why had I thought I wanted to die, when Elizabeth was there . . . needing me?

If I could take my child to Antwerp with me, perhaps we could live there simply . . . like an ordinary mother and daughter.

I was soon to discover the meaning of this hope and why it had been put to me.

The very next day I received a summons to appear at Lambeth to answer certain questions as to the validity of my marriage with the King.

The pattern was getting more and more like Katharine's – except, of course, that, being the aunt of the Emperor, she could not be condemned to death.

In a chapel in Cranmer's house in Lambeth I was confronted by Cranmer and others and urged to admit that there had been a contract of marriage between Henry Percy and me, before I married the King.

Cranmer had hinted that, if I agreed to this, not only could I save my life and leave the country with my daughter but the lives of the gentlemen might be saved.

How could I do anything but agree? We *had* talked of marriage, I said. If the King had not prevented us, we should have married and none of this would have happened.

It is easy to be wise after the event. I agreed. And Cranmer pronounced the marriage between the King and myself null and void.

I felt a little better; the remoteness of reality was lifting. I could plan. If I had not been married to the King, the adultery of which I was accused could not be called treason. The men would be free. I should be free. I should still be an encumbrance but if I were out of the country I could be forgotten.

I slept a little better that night.

*

How could I have been so foolish? It seemed that even now I did not know my husband.

The lives of other people meant nothing to him. All those young men who had been his friends, who had joked and laughed and hawked and hunted with him, meant nothing to him, and if their death could help him to his goal, he would have no compunction in sweeping them aside.

What a terrible day that was! The most wretched of my life.

They had erected a scaffold on Tower Hill. My brother went first – my dear, sweet brother, whom I had loved so dearly, the one of all on Earth whom I trusted completely. They said he died calmly and most bravely.

Poor Francis Weston. His family was desolate. His wife and mother entreated the King to spare his life. They were rich and they offered 100,000 crowns for him. Henry rejected the offer.

And Weston, Norris and Brereton submitted their heads to the axe.

Mark Smeaton was hanged. I had hoped he would retract his admission of guilt on the scaffold.

'Has he cleared me?' I asked.

They told me he had not.

'His soul will suffer for the false witness he has borne,' I said.

Mary Wyatt laid a hand on my shoulder, and when I lifted my eyes, I saw tears on her cheeks.

'Do not weep, Mary,' I said. 'My brother and the rest are now, I doubt not, before the great King, and I shall follow tomorrow.'

*

When death is close, one thinks back over the past, and what looms large in one's mind are the actions one regrets.

I wished that I had been a better person. I could see clearly now my folly at every turn. I am not sure whether any action of mine could have altered my fate. I was dealing with a man who was corrupted by the great power he possessed, a mean, selfish man, a monster of a man, a murderer.

I had never really wanted him. He had forced himself upon me. I had been enamoured of pomp and power, I admit. I had grasped at those things in life which had seemed the greatest prizes, for I had been blinded by the glitter of all that had been laid before me. I had been tempted, as Christ was by

475

Satan, but I had not had the good sense to turn away from temptation.

And I had done many cruel things.

I had hated Katharine. I had hated the Princess Mary. True, they has been no good friends to me. How could they be, when I was the one whom they accused of robbing them of their rights?

But I could have been kinder to Mary.

How I had disliked that girl. I had wanted to humiliate her. I wanted her out of the way because I wanted her position for my daughter.

I asked Lady Kingston to come to me.

I made her sit, which she was reluctant to do. She still regarded me as the Queen, and that was my chair in which nobody sat but myself.

I said: 'My title has gone. I am condemned to death. All I wish now is to clear my conscience.'

So I forced her to sit and I knelt before her. I asked her, as in the presence of God and His angels, to go from me to the Princess Mary and to kneel before her as I now knelt before *her*, and ask her forgiveness for the wrongs I had done her.

'Until that is done, my conscience cannot be stilled,' I told her.

She promised me she would do this, and I knew she would, for Lady Kingston was a good woman.

*

This is my last day on Earth. Tomorrow I shall be gone. I am twenty-nine years of age. It is young to die.

I have lost my beloved brother. I shall never see my child again. I pray for her and I have exhorted Lady Bryan to care for her. She will know what to say when Elizabeth asks why I do not come to her.

A sword has arrived, especially for me. It comes from

France. I did not want the axe. It is a last concession from the King.

Kingston came to see me.

I said to him: 'I hear I shall die before noon tomorrow. I am sorry. I had hoped to be dead by this time and past my pain.'

'The pain is very little, Madam,' he told me. 'It is over in an instant. The executioner is very good.'

I put my hands about my neck and laughed. 'And I have a little neck,' I said.

He turned away. I think he was moved by my calm acceptance of death.

I wondered whether I should request to see Elizabeth. Would that request be granted? I wondered. Henry would have decided.

What should I say to her? How does one say goodbye to a child? 'My darling, I shall not see you again. Tomorrow they are going to cut off my head. Your father, in the great goodness of his heart, has allowed me to escape the terrible death by fire. He will be content to have my head removed by a very fine sword which has been sent from France for the purpose.'

Now I was getting hysterical.

I must not see Elizabeth. I could trust Lady Bryan.

I wrote a letter – not to the King but to be shown to him. I would ask Mary to give it to one of the gentlemen of the Privy Chamber.

'Commend me to His Majesty and tell him that he hath been ever constant in his career of advancing me; from private gentlewoman he made me a marquess; from a marquess to a queen; and now he hath no higher honour of degree, he gives my innocency the crown of martyrdom.'

I hoped those words would make a mark on that conscience of his. I hoped they would be so telling that he would not be able to shrug them aside. I hoped he would be haunted by them for a long time to come.

There were moments when I longed to see him, that I

might say to him what was in my mind, tell him that I saw clearly behind the mask of geniality – though that had been used less and less as time passed. Bluff King Hal was Henry the all-powerful, the selfish monster, the murderer.

I did not so much hate as despise him. He would be remembered throughout the ages to come as the King who because of his carnal desires, had discarded the wife of twenty years on a trumped-up charge; and having succeeded in that he murdered his second. I wondered what would be the fate of the next ... and the next ... and the next ...

But I must calm myself. I must prepare myself for departure.

I would dress with care. I should be elegant to the end. I should wear a robe of black damask with a white cape, and my hat with ornamental coifs under it.

I would calm myself. Indeed – but for leaving Elizabeth – I should have gone gratefully to my death. I would not want to live again through the last year of my life.

Perhaps I shall not be forgotten, but remembered as the Queen who was murdered because she stood in the way of one who had the power, cruelly and most unjustly, to murder those who were an encumbrance to him.

I did not retire that night. What use? Tomorrow I should no longer need sleep.

I was inspired to express my feelings in verse.

> Oh, death rock me to sleep [I wrote]
> Bring on my quiet rest,
> Let pass my very guiltless ghost
> Out of my careful breast.

The clocks have struck midnight. The new day has come. Very soon now they will be leading me out to the Green. Before this day is over, my life will be no more.

Bibliography

Aubrey, William Hickman Smith, *The National and Domestic History of England*

Bagley, J.J., *Henry VIII*

Barrington, E., *Anne Boleyn*

Batiffol, Louis (translated by Elsie Finnimore Buckley), *National History of France*

Bigland, Eileen (editor), *Henry VIII*

Bowle, John, *Henry VIII*

Bruce, Marie Louise, *The Making of Henry VIII*

Bruce, Marie Louise, *Anne Boleyn*

Castries, Duc de (translated by Anne Dobell), *Lives of the Kings and Queens of France*

Cavendish, George, *The Life of Cardinal Wolsey*

Chamberlin, Frederick, *The Private Character of Henry VIII*

Chambers, R.W., *Thomas More*

Fisher, H.A.L., *Political History of England*

Froude, James Anthony, *The Divorce of Catherine of Aragon*

Froude, James Anthony, *History of England*

Gairdner, James (editor), *Memorials of Henry VII*

Green, Mary Anne Everett, *Lives of the Princesses of England*

Green, Mary Anne Everett, *Letters of Royal Illustrious Ladies*

Guizot, M. (translated by Robert Black), *The History of France*

Hackett, Francis, *Henry VIII*

Hackett, Francis, *Francis the First*

Herbert, Edward, Lord of Cherbury, *The History of England under Henry VII*

Hudson, Henry William, *France*

Hume, Martin, *The Wives of Henry VIII*

Jackson, Catherine Charlotte, Lady, *The Court of France in the Sixteenth Century*

Lingard, John, *History of England*

Luke, Mary, *Catherine of Aragon*

Mattingly, Garrett, *Catherine of Aragon*

Pollard A.F., *Henry VIII*

Prescott, H.F.M., *Mary Tudor*

Roper, William, *The Life of Sir Thomas More*

Sergeant, Philip W., *The Life of Anne Boleyn*

Scarisbrick, J.J., *Henry VIII*

Smith, Lacy Baldwin, *Henry VIII*

Salzman, F., *England in Tudor Times*

Stephens, Sir Leslie and Lee, Sir Sidney (editors), *Dictionary of National Biography*

Strickland, Agnes, *Lives of the Queens of England*

Trevelyan, G.M., *History of England*

Wade, John, *British History*